. . . and you'll love

Var...

Hunter's partner and a seriously SEXY, ballsy lady . . .

✓ **She's tough**

✓ **She's beautiful**

✓ **Look at those legs**

Wait till you see the slam-bang hi-octane stuff she gets up to in this awesome thriller.

And get ready to go right to the snowy edge when she's chased through an arctic wilderness by a computer-driven, missile-loaded 4x4 that shoots bad guys to bits.

Something big and Bond-like is happening and nobody can figure out the hell what . . .

But who's this getting off the plane?

✓ **She's also tough**

✓ **She's also beautiful**

✓ **And she's after Hunter**

BIG TIME!

To Josh

Thank you for buying this book.
You are helping in the fight against
testicular and prostate cancers.

www.everyman-campaign.org

Steve Caze

2011

Steve Cage has worked in film, TV, and advertising for nearly thirty years. During that time he's created spaceships and sci-fi hardware for movies and TV shows, run a small visual effects studio, and contributed to numerous high-end ad campaigns for many of Britain's top industrial companies. Using various assumed names he's published fiction and non-fiction books—serialising two for BBC radio—and written as a newspaper leader-page columnist. He is also an award-winning movie producer, writer, and director.

INTRO

Check your balls, guys!
Or how I survived testicular cancer and why
Google could help save your life too.

(1)

I spent most of last year getting a buzz from writing this book. Still in my pyjamas I'd crack on each day by 8.15am, showering and dressing mid-morning, working through till 6.30pm. I'd break off for twenty minutes at lunchtime and again for a brisk half-hour walk mid-afternoon. After dinner I listened to music and sat with my notebook, planning where my story might go next. I was back at the PC between 9.30-11.00pm, going over what I'd written since breakfast. I stuck to this routine for nine months solid. We even cancelled our summer holiday because I was on a roll and didn't want to break off.

As the months passed a dull ache began in my groin and lower back. I assumed it was from sitting for long stretches at a PC. I'd invested in a good office chair but my wife was always banging on at me for contorting in weird positions with my legs knotted while I worked. The ache came and went but wasn't too painful. Sometimes it spread down to my buttocks and some days it was worse than others. It was more of a nagging discomfort, which I guessed would eventually go away.

I Googled the symptoms and pulled up grim warnings about testicular cancer (TC). But the same websites said it might not be TC. Like many guys must do in my position, I got hooked on the safer option. I was fit as a fiddle, had never smoked, and because I ate sensibly I wasn't fat. My middle names were "fitness" and "good health" and it was fair to say that I didn't look my age. Because of this, each time I Googled (more obsessively as time went by) I gave myself the benefit of the doubt. To be honest, I was afraid that if it was cancer I'd have to break off writing my book and all that mattered was that I finished it ASAP. This seems crazy when I look back but it shows how much the writing had taken over. Behind it was the fairly sound belief that cancer seemed to happen to people who abused themselves or their bodies. It didn't hit guys like me who, at nearly 50, could run half-a-mile (as I sometimes did to the post office, so I could get back to my writing) and not be out of breath.

The shower in our en-suite developed a problem, meaning we had to use the bath for a few days while we waited for a plumber. One Saturday morning when I was sitting in the bath, trying to figure out where the ache was coming from, I found a lump in my right ball. It was rock hard, like a small stone at one end. I'd felt something there before, when it was smaller, but when I Googled it I discovered that bits of stuff were going on where the testicles joined the body, which could be mistaken for tumours. On that occasion I'd stayed cool. Not because I was scared of finding something dodgy but because I couldn't believe it was the Big C. Lesson number one for you guys who don't perform what in TC circles is known as the monthly self-exam.

After my bath—and just as I'd finished the first 140,000 word draft of this book—I reluctantly made an appointment to see my GP. Fast forward to me being swept up by the colossal, much maligned monster known as the British NHS. I'd heard the horror stories about the NHS, as you will have, but from the word go I experienced a world-class healthcare service. This not only made me wonder if I lived on a different planet to the gloom-obsessed media but left me gobsmacked at the professionalism of the NHS and its doctors and nurses.

I was referred to a urologist-surgeon, Mr Gupta, at the Royal Oldham Hospital near Manchester. The NHS has the Two Week Rule for suspected cancer patients, meaning Mr Gupta saw me quickly, the next Thursday afternoon. He examined me and booked me in for an ultrasound scan at 10.30am the following Monday. The fancy computer kit they used was impressive and looked like something out of a sci-fi movie. Most guys balk at the idea of being asked to drop their togs so another guy can fondle their packet. It's why plenty of proud young guys end up being diagnosed with TC when it's too effing late. Trust me on this one, guys. If the Big C's on the cards, as is the prospect of you pushing up daisies, having some other guy grope between your legs is no big deal.

The young guy who got stuck into me wiped some clear gel on my balls and slid something around, which sent a picture to his computer. He wasn't happy. I told him to cut the BS and hit me with it straight. He turned the screen to show me a solid black lump in my right ball. He said it might not be a tumour but probably was. While I got dressed behind a curtain, trying to get my head round TC, the guy murmured gravely at a phone. When he'd finished he

ix

told me to call Mr Gupta's PA right away. I hung around at the hospital for a while, trying to phone her, but the line was busy. Driving home I pulled over for a few minutes to get it together while it sank in that chances were I had cancer. I kept thinking it must be a false alarm. I'd made it to age 47 without a hitch and had never had anything medically wrong with me. I was super-fit. Then the bomb went off when I remembered first seeing my GP about my ache. He'd nonchalantly said that if it was TC he couldn't guarantee it wouldn't be fatal.

I knew from Googling that there were two types of TC, both potential killers. One, a seminoma, was less risky and slower to develop. The other, a nonseminoma, was aggressive and could spread quickly to the lungs and brain. The scary thing about most cancers is how they get to work on you without you realising. Mine must have been growing while I'd slogged away at my PC.

When I got home Mr Gupta's PA phoned and asked me to go back to the hospital after lunch. When I got there Mr Gupta had seen the scan. He told me the problem with TC is that the only way they can find out if it is TC is to cut out the ball. In the UK this is known as an orchidectomy. (They seem to miss out the letter "d" in the States.) If they try to check the ball in situ, and it turns out to be cancer, malicious cells can enter the bloodstream. By now I was floating. Mr Gupta talked me through how he'd open me up and what he'd do then—wham! Ten minutes later they whisked me off to pre-op and within twenty-four hours I was in theatre. That's how fast these guys—in other words the NHS—moved to save my life.

The op was a success but even when the testicle was out it wasn't the end of it. They sent it away for a biopsy, to check if it was cancer, which it was, and in the majority of cases is. I went through more tests and got hooked up to a CT scanner and had needles stuck in my hand and coloured liquids pumped round my body to see if they'd caught it in time. Over Christmas and New Year I had radiotherapy at Christie's in Manchester. Each day some serious sci-fi looking kit angled round and dosed my para-aorta with radiation. I felt like Bruce Banner being blasted by gamma rays before he morphed into the Hulk. And like all writers, I viewed my experience as potential material. I knew that the book you're holding would be the first in a continuing series of tough thrillers. Lying on my back at Christie's I decided that Hunter, the lead guy, would get hit by TC in book three or four. It will go back to a bloody scene in this book when he comes in for some aggro and gets kicked between the legs by a nasty bent cop.

I was lucky. TC turned my life upside down but we'd caught it in time, although there was a two week period after my op, while I waited for the CT scan results, when I didn't know 100% for sure if I'd live. There's a bit towards the end of this book where Hunter decides to stop belly-aching like a spoilt tosser and realises—after nearly being slaughtered twice—how much his kids matter and that life itself is the most precious thing of all. That's pretty much me speaking because I think something shifted after I'd faced cancer.

(2)

So what's the moral of my story?

Why the PR and the link to the Everyman cancer campaign with this book?

Before my op I'd trawled Google, reading heart-wrenching stories about guys from all walks of life who weren't so lucky at confronting TC. They found something suspect but kept it to themselves, partly out of fear, maybe from embarrassment, and paid the ultimate price. Young guys between 18 and 35 are the most susceptible and more often than not they get the virulent strain. TC is also the most common cancer in men aged 18 to 44.

I want to raise awareness of TC because I could have acted faster than I did. OK I was vigilant but I kept thinking I was spooking myself. I was wrong and so might you be. I'm not exactly a household name but I'd set out to re-invent the British crime-adventure thriller for the 21st century, targeting that crucial 18 to 35 male age group. Recent surveys show that only 1 in 5 guys check their balls. They know more about getting their girls to check their boobs. Maybe I could target with-it young guys everywhere by tying the book's release to a frontline TC charity and splitting the proceeds. If I'd written a flowery literary novel I'd struggle. But a Hollywood style fast-action gorefest, written with attitude, was another matter.

There's another reason why I was able to consider doing this. I'd had Critical Illness Health Cover and had hit pay day. Ten years earlier my wife and I had cancelled a whole stack of insurance policies to reduce our monthly outgoings. Our financial advisor at St James's Place, Alan Graham, said that if we cancelled our Critical Illness cover *he'd* carry on paying it for us. That's how seriously he takes it because people think it's a waste of time. But think of how many people you know who've been touched by cancer and you begin to suss it's not a bad idea. I'd Alan to thank when I found out my policy covered TC. In a roundabout way, I'd kinda got the big publishing advance I'd hoped for when I started writing my book. Some people believe that if you put out to the Universe for something you want you get it (as sexy Vanessa decides in this book) but not always how you expect.

I could afford to give something back. TC has been flagged up to you because you've bought this book. You've also donated to Everyman so it can help tons of guys become aware of TC and other male specific cancers, and the benefits of a simple monthly self-exam. Of course it's still a commercial venture. Of course I want to sell lots of books so I can keep writing them and keep donating. Unfortunately, even a low-cost product like a paperback has to be designed and manufactured and various people need to take their cut. But it's a two-way thing. The more books we shift, the more my charity makes because we're splitting my royalty 50-50. Magnum has also chipped in, meaning Everyman gets £1 for every copy that's sold. That's way more than most writers get from each paperback they sell. Not bad for something costing a few quid, which you can ask your friends to buy, spreading the word, so that more lives can be saved. Or as I prefer to see it—so that more lives aren't needlessly wasted.

(3)

Cases of TC have doubled since 1975 but nobody knows why. Although there isn't any convincing evidence to support this, I've heard about a possible link to the amount of estrogen that's in our recycled drinking water due to the number of women who are on the pill. In other words, guys (and girls), it might be linked to sex. Which is another way of saying it could be linked—like much that's wrong with the world—to our modern lifestyle. But if you have a ball removed the other one copes fine, meaning you can still have kids and have sex and carry on as normal. You can even have a synthetic ball put in if you think you might get hung up about having just one. In the rare event that you end up losing both balls you won't be able to father kids but your sperm can be frozen before the op and you can take replacement testosterone.

Some more good news is that, even though TC is one of the lesser-known cancers, it's one of the most curable with a 99% all-clear rate if caught soon enough. Don't get me wrong. It's deadly and can kill you just like any other cancer. If you don't get to it in time you're up shit creek. Nor does its cure rate (falling off to 87% in later stage disease) mean you can stick your head in the sand. It means that if you find you've got TC, and you *get to it in time*, there's a 99% chance you'll live.

That's the big idea behind this book. It's why I was determined to use it as a marketing vehicle that raises money and helps young guys (and their girls) to sit up and take notice of TC. Everyman also works to stamp out prostate cancer, which kills a guy *every hour* in the UK. Buying this book means you're supporting these men too. Check out Everyman's website (URL on the Thank You page near the front of the book) and please, please, please start checking yourself regularly while in the bath or shower. Checking your balls takes hardly any time and it could save your life. Tell your sons, brothers, dads, boyfriends, workmates, neighbours. Don't think TC can't happen to you. That's what I used to think. But it did happen to me. Sometimes I still can't believe it.

I was unusual, contracting it when I was 47. I'm even a medical novelty according to my Christie's clinical oncologist, Dr Jacqui Livsey, who's looking after me till 2013. My cancer was the least virulent. They don't know what caused it and never will. When they took out the testicle they discovered it had atrophied, which might have been down to an infection many years ago. My cancer is almost unknown in somebody as "old" (groan) as me. They said that it suggested I was aging more slowly and had the metabolism of a younger, fitter guy. That's OK then. Seems that taking care of myself and carrying on like I did when I was 21 is paying off.

And if it wasn't for Google — which is a gigantic encyclopaedia, instantly available to most of us without trailing to a library — I might not have acted quickly enough. Like the NHS, Google is criticised as an out-of-control monster. Yet it's arguably true that, like the NHS, it helped save my life because what I pulled up on Google meant I took action sooner rather than later.

Before I forget, I didn't have an artificial ball put in. But get this. When I now write at the PC I can cross my legs a whole lot easier.

STEVE CAGE

NOW THE KILLING STARTS

MAGNUM
LONDON

NOW THE KILLING STARTS

First published in 2010 by Magnum Publishing Ltd
14 Hanover Street, Mayfair, London, W1S 1YH

Everyman is run by the Institute of Cancer Research
Company limited by guarantee. Registered in England No 534147
A Charity, Not for Profit. VAT registration No 849 0581 02

Steve Cage has asserted his moral rights
CIP catalogue available at the British Library

ISBN 978-0-9565914-0-1

Typset in Palatino by Hot Metal Retro
Hunter photo figure © Blacksheep, London
Cover figure © Madeleine Abrahamsson, Sweden
Extra special thanks to everybody at Amtrak

The paper used to make this book has been produced
from trees that have been legally sourced from well-
managed and credibly certified forests

Printed and bound in the UK by
CPI Bookmarque, Croydon, CR0 4TD

Big thanks due

To literary agent John Jarrold for editing this book.

Having made movies I know that good fiction editors are like good film editors. They see things you don't and help you get the best from your material. John is an ex-publisher who knows his stuff.

To publisher Patrick Janson-Smith.

Former head of Transworld, and a friend of my non-fiction publisher, Patrick advised me on an early, more literary, draft of this book. He encouraged me to go after the commercial end of the market and recommended a stack of energetic thriller writers whom he thought did it best—all of them American. At Transworld Patrick first published Terry Pratchett, Lee Child, Robert Goddard, Andy McNab, Jilly Cooper, and many others. His input shows in the book you're holding, as does JJ's.

Thanks guys.

Finally, and most importantly, to my amazing wife Julie. For the past twenty years she's driven everything I've done and made it all worthwhile. She raised millions to exec produce my movies and none of my creative work could have happened without her unstinting support, including this book.

Thanks darling.

I love you.

WAtCHMAN, WHAt OF tHE NiGHt?

iSAiAH 21:11

Michael Greenhalgh's head was throbbing and his stomach had started to hurt. He didn't know why he was still standing up. He was bleeding so much and his body was so trashed that by now he should be falling, he should be slumping to the floor.

Three young thugs stood before him but he towered over them all. He couldn't see their faces. They were clear enough but he'd no wish to linger over the details for their faces must not matter. Ever since his nightmare had begun he'd not wanted to admit

7

their ugly faces were real. It would mean the bastards were going to kill him. And that would send him mad. It would mean the manimals had won.

One of them tough-guy talked and flicked open a switchblade. Dumb gangsta speak streamed from between jewel-studded teeth riding a shit-like stink of bad breath. The blade came up and slit Greenhalgh's septum, making him snarl from pain. His mouth was so swollen he couldn't speak properly but he dissed the pint-sized tosser anyway. Instantly feet dropkicked him and something hit his nose so hard he might have collided with an anvil. It was the grubby lino slamming into his face like the cobbles did in the alley when he took a dive after he'd been shot. A carbonated water sensation filled his nostrils. He sensed the crunch of his breaking teeth.

Then it was human punch-bag time and they laced into him again. As the frenzy of violence advanced he writhed and swore at them from a puddle of his skidmarked blood. The Nikes came at him relentlessly. Something happened up his arse. Before he passed out he saw a dozen squashed cigarette ends fanned about his face.

*

Events were moving quickly.

The brittle blackness parted, as though he were emerging from beneath a heavy veil. Another pain came from his body. At first he thought it was the bullet wound but then he saw a syringe with a teardrop hanging from the end. The needle pricked him again and the hot liquid it injected made his muscles relax then spasm and contract. He sensed an expanding pressure, a liquid pressure, drilling at his flesh. It pumped into his arms, his legs, his body. The needle plunged horribly deep, the cold less excru-

ciating as a drugs-induced orgasmic heat quickly filled him up. And now a wonderful expanding heaviness, sexual in its potency. He was strapped face down on a bed, spreadeagled naked across a filthy bloody mattress. The scum squabbled behind him like dogs fighting over a bitch on heat. Darkness came again then light came again while sweaty hands mauled him and he heard obscene gasping cries as the bastards took their turn, tanked on the designer drug called spunk.

Animals, he thought again, gritting what was left of his front teeth, ODing on adrenalin as they started beating him senseless when they'd finished. Fucking animals.

*

Losing it now, really fucking losing it.

Outside in the freezing fucking cold, somewhere in the filthy inner city. Boarded windows. Old stone flags. The stink of crap. Still naked, being dragged from the blood-soaked boot of a car. Something was hooked over his head then he saw a rope thrown over a streetlamp. Suddenly he was being throttled and flying off the ground. Verticals went kaleidoscope crazy. The light of day passed to a frosty night as the weight of his body seemed to snap his neck and a noose hoisted him up by his fucking head.

*

Still going higher, up to the stretching lights of a distant city, up to the stars. Unable to breathe. Seeing Francis Bacon's Screaming Man *superimposed with the huge gob of Michael Greenhalgh. By the big backbencher himself, the working-class kid who made good surrounded by a bouquet of greedy microphones, jabbing his forefinger at a massive Westminster crowd, timing ano-*

9

ther cluster bomb of words. The notorious Tory MP for Acke-
bourne East, the papers had said. The fascist bastard who wanted
to bring back hanging, some of the nastier editors said. But it
was a damned good speech, a fucking brilliant speech, a flagship
speech of Prime Minister material that captured the mood of a
nation. Now the maverick speaker was squealing like a terrified
child. He'd become the frightened baby contained within all men
suddenly released, screaming, crying, screaming, crying. Party
and politics, that satisfying feeling of adulation before fawning
subjects, the lust for power and prestige—each took on its true
significance and mattered not a damn.

The streetlight's galvanized-metal stem bent above him as he
kicked helplessly and began to die. The shadow of his lynching
stretched across graffiti-caked walls, his wrists Duck-taped behind him, his feet slashed open so the blood would fetch the dogs.
As he thrashed and choked and spun and bled he kept seeing a
million streetlights flung across the clear Mancunian night.

*

Cold sweetish-smelling liquid drenched him then pump-action
shots started blowing bits of him away. Then a huge blinding
flash and flames leapt up. The weight of his body pulled unbear-
ably, making his eyes petechia pop, but the curtains were closing
now. The struggle was at an end.

Heavy curtains. Salubrious curtains. The most wonderful
curtains he'd ever known.

PARt ONE

ONE

DS David Kowalski watched the opening titles to ITV1's *Early Evening News* do the crazy aerial zoom thing as the camera raced up the Thames.

Skyscrapers flew past then Big Ben whizzed close and morphed into the new ITN studios at Marsh Wall, emblazoned like a giant Wurlitzer against the night sky. CG letters rolled in as a guy's OTT tabloid telly voice announced the show was coming live from London.

Next came the fit girly Newscaster, a super-slick blonde-haired young black woman who arrived on screen so fast it's a wonder the camera didn't knock her off her feet as it swept in riding the *swish*, flash, and subwoofed *thud* of a laser-bolt. While hi-octane music *vadoomed* she stalked out of white neon, seeming to be all tits, legs, and high heels with a wet-look skirt chopped off just below her naughty bit and her cuffs shoved back. Voiceover man introduced her and the big music died.

'Hello,' she said chummily. A CG hotspot pinged from her digitally enhanced teeth before she turned to camera two and got to it, saying gravely, 'Britain could see the return of capital punishment, civil liberties groups are warning tonight. The public outrage that has swept the country since the brutal murder of Tory MP Michael Greenhalgh has finally prompted Ministers to act. Rumour has it the controversial new Crime and Punishment Bill could soon be passed, while the *Guardian* newspaper claims that secret "death chambers" could be commissioned at our biggest prisons. As if these allegations aren't enough, ITN can reveal that secret meetings have taken place at Chequers. We understand senior civil servants and police chiefs attended, along with prison governors from the United States and representatives from the European Court of Human Rights.

'Meanwhile, will the Prime Minister address calls for a referendum on capital punishment? If so, when might it be? Let's go live to our political editor to find out.' High-angle shots of a vast angry crowd had crept slow-mo behind her while she shot her intro. Now they did a neat CG wipe as she swung to face them, asking, 'How's the atmosphere at Westminster, Richard?'

Kowalski saw a bespectacled fat face filling the screen. Snow cut through the shot as the guy observed gloomily, 'It's electric, Sam. As you can see thousands have gathered in anticipation of the dead MP's Bill passing successfully through its first reading.'

In front of the crowd a huge laser videowall ran Greenhalgh's final public speech. Enormous speakers pumped his booming voice around the square. A gunship searchlight swept the sea of tiny heads, making it look like a pop concert instead of a political rally. Fists punching, Greenhalgh was banging on about his pet subject—hanging the bastards, flogging them, stringing the buggers up. He was an ex-coal miner and remnants of his Yorkshire accent still worked his vowels.

'Our society's deteriorating ladies and gentlemen! Crime is the dominant factor affecting our way of life! But are our children encouraged to nurture civilized moral values by those who excuse bad behaviour on account of the socio-economic forces they claim *produce* crime?'

'No!' roared back the crowd.

'No!' he agreed, braced against the lectern so firmly it looked as if he might wrench it free and toss it from the screen. 'I ask you to question the morally reprehensible forces destroying our society! As the most important General Election of modern times draws near, I implore you! Support the return of capital punishment, before it's too late!'

Another roar erupted from the crowd, accompanied by masses of tiny handheld Union Jacks waving patriotically. Then Kowalski saw Greenhalgh's gargantuan leering face switch to hundreds of tiny facsimiles, each the size of a domestic TV screen. Just as quickly the massive face resumed

15

from another angle, working with the robust voice to deliver a stream of acoustic energy relentlessly bombarding the night.

The woman again: 'We can see the size of the crowd, Richard. But is the mood confrontational? Will demonstrators clash with the police?'

'I think it's unlikely Sam. This rally has been orchestrated to show how angry the public is about crime and punishment, while Parliament debates the hottest piece of legislation since the Second World War. The police aren't here to provoke the demonstrators but to protect them from a number of subversive left-wing groups that have gathered in London this afternoon.' Punctuating his observations were hand-held shots of leather-clad riot cops stalking the crowd, night visors down, machineguns ready, looking like low-budget rejects from the *Terminator* movies. Gunships thudded eerily overhead, fighting the monotonous voice blaring from the big screen. Then back to the correspondent, with snow-crusted hair, going on about Greenhalgh's forceful personality and how he continued to make his extraordinary presence felt after his death. 'He dared to say things which, till recently, would have been considered so politically incorrect as to be unthinkable. He voiced a popular concern that everything is on the slide and that, unless something is done soon, the crimewave will undermine the stability of British society.'

The woman was now stuck behind a cool sci-fi CG desk that looked to be made from shifting light. 'And by lynching him,' she said, heading to break number one and the first bunch of ads, 'it's as if the forces of lawlessness deliberately thumbed their noses at the popular desire to bring back capital punishment?'

'Absolutely. And with the Tories at an all-time high in the polls, and no Free Vote in the Commons, the Government will be accused of seizing political advantage. Especially if it uses its powers of veto if the Bill is blocked by the Lords.'

Kowalski had seen enough.

Nodding to himself knowingly he sent away the noise of the TV and opened a can of Stella. He was heading the investigation into Greenhalgh's horrific murder but needed to see what was happening in London to try and get his head round what he'd uncovered. He thought about this as he took out his phone and switched it back on. While he waited for it to jingle-jangle to life his eyes wandered onto a glossy *Weekend* magazine on the couch, reminding him of the day when his life caved in and his nightmare began. No, his living fucking hell. His squeaky-clean photo filled the cover, his hi-tech gunship helmet stuck proudly under his arm like a football. The posh woman journalist had described him as a tall, strongly built 28 year old air cop, outward-going with intense green eyes, known for his relentless determination and his cool demeanour. It was the butter-coloured hair bit he didn't like because it sounded peroxide gay. But she'd meant well and made the effort to come up north and interview him for real before writing the moving copy to go with:

YOUNG POLICE HERO'S TRAGEDY
TOUCHES THE HEARTS OF MILLIONS

They were in the wrong place at the wrong time. Caught between a shop window and a stolen Transit. The patho-

17

logist said death would have been instant, but Kowalski knew what that meant. Human bodies were basically bags of water. If they collided with something at high speed they totally fucking splattered.

He flicked through his address book till he found Vanessa Aysgarth's gorgeous face. Although her platinum hair had been cut shorter when Central Matrix captured her ID holograph it was the unique print of her sincere pale-blue eyes that mattered to the bastards in control. Unlike a lot of snotty middle-class birds working in TV, she'd a lovely refined voice that was always open, never condescending. He liked her because he could talk to her as if she was another guy. She was interviewing him again tomorrow for a *Crime in Britain* special she and Hunter were making about Greenhalgh's killing. Kowalski wondered if he should potentially endanger her life and hesitated before thumbing the green rubber button. If he shot the call he'd breach his employment contract.

Fuck that for a lark he thought, scrambling the transmission in case anybody was snooping.

TWO

Mark Addison swore, 'About fucking time,' as the red lights made green and he trod the X6's gas pedal with a size-thirteen booted foot.

Twin tramlines split the snowy dual carriageway down the middle. Ashton Road East, it was called. The A656 if you punched it into Streetmap, running straight out of Manchester's New Central Square. It was the usual mess of fast-food drive-ins and inner-city crap tangling in front of plastic-skinned space-age tower blocks. Locals took the piss and knew it as downtown Droylsden. It wasn't somewhere Les Dawson thought up for a mother-in-law gag but was home to Robertson's jam and the first place in the world to weave towels by machine loom—as if anybody gave a toss about that. Notables included guys from pop groups 10cc, Take That. Incredibly, Davy Jones, lead singer with The Monkees, grew up there.

Addison was a big ex-cop. Way over six foot. Pushing fifteen stone but all solid, no fat, with short prematurely grey hair. His hands took up as much space at the leather-skinned wheel as two bunches of bananas. Some cops disliked him, saying he'd the kind of face you never got tired of kicking in. Not that they'd had chance. Addison knew the value of good PR for enhancing the reputation of a tough cop and once set the rumour going that he'd snapped a pimp's back over his knee like a twig. He packed in policing when he realised there was more money in IT. He was no fucking ball brain either when it came to business but was a legit limited company whose last filed accounts showed a pre-tax profit of £150k. From his finger being in various dodgy corporate pies such as Chief Commissioner Driscoll's two fat companies. Think of the devil. As he did sixth gear then went for a head scratch, up flashed Driscoll's mug on the phone parked at the dash.

'Yeah,' Addison said, his voice so slickly deep it might have been put through a voice morpher for *Dr Who*.

'Leviathan has landed.'

'What, so fucking soon?'

'He's gone home and called Vanessa but she's just had a shower and asked him to ring back.'

'Any idea where he went?' Kowalski was up to no good. They'd tailed him when he left the station but lost him because he'd switched off his phone.

'No, but he probably sussed he was being followed. As a consequence you're on your way over to check his PC for a virus. There's a nasty one going round.' Unable to contain his dry wit he threw down one of his trademark measured pauses. He was young for a chief cop, his hair cut so short that when he was tiny on a phone his bullet head looked shaved. His dark eyes dominated his sallow face, giving him a mean look that played games with his pseudo-piss-posh voice, which was forever tanked on sarcasm.

'Let me guess,' Addison said, picking up the pause and running, 'I'm to waste his hard drive.'

'Totally and absolutely.'

'Any special instructions?'

'I'll sort everything with forensic.'

'Understood.'

Addison finished his cigarette. Out came smoke. Down went the driver's window. Through it went the butt. Screw the fucking fine if a camera clocks me, he thought, as the window came up and he took off. Most drivers were only touching thirty when they could have done forty, but Addison did sixty thinking bollocks to the snow. When you'd got friends in high places speed traps didn't matter.

In her hotel room overlooking New Central Square Vanessa was sitting naked in front of the dressing table, drying her hair. Next to her was a cartoon birthday card declaring that 'Orgasms start for beautiful birds at 40'. Some clever dick had crossed out the number forty and scribbled '42' above it in felt-tip. She was 41 for another week but an old friend had got to her early from the States.

When she'd finished she crossed to the wardrobe and unhooked a sleeveless black 1960s dress that she'd picked up on Saturday from an antique clothes fair in Harrogate. She'd spent the weekend up north because her partner Max was in New York. There'd been no point in returning to Hampstead to be pissed off on her own for two days, after Hunter flew back to London on Friday to be with his kids. Instead she drove across to Yorkshire to see her dad and younger sister Jackie. It had been like old times, when mum was alive. She got back to the hotel a couple of hours ago. Had a workout in the gym then a shower before dinner, missing Hunter already, feeling like she wanted to dress up for him, buzzing like a kid getting ready for her first date. It was crazy. He was ten years younger than her. Nine and a bit actually but there it was. He was getting to her more than she'd realised.

Looking at the dress she decided it was too sexy for dinner with him on a Sunday evening and hung it back. She got out a cream t-shirt, a long olive-green crinkly skirt and her favourite bomber jacket made from bottle-green suede. It was masculine looking, covered in zips and studs like a biker's jacket.

David Kowalski rang back when she'd finished getting dressed. They were interviewing him at the Greenhalgh lynch scene in the morning, on his day off. Picking up where he'd left off when he rang earlier he slurped from a can then cut to the chase.

'Listen love. I trust you guys because I know you but I probably shouldn't say anything till I'm sure.'

'About what?'

'I think Greenhalgh might have been a sacrifice to forward the cause. He tables a motion to bring back hanging. The Government's determined to get it through. A surefire way to get the country behind it would be to bump him off and get the public baying for blood. There's other stuff, such as how anybody outside a SWAT team could shoot so accurately from that distance.'

Vanessa had to admit that Greenhalgh's death was convenient but crazier things had happened. She knew he'd been snatched from his Jag after the chauffeur was shot by a sniper. An unpronounceable Islamic terrorist fundamentalist group, known for its crack military training, proudly squared fuck for the MP's murder soon after the body was found. But just as quickly it denied it and posted an angry adjuration on its website.

'Can you prove anything?'

'Not yet. But Driscoll showed me the interim report this afternoon and it's gonna be a whitewash. Only he doesn't know what I've just dug up.'

'Meaning?'

'I'm onto something that'll blow the lid off this whole bastard thing. But I need to go back to CPHQ first to check some HD footage.'

'What of?'

'I'll tell you tomorrow, love.'

'Jesus Christ, David! Why ring to say you might be onto something if you won't tell me what?'

'Trust me love. I'll cozy with you when I know. I need to be sure to protect my informant.'

She didn't push it, partly because she could have done without this tonight, which she wanted to be cosy, candle-lit, romantic, partly because she knew him well enough to know that he was lonely and would talk about the serious stuff when he was ready. They'd first interviewed him for a series they made about modern police life. Instead of the usual fly-on-the-wall tosh showing stupid people abusing their democratic freedoms it focused on the domestic lives of the officers. David was one of the featured cops but by a terrible fateful coincidence during filming he lost his wife and daughter when they were killed in a police chase. His story made for heartbreaking TV and was tipped to win a BAFTA. Recently, he'd been back in the public eye when, to a certain amount of stagy police hoo-ha, he was put in charge of the Greenhalgh case. But privately Vanessa was amazed he hadn't fallen to pieces in the face of so much misery. Whenever they spoke she'd to keep a commiserating tone from her voice. 'Are you willing to say anything on camera?'

'I think I've got to, love.'

'Won't you need permission?'

'Strictly speaking, yes.'

'But?'

'I'll use the right language.' Before he could say anything else she heard his doorbell buzz then Ted started barking in the background. 'Shit. I'll call you back, love. Maybe I will tell you tonight.'

Kowalski heard a freight train passing the house, seemingly endless but muted by the triple-glazed uPVC. He stuffed a biscuit in his mouth and sprayed crumbs shouting, 'Shut it, Ted,' at the shut kitchen door while he killed the call. Waving the TV remote he sent away the telly, crossed to the front door, and asked the caller for his ID over the intercom.

'It's Addison,' said Addison. The noise of the train and Ted fought his boomy voice.

Kowalski despaired again. 'I thought I told you not to fucking bother me!'

'There's a virus going round. They asked me to do it on my way home. Some nutter's targeting cops. If you're infected you're fucked.'

Pissed off, Kowalski flicked the switch that shot back the bolts and let his visitor in. Container wagons groaned past on an embankment next to the house, some with wheels binding as hideously as fingernails clawing down a blackboard. Of all fucking times for Addison to show. He shouted angrily, 'For fuck's sake, shut it Ted!' as he came back to the lounge checking his phone while the dog went crazy in the kitchen. He sussed that he hadn't killed the call and thumbed the red button as Addison banged his snowy feet on the step and followed him in. Conscious of Ted his eyes went to the kitchen door. The dog's shadow moved in the gap at the bottom, its claws scratching tiles while it barked and sniffed, checking out the new guy's smell. Kowalski seriously mean-mugged Addison and reached for his Stella. 'Couldn't it fucking wait?'

'It's standard procedure for all PCs over two years old,' Addison reeled off. He dumped his case and switched on the PC, which stood on a clear plastic table under the staircase bulkhead.

To show that he didn't want to talk Kowalski aimed the TV remote and brought back the *Early Evening News*, way too loudly. Greenhalgh was back on screen, shouting and waving. The political correspondent now had snow hair. Contending with the pounding of rotor blades he rounded off his report saying, 'Passionate, gregarious, a brilliant orator forever thumping clenched fists at the air he seemed to drag the words from his mouth and mould them in front of his face with his hands. He was the quintessential example of our new breed of PR obsessed showbiz politicians who depend on showbusiness techniques to market themselves.'

Cut to sexy black woman thanking him then cueing the next break from her sci-fi desk. The pulse of CG light OTT Colgate-pinged from her teeth as she smiled into the music sting then fancy chrome graphics wiped her out as commercials crashed in.

Addison opened his case and rooted through it. 'It's a shame about Greenhalgh,' he lamented. 'He was developing a Powellian notoriety.' While the PC booted he crossed to the mantelpiece and held up his cigarettes. 'Would you mind?' he asked over the TV din, which seemed to drive a tension that was building.

'Yes I fucking would,' Kowalski told him, knocking back Stella.

Addison stuck away the pack.

'How's it been going?'

'It's been fucking difficult,' Kowalski replied, giving the big tosser a hard stare. 'But I manage.' The new commercial was more sedate. Surround-sound bees buzzed so realistically they might have been released from a hive into the room. Still the PC booted, digi-chattering merrily, the green diodes flashing. 'You're married, aren't you?' Kowalski observed.

'Yes I am.'

'And you have kids.'

'Two boys.'

'You can imagine then.'

'I suppose I can,' he said, pasting an appropriate expression across his ugly mug before turning to regard the mantelpiece with increasing interest.

In pride of place was a photo of Lucy and Melinda, both bright with summer clothes. Sitting between them was dumb-looking Ted. Melinda was red-haired, round faced, with big blue eyes and a slightly puzzled expression. She held an ice-cream cornet in one hand and clutched Ted's collar with the other. Little Lucy spookily resembled her daddy and would have been a stunner if she'd made it to womanhood. The smallness of her milk teeth emphasized the innocent vulnerability of her age, despite a compelling feminine maturity to her grin.

Addison went back to the PC when it had booted up. He typed and got preoccupied as he checked stuff, his attention not fully on what came out of his gob. 'If it happened to me,' he said, stooping his massive body, hitting Return when the black bird welcomed everybody back on TV, 'I reckon I'd fuck off to Spain as well.'

Kowalski had told nobody but Vanessa where he was thinking of going to live, when they spoke earlier. His face dropped, in cahoots with the proverbial penny. He knew Addison clocked that he'd put his stupid fucking foot in it when he whipped out his Sheuze and spun to face him. Sheuzes were standard police-issue and silencered with a slimline acoustic barrel. Some cops said the noise of them firing was imagined instead of felt. Although Addison was an ex-cop it was illegal for him to own one. He'd have got hold of it because he was close to Driscoll. Kowalski went

26

cold when he sussed what the fuck was going on. He auto reached for his Sheuze at his belt but realised the holster was hanging on a chair by the window before his hand set off moving.

Mexican trade-off time.

'You know I don't want to do this,' Addison assured him, nodding for him to shove up his hands.

'Then fucking don't,' Kowalski said as Addison picked up the TV remote and killed the telly. A sudden, almost deafening silence. 'Driscoll sent you, didn't he?' No need for the bastard to answer. Ted muttered and whined at the kitchen door. 'What's it about, Mark?'

'I don't know.'

'Yes you fucking do.'

'I fucking don't.'

'Greenhalgh was killed to order, wasn't he?'

'I honestly have no idea.'

'Driscoll knows that I know.'

'Does he?'

'What the fuck's going on?'

'I don't fucking know!'

Kowalski felt to be disengaging from the situation. The lower his spirits sank, as he became reconciled to the real reason for Addison's visit, the more certain he was of the devastating truth about Greenhalgh's death. In his mind's eye he saw his tiny house from the immensity of space, zooming up at light-speed on Google Earth. He was aware of his miniscule insignificance in the scheme of things yet overwhelmed by the importance of what he now knew. Simultaneously he was demoralized by the essential corruptibility of the human condition. *It all boiled down to the power of the gun.*

27

'But what I do know is that you're depressed,' Addison said. He'd put on some blue latex gloves when he'd taken the stack apart. To kill static, Kowalski assumed. He knew the real reason why when Addison reached for the holster hanging on the chair and unclipped the gun. He checked it was loaded then coolly flicked on the laser and waved the thin red beam to and fro. 'You're so pissed off at being left on your tod you've been contemplating suicide,' he added, stuffing his own Sheuze back in his coat in the holster near his tit.

'Is that what Driscoll will put out? I don't suppose any war's fought without casualties is it? Did the bastard quote *Leviathan*?' He considered trying to appease Addison but instead grinned and tightened his grip on the can of Stella. 'Tell him I told you the one about force and fraud being the cardinal virtues of war. He'll realise I wasn't a fucking working-class dickhead after all.' Furious at being duped, he crushed the can like paper in his hand and said through gritted teeth, 'I remain the victor in death while scum like you will enter hell, only to find you're wading through your own shite.'

Suddenly, as the laser hotspot hit his forehead, he saw Lucy and Melinda reaching out for him. Jesus, he thought. It's true what they say.

The gun made scarcely a sound, just a hollow *phut* not unlike the dull thud of an airgun but more ballsy and very un-Hollywood. To his surprise he saw the slug for a split second, frozen real big, like one of those silly CGI effects in movies. He even clocked the fine lines machined at the chrome shaft. Seeing it was more of a subliminal impression, bolted to the realisation that nobody would ever see a bullet that was about to blow their fucking head off and live to tell the tale. It was the last thing he started sensing as a nano impulse. There was a sort of dull explosion then everything began to expand.

Addison eased his finger off the trigger.

The cool thing about lasers was that you didn't waste so many fucking bullets. Where the hotspot went, so went the slug.

He heard the dull pop from Kowalski's head as it came apart and the dumdum bullet justified its fancy tech spec. As the head's contents flew back they splattered across the tacky embossed retro plastic stones glued randomly across the chimneybreast. The dog went fucking spare next door when it heard the body slam into the fireplace with out-stretchy arms. The crumpled can of Stella flew up, spraying its contents in a frothy mess. Stuff fell from the mantel-piece. The bird and the kid eyeballed from the photo. And as part of Kowalski's skull shot towards him in such a con-fined space, Addison ducked.

Fucking fast.

THREE

The woman was facing Hunter from a few seats further along the cabin, typing at her laptop and glancing across discreetly whenever she paused to think.

He'd noticed her watching him in the lounge back at Heathrow. When they'd boarded the flight he was sure she'd lagged behind so she could see where he sat. Catching a helijet was like catching a train to fly. Not surprising because of who'd won the franchise. As at Euston or Kings Cross passengers queued at the barriers till they were allowed through at the last minute. He'd kept well back, so he could work his way alongside her to try and chat her up. But when they'd crossed the skybridge to the plane she'd stopped to check her phone and before he knew it he'd gone past her.

She was executively dressed in a shiny two-piece with a short skirt instead of trousers. Was about his age (32) with long, wavy dark hair and the most beautiful, penetrating deep-brown eyes. She'd deliberately kept crossing and uncrossing her perfect long legs but it was her eyes that had got to him. They'd a weird luminous intensity and seemed to pierce through him when she looked at him, giving her stage presence. Later, he'd realise it was the sandy-coloured edges of her pupils that did this, contrasting with the darker middles. Feeling her eyes drill into his that snowy winter's evening, when he flew back up to Manchester, she oozed elegance and sophistication. Everything about her did.

When she got up and headed for the sliding door at the end of the gangway he noticed Vanessa's face flashing on his phone. After a spate of phone-rage killings Virgin had banned ringtones aboard its public transport. You'd either to feel your phone vibrate or catch it flashing.

'What?' he asked, taking the call, clocking the ENGAGED sign doing its thing after the woman disappeared.

'Has David phoned you?'

'No. Why?'

'He phoned me about ten minutes ago but had to answer the door and said he'd call back but hasn't. Now both his phones are going to voicemail.'

'Maybe he had visitors.'

'Maybe,' she agreed. 'But he wasn't happy when his door buzzed. He suspects something serious about the killing and wants to talk.'

'What about?'

'I don't know. He said he'd tell us tomorrow then said he might tell me tonight. I'll explain over dinner, in case he's trying to ring back.'

She hung up quickly.

It was probably nothing to worry about because neighbours were always looking in on David, to keep an eye on him or do his washing and ironing.

Hunter sank down but kept his phone open so that he could look at Vanessa's photo. Something was bubbling between them. Conventional wisdom warned you not to sleep with your business partner but it had nothing to say about what the fuck you should do if the idea kept popping into your head against your will. He'd been with her for nearly three years, since they'd left the BBC to set up Real Life Pictures. They'd never slept together but were so close they had a rare understanding for men and women outside of the same bed. They spent so much time together that if people didn't think they were brother and sister, or bizarrely on occasion mother and son, it was because they took it for granted they were lovers. And there was the rub, he decided, shutting his phone when he saw the dark-haired woman heading back to her seat as brazenly as a model hitting the catwalk.

31

She did the flirty eye thing as she sat down then clocked her phone flashing. When she answered it and digested something her face dropped, big time, as she shifted into the empty seat next to her and was hidden. Hunter felt his adolescent excitement slipping away. The prospect of getting to know somebody new after nine years and a wrecked marriage suddenly filled him with an immense fucking desolation.

He sensed the helijet turn as it banked through the blizzard into its final descent and the clumsy conical-shaped VTOL engines began shifting to their vertical position. The introduction of an hourly service in and out of central Manchester had been its most successful business initiative of recent years, boosting its international profile and finally enabling it to pull off the Olympic Games. Various high-profile shebangs had come to the city's new international conference centre, including the Labour and Conservatives' annual get-togethers. This had pissed off Brighton and Blackpool, which now had to settle for the crank parties instead of the two major corrupt ones. It was at the recent Tory bash in Manchester that Greenhalgh had made his flagship speech.

Take-offs and landings always brought out a schoolboy enthusiasm in Hunter. Through his snowy window he saw chaser lights flash on round the landing pad atop New Piccadilly Plaza as it angled round to meet them. At eighty-eight storeys it was the tallest building in the UK, housing a five star Hilton, penthouse apartments, offices, shops. It was built in the shape of a gigantic glass tuning fork clad in chrome, red, and grey ribbed laminate with the skyport running across the top. Hamster tubes carrying the lifts went down between the prongs. Huge neon-rimmed stainless-steel letters hung on a mess of girders at each side, announcing boldly:

As the helijet swooped in to land the four massive deflector panels began to move. Snow, which had laid over the past hour, cascaded from them as they lumbered up into position. They stuck out like giant mechanical cloverleaves and enclosed the helijet like a Venus flytrap when finally it touched down.

The PA system chimed then Henry, the Indian-sounding gay flight manager, reminded everybody to take their bags and belongings with them and to have their tickets and ID cards ready. The dark-haired woman was already on her feet, still avoiding Hunter's eye. He was convinced he'd seen her some place before but couldn't figure out the hell where. Maybe at a news conference or a TV bash. It stuck in his mind that she'd eyeballed him on that occasion too. As he gathered up his stuff he made a decision. She hadn't been taking the piss. Whatever had caused her to go cold over the past ten minutes wasn't because of anything he'd done. He followed her into the travel tube, its flimsiness spooking him when the wind suddenly shook and rattled it a quarter of a mile up.

Before he entered the lift he remembered Vanessa's concern about David and snapped open his phone again. He checked he'd no new e-mail then scrolled quickly through his address book.

Kowalski's mobile stopped ringing for a third time. It was still clipped to his bloody utility belt. Addison checked the name and photo on the display. Hunter's partner Vanessa Aysgarth again. A fit platinum blonde with some serious chest, the trendy specs making her look too sophisticated for a thick ex-copper like him.

He went back to the PC and copied the Greenhalgh files onto his memory stick. He'd done the same with Kowalski's e-mail Personal Filing Cabinet. He'd scan it later, to see if DK had written anything that might give a clue as to what he suspected, or if he'd e-mailed anything to Hunter or the blonde bit with the tits. Driscoll was sorting stuff with forensic. The cops who'd find the body would know the score. What would tip them off was a suicide e-note on the PC screen. Addison had primed it to hit Central Police Headquarters just after midnight. It said:

Subj:	**Re: DEATH OF DAVID KOWALSKI**
Date:	GMT Standard Time
From:	d.kowalski@whizzointernet.co.uk
To:	crimestoppers@CPHQ.gov.uk

Sent from the Internet (Details)

Sorry to leave such a fucking mess guys but
I had to be sure I did the job properly. It's not
been the same since I lost Lucy and Melinda.
I've struggled on for nearly a year but I've
had enough. The house is too quiet. I can't
face Christmas without them.

Keep up the good work.

Ciao
Dave K

Addison knew that should do the trick and tug at millions of heartstrings when it got splashed across the fucking papers. He was almost outta there but needed Driscoll to OK the names of Kowalski's wife and kid because he wasn't sure if he'd got them right. He snapped open his phone but then Kowalski's landline set off ringing. An old-style answerphone kicked in and Kowalski greeted the caller. The dog had stopped barking. Instead it whimpered and scratched at the kitchen door. Still its shadow buzzed up and down in the slit of light, its claws tapping ceramic as it tried to sniff under the gap.

Kowalski asked the caller to please leave a message after the beep. It sounded, then Addison recognised Hunter's voice. It said, 'Hi Dave. Vanessa says you've something mega to tell us about the killing. Can you e-mail it ASAP? Otherwise we'll see you in the morning.'

Message end.

The answerphone beeped and settled. Silence except for the yattering fucking dog.

Addison got back to his phone but turned to frown at the kitchen door. The dog was pissing him off. Still wearing the gloves to hide his prints he picked up Kowalski's Sheuze and stepped past the headless body, being careful where he plonked his big feet. Smashed chunks of skull covered the carpet like bits of eggshell, replete with flesh and bits of bloody blond hair.

Taking his position Addison looked up at the spattered ceiling. Human brain, he thought with amusement, and imagined Hannibal Lecter with his knife and fucking fork. Luckily nothing was dripping. He aimed above the dog's shadow and rapid-fired several times. The silencered high-velocity slugs went *phut phut phut*, sounding not so much like gunfire as the sound of automatic impact. The door splintered as the dog exploded. Its food and water bowls clattered. Goodbye Muttley, Addison thought. Impressed by his marksmanship he squinted at the bullet holes, spinning the gun like the Outlaw Kid.

Before he could get back to calling Driscoll his mobile went off. He swore when he clocked the face and stuck the phone to his ear. His wife swore at him and asked if he was going to bother fucking come home. 'I've had some work to do, love,' he said, stepping over a chunk of bloody jawbone studded with amalgam-filled molars. He'd none of his usual steady assurance.

'Work?' she mocked. 'I work all fucking day and cook and fucking clean but you never lift a fucking finger.' She saw the joke in what she'd said. 'There's only one fucking finger you ever fucking lift. It's all you think women are fucking for, isn't it?'

36

'No love,' he implored, appalled by her language. He looked awkwardly at his feet as she reprimanded him then he felt something squirm like a mouse under his shoe and stepped back. He'd stood on a human ear. Wincing, he wiped his foot on the carpet as though he'd stood in dog shit. Got out his handkerchief and kept the phone at his ear with his free hand while he pogoed about on one leg, trying to clean his shoe. Something burst under his other foot as he hopped, and stuff in the room vibrated. He'd landed on an eyeball. 'Shit,' he said, stopping to wipe the snot-like mess from his heel.

'Are you fucking swearing at me?'

When she hung up he decided he'd been a total fucking pillock for marrying her. He stuck the gun in Kowalski's right hand and threaded the forefinger through the trigger cowl then glanced up at the mantelpiece at another photo of the dead cop, standing with his wife and kid. A bouquet of human happiness, snapped at a GMP presentation for bravery. Blood and bits of Kowalski's real face, which was splattered with his brains across the fireplace wall, obscured his proud gawping mug. Curiously, the wife and kid's faces were clean. Addison wondered if they were watching him accusingly when finally he called Driscoll to check their names.

FOUR

Vanessa was calling David again, getting bad vibes while she crossed to stand by the window, phone at ear, as the third ring rang.

When they'd talked earlier, and he'd answered the door, he must have thought he'd cut her off when he hadn't. She'd heard somebody over the intercom but couldn't tell what they'd said because of Ted barking. But she'd heard a guy's voice when the phone was near the speaker. David swore at him and opened up to let him in then must have sussed the call was still live. Before he'd killed it the somebody came in and shut the front door behind them over a passing train. It was the last thing Vanessa heard. Now she sensed something was seriously up.

The fifth ring happened.

With the sixth his mobile ran to voicemail again. She cut off the 02 girl and tried his landline one more time.

Answerphone.

She cancelled the call and wondered what the hell to do. Through the window she saw the dot of the lift that would be carrying Hunter, dropping between the twin towers of the Plaza in a tinted yellow hamster tube, on its way to the transport interchange that formed the ground floor. He always walked back to the hotel for the exercise. Meaning she'd maybe fifteen minutes before she needed to be in the restaurant.

Still fretting about David she decided to try something. It was a long shot but her instincts told her that whatever he'd dug up was connected to one particular guy. She'd no idea how she knew. Call it gut feel. Call it women's intuition. Crossing back to the bed she sat down and started Googling the number of a newsagent's shop.

Driscoll was in his office and just sitting down in front of his enormous glass-slab desk when his mobile rang. The desk was so fucking OTT it made him think of an Egyptian Pharaoh's tomb because of the way it dominated the airy, simply furnished room. Although transparent it was filled with water and carbon tetrachloride contaminated with multi-coloured amoeba-like swirls. These constantly shifted and collided before splitting like the blobs of wax in a lava lamp, kicking light.

He OK'd the names for Addison and watched his phone screensaver collapse, playing its cheesy jingle as it settled into park mode. So that was it. Kowalski had become the proverbial meatified funny. Whatever he knew should have died with him. But had it? Driscoll sensed big time shit was headed his way.

He spun to face the nighttime city view through his tinted picture window thirty-five storeys up. He'd intended to go home but after hearing Vanessa's little confab with Kowalski decided to stay behind to check something out. He kept going over what Kowalski had said. *I'm onto something that'll blow the lid off this whole bastard thing.* He hadn't told Vanessa what but she now knew that he'd suspected something. She and Hunter were shooting a film about the Greenhalgh killing and would be under surveillance from tomorrow because of it. When they found out Kowalski was history the shit would hit the fan. Hunter would start digging because he was a persistent bastard with his unfashionably long hair and trendy leather trenchcoat, making him look like some useless fucking dolebrain out of *The Matrix*.

So what did Kowalski know? Why had he wanted to check some CCTV footage? There was indeed a tiny detail that could blow the lid off this whole fucking thing and send the balloon up. Driscoll had voiced his concern but it had been pooh-poohed because chances were millions to one against anybody noticing.

His console beeped. Snow slashed at the window as he spun back in his chair and took the call. It was Collins, a young Scot in Communications Surveillance.

'She's on the phone again, sir.'

'Who to this time?'

'Samrah.'

'Really?' He didn't know why but suddenly alarm bells were blaring in his fucking face.

Samrah was a key witness to Greenhalgh's kidnapping. His scruffy newsagent's was a hundred yards from where the MP's car was attacked. Samrah saw the chauffeur get his head blown off and saw the gunmen chase Greenhalgh into an alley. He'd provided descriptions of the gang of black thugs. Not that he'd seen much because they'd worn plastic joke masks and balaclava hoods. If he'd seen anything worthwhile he wouldn't be alive.

'I've MP3'd it for you from the top, sir.'

He typed then whacked Enter to patch through the call. Up it pinged onto the PC, the green Audio Wave Form bouncing merrily as Vanessa reminded Samrah who she was. Driscoll put the call through the room speakers then with folded arms sat back to listen.

Samrah had remembered her straight away.

'You were with the guy in the long leather coat weren't you?'

'That's right,' she said.

'Aye, I remember you love.'

Something in his voice indicated that what he remembered was that he found her attractive. He was a likeable little Indian guy from Bradford who sounded more broad-Yorkshire than most OAPs who remembered when Bradford had only a few hundred Asians working in the mills and Britain was a different place. She was a good judge of accents herself because she also came from Yorkshire, albeit the more genteel rural bit to the north of the old industrial heartlands.

She'd bantered a bit while she reminded him who she was but now got to it. 'I know you declined to be interviewed for the film, but I wondered if you'd be willing to talk off the record.'

'What about?'

'David Kowalski.'

He hesitated before saying, 'The cop?' stating the obvious to buy some time.

She sensed his unease and knew she'd struck a nerve. Buoyed, she stood up and stepped into her brown suede high heels, a favourite ploy of hers to help stay ascendant. She was a gnat's twitch under five-eight-and-a-half but the shoes took her nearer six foot. Maybe phoning Samrah had been a panic move but she said from the hip anyway, 'I'm worried about him. He phoned me tonight and told me he suspects something big about the Greenhalgh killing. Then we got cut off.'

She let the observation dangle.

'Did he say what?'

'No. And he isn't answering his phone.'

Now the defensiveness cranked, the shutters slammed down. 'You can film outside tomorrow, love. I can't stop you doing that. But don't come in with a camera or I'll ring the police.'

'Is there anything you can tell me?'

'No love, there isn't.' He seemed pissed off, which only implied there was something else he knew. She'd spoken to him once in person, when they did a recce for the shoot and he refused to be interviewed. That was how he'd remembered her. He'd struck her as being a nice guy, with no axe to grind. As if hearing her think this he countered guiltily with, 'Look love, I've got nothing against you and your boyfriend.'

'He isn't my boyfriend.'

'Every bugger who's crawled over this place from the press or TV has offered me a bribe. You and your boyfriend haven't. I liked you both.' He primed another pause so he could lay it on. 'I know you're only doing your job but for God's sake just leave it. It ain't worth it.' She heard his shop door's groovy electro-jingle and some kids laughing as they tough-guyed in, no doubt for an Alcopops fix. 'Customers, love. I'll have to go.'

He put down the receiver slowly, like he didn't want to fob her off.

She stared at her phone. His ID photo made him look like a Middle Eastern hitman. It was the big brow that did it, the strangely inebriated look to the dark eyes, the shiny pockmarked cheeks. But what the fuck was that about? All that had rebounded from her phoning him was that she was more concerned than ever about David's silence.

FiVE

Everybody stampeded across to the barriers.

Hunter took his time, bringing up the rear with his long coat flowing, so he could see where the woman went. She answered her phone as she joined another queue but still avoided his eye. Part of him couldn't be arsed with her and wanted to get back to Vanessa ASAP. And yet, as he watched her talking and flicking back her hair, something about her offered a chance to escape. From what he wasn't sure. She seemed assertive but calm and composed, like a cat caught by headlights. It was as if he were being granted a special dispensation to look at her.

When she'd finished on the phone and was sticking it away she accidentally caught his eye and smiled. He did it back, nodding at a bar on the concourse, and raised a hand to suggest having a drink. She frowned and looked away. Getting the message he didn't look at her again till he was going through the barrier.

He heard her block heels clumping and turned to see her coming up behind.

'Actually, I don't like pubs,' he said, inhaling her wonderful feminine scent.

'Neither do I.'

'Can I get you a coffee?'

'No you can't.'

'We've met before.'

'I don't think so.'

'We have.'

'No we haven't.'

Fuck you then, he thought resentfully, letting her go. Cock-teaser he tacked on, with a spasm of juvenile anger as he fell back. Talk about shoulders doing the fucking low temp thing. It was the first pass he'd made in ten years. He wondered what the hell she'd been playing at when she moved briskly away to join a thin, severe-looking young black guy who was waiting for her near the entrance. The boyfriend, no doubt. Tall and slick in a snazzy brushed-steel looking suit, standing by a couple of frowning, gun-toting, gum-chewing cops packaged in bulletproof body kit. Hunter heard the black guy ask her something with a deep concerned voice that seemed way too Bolshie for his lanky frame. It was more like a rhetorical statement than a question.

She passed her case to Mark and followed him through the revolving door onto the busy street. They moved quickly because the Lexus was parked on the short-wait pick-up bit, its hazards partying at the wet.

'What did Hunter want?' he asked her again, dodging people.

'Nothing,' she said, heels clumping, brolly going up.

'What did he want, Abigail?'

'Nothing.'

She saw Hunter arrive outside in time to see her getting into the Lexus. She'd hated pissing him about. When she wanted something she went for it. He was right. They'd met before. She knew all about him and the film he was shooting. She'd wanted to liaise with him, as Sir Ian would say, aboard the helijet. Had been getting ready to go over to ask if the seat next to him was free when her phone had rung and she'd discovered that Simon had been found murdered at Felixstowe Docks. Mark was in town and came straight over to pick her up, to whisk her back to an emergency meeting at Copley Hall. If he'd seen her with Hunter questions would have been asked.

Computer started filling her in when she sat down but her attention was on Hunter. She'd waited weeks for to-night, getting Computer to flag up Hunter's ticket so that she could catch his flight. He watched her as he stood buttoning his coat and people wiped in front of him this way and that. The snow swirled more lazily down here than in the sky. She knew he was trying to figure out why she'd cold-shouldered him after coming on at Heathrow and during the early part of the flight.

Kareem's voice came from the 4x4's speakers. 'What's the verdict, Abigail?'

'Sorry?'

'Was Driscoll involved in Simon's death?'

She told him what she thought. Simon was a young guy who'd had a crush on her. His hologram revolved in front of Computer's screen. She could only bring herself to look at him when he was in profile, or showing the back of his head. 'He was onto the stainless steel run,' she said. 'It was the same lorry at Trafford Park yesterday.'

'Fucking hell,' Mark retorted knowingly as he pressed the ignition button and the Lexus rose.

'That points to Driscoll,' Kareem chipped in.

'Indubitably,' threw in Computer, his vectorscope syllable-bumping at the dash.

'I'm going back first thing in the morning,' Mark said. 'And this time we fucking nail it.'

The guys were gunning for blood because Simon was their first fatality.

While Mark waited for a break in the traffic so he could pull out she watched Hunter. She found him so attractive it scared her. If she'd got to him on the plane she was sure she'd have spent the night with him. Avoiding his eye she clunk-clicked her seatbelt and half-covered her face when Mark stuck his foot down and took off, splashing slush as they joined the traffic.

siX

Driscoll had been frowning at his PC, wondering, since the call ended. It was such a fucking pain to think about doing it he wasn't sure if he could be arsed. But after listening to Samrah and Vanessa he stood up and took off his jacket then loosened his tie like a man on a mission.

There was no need for him to play back the Samrah call because he doubted if there was anything to read between the lines. Instinctively he knew that Samrah had played schtum with Vanessa because he was scared of the gang coming back. The cops who took his statement had planted this possibility in his mind, as they did with all witnesses. Until Kowalski they hadn't needed to kill anybody because everything had been planned with a military precision, right down to the bogus roadworks that diverted Greenhalgh's Jag.

It was what Kowalski had said about checking CCTV footage that galvanized Driscoll. There'd been a thorough post-mortem of every aspect of the kidnap but something was at the back of his mind. They'd checked the HD footage closely but had made a couple of gaffes. The first was to assume the witnesses had told the truth. The second was not asking the computer to speculate because, on the back of mistake number one, there was nothing for it to speculate about. AI was happening but computers could still only respond to questions they were asked. It was this that was bugging him.

So it was Edward de Bono time. Time to remember a tatty Pelican from when he was an undergrad and do a spot of lateral thinking. *About Samrah's Transit van.* Some detail, winking at the edge of his mind.

Snow still slashed at the window as he hooked his jacket over his chair then sat back down and poked a button at his console.

'Yes sir?'

'I want to see the recording of the Michael Greenhalgh kidnapping.'

'The digitally enhanced stuff?'

47

'Yes please.'

One of the beauties of today's State snooping world was that it had HD CCTV cameras every fucking where, paid for by those whom they snooped on. The excuse was that they were needed in the fight against international terrorism. The real reason was that they enabled Snoopsville to raise extra revenue by petty-fining people with money in their pockets.

He typed his Password then up popped the CCTV tiles in sequence, each one a different camera POV freeze-frame parked. He maximized # 1. Knew roughly whereabouts on the universal timeline he needed to be. Found it. Hit Play Movie. Entered a crystal-clear 1920x1080 HD world.

A high-angle CCTV view showed an inner-city pavement drenched in autumn sunshine. Midway across it a phone box tapered away due to the wide-angle lens looking down from above. Greenhalgh's blue Jag pulled up, its nearside front tyre clearly blown. When the car had stopped Greenhalgh's grey-uniformed chauffeur, George, got out wearing sunglasses and a peaked hat. He took off his super-cool shades to squint up at the Indian Summer sun then hooked them back and walked round to the kerb to check the dead tyre. Normanshaw was a dangerous place. Obviously au fait with this George glanced uneasily at the street and said something to Greenhalgh, who was reading a paper in the back of the car and had sent down his window. Neither of them knew that a sniper blew out the tyre using a silencered automatic rifle seconds before the Jag hit the CCTV's view.

Although the camera had recorded audio, the constant drone of passing traffic drowned out the conversation. But enough of the MP's face showed on the ultra-sharp footage for the computer to scan his mouth, enabling it to play a digi simulation. Unfortunately Greenhalgh swore, which the computer considered to be inappropriate. It auto-censored the offending words and froze the action. A camp CG voice said, *'But the tyres can't [BEEP] blow out, George! They're [BEEP] run-flats!'*

The computer also superimposed the words letter-by-letter, blink-fast-rapido across the screen:

> **BUT THE TYRES CAN'T F*****G BLOW OUT GEORGE! THEY'RE F*****G RUN-FLATS!**

Then it *gerdunged*:

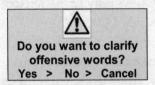

> ⚠
> **Do you want to clarify offensive words?**
> Yes > No > Cancel

Driscoll frowned.

Like smoking, the use of bad language in public was becoming stigmatized. Instant fines and the Exchequer gleefully rubbing its hands at the prospect of exploiting a foulmouthed nation were just round the corner. He clicked NO and told the computer to keep going.

Walking like a man used to wearing stilettos instead of moccasins George pranced effeminately back round the front of the car with his shadow leading. He paused to let a 16-wheeler roar past, its fat twin-tyres cutting through frame-top. He waved a hand nimbly at the fumes then stiffened. He'd heard a high-velocity slug coming straight at him. In the split-second it took him to clock it his head had exploded exactly like when The Jackal shot the watermelon. His body jerked back. His hat flew up and swelled huge into the camera then flipped out of frame just before it hit. A moment later it reappeared as it rebounded from the brickwork under the lens. Beneath it George's headless body was falling from the first bullet hit among a spray of blood and brains. Another shot holed his back and popped out some ribs. Another demolished his shoulder. In the back of the car Greenhalgh dived, sending his newspaper flying. As George crashed onto the car bonnet his arm that took the hit to the shoulder separated and boomeranged over the Jag's roof into the road where a truck ran over it, crunching it and burning rubber as it got jammed round the inside wheel arch.

Unaffected by the grisly scene Driscoll paused to bring up tile # 2 and a new POV.

The van.

He needed to see Samrah's fucking van.

The new POV auto-picked-up where the old view left off because everything had been recorded multi camera and was timecode linked by Central Matrix. He whizzed on till he found the same place in the movie. In the new view the phone box had shifted across frame. Greenhalgh was scrambling on all fours towards it away from the open back door of the Jag. Holes turned the car into a colander, aureoles of shiny steel zinging-zanging each time a bullet went in machinegun quick. There was a terrific Hollywood energy to the slug hits and the frenetic noise of windows popping like light bulbs. It was a disconcerting effect, but not as disconcerting as the passing traffic, which seemed to Driscoll not to give a shit about the attack as it tootled merrily about its fucking business.

He changed angle again and picked up camera # 3 from across the road, in time to catch Greenhalgh making it to his feet and stumbling into a cobbled back alley further along the street. Samrah's silver Transit was parked outside a row of tatty old shops in a brick-and-ferro-concrete ghetto where jazzy urban Wiggles Bboy caked every vertical surface. Driscoll clocked straight away what had bugged him about the van. It was so obvious it was fucking crazy. Greenhalgh's Jag had stopped a few hundred yards from it. Jumping on again, still watching from across the road, he picked up the action when three masked gunmen were striding along the pavement blasting at the shop windows randomly with pump-action shotguns. Although disguised with plastic Halloween joke masks the guys wore black balaclavas underneath.

Suddenly the sniper who'd shot at the Jag ran out from behind the Transit. Unlike the other gunmen his joke mask was missing. Driscoll knew it had fallen off when the guy had sniped from a nearby rooftop. He wore only a black balaclava. Black skin showed round his eye sockets and wrists. When he went behind the Transit (on the opposite pavement to the camera) Driscoll paused again, swearing to himself as a realisation hit him.

When the sniper was hidden behind the van he swapped his rifle for two shotguns, Duck-taped together, which were lobbed across by the nearest gunman. The Jag was parked arse facing. As he stalked back into view the sniper aimed at the Jag's fuel tank and coolly jerked off several rounds. With the third shot the car spectacularly exploded, flames tongue-wagging through its blasted window sockets. Driscoll paused again and hit slow-mo Rewind. Everything crept backwards till the sniper came out from behind the Transit. The ball of fire sucked itself back into the Jag. Comically, the sniper pranced in reverse and threw the shotguns back to the other gunman then went behind the Transit.

Now Driscoll went for camera # 4. It was similar to the first POV, looking down at the pavement and phone box, but wider and aimed the other way. This time the Transit was in full view from the front. The sniper came in from the bottom corner, still running backwards along the pavement. Driscoll crept the action back a frame at a time till the sniper backed up next to the driver's window of the Transit.

Then he killed the action and zoomed close. It was plain to see what had been prying at the back of his mind. The van's windows were *mirror-finished. You couldn't see inside the fucking Transit.*

Meaning you couldn't suss if anybody had been fucking well sitting in it either.

Driscoll toggled in and asked the computer to assess the distance between the driver's window and the head of the sniper. Then he asked it to imagine if somebody sitting in the Transit could have been close enough to give a description. The computer regretted that it lacked sufficient information to reach a formal extrapolation. Driscoll asked it to speculate. It said that an eyewitness account being good enough to grab a conviction was unlikely because of the sniper's disguise. Even if the scene were recalled under hypnosis he wasn't clear enough to be identifiable. Driscoll asked it to assess the same probability if anybody sitting in the van had been looking at the gunman through a tinted mirror window. Even less likely, the computer said. Not impossible but the number it threw up to indicate the odds stacked against was so long that Driscoll couldn't get his head round it.

He sat back with compressed lips and folded arms. The tension he'd started feeling earlier was easing. Maybe he'd been paranoid. But still he stared thoughtfully at the image on screen, weighing things up.

Several minutes later he was still staring. Sleet and hail slashed at the window.

MONDAY

SEVEN

Mark was there before dawn, driving his cherished 1975 silver XJS into the sprawling Trafford industrial park at the western edge of Manchester.

He passed MUFC's vast empty snow-dusted car parks then took a left at the bottom of Sir Matt Busby Way and headed into the misty darkness. The roads were quiet at that hour. Only a few taillights faded on the dual carriageway up ahead.

He was careful not to excite the speed cameras but stuck his foot down between them with Gary Numan's *Dominion Day* going at the speakers. He'd intended to take the same route Simon did yesterday but by a fluke had seen the target lorry coming from the other direction when he'd hit Chester Road. He needed to stay low in case it passed him again. He was sure the driver had given him the big stare when they'd tried to give way to each other. Plus a classic car stuck out on the quiet roads. He'd also assumed the rig was making for the freight depot. A few days ago they'd tracked its sister to the Dunford Bridge Freightliner Terminal across the Pennines, where Mark would be going tomorrow night. There might even be a rig number three. He wouldn't know for sure till he'd videoed the one going the other way because all the rigs had false plates.

He met a convoy of juggernauts coming towards him. As soon as he crossed over the next roundabout a derelict Victorian brewery started passing on his right. When the road was clear up ahead, and in his rearview, he swerved into a street on the left. It faced the grand brick façade of the brewery offices, which were being demolished. Embedded in the cobbles was a rusty railway line that would have led to the brewery sidings before the new road had thwarted it.

Mark did a fast three-point turn and pulled up five hundred yards from the main road under a dead streetlight. He killed the car's lights and engine then snapped loose his seatbelt, sank down, and lit a cigarette. He hoped the XJS wasn't obvious against the freezing-cold darkness of the impending dawn and said to his Bluetooth, 'It's on its way. Assuming that working on my tod I haven't been dumb enough to fucking lose it.' He sensed Abigail wasn't at the other end of the line because she didn't insult him. Kareem said she was on her way back up from a meeting with Sir Ian, following the announcement of Kowalski's death on TV.

Across some wasteground to Mark's right the demolition bulldozers had been barricaded overnight in a wire-fenced compound, their windows hidden by graffiti-caked steel plates. Through the fencing he saw the blue-and-yellow rig he was waiting for, powering across the roundabout towards him on the main road.

'Here it comes,' he said. He got ready to hightail after it but the lorry suddenly slowed as it neared the brewery offices. 'Shit,' he tacked on.

Abigail responded from the speakers, rustling and bumping stuff as she sat down. 'I can't hear you Mark.' She meant because of the music.

'Sorry,' he said and killed it.

She told him where she'd been and that she was going into Manchester to a snap news conference at CPHQ at 10.00am.

'What's happening?'

'It's stopping,' he said, watching it slow, sinking in his seat. 'Come on, you fucker,' he added, coaxing the moment. The lorry drew up at the bottom of the street with its airbrakes complaining. Chrome writing on the sides of the trailer and the cab kicked back the streetlight glow. The rig belonged to an old family firm of stainless-steel fabricators. 'It's pulled up in front of me,' he said, riding his enthusiasm. 'The driver's getting out.' He eased up to peep through the crook of the steering wheel where it curved above the lovingly polished walnut dashboard. The driver made for the back of the trailer with lit cigarette in mouth and phone stuck at ear, shooting breath and smoke. 'Shit,' Mark said, sinking down again.

'What?' she asked.

'He looked straight at me but I don't think he saw me.' He edged up. The driver stuffed his phone away when he hit the back of the trailer. Glancing round furtively at the deserted road he quickly unbolted the doors.

'What's he doing?'

'Opening up.'

'Be careful. They might be onto you.'

'I don't think so.' He reached for his infrared binocs on the seat next to him. Brought them up to his eyes and hit scan. 'I'm sure there are guys inside. I can see something moving.'

'So Simon was right,' she said.

'Looks like it.'

'Video it.'

'Will do.'

He adjusted the scanner. Digi chatter kicked in and the image whizzed up, throbbing concentrically red. The HD guidance locked on like a laser gunsight through the 235:1 sight-masking as Record mode began.

Mark saw the driver look round again. Oblivious to the XJS he threw a box of matches into the back of the lorry then banged shut the doors and whacked across the bolts. But not before a cigarette butt flew out and landed in the road. Mark saw it and swung down the binocs.

'Ah hah,' he said, hitting macro zoom, reaching to stub his own cigarette with his free hand. The smouldering butt came up massively clear. 'Looks like he stopped because a wanker in the back of the lorry phoned through to ask for a fucking light.'

The driver climbed back in and revved up. Smoke shot from the exhaust pipe behind the cab then its airbrakes creaked and hissed while it hauled ass, trailing fumes.

'It's setting off,' he said.

'Towards the terminal?'

'Yes.'

'Follow it,' she ordered.

'Not yet.'

'Why?'

'I'll tell you in a mo.' When the lorry had gone he got out and hurried down the frosty pavement puffing breath, rubbing his hands in the bitter cold. He let the road clear then ran over, picked up the butt, and crossed back to the pavement to check it under a streetlight. Gold writing on the stem ID'd it as hailing from Eastern Europe. 'Bingo!' he said triumphantly.

Abigail asked him to explain. He tried to prattle stupidly in Polish but sounded more like a dumb Russian, filling her in as he zipped the butt in a forensic bag and headed back to his car.

EiGHT

Hunter was stuck in never-never land, in Vanessa's room late the previous evening. The lights were romantically dim. Snowflakes chased outside the window.

61

Over dinner she'd explained what David had said about Driscoll and how he'd suddenly ended the call to answer the door. His phones had rung out ever since. E-mails to him were being ignored. They'd speculated about what could have happened then wondered if he'd had second thoughts about talking, because of his accountability as a cop. The dream felt real enough even though Hunter knew it wasn't. Him sitting on the buffet in front of Vanessa's dressing table an hour after they'd come back up from dinner. Her sitting against the pillows on her bed with folded arms and legs thrust out, high heels slipped off, long skirt spread, pale eyes sparkling sexily in lamplight. They often sat up late chatting when they worked away. She was a good listener and during the dark days of his divorce had been there when he'd needed her, especially when he lost custody of his kids and his world ended.

Withdrawing from a long relationship after being crapped on had damaged him. The thought of getting to know somebody new was scary. He doubted sometimes if he'd have the urge to find another mate. For most of the past year work had consumed him. But flying back from London that night his body had started working again and he'd opened up to Vanessa about the beautiful dark-haired woman. Despite her cold-shoulder job she'd been on his mind ever since. As he described her, he noticed how Vanessa's feet, which were crossed at the ankles, started twitching against each other involuntarily. He sensed it was an unconscious reaction to her inner thoughts, perhaps her embarrassment, as he talked about the woman and wondered if it was time he went for another relationship. And yet, paradoxically, the more he said how much he wanted to find the woman, the more turned on he got watching Vanessa sitting on the bed. Now his dream took a reality check, sparked by something minor that had happened back in the carvery.

When they were eating he'd glanced across at Vanessa when she went to the salad bar. He'd been thinking about the film they were shooting, and what great company she was, when he got caught off-guard, like he was looking at somebody else. He saw a tall, beautiful blonde wearing a shiny crinkly skirt, which hung nearly to her ankles, and a t-shirt that couldn't have been tighter if it had been soaking fucking wet. Suddenly he'd realised that he fancied her like crazy. For the first time he imagined not just going to bed with her, but being.

In love with her.

It hit him like a bolt from the blue because he'd seen her as he really saw her, eclipsed sexily as somebody else. But something else egged him on, which was the kicker. In his dream it made him wonder if something was happening between them when he was awake. He usually brushed it off as being driven by the pain of losing Hayley and Jenny, or some obtuse reaction to his divorce and long celibacy. After all, Vanessa was an incredibly attractive woman and he was a no shit, HS guy.

But in recent weeks he'd sensed a change in her. An encroaching loneliness, unnoticeable to most people but a no brainer to him because they worked together. It squared with the shift in how he related to her and seemed to have stirred his growing unease. It was like they were facing up to an abstraction materialising through a mist between them but avoided talking about it. As soon as this awareness arrived in his dream he began to panic. He knew he was in morally dangerous territory from which he should keep away. He didn't articulate it but felt it as a kind of suppressed emotional impulse. Told himself coolly, rationally, that he must forget he was falling in love with Vanessa, just as somebody might be programmed to break a bad habit during hypnotherapy and have no memory of it when they resurfaced.

They were still together in her room in his dream but now a gun started hammering, remote to begin with, battering the edges, deflecting his thoughts. He was still submerged, swimming up but also sinking back, fighting himself he knew in his heart.

With an overwhelming sense of relief he started to wake up, but not before Vanessa drew up her long legs on the bed and her skirt rode up. Lightning struck him between his legs when he saw that she'd nothing on underneath. He heard himself moan at the sight of her then stood up and headed straight across. He fell to his knees, literally slavering like a dog, fighting it, begging her not to but fighting it, unable to take his eyes off it. *I can't go on like this*, he despaired, somehow independent of his dream. *It's fucking tearing me apart.*

Sending his tongue into her he moaned out loud in his sleep and could have sworn he'd called her name. The gun was still fucking hammering, banging at his head, blowing everything apart.

It was his room phone next to the bed, going off in his face like a machinegun, blasting his brain as his dream caved in. It was the second in as many days and they were getting worse. He saw Vanessa spinning away naked as the sound of the real world crashed in, like faders shoved up on a dubbing console. Wailing sirens cut across the city.

The rush-hour traffic churned New Central Square, flooding his room with its familiar steady rhythm.

'Vanessa,' he moaned, unsure if he'd heard it right but fighting it in case he had. As his eyes cracked open he saw the digi clock next to the bed glowing 07:23 in bright red. Still the gun hammered. 'Vanessa.'

He blinked awake in time to see the clock make it to 07:24. He dragged the receiver across, nearly dropping it, and heard her voice.

She sounded shocked.

'Are you up?' she asked.

'Hang on,' he slurred back.

'Have you seen the news?'

He usually slept deeply and for a moment, lost in the early morning darkness of the bleak midwinter, he'd no idea where the fuck he was. He tried to remember what he'd been dreaming about but couldn't. He thought he'd said something in his sleep just now but couldn't remember what. It left him feeling anxious. As the fog cleared he realised that he was covered in sweat with his cock full on. He automatically pulled up the quilt to hide it.

'Have you seen the news?' she insisted.

'You woke me up,' he said. He flopped back shellshocked. Normally he'd have been up for an hour at this time but they were starting and finishing later today.

'David's dead.'

'What?'

'They're saying he's committed suicide.'

'Shit no.' Coming round quickly, he elbowed himself up and switched on the bedside lamp.

'Sarah phoned to tell me. They've called a conference at CPHQ at ten.'

65

'I don't believe he'd top himself for a minute,' he said, still dazzled.

'Neither do I.'

'Are you OK?'

'I'm not sure,' she said, her voice trailing. 'I heard him let somebody in . . . he was such a nice guy.'

Hunter knew she was filling up. 'Something fucking stinks. I can sense it.'

'So can I,' she managed. 'There's no way he'd kill himself. And after what he said about Driscoll. What if they were listening?' She was shit scared. Not a state of mind he associated with her.

'I'm coming up,' he said, banging down the phone, knowing she needed him.

He took a squirt then threw on some jeans, a t-shirt, and boots. They usually had rooms next to each other. Because he'd been home for the weekend, and the hotel was busy, he'd been moved down to the third floor. She was still way up on twenty-fucking-six.

NiNE

When Abigail swung the Lexus into the snowy approach road leading to Central Police Headquarters she clocked the pair of traditional blue police lamps (no doubt fitted with EU regulation low-energy bulbs) hanging incongruously from the impressive sci-fi portico. They were Driscoll's personal stamp on his home patch after he took over as Manchester's zero tolerant chief cop in 2014. They looked as out of place in today's super-slick, ultra-violent, foulmouthed world as PC George Dixon bidding a good evening to all from quaint old Dock fucking Green.

Despite its trendy prefix the building wasn't, strictly speaking, in the centre of Manchester. It stood south of Deansgate, nearer Salford on the map, just across the river from the acclaimed Civil Justice Courts (CJC) completed at Bridge Street West in 2007. At forty-six storeys CPHQ was only two short of nearby Beetham Tower's forty-eight and equally as impressive in the way it struck at the sky like a massive obelisk.

In line with modern architectural trends giant chrome letters ran up it, across it, and hung asymmetrically off it, saying bluntly:

$$\begin{array}{c} \textbf{C} \\ \textbf{POLIC} \textbf{E} \\ \textbf{N} \\ \textbf{T} \\ \textbf{R} \\ \textbf{HEADQUARTER} \textbf{S} \\ \underline{\textbf{L}} \end{array}$$

The italicized letters were primrose yellow, complementing the colours of the adjacent CJC with its daring tinted-glass slab cantilevered offices, jutting like half-open filing cabinet drawers above the busy piazzas.

In Abigail's opinion CPHQ was bolder, built when the Modernist Revival started to influence British architecture. It was finished in stylish black glass and chrome with lilac and primrose yellow highlights, not unlike the old Lloyds Building of London to look at but more strikingly futuristic, with its mess of exposed girders and pipes. Circular helipads stuck out from the four sides at the top so that from the ground it resembled a giant cloverleaf. Only two of the helipads had so far been commissioned. Police gunships flying to and fro, and helijets twice hourly at Piccadilly, caused problems for the *Coronation Street* exterior set at Granada TV. Despite intervention from the EU's Environmental Nuisance rottweilers Driscoll ran them out of town and the noise carried on.

She was in good spirits at the prospect of seeing Hunter after yesterday's fuck up. She'd dressed up for him in an orange-pinstripe mini-skirted business suit and a matching tan blouse embossed with a subtle shiny pattern. Her hair was stacked, showing her elegant neck, with strands hanging stylishly at each cheek. As she joined the queue of cars leading to CPHQ's underground multi-storey she decided that Hunter should be at the conference because he knew Kowalski and had been due to interview him that morning for his film. This time she intended to go for him if she got the chance because she was sure he was available. But she'd need to be careful. CPHQ was riddled with CCTVs. She didn't want any conversation recorded in HD with the possibility of the footage being scanned and lip-read by senior bent cops.

Her phone rang as she neared the barrier. She was still wearing her Bluetooth after the drive in from Cheshire and thumbed a button at the steering wheel.

'Abigail,' she said.

'Are you presentable my dear?' asked Kareem.

'I'm always presentable,' she said. 'I'm a beautiful leggy woman.' He didn't bite at the humour, even though he'd fed her some.

Which meant it was serious.

'I've got Sir Ian for you.'

Here we go, she thought. She'd an instinct like a water diviner's. Sir Ian was one of the busiest billionaires on the planet and flew by private chopper between north and south two or three times daily. If he didn't speak to her through a subordinate it meant one thing. He was fishing.

A smooth upper-middle-class voice came from the speakers. 'Abigail, my dear. I do hope you're not driving while using your mobile phone.'

'I'm a good girl, Sir Ian. I'm in hand's-off.'

'Goodness me, I wouldn't know about such things. All my phones are still made from Bakelite.'

She grinned. The self-deprecation was bogus. An elderly rich man's attempt at charming a smart young woman in a thoroughly modern world. He knew all about phones because he owned a company that made them. His money had converted the RX 500 she was driving into a machine so advanced it wouldn't have been out of place in a Bond movie. It was armed with some of the most powerful computer kit as yet generally unknown to man. Plus heat-seeking missiles. Sir Ian knew the spec better than anybody because it was his. If only PC Plod, who was eyeing her from his booth as she crept nearer, knew.

'I gather this morning's stainless-steel run was pretty significant,' he was saying.

'Yes Sir Ian.'

'Mark's convinced that Poles are in the lorries.'

'It would seem so.'

'And this dead policeman,' he said, moving on quickly. 'David Kowalski?'

'What do we know about him?'

'In what way, Sir Ian?'

'His apparent suicide.'

'That's what I'm on my way to find out.'

'It seems convenient, don't you think?'

'Yes, Sir Ian. But a lot of what we do is informed by strange coincidence.' His small talk was to try and cover the fact that he was gunning for something. She knew why he'd phoned. Had been expecting it since she left the heliport with Mark last night. As she inched forward she felt her heckles rising.

He said, 'Wasn't he on TV, in a documentary about the police?' Here it comes she thought. 'What was the young chap's name?'

'The guy who made the programme?'

'Yes.'

'Hunter, Sir Ian.'

'Ah yes. The series is up for an Oscar isn't it?'

'A BAFTA, Sir Ian. Oscars are for movies.'

'Of course. What do we know about him and the most engaging looking woman he works with?'

She said Vanessa's name but he spoke over her, an annoying habit of his reflecting his superior social standing. Now for the humdinger quip.

'Married to her isn't he?'

'I think you'll find, Sir Ian,' she said, her heckles going ballistic, 'that they aren't married and that he isn't fucking her.'

70

She wasn't sure if sex was happening between Hunter and Vanessa but was impressed at how quickly she'd put Sir Ian in his place. Her tyres squeaked at the lacquered concrete as she turned in through the chicane and hit the barrier. The bovine-faced cop standing in the booth twitched his zapata moustache at her when she sent down her window and stuck her ID card in the slot. Her hologram revolved as Central Matrix swiped her eyeprint and made it beep green. As the barrier lifted she reached for her card and set off but couldn't resist winding Sir Ian up when she tipped down the ramp. She sent her husky voice down a notch, asking suggestively, 'Would you like me to liaise with him, Sir Ian?'

'Goodness me, no,' he said, flustered. 'The committee must approve liaisons. You know that.'

'Of course, Sir Ian.'

He was a nice guy but from a generation that couldn't get its head round strong independent women. His young advisors did much of his social thinking for him, to keep him up to date. A sound came from his throat but it didn't quite make a chuckle. Now that his control of the conversation was slipping he'd lost interest in it. 'It'd be worth you looking into his background though,' he waffled. 'See what connections he has. Meanwhile, see if you can uncover anything about this Kowalski chap and keep me informed.'

'Yes, Sir Ian.'

He hastily killed the call.

Which had been pretty damned pointless really, she decided, like somebody had egged him into making it. She saw a parking space big enough for the Lexus and thumbed a button at the wheel.

'Mark Halliday,' she said, prompting Computer to auto-dial the number.

Mark answered straight away.

'Fuck you,' she said.

'I beg your pardon?'

'You heard. You've been poking your nose into my affairs and blabbing to Sir Ian.'

'I have not.'

'Yes you fucking well have. Hunter made a pass at me when we got off the plane. That was all.' She pulled up, checked there were no CCTVs and that nobody could see her let go of the wheel, then folded her arms defensively while Computer parked.

'There must have been a reason,' Mark said mulishly.

'In case you haven't noticed he's making a film about Greenhalgh. And he knew David Kowalski. It would be in our interests to get to know him.'

'Have you told Sir Ian that?'

'Not yet.'

Through the prison-barred windows on the far wall she saw the sky darken as a blizzard swept across the river but suddenly the day was becoming clearer. Everything was. If he weren't getting married next summer she'd have said Mark was jealous. But he wasn't. He was trying to protect her. He was younger than her and dedicated and extremely good at his job, but his well-meaning possessiveness reflected his old-fashioned view of women. Like Sir Ian, he couldn't believe a woman was tough enough to look after herself. She was touched and felt the tension of the past few minutes slip away.

'Mark?' she said.

'What?'

'I'm sorry.'

'You can be a nasty bitch sometimes,' he grunted, popping a short raspberry. 'What I'd be asking myself if I were you,' he added, reading the situation, 'is why I got so fucking wound up in the first place.'

He cut her off before she could bite back.

Smiling to herself she revised her opinion of his old-fashioned outlook and got back to thinking about Hunter. Suddenly aware of her naked body inside her slick clothes she allowed a look of quiet expectation to settle on her face while she gathered up her things.

TEN

Hunter hurried across the hotel Reception and headed for the stairs to the basement car park, on his way to missing the conference if he didn't move it.

Normally he'd have walked down to CPHQ but he'd had a late breakfast because he'd been with Vanessa longer than expected. She'd been shaken by David's death and had seemed unusually vulnerable, as if something was going on emotionally in her life that she was keeping to herself. At one point she'd looked at him from under the lids of her eyes like a young girl hiding a guilty secret. Something similar happened in her room last night. Because of the sledgehammer moment when he'd clocked her at the salad bar during dinner he'd had a few glasses too many of red wine and thought bollocks to the consequences. Bad move. Last night watching her sitting on her bed, this morning sitting with her on it, it would have been so fucking easy, he was sure of it.

He saw Sarah coming up the hotel steps and hung on to brief her. She was 23. Tall and slim with short black hair and those cool, girly good looks, backed up by a high IQ, which American women did best. The lenses of her trendy designer specs made her bush baby blue eyes intense and staring. She was wearing black platform boots, sheer black tights, and a short black leather skirt and matching bomber jacket. Seemed to be mostly legs and, because of her clashing bright pink gloves and scarf, looked edible. Her chief difference to the other woman in his life was that she had a much flatter chest. Originally from Wisconsin she'd settled locally after coming to the UK to attend film school. They went out of their way to hire her when they worked up north.

'Hey,' she said.

'Hey,' he said, giving her a quick hug, not quite pulling off the Stateside greeting.

'How is she?'

'Fine,' he said. 'She was cut up first thing.'

'Understandably.'

'Yeah.'

'Dave was a real sweet guy.'

He told her the heavy snow forecast for Wednesday was due to arrive tomorrow instead. Because they'd booked the crew that day for a 12.00pm start, to do David's interview, they'd decided to shoot the exteriors outside Samrah's shop. In the meantime they were going to record the live news broadcasts from the conference, to see if they could work out what David had been going to tell them. It was a long shot but they'd nothing else to go on. He told her to go up to Vanessa's room and said he'd see her when he got back.

When he made the stairs he decided to take the lift. As he hit the buttons Sarah turned back, saying, 'Hey by the way, Julia Hall's in the building.'

'Bloody hell no,' he said.

'She made a pass at me in the elevator last night.'

'Unlucky you.'

'Maybe you should take the stairs.'

'Yeah,' he said, his eyes going straight to her leather-clad buttocks when she turned. She was a great kid but he didn't like the cradle-snatcher thoughts that were darkening his mood.

At last a lift pinged apart.

'Darling,' said a small husky-voiced, red-haired, gushing nymphomaniac. Her piggy eyes went up to meet his only after they'd been down to his groin.

'Julia,' he said, as she stepped out and greeted him in a manner so OTT even the Germans stopped swearing by the vending machines. 'It's always a pleasure.'

Two suits had been marooned with her and looked relieved to be gulping new air.

ELEVEN

The conference suite was on the tenth floor of CPHQ. When Abigail arrived it was nearly full.

Most of the scruffy journalists blocking the door were shorter than her. They parted like peasants making way for royalty as she squeezed past and made her way across to a seat near the front. At the back of the room TV crews were still taping down cables and setting up equipment. At the front a clear-plastic counter awaited the senior officers. An embossed police authority emblem hung like the Star of David on the wall behind it. Sitting alone, looking self-conscious, was a fat, middle-aged, plainclothes cop with a birthmarked bald head and several chins. As Abigail sat down and checked her phone for e-mails the cop eyeballed her smarmily, turning to page three of his *Sport*. He must have thought she didn't notice him tilting on his chair as if to discreetly let out a fart.

Within easy reach of any methane that might be headed her way was a young black secretary, typing names into the digi panes in front of where three senior cops would sit. Driscoll's name popped up centre stage, green lettering burning against black. The fat guy was next, misspelt after the black kid stuck a hand across her nose but quickly corrected when laughter rippled across the room:

< DETECTIVE SERGEANT >
< WAKERN >

Then a third name. Abigail recognised him from the Greenhalgh hoo-ha, meaning he must have flown up that morning from New Scotland Yard:

< DETECTIVE SUPERINTENDENT >
< STONEHAM >

Behind the fat cop a TV cameraman was panning slowly across the audience. She saw him crank in the zoom before he made another pass. Some instinct told her to turn away when the camera was nearly on her.

She took her cue, hoping to see Hunter. More people were coming in. Snow slashed at the big aquatinted back windows but still no sign of him.

He was sardined with half-a-dozen journalists and Julia Hall in the tiny lift down in the car park, wondering if the doors would shut. It had turned out that she was gracing Manchester with her presence for some self-indulgent TV quiz tomfoolery, which was being shot that afternoon. The *Guardian* had phoned her and told her to get over to the conference. Hunter had offered her a lift, God knew why. She was a formidable middle-aged columnist who'd always flirted with him, widening her heavily made-up eyes at the end of every sentence. By all accounts she sucked young men, and the occasional young woman, in at one end and crapped them out from the other. She reminded him of a *New Monty Python* cartoon where a dwarf trampolined on a fat bird's stomach, making her legs kick to a farting noise each time he *boinged*.

This morning, as she wittered on conceitedly about herself, he regarded her with contempt and wished she'd shut the fuck up. Like some other puffed-up newspaper hacks he knew he didn't trust her as far as he could throw her, which wouldn't have been far without rupturing himself. Everything about her was vain and unsophisticated, from her agonising preoccupation with herself to her vivid drag queen make-up and coarse black denier encasing her short stubby legs. There was no comparison between pointless, coke-sniffing sluts like her and classy women like Vanessa. It was as if they were from different species. The older and wiser he got, the more conservative he sensed he was becoming.

Since they'd got out of the car she'd acquired an interest in why she was visiting the conference. As the lift began to rise she said over her shoulder, 'I've never been convinced about cops saying they've become hardened to the job. It was a nasty murder and his unit discovered what was left of the corpse.'

'Yes,' he said, as the first floor went by.

'A steady exposure to violent crime is bound to have a detrimental effect on their psychology.'

'Yes,' he said again.

At the panel a neat CG diagram of CPHQ flicked each passing floor and zinged it green. Everything shifted with a movie-like CG perspective, which struck Hunter as being nerdish and OTT. Numbers would have done just fine. He heard her saying, 'But I don't suppose you could get over having your family wiped out like that.'

'No,' he said through a reflex yawn.

'I had my reservations about him but he didn't strike me as being the sort of working-class dope who'd throw in the towel because he couldn't manage.'

He felt obliged to defend David with, 'It's bright guys like him who commit suicide because they reason everything out,' then stifled another yawn.

As she prattled on he wondered, bleakly, if somebody ought to whack her over the head with a shovel and put her out of her misery.

Then *bang*. Something whacked him when he glanced at the phone which the guy next to him was holding. It was tuned to a live TV broadcast coming from upstairs. Hunter's heart jumped when he saw the dark-haired woman in close-up. He'd to look twice at the tiny widescreen picture but couldn't believe his luck. She was so fucking beautiful it hurt.

TWELVE

Abigail looked round when Driscoll swept in wearing his uniform, carrying his hat, his bullet head shining under the striplights.

Stoneham tagged on red-haired, strongly built, square faced, watery blue-eyed, Germanic mean-looking with a beetle brow so pronounced it might have been a prosthetic effect. He wore a retro-groovy *Colombo* mac, which Abigail remembered from the Greenhalgh press calls as being his sartorial trademark. In today's increasingly nasty, zero tolerant world he looked like the sort of cop who stamped on a crook's head and asked questions later. A gang of uniformed officers, looking like a Nazi death squad, backed him up. As they bulldozed delegates down the side of the packed room Driscoll frowned with disapproval, no doubt pissed off by the dirty-dog smell of damp clothes and wet hair. No, at the plebeian germs he was obliged to inhale as a superior human.

Hunter came in last, preceded by Miss Piggy from the *Guardian*, who disappeared in the scrum of figures by the door because she was small. Hunter joined the crush lining the windows, through which snow raged, although the sun was trying to make a hole. Abigail saw his eyes make contact with hers across the sea of heads like a heat-seeking missile locking onto its target. This time she offered no resistance and fired back his animal sex look. *I want to fuck you*, it said, not mincing shit. As she turned back to the job at hand she'd a mental picture of him going at her, their naked limbs grittily intertwined, like a dated flash-frame cut in a *CSI New York* rerun.

Driscoll and Stoneham took up their positions next to Wakern, who gave a formal cough before struggling to his feet as the signal for everybody to shut gob. Again Driscoll frowned while a hush descended and Wakern sank down, his chair groaning under its load.

Then Driscoll got to it.

'Good morning ladies and gentlemen. We thought we'd better hold a press call quickly so if you don't mind I'll declare it open.

'As you all know, Detective Sergeant David Kowalski tragically died last evening. The death of a policeman is always an unpleasant affair. Bearing in mind he was in the headlines after the loss of his wife and daughter we're anxious to stem speculation about the circumstances of his death. We're living through an unusually sensitive time, with serious matters being debated in Parliament, and we wouldn't wish to throw fuel on the fire.

'Normally I'd delegate a meeting like this but because of David's profile and popularity in the force I thought I'd chair it myself and make it clear from the start that we'll not be looking for anybody in connection with our investigations.' A murmur passed round the room. He let it subside, along with various congested sniffing noses, before adding, 'Meanwhile, we'll answer your questions as thoroughly as we can.' After some more formalities he introduced his colleagues and revealed that Stoneham was now with Special Branch. Then he fielded the questions. Hands shot up. Voices erupted. Photoflashes went off.

Driscoll pointed at somebody near the front but Abigail couldn't see whom.

'Carol Cruickshank, *Northwest Tonight*. When you announced David Kowalski's death this morning you implied that he might have been contemplating suicide. You've also said you won't be looking for anybody else. Was the DS depressed?' Her lugubrious voice made her sound like a stav queen on acid.

'It's fair to say that he hadn't been in the best of spirits,' Driscoll said. 'I noticed this yesterday, when he spent an hour in my office. Statements from his colleagues will help us build a picture of what he was going through emotionally in the weeks leading up to his death.'

81

Abigail was about to raise a hand when Carol Cruick-shank cut in again. 'Are you suggesting he was still upset about losing his wife and daughter?'

'The general consensus is that he was still grieving Ms Cruickshank, yes. He lived alone and rarely socialized and was committed to his work. He was an experienced, capable young officer who would have gone far.'

Hunter was bugged because he was too near the window. He tried to look past some TV cameras and saw the dark-haired woman write something down. The meeting Driscoll had referred to would be when Kowalski saw the interim report which had spooked him.

Julia Hall, whose thick black-stockinged legs were crossed with difficulty, piped up. 'Why was he heading the inquiry into Greenhalgh's killing? I thought Special Branch took over high-profile political incidents.'

Stoneham straightened on his chair and answered, his voice unexpectedly smooth and articulate. To Hunter his eyes had a strange feminine intensity which played weird games with the Incredible Hulk physique. 'Not necessarily,' he said. 'Although Special Branch was involved, David's unit discovered the MP's body and he asked if he could take charge of the investigation.'

'Do you think he might have been adversely affected by the politician's death? After all it was a brutal murder that may have aroused memories of his domestic tragedy.' The question, still aimed at Stoneham, had come again from Julia Hall. Hunter clocked straight away that she was eye-balling the DS because she never let the fucking sex thing rest. Ignoring her on both counts Stoneham turned to Driscoll for help.

'You're asking us to speculate, madam. It would be unwise for us to make assumptions at this stage, although clearly we shan't discount them.' Pointing again he looked increasingly resentful, as if the way the questions were going was pissing him off.

'Who discovered the body at the scene of the crime?' It was a trick question from one of the tabloids, underplayed to trip Driscoll up. He spotted it immediately.

'Technically we're not discussing a "crime", young man. David was found dead in his lounge. He appeared to have taken his own life using a police firearm, which was still in his hand.' Everybody scribbled when the lounge and firearm details were revealed.

The questions and answers went round in circles until Driscoll pointed at a stunning, well-spoken young Asian girl. She obviously thought Hunter was eyeing her up, instead of the dark-haired woman, because she was in the same line of fire each time she turned round. She announced herself and said, 'Sir, didn't the dead officer have a pet dog? TV reports showed him frolicking with it earlier this year.'

'Yes madam, he did.' He seemed to cut his answer short. Immediately a dozen hands shot up with a babble of questions. It was the tabloids, galvanized at the prospect of writing sentimental headlines about an abandoned domestic pet.

'Is the dog alive or dead?'

'Where's the dog?'

'What about the dog?'

They'd asked the same thing from across the room. Hunter's mind raced as Driscoll raised a hand like he was holding back traffic then pointed again at the Asian bird, allowing her to keep pole position. 'Can you confirm if the dog is alive or dead?'

'Not at this stage of the inquiry, no.'

Definitely sensing something, Hunter raised a hand but was ignored. He wondered if Driscoll was drawing attention to Ted to divert it away from David. Or maybe he was being vague because he knew everybody would jump. If so it had worked. The audience was livening up since the mention of the dog.

Driscoll let some tension crank before nodding for the Asian bird to go again. 'Early reports suggest neighbours heard the howling of a dog.'

It was like electricity had sparked the room. Frowning, Driscoll ignored her and pointed at somebody else but a Scottish guy, his nose bunged with catarrh, butted in. 'Witnesses say they heard a distressed dog.'

Somebody else: 'Tell us about the dog, sir.'

'The dog,' again.

'The dog.'

'The dog.'

'The dog.'

Driscoll knew there weren't any witnesses and that nobody had mentioned hearing a howling fucking dog. They were trick questions being fired by these bog-eyed vultures in the hope of bumping their rags' slumping sales before the web killed them off once and for all. He resisted any more nonsense about the dog and scanned the room. Finally he saw Hunter, who grabbed his chance and sent the questions off on a tangent.

'Chief Commissioner, you said David was found with a police gun in his hand. In which hand,' he added, seeming to Driscoll like he was eyeballing somebody a few rows from the front, 'was he holding it?' Driscoll's mind raced as he checked some papers on the desk.

'In his right hand,' he said back.

'But David was left-handed,' Hunter countered.

A murmur ran across the room like another electric jolt. *Shit*, Driscoll thought, feeling the banana skin underfoot. He sensed TV cameras zoom in at his face at the same time as he remembered that *Kowalski was left-handed*. Addison had dropped a serious fucking bollock when he stuck the gun in Kowalski's right hand.

Driscoll sympathised with politicians who spouted bull-shit during live TV interviews. When an interviewer had you by the bollocks you'd to try and think through your answer without seeming to pick your words. It meant you sometimes opened your mouth before you were ready and came out with crap. Or seemed to avoid answering *because you didn't have time to fucking think*, like happened just now. Trust Hunter to stick a lit firecracker up the horse's arse. Stoneham bailed out the moment by lifting a page of notes so they could fake a consultation.

'My mistake,' Driscoll said. 'Apparently the gun was in his left hand.'

Before he could move on, the young Asian bird, spurred by Hunter's torpedo question, demanded: 'Do you think there's a pattern to these two killings?'

The question went off like the firecracker had exploded up the horse's arse and showered the room with its shit. In the ensuing lull Driscoll heard only the thudding of a gun-ship high above CPHQ.

'I don't know what you mean, young lady.'

Hunter dived in again.

Driscoll saw the bastard eyeballing him when he ganged up with the Asian bit for a double whammy to insist: 'Do you think there's a pattern to the deaths of Michael Greenhalgh and David Kowalski?'

Driscoll met nobody's eye. Instead, boiling with rage yet hiding it with icy professional calm, he directed his rapier-like answer as though it were a formal statement. 'I see no pattern except the familiar pattern of lawlessness. I see no pattern except a vicious underworld undermining the conduct of civilized people as they go about their lives.' He wanted to bang down his fist and smash the fucking table but resisted the temptation.

Everybody was getting excited but Hunter managed to intercede: 'You say David was assigned to the Greenhalgh case because he requested it. But wasn't he on an area exchange when the MP disappeared? Didn't you order him back here to take over the case?'

How the fuck did he know that?

'No Mr Hunter, I didn't. I don't know where you've obtained that information.'

'From David,' he said. Seeming to overplay the presentiment he added, 'Don't you agree that his death is mightily convenient?'

Abigail joined in with most of the audience and turned to face Hunter. Until then she'd been quietly admiring him. He was always a few days charismatically unshaven and seemed more like a rock star than a current affairs journalist. There was something about him that was rebellious. Not in the sense of the usual people-hating scruffbag but more the unruly sixth former letting stink bombs off at a debating society because it wound him up to hear anally-

86

retentive tossers talking pretentious rubbish. But now that he was going for Driscoll's throat her alarm bells started ringing big time. She watched him inquisitively, wondering what the hell he was getting at. Everybody else was wondering too.

Driscoll retorted, 'My priority is to report the facts, not to speculate about why David Kowalski was killed' — but he'd fallen straight into Hunter's trap.

'Ah, so you're admitting he was murdered?'

'No I am not!' He was flushing but managed to keep it together. He searched for another raised hand but there weren't any.

Clearly knowing, like any reporter rocking and rolling, that the confrontation would go out on TV Hunter went for Driscoll's jugular. 'And is it not a well-established fact, Chief Commissioner, that you're behind the Police Federation's lobbying of ministers for the reintroduction of capital punishment? Isn't that why this conference was staged quickly — to egg the public into linking David's Kowalski's "suicide" with high-profile murders, capitalizing on a popular desire to tackle drugs and gun crime and "see the bastards hanged"?'

Shit, Abigail thought. Talk about waving a red rag to a bull. Driscoll was a seriously nasty piece of work. She tried to tell Hunter to back off by looking straight at him, trying to conceal it from everybody around her, trying to tell him *No*. Sussing it, he lost his verbal footing enabling Driscoll to grab his opportunity.

'I shall say this once, Mr Hunter. Your allegations have no relevance to this conference. If you've any more questions we'll answer them if we can. But any more remarks like that and I'll have you escorted from the building.'

Journalists were getting up to leave, which kicked off a noisy minute where everybody yacked at each other or at their phones. Abigail could see that Driscoll was grateful for the commotion. Over the din he mouthed something to Stoneham under his breath then they threw Hunter hard stares. Some guys were clamouring to talk to him but he'd switched his attention to her.

She was fighting through the crowd towards the door but locked eyes with Hunter. She knew from his expression that he was pissed off because she was doing what she did to him on the plane last night. Except this time she was on the run.

THiRTEEN

She made it out of the conference room and hurried across to the lifts. She was sure that Driscoll had clocked her and Hunter eyeballing. After what just happened she couldn't afford to let the cops think they'd something going or her cover could be blown.

She'd intended to go out of the building's front entrance to try and fox him. But the doors to the empty lift leading down to the car park were open so she nipped inside and smacked the button. As the doors came together she saw Hunter burst out of the conference. He saw her and ran through a live Sky News broadcast towards her, nearly bowling over the woman presenter. But when he was half-way there the doors met, the lift pinged, and Abigail started to go down.

Hunter didn't waste time with the fucking lift but barged through to the staircase and took the steps down as fast as he could. His long coat flew out behind him, slowing him as he jumped the last half-dozen steps to each deck, nearly losing it on his dodgy ankle. She was wearing high heels and a mini skirt, meaning she couldn't move fast. She'd have to find her car, unlock it, get in. He'd ten floors to get through but reckoned he could be halfway before she was anywhere near the bottom.

She dashed out between the parting doors when the lift hit the basement car park. In the muggy hush of the low-ceilinged space her heels echoed dully as she hurried across, looking for the Lexus. Nobody about so she slowed, lifting her wrist to hit a button on her watch to say, 'Emergency, Computer.'

A few aisles away she heard the Lexus's alarm *pip-pip* as it de-armed itself and fired up. Behind her Hunter bulldozed through the metal staircase door, making it clang into breezeblock.

Puffing, he scanned the car park, heard her heels *clump-clumping* over a big 4x4 engine, tyres squeaking as it turned to meet her. Then he heard a door slide open and shut. Somebody was rescuing her. He assumed the black guy from the heliport then saw the Lexus a few rows away. Because of its size it manoeuvred slowly. Hang on a mo, he thought. He lost his bearings while he digested what he'd heard. He'd clocked the Lexus driving with her heels still running *over it*. Yet she was on her own, sitting behind the wheel. The Lexus was *driving itself* while she seat-belted up. He ran across. Managed to jump on the running board next to the driver's door and fought with the handle. He couldn't slide open the door because the central locking had auto-kicked in.

'Please get off!' she shouted, muted through the glass, hitting the brakes.

'Why were you trying to warn me?'

Ignoring him she banged her hand on the horn and kept it down. Then they saw macho man hurrying down the ramp from his booth up at the barrier, spooked by the din. In the heat of the moment Hunter had remembered where he'd seen her before. At the Tory conference when Greenhalgh made his swan song speech, then at the press calls after his murder. He didn't know if she could hear him over the blaring horn but said anyway, 'You're no journalist, yet you've been at big political events and some high-profile press calls. Who the hell are you'—he saw her conference ID badge still stuck to her lapel and managed to read—'Abigail?'

To know her Christian name made him want to whoop with joy. He'd wanted to call Jenny Abigail but had let Vicky override him, seeing as she'd endured the agony of childbirth.

As the cop neared, Hunter stood off the running board. She let go of the horn and sent down her window to say, 'Officer, this man is bothering me.'

The cop still had some yards to cover. She gripped the wheel and gazed resolutely ahead. Hunter said to her, 'I don't know who you are but David Kowalski was murder-

ed. He phoned my producer last night to say he'd uncovered something big about the Greenhalgh case.' She turned to eye him uncertainly but an understanding seemed to
pass between them.

When the cop arrived his nominally bovine expression
hardened to complement his Groucho Marx moustache.
He weighed up the false alarm but as a precaution unclipped his holster with a hard man, movie actor timing.

'Is everything OK Miss?'

'Yes, officer.'

'You said he was bothering you.'

'Not any more he isn't.'

Hunter looked at her despondently, trying to work out
what fucking game she was playing. She set off, driving
smoothly up the ramp, but had to wait for the exit barrier
to shift. Then she was away into the blizzard.

As if reading Hunter's mind the cop said, 'I don't blame
you, man,' as they watched the Lexus's tails fade through
the snow. Hunter shrugged and shook his head. 'Some ID,
please,' the guy added, turning serious.

'I wasn't hassling her.'

'Some ID.'

He felt for his ID card and held it out.

'A lovers' tiff?'

'Something like that.'

The cop handed back the card. Saying nothing else, he
loped back towards the ramp.

Hunter asked, 'Any chance of me seeing who she works
for on the list of conference guests?' Without turning the
cop waved a fat stubby hand dismissively and muttered
something through a yawn but Hunter couldn't tell what.
'Point taken,' he said anyway.

He turned then turned back, intending to be sarky, but thought twice. Instead he crossed to Vanessa's Volvo and stood next to it thinking about Abigail. He was pissed off because she'd run away from him again but buzzing because he knew it wasn't the last he'd seen of her.

FOURtEEN

Abigail phoned Kareem when she was driving away and asked him to e-mail through Hunter's OPQ report.

Journalists were always having TV spats with the police and this morning's would soon be forgotten. What set her mind going about Hunter was the way he'd nailed Driscoll, implying that he suspected something fishy about Kowalski's death. She'd been watching Driscoll for most of the past year. He was at the root of something big, though as yet they didn't know what. He was also dangerous, with a history of sexual violence towards women that you could find if you dug deep enough. Sir Ian would pick up on the TV broadcasts and ask her to find out what lay behind Hunter's accusations. Meaning he'd approve a liaison, in spite of the crap he'd spouted about the committee needing to give it the A-OK. Downloading a copy of Hunter's Psychometric Report was the quickest way she had of finding out what kind of a guy he was and learning more about his personal and private life.

Since leaving CPHQ she'd shaken out her hair and was in the middle of a hands-off conversation with Kareem.

'I'm on the BBC mainframe,' he said, 'highly illegally, of course.'

It was only late morning but the high-rise piled around was so brightly lit through the swirling snow it might have been the end of a miserable afternoon.

The stack beeped when the files arrived. On Computer's screen Hunter's holographic head popped up and revolved slowly, the resolution so lifelike he could have been patched via a video link.

'I've got him on Central Matrix as well,' Kareem said. 'He's divorced. Do you want the settlement files?'

She hesitated, but not long enough for him to notice.

'Yes please.'

'They'll take a few hours.'

'That's OK,' she said. Parrying quickly she asked, 'While you're on, can you get me another OPQ report?'

'Fire away.'

'His business partner Vanessa Aysgarth. She's also ex-BBC.' As she slowed for some red lights at White City the snow got its act together and came straight down. 'Can you get her stuff from Central Matrix as well?'

By the time the traffic lights hit green she saw Vanessa's head replace Hunter's and the matrix stacking down the right-hand side. Before she switched her eyes back to the road she managed to read:

AYSGARTH>	VANESSA ELIZABETH
AGE>	FORTY-ONE (41) YEARS
MARITAL STATUS>	SINGLE

And further down the same column:

HAIR>	PLATINUM
EYES>	LIGHT BLUE
HEIGHT>	1.7374 metres
WEIGHT>	58.9670081 kilograms

'Thanks Kareem,' she said.

She was surprised to find that Vanessa was nine years older than her. This came as something of a relief because of what she was about to do. She ended the call and touched a button at the wheel.

'Computer?'

'Good morning, Abigail.' At any time he responded to her commands without necessarily engaging in dialogue, as happened back at CPHQ. He conversed only if she cued him. She could believe his booming voice had been sampled from a recording of Sir Ian and camped up by some slamstick in Technical. 'How are you?'

'I'm fine,' she said, knocking back the volume. 'How're you?'

'Very well, thank you. I believe it's snowing where you are.' He'd have scanned the Met Office website, instantly correlating it to her satnav position when she started a dialogue. 'Would you like me to forecast the weather?'

'No thanks. I'd like you to open the two psychometric profiles we've just downloaded.'

'Which one would you like me to scan first?'

She was passing the slums along the southern edge of the city. The old terraced houses, many of them derelict with their roofslates looted, came up to the elevated inner ring road and in places disappeared under it. Adding a bizarre contrast in the distance was a monorail, slicing past a row of massive Chinese distribution warehouses, which struck hangar-like from the horizon.

She decided not to beat about the bush. The age gap between Hunter and Vanessa reassured her but she couldn't be sure sex wasn't happening because nowadays it was common for strong older women to screw fit young guys. Plus Vanessa was stunning, regardless of her age if not because of it, and a refreshing contrast to the dumpy hags who were typical of the mysterious closed-shop world of TV's above-the-line. More nigglingly, something about her made her look right with Hunter.

'Let's start with Vanessa,' she said.

'Analysis or overview?'

'Overview please. Some general info. Where's she from? She looks Swedish to me, yet Aysgarth's an unusual English-sounding name.'

'Her Nordic demeanour comes from her great-grandfather, who was Icelandic,' Computer said. 'He came to this country in 1898. His name was Gunarsdotter but with the outbreak of the First World War he feared the family would be ostracised with a German sounding surname. So he took the name of the Yorkshire village where he'd settled as a farm labourer and changed it to Aysgarth.'

'Of course,' she said. 'Aysgarth Falls.'

'Correct,' Computer said, and flashed a Google grab of the famous waterfalls on his screen.

'She's not married but is she in a relationship?'

'She was when the report was compiled.'

'Was it long term?'

'Five point three years, as of thirty-seven months ago. As the report is not current I cannot speculate about the longevity of the relationship.'

'Was it with a male or female partner?'

'Male.'

'OK, please scan the Hunter files.'

'Yes Abigail.'

The dashboard analyzer showed that nobody was monitoring their talk so she got to it. 'Is anything sexual going on between Hunter and Vanessa?'

'You're asking me to speculate, Abigail. The reports are over three years old. As I explained they indicate that Vanessa was in a committed relationship.'

'Let me try again. Scan their OPQ reports and advise me on the compatibility of their personality types.'

'Analysis or overview?'

'Analysis please.'

There was a digi-chatter pause. 'Analysis complete,' he said, vectorscope bouncing.

On his screen the profiled heads of Hunter and Vanessa faced each other off. 'OK, now you can speculate,' she added, smiling to herself at out-manoeuvring him and pushing her hair behind her ear. Although snow was still swirling dull sunlight filled the car, gilding every surface. As she joined the M56 she stuck her foot down and moved to the new high-speed lane. Effortlessly tore past the traffic in a 120mph low-profile-tyred blur.

He said, 'I would speculate that sexual intercourse between them is likely.'

'But you can't tell me if it's happened?'

'I'm afraid not, Abigail.'

'OK,' she said. 'I'd like you to open another file.'

'Yes Abigail.'

'Open my OPQ report.' Her face revolved on screen, her head having been scanned when her hair was shorter and dyed a honey colour. 'Compare Vanessa's Psychometric Report with mine.'

'Analysis or overview?'

'Analysis please.'

'Yes Abigail.'

'How much alike are we as women?'

'Analysis or overview?'

'Overview please.'

Computer was scarcely able to contain himself, which made his vectorscope bump rhythmically when he started chuckling.

'What's the matter?' she said, smiling because she knew what was coming.

'You and Vanessa are very similar as women.'

'I thought you might reach that informal conclusion.'

'It's a formal extrapolation, Abigail.'

'Sorry,' she said, feeling happy. 'Extrapolation.'

She was into rural Cheshire now. Snow was still falling, knocking back the rolling fields to an undulating grey-white haze where they raced past with the bare winter trees. Smiling to herself she came off at the next exit and saw a helijet descending on Manchester, its red-and-white livery muted through the blizzard. Not many guys could handle a woman like Vanessa because they'd find her difficult to dominate. She'd had her fifteen minutes in the celeb press, after she'd broken the jaw of a big-time American film director when he groped her bum in a Hollywood bar. This still amused Abigail when she hit the village and turned left at the church, reflecting on what she'd really sussed from the three OPQ reports about Hunter and Vanessa as matching personality types.

FiFtEeN

Driscoll's office was under the south-facing helipad where it got the most sun. It was connected to the basement car park by an exposed private lift which ran in a tinted glass tube up the outside wall.

An hour after the news conference he was sitting at his desk. Addison and Stoneham were sitting in front of him. The snow had stopped and strong winter sunlight shone through the window, pinging from Kowalski's badly scratched helmet. Addison had just thrown it across, having stripped its computer. Driscoll turned it speculatively in his hands. 'Are you sure his PC was clean?' he asked, feeling relieved.

'Quite sure,' Addison replied. 'I took it apart. He hasn't typed a fucking thing. I ran a search and he hasn't uploaded anything new for two weeks. I'll scan the PFC files, in case he converted it to Arabic to try and fuck anybody off. He hasn't e-mailed Hunter or Vanessa since August 4th. I'll run checks to make sure he hasn't used another screen name. I reckon he didn't give anybody the heads-up after you showed him the report. He wouldn't have had time before I got there.'

'We still don't know where he went on his way home or who the informant is.' He compressed his lips and thought about it for a moment. 'At least the only evidence Vanessa's got about what he told her is what he told her.'

'That's right,' they agreed.

'And now he's dead. In which case it's an allegation and she can't prove a fucking thing. This morning's row will soon be forgotten.' He threw the helmet back to Addison and filled them in about Vanessa's phone call to Samrah last night, as a way of trying to weigh things up. 'Something about that little shit doesn't stack up but I can't put my finger on what. The cameras in his shop are patched to us, aren't they?'

'Yeah,' Addison confirmed. 'He'd not have got the insurance without.'

'So if Hunter goes in we'll know about it.' Thinking it would be useful to see what Hunter and Vanessa had shot so far for their film he told Stoneham to get onto Sumners, the local post-production house they used when they were up north.

'They're down-converting their rushes at the BBC because Sumners is installing some new kit.'

'Tell the BBC whatever's necessary to get us access to a copy of the shot material before it's edited. But be discreet. I don't want Hunter or Aysgarth to know.'

Stoneham OK'd then got up and left with Addison in tow, still carrying the helmet.

When they'd gone Driscoll sat back with his hands stuck behind his head and mulled things over. Embedded in the opposite wall were several rows of mute TV screens tuned to daytime shows. *BBC News* was looking back over Kowalski's life. A report showed him playing with his dog, not long after he'd lost his wife and kid. Then some footage ran from the cop series that Hunter made. Up came the spontaneously captured moment when Kowalski found out what had just happened to Lucy and Melinda. He'd agreed for it to be kept in the film, making for one of the most powerful scenes in British fly-on-the-wall TV history. A nation had wept when it saw a good man's life shattered. Driscoll shook his head but felt no remorse after what they'd done to Kowalski. Focusing on the bigger picture was what mattered. Sacrifices were sometimes necessary to benefit the greater cause.

Earlier he'd checked the video footage from the car park. It showed Hunter chasing the brunette but a partition wall hid the camera from her Lexus so the pictures couldn't be scanned. Whatever Hunter had said to her when she'd killed the horn was so low on the Richter scale the computer couldn't notch up the audio. The cop who saw it reckoned Hunter had been trying to pop his cork but she'd told him to piss off. Driscoll wasn't convinced. He was also still unsure about Samrah. EU regs made the police jump through hoops when it came to grilling witnesses. They could wave a subpoena at Samrah or try to threaten him, but threaten him with what? Something told Driscoll to bide his time. Suddenly wondering how Hunter was getting on with his filming outside Samrah's shop he decided to catch up with Surveillance.

Hunter stood in crisp sunshine, checking his script, halfway along the cobbled alley that Greenhalgh ran into after he'd escaped from his car. Shabby back yards lined each side, some with incongruous uPVC doors opening onto it. The small redbrick terraced houses ran away, many barricaded with B&Q's popular wrought-iron budget security grilles. Satellite TV was a thing of the past but numerous rusty old dishes still sprouted from the dormer-knackered roofscape because nobody could be bothered to take them down.

In front of Hunter a TV documentary crew was gearing up for a take. Graeme, their strongly built temp cameraman, lifted the HD kit onto his shoulder and tweaked the heated viewfinder to stop it steaming up. Harry, their elderly, portly, white-haired sound guy, checked the radio mike by asking Hunter for some level.

'The Killing of Michael Greenhalgh,' he said, stating the film's title. The mike was clipped to his lapel. Harry nudged it then asked him to go for it again.

Vanessa was huddled girlishly against the cold in her green suede bomber jacket with a pair of mirror shades propped on top of her head. Her stylish platform shoe-boots made her legs look even longer, complementing the way she strutted up and down with an assertive upright posture, which Hunter knew could intimidate other strong women. She was going over the script with Sarah. Two runners were stationed one at either end of the alley. The guy on the main road was guarding the Volvo and Harry's royal blue Patriot.

Vanessa finished with Sarah then shouted for a kid who was on work experience from a city media school. He was pacing near the cars, smoking furtively. When he heard Vanessa he broke the law and trod on his cigarette then made a big thing of jogging towards her. He was excited to be participating in real TV production. The naïve seriousness with which he took humble cable bashing lit up his acned but well-meaning face. When he arrived Vanessa

101

waved at the runner furthest away. He did a thumbs-up and stepped out of sight, to avoid showing behind Hunter when they were shooting.

While Sarah dabbed some powder onto Hunter's face to take away the shine he reflected on what had happened at CPHQ. After the stand-off in the car park he'd had a coffee with a guy he knew from M Channel who confirmed what Hunter had sussed as an experienced filmmaker. That his row with Driscoll didn't come across on TV anything like it did in the conference room. The microphones fanned in front of the cops picked up what Driscoll had said clearly enough. But the voice mortar bombing him with accusations echoed vaguely from off camera, with not much standing out. As for Abigail, she was a mystery and keeping her distance for some reason. She wasn't a journalist. You got to know faces in the news trade, even the provincials. She might be a writer researching a book, as Sarah mooted during the drive out to Normanshaw, but Hunter doubted it. She looked and behaved more like a high-powered businesswoman than any writer or journalist he'd come across. Whoever she was it was obvious what was going to happen between them sooner or later. When it did, he sensed theirs would be one of those relationships that wouldn't need much breaking in.

Vanessa called chop-chop by clapping her hands and stamping her feet from the cold. The sun shone obliquely along the alley picking out everybody's puffing breath and highlighting the scaly texture of the cobbles, which were still frosty in the shadows. She lowered her shades then drew on her fluffy mittens saying, 'OK guys?'

'Ready,' Graeme said, assuming his first position.

'Harry?'

'Ready folks,' he replied, adjusting his cans. The kid ceremoniously picked up the cable joining Harry's old DAT recorder to the camera, so that nobody tripped up as they backed away from Hunter during the take.

Vanessa said to Harry, 'Turn over.'

To keep costs down with such a tiny crew they didn't slate the shots. Instead Harry announced them impeccably in public school English. He watched the LEDs on his kit. 'I'm turning,' he said, anticipating, 'and I'm at speed.'

'Action,' said Vanessa, her eyes blanked by her shades. She lifted them back up as soon as she'd called and gave Hunter her director's stare. He wondered if the guys could sense the special thing they shared when they were shooting. With his breath surrounding his face and her beautiful eyes drawing out his performance he advanced slowly towards her and began to speak.

When they'd finished, and the guys were packing up, Hunter ran through the schedule with Vanessa and Sarah next to the car. Prompted by some of the questions he'd asked on camera he tried to imagine the scene in the alley when Greenhalgh ran into it and got shot. The sun shone straight along it. Forensic had picked it over so thoroughly he could believe they'd hoovered the cobbles to finish the job off. A few yards away was the phone box that got totalled, wrapped in green plastic sheeting secured by scene-of-crime tape. Any paving slabs that had been hit by bullets had been dug up and taken away, the holes filled with blobs of fresh tarmac.

There was only a scorch-mark where the Jag had exploded. The people walking the street hardly gave it a second glance, just as they'd hardly noticed the presence of another film crew drawn by the killing. It was obvious that, to them, nothing unusual had happened because shootings from rival drugs gangs were common. Regardless of this, Hunter often thought the inner cities weren't as bad as the media made out. He looked at the row of crappy shops. Plywood boards had been bolted over Samrah's window from when it got blasted through. Messy legend, daubed across them, said he was open as usual. New glass hadn't been fitted yet because the insurers were saying the damage was the result of a terrorist attack so tough titty. Parked outside was an old silver Transit with mirror-finished windows and paintwork dulled by the sun.

Because they'd rattled quickly through the shoot the kid had gone to fetch some hot drinks from a cafe. It would be a good twenty minutes yet before they set off back to town so Hunter told everybody he was going for a wander. He headed off, in front of the shops, and took a left into the next sidestreet. Union Street, it was called. He walked a short distance then took another left into the cobbled alley that ran straight behind the shops, parallel with the main road. The rumble of traffic quickly faded. Knowing north country custom he reckoned he was in Back Union Street and looked round, searching for the sign.

Wrong, when he clocked it.

Union Street West.

siXteeN

Samrah made sure the two plainclothes cops sitting in the car outside the shop were still there then picked up a *Daily Mirror* and told Nosheen he was off to the bog. Both cameras hanging from the ceiling were linked to CPHQ. If Big Brother was watching it would look innocent enough if he disappeared with his paper for ten or fifteen minutes to have a crap.

He'd watched Hunter filming outside on the street. Saw him toddle off on his own and realised, when he'd nipped upstairs a few minutes ago to check, that he was coming round the back. Meaning he was away from the CCTVs that covered the shops out front. A few had mute cameras stuck above their back doors and one had a dummy. Samrah's insurers had stipulated a rollershutter only so he'd avoided spending the money.

There was no going back, not after what had happened to David Kowalski. If the film crew had gone after they'd finished he'd still have gotten in touch with Hunter and Vanessa. Last night Kowalski had come to the shop after he came off duty. They went into the back office and Samrah had shut the inner doors so the cameras couldn't see or

105

hear then did the right thing and told Kowalski what he'd seen during Greenhalgh's kidnap. Kowalski was gobsmacked and asked him if he was sure. Samrah told him there was no mistake. He knew DK was a good cop, too good to be a fucking goon. Was assured of police anonymity and thought that would be the end of it. Before he left, Kowalski said he didn't blame him for playing schtum.

But, he'd added ominously, *if anything happens to me, you can trust Hunter and Vanessa. They're two of the coolest people you'll ever meet.*

And now Kowalski was dead.

So Samrah had decided it was time for action. Bollocks to sticking his head in the sand. Whistling cheerily he went through to the back of the shop. Before he shut the door behind him he opened the bog door at the foot of the stairs so that camera # 1 clocked where he seemed to be going. He went inside, banged down the toilet lid, noisily latched the door, and waited. After a few seconds he unlatched the door soundlessly and crept outside into the yard.

In comparison to the alley where he'd filmed Hunter decided this place was the local shit heap. Running parallel, over a graffiti-daubed wall, was a disused railway in a deep rubbish-filled cutting watched over by a derelict mill. Everything underfoot was frosty-white and in shadow because the mill had snuck out the low winter sun. Coming from the Balti house at the end of the terrace was a mouthwatering spicy smell, which shot through the air of northern decrepitude. It wasn't so much the bogus innocence of *Coronation Street* as gangsta turf with one foot stuck in NYC and the other in the grave of *Saturday Night and Sunday Morning*. Hunter shook his head, finding it hard to believe that the industrial workers who'd first thrived there might have bumped into Friedrich Engels when he'd trudged through the stinking pigsty of their lives.

He made his way along, crunching broken glass, till a big alley gate stopped him halfway, incongruous and new against the decay. He put his hands up to the bars and looked through, the prison sensation intensifying. Such gates were common throughout the old industrial towns now, to stop the alleys being used as escape routes. Crime had dropped by 90% in some places because of them. This one was covered in withered wreaths hung in memory of Greenhalgh. It wasn't the alley where he'd been shot but the gates thereabouts were obvious targets for floral tributes. Only deceased members of the Royal Family had matched the sentimental outpouring shown by the public after the MP's death.

Puffing steam in the freezing cold, Hunter looked up. From a topmost spike a cute cuddly toy was hanging by its neck on a noose made from a piece of string. Somebody had scribbled on its pink PVC vest in blue felt-tip:

A FASCIST BASTARD
DIED HERE

Thinking of his girls and their cherished collection of cuddly toys he felt obliged to reach up and rescue it. Took off the noose and tore away its vest and stroked its soft furry face. Its painted cartoon eyes seemed to look up at him mournfully. Maybe his spirits were low because of David's death, which had sunk in while he'd talked about it on camera. But seeing a kid's cuddly toy callously hung disconcerted him because, like any dad humble enough to

107

be in tune with the needs of kids, they struck at something deep in western culture. Being appalled by the insensitivity of the nasty-minded shit who hung it took him closer not only to his own kids but to the innocence of childhood and a profound realisation. How lucky his kids were not to be trapped in a fucking hellhole like this.

Driscoll was on the phone to the surveillance guys in the car. The live cameras inside and outside Samrah's shop were patched through to his PC.

The spotty-faced kid working with Hunter had been to fetch some teas and coffees. He was now in Samrah's shop buying cigarettes and a *Daily Telegraph*, presumably for the Godfrey with the headphones.

A gauze screen fastened to bullet-proof glass administered the inhuman space from floor to ceiling, segregating where customers stood from anything of value. A tiny serving hatch permitted the exchange of goods and money. The kid was being served by Samrah's sexy daughter. The diamond-shapes of the gauze threw a fishnet pattern of thin black lines across her face. Her hair hung nearly to her waist and she wore a zip-covered denim jacket and a mini skirt. She looked like she should be a Bollywood actress but was at uni, training to be a doctor. A few minutes ago Samrah had gone to the bog. The HD cameras showed wide-angle views of each side of the partition. Everything was crazily sharp. Driscoll could toggle in to any part of either picture and enlarge it so clearly he could nearly read the newspapers on the counter. Everything was artificially lit because of the makeshift boards covering the window. No daylight came through the door because it was made from solid steel-plated uPVC.

Costello, an Irish guy, said, 'He fucked off down the street on his own less than ten minutes ago, sir.'

'I know,' he said. 'I saw it on the camera out front. He's probably gone for a poke round.'

'Yes sir. What do you want us to do?'

'See what he's up to. I'm sure he's minding his own business but with him you can never tell.' Even as he spoke, those damned alarm bells rang at the back of his mind.

'Yes sir.' Traffic whizzed this way and that through an open window on the guy's phone. 'There's something else though.'

'What?'

'Just a feeling, but a souped-up XJS driven by a young black guy was cruising earlier.'

'Probably a dealer.'

'I don't think so, sir. We ran a check on the plate. Mark Halliday. An industrial chemist. Ex-Zeneca.'

'Where is he now?'

'Don't know, sir.'

'I'm sure it's nothing. But keep me informed.'

'Yes sir.'

He heard their car start before he killed the call. On his PC the nuclear fallout bunker of the shop looked unassuming enough, but something was in the air. He couldn't put his finger on the fuck what. It was like arriving early for a late train that you sensed wasn't coming.

When Hunter made his way back along the alley he was surprised to see Samrah coming out of his yard. They'd met before when they did a recce for the shoot. He'd seemed like a nice guy but they hadn't pushed it when he said he didn't want to be filmed.

As Hunter arrived they nodded their heads and had a few words about the weather and the state of the nation as they weighed each other up. Samrah lit a cigarette and said he'd come outside to say thank you.

'What for?' Hunter asked.

'You and your girlfriend didn't come in to hassle me when you were filming.'

'She's not my girlfriend.'

'That's what she said about you,' he said, amused by something. His cheeks were so heavily pockmarked it was easier to think of his weathered face as being debossed with numerous tiny craters. 'She's from Yorkshire you know. Like me.'

'How can you tell?'

'By her accent.'

'She hasn't got an accent.'

'Yes she has. It might be posh but it's still Yorkshire.' Impressed by his one-upmanship he sucked at his cigarette, making the end glow.

'How long have you lived here?' Hunter asked him.

'Ten years. The mill where I worked in Bradford went bump so I moved over. The shop used to be my uncle's. He bought it in 1979, just as the old order crumbled.' Hunter knew he meant Thatcher. 'They were simpler times, even so recently. Back then this place hadn't changed since the Fifties.' He nodded at the derelict mill. 'That was still going. Folk were involved with the place where they lived and worked. They queued outside the shop at dinnertimes for butties. Dripping teacakes that were bad for your cholesterol, and potted meat. Aye,' he lamented, cigarette going to mouth, end going bright. 'We haven't done fresh sarnies for a long time.' Now he sent out smoke and got to it. 'I wondered if you might come round to ask me some questions.'

'I haven't come to ask you any questions. I thought I'd have a look round.' He was getting cold and pulled on his gloves, watching where he put his feet when he stunk dog shit. 'David Kowalski interviewed you, didn't he?'

'Aye. He was a good lad.'

'We made a TV series with him.'

'I know. He spoke highly of you and your nice lady.'

'She didn't mean to upset you when she rang last night. She was worried about him.'

'I know,' he said, meaning it, sending out smoke. 'And it looks like she was right to be.'

'You've heard?'

'Course I fucking have.' He leant against the wall. The old bruised-looking brickwork had a similar texture to his face. Above the frosty roofslates Hunter saw a mill chimney with a sapling growing from the top, poking at the clear sky. 'It seems a bit iffy to me,' Samrah went on.

'What does?'

'That he should go and top himsen even if he was pissed off about losing his wife and kid. It's what they're saying, isn't it?' He kept his eyes on him as he tried unsuccessfully to blow his smoke across the alley. Hunter sensed something coming. Knew it as soon as he'd seen the newsagent mooching in his yard. Samrah said, 'You know they've been watching you, don't you?'

'Who?'

'The cops. There are two pricks in a red Shado out front. They've been spying on you since you got here. There's a dodgy-looking XJS an' all. The cops must think folk are fucking stupid.' He sucked his cigarette again.

111

Despite Samrah not playing ball during the recce Hunter decided to give it another whirl. The guy was obviously gunning to talk about something deadly fucking serious. 'What did you see when the MP got shot?'

'You'll know from the papers,' he said. Amused, he added, 'I thought you weren't gonna ask me any questions?' Hunter said nothing but stayed cool. He knew his instincts had been right when, like he'd been cued, Samrah portentously stubbed out his cigarette against the wall. Then, as though inviting Hunter into a secret den, he shoved open the knackered wooden door leading to the yard. The hinges were shot, causing the bottom edge to bind across the old stone slabs. It had done it for so long it had scribed a radius. 'Why don't you come in, lad?'

Hunter followed him obediently. Just before he stepped into the yard he saw a red car bonnet creep into view at the end of the alley. He made sure he'd nipped out of sight before he clocked who was in the car. Or before they could see him.

SEVENtEEN

Hunter was shown into a freezing cold, untidy back office that used to be a living room. There was a painted Victorian cast-iron fireplace with a sink cupboard between it and the window. The faded wallpaper was original 1950s. Pale grey, with blobs of primary colour floating on a fretwork of thin black lines that might have been deliberately badly drawn. He'd seen a similar pattern before. Fablon, when he was a kid. No, his grandma's old shopping bag, except the background colour was different. Her bag was white, not grey.

Samrah pulled up an old wooden chair for him and told him for a third time to keep his fucking voice down. They were at the back of the building, meaning the shop cameras couldn't snoop audio with the inner doors being shut. But the guy wasn't taking any chances.

'I was sitting in my van when I saw the Jag pull up,' he said, cutting just above a murmur. 'Before I knew it the chauffeur's head went pop and the Jag was being shot to bits. I wondered what the fuck was happening. The gang came from nowhere. Blew up the Jag. Blasted my shop window through then chased the MP into the alley, shot him, and dragged him across to a getaway car. It was over in minutes.'

'What were they like?'

'They were all masked up with black balaclavas on and kids' clown masks or something.' He hesitated. 'Except for the guy who only had a hood.'

'Hang on,' Hunter said remembering. 'You're right. I've read the papers. But I thought you were upstairs above the shop when the window went through?'

'Aye I was.'

'But you just said you were in your van.'

'The upstairs POV's the official story to explain why I wasn't on the CCTVs downstairs but could still say I saw what happened.' He let a silence get pregnant and felt for his cigarettes. Hunter hated smoking but needed to give

113

the guy some space. Behind the friendly exterior Samrah was shit scared. Told him he'd come up with the official story because he was terrified of gang revenge if they'd found out he'd been in the van. Sensing that smoking pissed Hunter off he opened the window. After a few inches it bumped against the iron bars on the outside. He'd had to stick his hand through those on the inside to shoot the latch. He sat on the edge of the desk and lit another cigarette, holding it to the fresh air, allowing another pause to fill before he let loose the showstopper. 'It's because I was sitting in my van that I noticed the guy next to my window had light-coloured eyes.'

'Jesus Christ.' Hunter knew the gunman was black. According to witnesses they all were. But pale eyes and black skin didn't tango.

'That's how DK reacted,' Samrah said.

'Go on,' he said, anticipating. His heart picked up speed now as he sensed he was headed for something mega.

'As I say I pulled up in my van before the chauffeur got shot. Before all hell broke loose I'd been sitting there for half-an-hour, reading my paper because my cousin Imran was minding the shop. When I saw the Jag pull up with a dead tyre I assumed the guy would change it, or call the RAC. I didn't know Greenhalgh was in the fucking back. I stayed put when I realised shooters were going, in case I got hit. The gang didn't know I was there. When the guy without a mask stopped to pump his gun right next to my window I noticed he'd got lightish eyes. I thought it odd for a bloke like me.' He meant because the gunman was black or of Asian or Middle Eastern origin. Too right, Hunter thought, his mind kicking into hyperdrive.

'So you were right up close to him?'

'About two feet away.'

'Did he see you?'

'No, none of 'em did. I shat myself and sat there for over two hours. I haven't had the van long. It still has one-way mirror stuff stuck to the windows.'

'Meaning you were totally hidden?'

'Aye, thank fuck. I was too scared to get out in case the gang was still around. After a couple of hours I started up and set off. The cops couldn't close a busy main road like this so they just taped off the alley and put a tent over the end. There was so much going on, and so many folk hanging round from the press and TV, that nobody noticed me drive away. It was the scariest moment of my life. Plus, there were the Big Brother cameras.'

'What do you mean?'

'If I'd got out of the van straight after Greenhalgh was taken they'd have clocked me.'

'They'll still have clocked you driving away.'

'Aye but not for two hours. Two-and-a-bit actually. And they still wouldn't see who was driving because of the windows. I've had no comeback so I assume they haven't checked the CCTVs that far ahead. The cops didn't come round to see anybody till teatime that day, when I'd had chance to think it through and talk to Imran. For two weeks I was scared if the phone rang or if a cop car pulled up outside.'

'You knew the gang was black because you could see the skin round their eyes and wrists, right?'

'Right.'

'What about the guy next to your van?'

'He was the same. And because he wasn't wearing a plastic mask the skin around his eyes showed a bit more.'

He drew a circle round one of his eyes with a forefinger, to show what he meant.

'The cops have fine-tooth combed this area trying to find his mask, haven't they?'

'Aye. They reckon he lost it before he ran out from further down the street.' He blew smoke at the ceiling. 'Except they've got it now.'

'What do you mean?'

'A kid had it. His mother brought it in to the shop last night, after she'd heard them appealing for it on TV. Said she found it under his bed and didn't want the cops crawling all over her flat.'

'You mean the mask was *here?*'

'Aye. In this office.'

Shit he thought, everything piling. Thinking quickly: 'Have you told the cops?'

'Aye.'

Thinking shit again: 'What did you say?'

'That she brought it here and gave it to me. Which is what she did and what the cameras shot. I told the cops ASAP, to make it look like I was playing the game.'

Praying no: 'Have they taken it?'

'Aye. They came round right away.'

Fuck, he thought. Fuck, fuck, fuck. His heart sank. For a moment he'd thought he was going to get hold of a key piece of forensic evidence. Then he remembered a *Tough Justice* doc he'd worked on. It was a long shot but worth a try. 'Where did you keep the mask?'

'Over here.' He crossed to the sink cupboard and opened it. Inside was an old pot sink. Brick-shaped white tiles, bordered by a thin black-and-white chequerboard, ran above it. Most of the big tiles were cracked or crazed. The

116

taps looked like they went out with the ark and had those perished, pink rubber bendy tube things on the ends.

'Can you show me where?'

'Now there's a funny thing.'

'What is?'

'That's what the police forensic bod asked.'

'You mean he's been?'

'No. He's coming this afternoon.' He quickly checked his watch, as if to reassure himself of the time.

'Please can you show me?'

'It depends.'

'On what?'

'On whether or not you came here today.'

'I haven't been here today.'

'I didn't think so. Just as I must have imagined it when that kid's mother brought the mask in last night.' He stood aside, so Hunter could get to the drainer. 'I put it here,' he said, 'where the pots dry.'

'Thanks,' he said, stooping to look.

He could see some tiny specks of dust and the odd hair. There was every chance they'd include crucial incriminating evidence from the mask. Microscopic flakes of human skin. Dandruff. Bits of shit he couldn't imagine. This was turning mega fucking serious. His old journalist's instincts were hotting up. 'Have you got some cellotape?'

Samrah found some in a drawer. Working across the drainer slowly a furrow at a time Hunter tore off strips of tape, laid them over the residue, and lifted it up. He saw an A4 plastic folder and a manila envelope on the desk. Asked Samrah if he could have them then pressed the lengths of tape across the inside pockets of the folder, to keep everything in place.

When he'd finished Samrah told him, 'You're gonna try and get a DNA profile done, aren't you?'

'Have you ever noticed how black people always seem to have brown eyes?'

'Aye, but not at first. When I did, I sent DK a snail mail note because I smelled shit.' He heard the electro-jingle in the shop as a customer came in. 'You'd better go, lad,' he said, getting up, suddenly oppressed by everything he'd disclosed. He told Hunter to shush and led him through to the steel-plated back door, letting in the smell of the freezing outside. 'Make sure nobody sees you,' he said, watching him stud his leather coat, 'when you bob back along the alley.'

Hunter OK'd and slipped the envelope in his coat, to deter any questions from the crew, then went out into the frosty yard. Except for the wheelie bins it was caught in a time warp. 'Why say you were upstairs?' he asked. 'Why not say you weren't here?'

'Because I'd have needed an alibi if the cops had run a check. There was no way I was gonna say I was in the van and risk the sniper sussing I might have clocked him. But I had to explain why I wasn't on-camera with Imran in the shop. So I pretended to be upstairs and said I went straight out the back when I came down.'

Hunter thanked him and got the hell outta there. A chill washed over him as he went down the yard but the bitter air didn't cause it when it stung his face.

EiGHtEEN

When he reached the car, Vanessa was sitting in the front passenger seat, on the phone. Sarah was pacing about on the pavement, also on her phone. Graeme was fingering froth from a cappuccino before dropping the empty carton in a new recycle bin. Harry and the others were waiting in the Patriot.

Hunter sank onto the back seat and reached for his seatbelt. He looked round discreetly but couldn't see the red Shado. As he clunk-clicked Sarah got in behind the wheel and pressed the ignition. 'We thought you'd gone on vacation,' she said via the rearview as she set off.

He slid back his cuff to check his watch. Twenty-seven minutes. It felt like he'd been gone much longer because during his time away his world had changed. His spirits took a nosedive as the enormity of what he'd uncovered sank in. In a way he wished he didn't know what he knew and wished that David hadn't phoned Vanessa last night. Now David was dead. Murdered, you could bet your bottom dollar. Except they (whoever they were) knew nothing about Samrah's spilled beans. Hunter knew this was his killer advantage.

Vanessa finished her call and turned to smile, button-holing him with her pale eyes. 'We thought you'd got lost, love.' He shook his head, desperate to tell her but desperate not to. *To protect her.* 'Where did you go?'

'For a wander,' he said neutrally. She sussed something was up straight away because she knew him so well. She seemed as if she might persist but backed off when she'd clocked the look on his face. Her invigorating lavender smell filled the car and had KO'd him when he sat down but something unexpected was happening. The further he got from Samrah's shop, and the more spooked he was by what a DNA profile might throw up, the more he couldn't take his eyes off Vanessa. Whatever he'd been dreaming about when she woke him that morning seemed about to focus then blurred, spooking him even more. He knew stress was driving it but it left him feeling so exposed that he'd to open his window to get some air. With an effort he thought back to Samrah's ice-cold, smoke-filled office. His broad-Yorkshire accent had mellowed when he'd taken control of the conversation. *I didn't say anything because I was scared the gang might come to get me,* he'd said. *And the MP was dead, so why drag myself into it any more? It wouldn't bring him back.*

Graeme's voice crashed in. Hunter couldn't remember him getting in the fucking car. He was strongly built, maybe 45, more like a track-and-field athlete than a TV cameraman. Their regular guy had an inner-ear infection and couldn't risk standing up holding £150k's worth of kit, in case he fell over. 'How long have you two guys been together?' The ambiguity of the question nearly made Hunter cry out. He saw by Vanessa's expression, as she turned quickly to face him, that she'd clocked it too. *He thinks we're shacked up.* She'd flushed but seemed a hair's breadth from winking her eye impishly at Hunter.

'Nearly three years,' he said, unsure what else to say, reaching self-consciously for a bottle of water.

'Where do you live?' Again the question was a double whammy, still discreetly probing.

'Vanessa lives with her partner in Hampstead,' he said, deciding to clear up any misconceptions, if there were any. 'I live nearer Camden.' He glugged water then smacked back the nozzle, his eye still on Vanessa. Then he caught Sarah's twinkling eye, watching him from her rearview as traffic bunched up front and she slowed the car. *She knows*, he thought, feeling even more exposed as ice-cold air blew in, everything fly-in-a-bottling.

Graeme OK'd but obviously had no comprehension of the geography of north London. 'Married?' he asked, turning and speaking directly to Hunter.

'Divorced,' he said, visualizing his girls.

Graeme nodded and waited to see if Vanessa might elaborate on her domestic situation but was distracted by his phone when it jingled to tell him he'd a message.

Thinking of Hayley and Jenny broke it, thank fuck. He closed his eyes tight. When he opened them Vanessa was looking straight at him. Her shades blanked her eyes now but, sensing his mood, she gave him one of her reassuring motherly smiles from under them. 'Were you happy,' she asked him.

'With the shoot?'

'Yes,' she said, watching him.

He nodded and said that he was.

'You seem a bit quiet.'

He shook his head and said that he wasn't.

A spot of colour appeared at each of her cheeks before she turned away. She'd recently grown her hair long and usually had it in a tail when they were shooting. Today it was hanging loose, layered exquisitely like the feathers of a bird's wing at the sides where it swept back across her shoulders.

They had three hours to kill before they could carry on working so Sarah drove them back to the hotel. To Hunter it was one of those awkward days that happen during the shooting of any documentary where there was a big gap in the middle, meaning everything could have fitted into a more affordable half day.

They'd booked an interview with a criminal psychologist at the university but he wasn't available till late that afternoon. So Vanessa told everybody to break for a long lunch. TV crews being TV crews they made sure they ate at their employers' expense before taking advantage of the free time. With them being in the way, and her phone going constantly, Hunter couldn't find the right moment to tell Vanessa about what he'd got from Samrah's shop. For safety's sake he was wary of saying anything. He feared every CCTV camera he could see would be linked to Central Matrix and able to scan and lip-read his mouth. His priority was to get to the Independent Forensic Institute (IFI) before the residue deteriorated. It would be safest to spill everything to her in her room before dinner that night when they were alone and away from the crew and prying cameras.

It wasn't until everybody was sitting round a long table in the carvery that he got an inkling why Vanessa hadn't been as scrupulous as she might at rescheduling the day.

As he sat down opposite her with a full plate she asked him, 'Do you fancy going out tonight?'

'Where?' he said, unsure what she meant and thinking, after what had happened at Samrah's, that going out was the last thing he wanted. He glanced along the table to see if the offer was open to anybody else.

Apparently not.

'I haven't decided,' she said, shaking vinegar across her fries. 'I want to go shopping this afternoon so I'll give it some thought.' The others had gone silent and were listening and quietly eating.

'Do you mean a night on the town?'

'Yes,' she said, watching him. 'We could eat here then go somewhere else.'

Since the smoking ban a new generation of exclusive nightclubs had sprung up aimed at discerning middle-class professionals, similar to the private member clubs in Soho. Binge drinking idiots and anthropoids below a certain IQ level were fiercely excluded. The new clubs catered for people who never used to go near such places because of the stink of smoke and pissed sub-humanity. The prosperous new client base had come out in droves and made a bunch of savvy club owners rich.

'I need to do a bit of shopping myself,' he said, grabbing his chance to get to the IFI unhindered.

'Shall we shop together?'

'Where do you want to go?'

'I thought I might buy a short skirt,' she said grinning. She picked up a fat steak chip, dipped it in mayo, and bit it slowly. 'I might drive over go to the Clothesdome,' she added, still watching him. 'I saw a sexy blue leather suit on their website the other day.'

'I think I'll stay in town,' he said, parrying to ensure he stayed alone.

Back went the chip to the mayo.

Up it came again.

'Are you sure?'

'Yes,' he said, watching her go for another bite. The unease he'd felt at deceiving her was cancelled when he remembered something. 'Anyway it's your birthday next week. I need to be on my own.'

He winked at her.

Now the kid blundered into the conversation from the far end of the table. 'How old are you then, Vanessa?'

'How old do you think?'

'Sixty?' he said, deliberately over-egging it. He grinned, exposing a mouthful of masticated potato as an excuse to eyeball Sarah.

Harry shook his head with despair. 'Goodness me, the manners of young people today,' he said, turning to the kid to wave his fork disapprovingly at him. 'When I was young it was considered highly improper to enquire after a lady's age.'

'That must have been a long time ago, Harry,' the kid said. A putrid sludge showed at his mouth now, framed by his pale pimpled face. When he laughed he bleated like a nanny goat, so loudly the restaurant manager threw him a hard stare from his workstation.

'I'm forty-two next week,' Vanessa said.

'You don't look it,' the kid said back, meaning it. Again his eyes went to Sarah, who made a conscious effort not to look in his direction.

Actually she did look it, Hunter thought. It was why she was so fucking charismatic.

His adrenalin rush when they'd driven away from Normanshaw had eased. But he decided that, because of how massively weighed down he felt by what he'd found out, and his weird state of mind when Vanessa had turned him on in the car, it was futile to resist how he felt about her any longer.

Something else had happened. When they came up from the car park she'd taken a phone call but quickly put a distance between herself and everybody else. Hunter thought he'd seen Max's face flashing. What he knew for sure, as she'd hurried back down the steps and into the car park to keep it private, was that it was a conversation she'd rather not have had. She'd been self-conscious ever since. Hunter hadn't pried, passing the call off as some domestic disagreement with Max that she'd doubtless explain when she was ready. But something had shifted, big time. When she asked him if he wanted to go out with her that night it was like she'd taken a baseball bat to something emotionally herself. Whatever was going on between them, just under the surface of everything they did, was getting worse. It was happening because they were always checking each other out but didn't push it because they were respectable middle-class guys. It was crazy. They wanted each other so they should fucking well go for it. On the back of everything which had happened that day his decision left him on edge but also incredibly sexually energized. Crazily, ironically, it was David's death and Samrah throwing shit at the fan that now forced him to confront what he hadn't wanted to face for a long time.

It's OK, it was saying.

It's OK to want her.

It's OK to—

125

That he couldn't admit.

Not yet.

The talk carried on in an upbeat fashion, helping everybody to bond. Half-an-hour later, Hunter was finally alone with Vanessa, and ready to tell her about Samrah after all, when her phone went off yet again. After the cancellation of David's interview she'd thought ahead and chased up some recent pitches. A commissioning editor had rung to wish her happy birthday, misjudging the date like the sender of the early card up in her room.

As they got down to negotiating a budget Hunter realised it would be a long call. Vanessa needed the Volvo to go shopping, meaning he'd need to hire a car to get to the IFI. Squeezing her arm he said he'd see her later and got up to leave. Hertz had a place behind the hotel. As he left the restaurant he noticed a tough-looking, forty-something business-suited bird, with enormous breasts, who seemed to catch his eye from above her *Times* when he passed the lounge. She was probably nothing to get uptight about but he was on edge after what Samrah had said about the guys in the Shado and couldn't shake off the feeling that he was being watched.

He'd intended to leave by the main entrance. At the last second he made sure nobody was tailing him and slipped down to a basement bar. It led to an exit near the service lift, which not many people knew about. He walked round to Hertz, hired a yellow Mini, and drove straight out to the IFI, checking his rearview all the way.

NiNEtEEN

Abigail was based at Copley Hall, at Siddington near Macclesfield. It was a Jacobean-style grand stately home, built between 1716 and 1735, set in two hundred acres of parkland, Grade 2 listed. She knew the imposing style was also known as Tudor-revival but to her its turrets and quasi-onion-domed towers made it look like it should be in Moscow when seen across the fields. Wild deer had roamed its grounds for nearly three hundred years.

Her boss Sir Ian Churchill, the latest owner, wasn't an aristocrat but a very rich man who'd made his first billion from selling the City Zone chain of multi-storey car parks that he'd built since 1971. By the time he'd made his third billion from Pink, an international phone network aimed at the pink pound (or any pink currency) he'd concluded that the corrupt nature of modern British public life meant its political system was stuffed. Sharing this view was a group of patriotic Tory grandees, judges, and industrialists with whom he became acquainted as he amassed his huge wealth. Sir Ian was a good man. When his twilight years approached he'd decided to use his money to infiltrate the institutionalized corruption that was killing the nation he loved. He fancied doing it from a big country house in his Cheshire birthplace and made the genuinely aristocratic owners of Copley Hall an offer they couldn't refuse. The real reason he bought it, as he'd confided to Abigail, was that he needed a house with a garden big enough to land his helicopter in, but far enough from the neighbours not to annoy them with it.

The first floor was comprised of immaculate exhibition rooms, each decorated in a different historical style from Tudor through to Regency. Here, Abigail's brilliant young colleagues assembled to help Sir Ian on his mission. A distinguishing prerequisite was their true patriotic outlook. They knew that genuine patriotism was something to do with loving the ground under their feet, cherishing its history and traditions, looking forward as well as back, not hanging St George's Day flags from bedroom windows during the World Cup. Other group members were based in Bracknell. They took care of the heavy technology, notably the conversion of Abigail's Lexus into a mobile fighting machine. To her the operation was more *Department S* than the Bond films or MI6. But the Lexus was an impressive piece of kit, costing Sir Ian a cool four million to hit spec, and would have done Q proud.

Abigail was close to Kareem, the lynchpin of the set-up. He was a good-looking gay 33 year-old known affectionately as the Terminator. Like most Indians he was hardworking, diligent, determined, and worked out of the Tudor Room with his equally brilliant techno nuts. Surrounded by dark oak panelling, pewter goblets, and fine linenfold patterns they used laptops and the Internet to strike at rotten apples festering in the national barrel. Computer, the onboard brain of the Lexus and the world's first true AI, was Kareem's baby. While university research labs of the globe still talked about doing it he'd gone ahead and done it. And it had boiled down to something so stupidly simple that nobody else had sussed it because they were too busy looking in rather than out. To Abigail's amazement Kareem had no formal university education but was self-taught. Set up his first IT company at the age of only 19 and sold it for ten million when he was 26. He was so gifted when it came to IT that he was the only known person who could hack into the supposedly impenetrable government fortress known as Central Matrix. Meaning he could clone or KO the biometric records and ID data of anybody in the UK.

Up to a dozen group members with special skills, ranging from undercover surveillance (Mark's forte) through to military combat training, were based at Copley Hall at any time. Abigail was Sir Ian's Chief of Staff, and staying in the Elizabethan Room. It overlooked the driveway at the front of the house, with its sweeping views down to the Middle Pool and arched brick bridge. Although it was a big room with ostentatious furniture, wide polished floorboards, priceless Turkish rugs, she found it cosy. In the country houses where she stayed that belonged to other committee members the bedrooms were often cold, even in summer. This one was different. Sir Ian had cut no corners updating the heating and insulation spec while staying sympathetic to planning regs. But he'd got the money to do it. Because of the circles she moved in, Abigail knew that nowadays many genuine aristocrats hadn't.

When she'd got back from CPHQ she'd gone into a two-hour lunch meeting with Sir Ian. For the past hour she'd been in her room, sitting crosslegged on the four-poster bed, going through Hunter and Vanessa's OPQ reports on her laptop. She'd also made some discreet phone calls to her contacts at the BBC. As far as they knew Hunter had nothing sexual going with Vanessa. Abigail wouldn't have wasted time with him if he had.

She got down to his divorce settlement files, which had just arrived. He'd told his BBC counsellor that he probably married Victoria Carlton for the wrong reasons and wondered in hindsight if her upper-middle-class background had represented a silly romantic social stability. She was of merchant banking stock, and ex-Rodean, ex-Cheltenham Ladies College. Her parents had disapproved of her marrying Hunter, dismissing him as a wayward film school thug with a humble librarian for a mother and a marginally less humble father who was an NHS GP in tough inner-city Birmingham. The marriage had lasted for seven years. Carlton was the adulterous half but retained custody of their two daughters on the grounds that their father was always off gallivanting around the country. Hunter was a shrewd character with both feet on the ground, but he was also a devoted dad. Losing his kids had cut him up badly. They seemed to be his weak spot.

Gentle knocking at the door interrupted her. 'Come in,' she said, minimizing what was on screen.

Ruth, the Senior Housekeeper, appeared looking like a template for English middle-aged spinsterhood. Grey hair. Silk blouse a shade up from her smart navy two-piece. A touch heavy at the jowl, a touch OTT on the face-paint. To Abigail, Ruth's duty to something above and beyond her humble self meant she'd somehow bypassed greed, sex, and the agonizing self-absorption that screwed up life for everybody else.

'Excuse me, madam,' she said, apparently moving forward on castors, 'but Sir Ian wondered if you'd like to join him with Lord and Lady Melford for afternoon tea.'

'That'll be fine, Ruth.'

'Yes, madam.' She nodded deferentially and left the room as quietly as she'd entered.

As Abigail had expected, Sir Ian had OK'd it for her to liaise with Hunter. Mark tracked him to Normanshaw at lunchtime before being spooked by two undercover cops who were watching the shoot. She opened Hunter's OPQ files again, glancing longingly through the window at the dusk deepening over Manchester while his hologram rendered. She wasn't sure of his movements tomorrow. Approaching him by phone or e-mail was risky. It would be best to go to his hotel first thing in the morning and catch him before he left. Looking forward to it she projected his face above the bed, touching him as he revolved in front of her, feeling what she'd felt when he'd eyeballed her in the conference at CPHQ that morning.

TWENtY

Driscoll wasn't convinced about what he'd seen on the CCTVs outside Samrah's shop when Hunter went walkies. It had bugged him all afternoon and did so again now as he spun in his chair to gaze out at the city lights.

He'd let his driver go early because he intended to stick around to check out the uncut footage Hunter shot at Normanshaw. The young yank bird dropped off the rushes at the BBC when they got back from the university. Driscoll knew that, to save money, Vanessa and Hunter down-converted their rushes from HD so they took up less memory on the Avid during editing. As instructed, Stoneham had fixed it for the raw footage to be piped illegally across to CPHQ as soon as it was digitized.

There was another reason why Driscoll hadn't gone home, something that set his mind going about the CCTV stuff during his meeting that afternoon with the new kick-ass woman Tory Chief of the City Council. He knew Hunter had hired the Mini as soon as his ID card went into the PC at Hertz and Central Matrix flagged it up. But it was a fluke they'd tracked him to the IFI because he'd hightailed it through backstreets and shitty industrial estates the closer he'd got. He'd parked a mile from the institute and walked all over the fucking place to get to it, suggesting he was up to no good. Addison and his new punk Naylor had cruised the area and by another fluke clocked Hunter emerging from a ginnel near the IFI. Seconds later and they'd have missed him.

But it was Hunter's phone being switched off that had set the alarm bells going. The Communications Police (CP) could scan for a phone's whereabouts by satellite and pinpoint its position to within a few yards. They'd put out a trace on Hunter's when he went for a nosy after he'd finished shooting, but it was switched off. He didn't switch it on again till he was on his way back to the car. Leaving it switched off in case it rang during filming was elementary. Leaving it switched off when he went walkies was dubious but excusable, in case he'd forgotten about it. But deliberately turning it off when he ponced out of Hertz to get in the Mini and drive to the IFI? Nowadays people didn't drive round with their phones switched off, not when they came with Bluetooths. And why did Hunter go to the IFI? Research for his film? Maybe. If so, why park a mile away and traipse round the houses to get to it? And why was he only there for ten minutes, like he was doing a drop-off or making a pick-up? Why not send a bike? Something was going on, hence Driscoll's itch about the CCTV stuff over the past few hours.

Knowing the bastard was getting to him he swung back in his chair to face his PC. He pulled up the CCTV cameras on the street outside Samrah's shop and popped open the tiles. Each 16x9 CCTV view *gerdunged* into real-time infrared, but what was happening at Normanshaw now didn't interest him. What had happened four hours ago, when Hunter fucked off for his walk, was what interested him. He maximized camera # 4, looking at Samrah's shop from across the street. Head and taillights constantly churned up the image. Neighbouring tacky junk-food-joint signs also did the flick. The time was 17:47. Driscoll pulled up the timecode box, remembered when Hunter went AWOL, typed in 13:25. The footage whizzed back timelapse fast. Night became day until, in a few blinks of an eye, he saw Hunter doing his fucking *Matrix* flowing coat thing as he toddled off in front of the shops, hit the end of the terrace, turned into Union Street, and disappeared because of the oblique angle.

Camera # 4 was the CCTV nearest to Union Street but it couldn't see down it. It looked across from two o'clock, meaning that when Hunter went round the corner he soon entered a blind spot. Only main roads tended to be covered by CCTVs, if there were enough commercial premises. Their field-of-vision covered plenty of sidestreets too but usually by chance. Union Street was such a place. Driscoll rewound a few seconds and zoomed in till Hunter nearly filled frame. The HD resolution was amazing. SuperHD would be even better, snooping through windows right up people's arses.

At the corner of Samrah's terrace was The True Taste of India. Driscoll let Hunter walk along to it but froze the action as soon as the leather-coated figure went round the corner. What he'd clocked over the Tory chief's shoulder in his earlier meeting was something as unassuming as the painting on the wall behind her. A contract company had supplied it to fill up wall space, not because it had much aesthetic merit. It was a bag of shit really. But it wasn't the picture that had caught his attention and got the de Bono lateral thing going again. It was something about it. *The glass covering it.* It reflected a tiny snapshot of what was going on *outside* the room—the view through the window —while he'd chatted up the city's glamorous new leader with the king-size hooters.

So what about CCTVs?

They videoed what they saw.

But what about what they *didn't* see?

Or didn't know they saw?

He toggled to the right on camera # 4, away from Hunter, and zoomed close. Facing the Indian take-away on the opposite corner was a junk shop. Next door, going down Union Street, was the Man Lee Chinese take-away—two old shops knocked into one with a double front window. Driscoll zoomed closer. No graininess because HD worked like a digital camera. The image made from millions of pixels, not tiny particles of chemical emulsion, stuck to a layer of plastic, reacting to light, which was what created film grain.

He toggled slowly across the big window, tweaking the contrast to make stuff show better, until he found Hunter *reflected* from the opposite pavement but unseen by camera # 4 because he was out of sight round the corner. Or so it seemed. Driscoll was really fucking buzzing. What had bugged him was the surveillance cops losing Hunter so quickly. Nobody thought much about it because they'd assumed he'd gone for a walk or even for a squirt. When the cops drove after him into Union Street they didn't see him in the alley running behind the shops, or anywhere thereabouts. They'd taken off to see if they could find him but didn't, assuming they'd driven down one street while he'd sauntered up another.

Wrong, Driscoll realised. He hit slow-mo and kept Hunter going down Union Street, reflected in the window for a few yards. He knew what was coming and swore when it did. Hunter turned into the alley running *behind Samrah's shop*. Driscoll played everything through again, to be sure, then zoomed out on camera # 4 to watch from across the main road. He nudged on a few minutes and hit Play. The Shado passed in front of the shops then turned left into Union Street. Its brake lights showed in the oblique angle as it hesitated at the end of the alley before disappearing when it took off.

Fuming, Driscoll jabbed a button at his console. A phone number did the auto-dial thing.

'Costello, sir,' said the Irish cop who'd been on surveillance duty at lunchtime.

'When you drove down Union Street after Hunter fuck-ed off you stopped at the end of the alley running behind the shops, didn't you?'

'Yes sir. To take a butchers.'

'And?'

'What do you mean, sir?'

'Did you see him?'

'Well, no sir,' he said, wondering. 'If he'd been there we'd have told you.'

'What if he went into the alley and walked out the other end before you got there?'

'He couldn't have, sir. There's an alley gate blocking it, covered in dead flowers.'

'There was no way out?'

'None sir. Not unless he jumped over the wall onto the railway. But it's a thirty-foot drop.'

'That's all I needed to know.'

'Yes sir,' he said, sounding nonplussed.

Driscoll killed the call and thought for a moment, drum-ming some fingers. He was absolutely fucking seething. Hunter goes for a fucking walk but disappears into fuck-ing thin air. Goes into the fucking alley behind Samrah's fucking shop but pops up twenty minutes later. Fucks off to the IFI sneakily, avoiding cameras, phone switched off, parking well away. Blood was banging in his ears but he needed to be sure.

He pulled up Street View and punched in M11. Found Union Street, toggled into the shitty alley. Bang. It was like he was in it for real, in widescreen HD. He went up to the alley gate. Google's car had scanned the area months be-fore Greenhalgh was kidnapped, meaning the gate was clean. It was springtime because dandelions were growing everywhere. Driscoll toggled left and right, to check there was no way to get past the gate, then did a hundred-and-eighty to look back at Union Street. The litter-strewn cobbles stretched away, glittering with smashed glass. Samrah's shop was fifth from the end. Driscoll turned forty-five degrees right, tilted up, counted five chimneystacks in. He turned left again and toggled along the alley. Stopped. Did another forty-five to the right, so he was in line with the back of the shop. Because of the wall and the wooden door at the bottom of Samrah's yard he couldn't see much. Just the rollershutter housing above the back door, its galvanized steel winking brightly against dirty Mancunian brick. Next to it was the small barred bog window where Samrah supposedly took a squeeze after Hunter took a hike.

He'd seen enough.

He punched another console button and sat through the auto-dial thing again.

'Addison,' said Addison.

'Where is he now?'

'Still in the bar at the hotel.'

'Doing what?'

'Gawping at his laptop.'

'Which website is he on?'

Via the CP they could trace his IP address and know in seconds which site he was on, right down to the page he was viewing.

'He isn't. We ran a check straight away. He's watching a DVD.'

Driscoll heard windscreen wipers make a dull *squeak* at the other end of the phone before he announced, 'I think Leviathan might have landed.'

'Fucking hell, not again?'

'We're going to bring him in.'

'For questioning?'

'Yes but no.'

'Meaning?'

'The police are going to find him very badly beaten up in his hotel room. As a persistent fucking documentary filmmaker he must have seriously pissed somebody off.' He threw down one of his measured pauses. The only thing missing was a bit of moody synth music, to back it up.

Addison picked up the pause and ran. 'Understood,' he said. 'Any special instructions?' he asked, sucking at his cigarette. *Squeak* came over the phone, muted like a metronome. Snow was fluttering lazily across the city. Driscoll knew it would be the dryness of the X6's windscreen making the rubber blades restless.

'He's good looking and his white teeth annoy me. Hurt him enough to scare the shit out of him and want to avoid being on camera for a very long time. He's an investigative journalist. They think they're immune to the way stuff gets sorted in the real world. Have you still got that metal fist thing with the bolts welded to it?'

'It's in the back.'

'Maybe lose him the use of an eye.'

'What about Vanessa?'

'She can find the fucking horrible mess. I might arrange for somebody to tell her she'd better get the hell down to his fucking room. He'll suspect something after this morning's upset at the press conference because he and I don't get on. But he won't be able to prove a fucking thing. Call me when it's done.'

He killed the call before Addison A-OK'd but heard another *squeak* just before it cut off. What he also heard, this time in his head, was the moody synth music, doing mangled industrial atmospherics. And fucking how.

TWENtY-ONE

The DVD had nearly finished.

It was a well-made corporate video about the amazing advances made in DNA profiling in recent years. Hollywood-style CGI work ran to moody sci-fi music while a gung-ho American OTT narrated like he was running with a multiplex trailer. The camera zoomed through an eye into a blood vessel then shot out and motion-controlled across a human brain like it was cruising above a planet to land. It was all Quicktimed on the IFI website but Hunter wasn't taking any chances by letting his IP address strike DNA page hits.

He'd just got the waiter to bring him another scotch and knocked it back in one because the day had left him feeling all over the fucking place. The evening ahead, as much as anything, left him on edge, wondering what the morning would bring when he got to it. He also felt hassled from covering his tracks all afternoon. If they knew he'd hired a car he was pretty sure nobody had followed him because of how he'd driven to the IFI.

He still hadn't said anything to Vanessa about the residue because of the crew being in the way till an hour ago. When they got back from the uni she went up to her room to get ready for dinner. Sarah went with her, so she could scrunch-dry her hair for her before she went home. He'd been alone in the bar weighing up the day, rounding it off with a shot of moonshine to try and KO the ache twisting his gut.

As he watched the DVD he played with a business card in his right hand, rotating it from its short to long edges:

Dr Steven Hamer
BSc, DPhil, Cbioll, FIBiol
Specialist Forensic Pathologist

The *Tough Justice* he'd remembered at Samrah's was about the corruption that crept into police forensic science after it was farmed out to the private sector during the 1990s. Some of the less reputable labs had colluded with big legal companies, who bribed them to try and stop their high-profile clients from being convicted. Steve was an old friend they'd interviewed for the film. It was largely because of it that tough Data Protection laws had been introduced, making forensic science one of the few areas which State crooks couldn't infiltrate.

Hunter could remember the old days, when DNA profiling was a basic but effective science. A blood, semen, or saliva sample swabbed from a crime scene could provide enough info for a DNA pattern to be assembled. DNA formed the genetic molecule of all living organisms, with the binary digits of each as individual as a fingerprint. Forensic samples were used to build a profile of a criminal's sex and blood type, or even their hair and eye colour.

Which was fine, as long as the suspect was in custody or the police held their DNA records.

In comparison to these crude beginnings DNA profiling was now so sophisticated its potential was scary. Computer scanners could not only build a full body matrix. They could extract such a minutiae of information from a blood, saliva, or microscopic skin-flake sample that recognisable photofit pictures could be rendered. As the info pack Steve had given him said:

> The technology has advanced rapidly.
> All DNA computer systems in the country are now linked to Central Matrix. A database has been created where forensic information is held about everybody in the UK, linked to their finger, eye, and audio prints.

And further down the same page:

> To allow the exchange of information quickly between institutes their computers are networked via the Internet. Hence the term 'intelligent buildings'.

Central Matrix was able to scan the forensic data when a DNA profile was generated. The holographs on everybody's ID cards were also computer generated, by a 3D scanner rotating three-hundred-and-sixty degrees around their heads. The eyeprint was key. When info from a DNA profile was fed into Central Matrix an instant comparison could be made. And because every DNA sample was unique, chances for error were billions to one against. The system was essentially foolproof, with the CG images guaranteeing the authenticity of the match.

Hunter had arranged to go back to the IFI in the morning, to see what the residue yielded, but hadn't told Steve where it was from or what it was for.

He popped out the DVD and switched off his laptop. When he stood up the whiskey did its thing after the stress of the afternoon. It had been a long day but snow was in the air, bringing a romantic Christmassy feel to the evening as he crossed the bar and gazed out at busy New Central Square. Now that he was resigned to what he sensed was coming with Vanessa he got ready. It was 19:11. Sarah would leave soon, if she hadn't already. Meaning he'd be alone with Vanessa, at last.

Addison was parked across from the hotel, watching Hunter exit the bar through his infrared binocs. The optitracker got to work, auto-zooming in as the laser crosspoint locked on and fired. Through the 235:1 sight-masking concentric squares throbbed smaller, pulsing red as they gained on the leather-coated figure crossing Reception to the lifts, whizzing his head up big.

Sitting next to Addison, getting ready to smash Hunter to a pulp, was Naylor, a seriously mean-looking fucker-and-a-half. Tall, in his twenties, with a scabby shaved head specked with pus-filled spots, and wearing a grey leather trenchcoat swiped from his all-action Gestapo heroes. To Addison, he wasn't so much ugly as something nasty that got puked up when mom Nature took the piss out of mater and pater Naylor by cloning their nasty bits. With gobshites like him walking his earth, surely God got it wrong when he said that all his subjects were equal. Maybe God was a comedian. Addison made a good living from violence but stayed dispassionate because he was an IT guy and no fucking fool. Not to put too fine a point on it, he took the money and ran. As a bright ex-cop he knew it was easy, if you were prosperous, naïve, remote, to lionize thuggery and glamorize a brutish underworld whose existence was a symptom of middle-class cowardice. The unpleasant reality of crime was guys such as Naylor. Like all tough-guy tossers whose life ran on boneheaded macho exhibitionism he was a total fucking imbecile, compensating for what hadn't developed upstairs with animal stupidity. This was his Achilles heel, making him accident-prone and a source of unintentional comedy. If an empty soccer pitch had a fresh dog turd lying in wait for the unwary foot, Naylor's would find it if he ran across. Addison, himself a comedian but wiser, older, sharper than his punk, had clocked this pronto, meaning Naylor was a permanent joke-butt.

They hadn't been together long and he was breaking the young fucker in. He was still a virgin, as they said in the trade. Tonight was his big night and Naylor was getting impatient. *Squeak* went the X6's wipers as he stuck the iron mace in his pocket and slid open the door.

'Do his fucking teeth,' Addison told him.

'Yeah sure,' Naylor said in his thick Scouse lingo, matchstick at gob corner.

'Use your heel,' he added. 'Aim under his nose. If you aim for his mouth you'll hit him too low and all you'll do is break his fucking jaw.'

'Yeah sure,' Naylor said, sticking on his mirror shades then getting out and sliding shut the door.

Behind the kid's evil cats' eyes, Addison decided as the shades snuck them, was something sinister, even to a cynical old soldier like him. It was the malicious glare of a soccer hooligan partying with the ugly depravity of Heath Ledger's Joker. This aspect of his retardation made him unpredictable and dangerous.

As Naylor walked away from the X6 with his long coat flowing and his feet tapping like some dodgy Foley effect in a 60s spy movie, Addison puffed his cheeks wearily and noted aloud, 'If that kid had a fucking brain he'd be dangerous.' Then he switched off the binocs and lit a fresh cigarette.

TWENtY-tWO

When Hunter entered Vanessa's room she was sitting in front of her dressing table wearing a pink towelling bathrobe, making up her face. Her scrunch-dried hair was puffed out, shaggy. She was so disconcertingly beautiful she almost looked predatory. He'd noticed before that when she got dolled up to go some place special she took longer doing her make-up, especially her eyes. They were on his from the mirror as soon as Sarah let him in and he crossed over to sit by the window. Tonight's the night, he thought bravely, as he sank down behind Vanessa, pulling a bottle of water from his coat and popping the nozzle. But was it? He was excited at the prospect but could hardly bring himself to look at her reflection when the smell of her clean flesh hit him. As he tipped back the bottle he felt simultaneously daunted by her presence and stupid for thinking what he'd thought since lunchtime, gearing up to it like a plonker.

Sarah broke it, thank God, as the bottle came down and his eyes went horizontal. She was sitting on the bed, typing at Vanessa's laptop. 'I'm nearly done,' she'd said and started hastily packing her stuff, obviously sensing she was in the way. *She knows,* Hunter thought for the second time that day, dropping back his head to see ceiling again while he glugged more water.

'Are you OK?' Vanessa asked him from the mirror.

He said he was but kept sipping from his bottle. There wasn't much water left but he needed it to last so that he'd got something to do.

Vanessa delicately brushed her eyelashes with mascara and said, 'Bishop's e-mailed some changes. They want to bring the transmission forward.'

'It means we'll get paid faster,' he said, clocking her bare feet. The toenails were subtly varnished, her smooth skin as perfect as Hayley's and Jenny's. His eyes filled up at the thought of his beautiful little girls. They always brought him down to earth with a bang. In that moment he knew he'd been kidding himself about laying Vanessa and sensed that whatever had been building had just fizzled out. He was relieved but in his head still heard an old Donna Summer disco song that had got him going in the lift when he came up. The iconic gay anthem from 1977. The chorus wouldn't stop mocking him when he asked her, 'Did you book a table?'

'Yes,' she said. 'The food's supposed to be good. Unless you'd rather eat at Zhivago's.'

'Here's fine,' he said. 'It's freezing out anyway.' He shoved away the bottle, deciding now wasn't the time to say he didn't want to go to a nightclub but paving the way with his observation about the weather. Failing to anticipate a yawn he said through it, 'I'd better go down and get ready,' as he hauled himself out of his chair.

'You needn't sound so enthusiastic,' she said flatly. She watched him cross the room from the mirror before she brushed mascara on her other eye. When he reached the door she spun on the buffet to face him with a twinkle in her eye. 'It's expensive here so you'd better put on your best frock.'

He OK'd and turned, grinning.

'Did you get the suit?'

'Yes. Five hundred it cost me. And that was in the sale. Plus new boots and a new top.'

'Does this mean you'll be showing your legs?'

'It might do,' she said, returning his grin yet catching his eye girlishly before she swung back.

'Wonders never cease,' he said, his eyes on the perfect legs where they stuck from her robe.

She said she'd be down in ten minutes but he wasn't sure if he heard because everything jingle fucking jangled in his brain when he clocked that her robe only just covered her pubic hair.

Hunter was on a sexual knife-edge by the time he unlocked his door, stuck on the lights, and threw off his coat.

Next to the bed was an American thriller he was reading. He felt to be living through an action thriller himself. The difference between fiction and reality was the unsettling effect of the plot on this flawed hero, trashing his ability to cope. Thrown into it was everything else going on in his life, and that nagging fucking fear about DNA profiles. What distracted him, as he pulled his shirt off over his head without unbuttoning it, was a determined-sounding knock at his door. Too soon for Vanessa, he decided, crossing over. He was confronted by an ugly guy somewhere in his twenties, nearly as tall as him with a scabby shaved head.

'Mr Hunter?'

'That's me.'

'I've got something for you.'

The whiskey had gone to his head and Patrick Cowley's fifteen minute Donna Summer megamix goaded him from the corridor. Meaning it took a nanosec for him to digest that standing in front of him was a UPS delivery guy, in sugar brown uniform.

'Special delivery,' he'd said in his nimble voice.

Hunter was stripped to the waist and all hairy chest, some six-pack, and a fair amount of tit muscle but something about the way the guy eyeballed him unsettled him as he took the ePad. 'I'm surprised they let you come up,' he noted, taking his ID card from his back pocket and slotting it in. The package had come overnight from the States. Stuff for the O2 film they were shooting in the New Year, judging by the bulky feel of the envelope.

'They know me downstairs, sir,' the guy said, zapping the barcode with his laser gun then waiting for Hunter to hit the green button. The ePad pinged, Hunter withdrew his ID card, and the guy gave him the package. 'Have a nice day,' he said, holding his customer's eye for a touch longer than necessary before turning to prance pigeonfootedly away.

TWENtY-tHREE

The raw footage had arrived.

Driscoll skimmed through it then rewound to check. It whizzed in reverse on a TV screen on the wall but was also minimized on his PC. His office was in darkness except for the light from the screens, bouncing from every shiny surface. He was going back to the key part of Hunter's filming. No need to get too uptight after all, it seemed. Maybe paranoia had got the better of him.

He found the action he wanted. Hunter was standing in the cobbled alley speaking to camera, gunning through the pre-credits hook to set the tone for the programme. He'd yacked about Greenhalgh's popularity with the electorate and had speculated about possible motives for his death, referring to what Kowalski had said to Vanessa last night but keeping it vague.

'Furthermore,' he was saying, 'I can reveal that DS Kowalski phoned one of my colleagues shortly before he died. He believed that the circumstances surrounding Michael Greenhalgh's death raised some serious questions and that certain aspects of the way he was murdered didn't stack up.' A pause while he paced forward, long coat flowing, looking annoyingly super-cool as he stuck on the obligatory mirror shades. Gone were the arse-faced public school nerds who used to front current affairs TV. These days it was all about high-powered macho packaging, striving for sexy *CSI*-style effect.

Now Hunter hit his *Matrix* move and launched into the shout lines. Said, 'Tonight on *Crime in Britain* we ask: was Michael Greenhalgh's death part of a politically motivated plot? Was it a premeditated killing of convenience?' A beat while he took some steps forward, before asking gravely, 'Was he deliberately *bumped off*?'

He turned away as the sun flared artily into the lens and his coat swept out behind him. Driscoll knew that Hunter wasn't being posey. In post-production he'd be knocked back to grainy monochrome to create a live background for *Crime in Britain*'s chrome CGI logo to meteor-spin out of nothingness, before the opening titles and music kicked in. Vanessa shouted, 'Cut', and Hunter relaxed. The sound spat and the mike rustled. The hand-held camera swung down to show cobbles and feet. The old boy who was the sound mixer said, 'Quiet folks, while I grab some atmos.' As if on cue the spotty-faced kid belched then the rushes switched to show Hunter going on about the gruesome nature of the murder.

Driscoll killed everything and sat mulling, elbow to chair arm, clenched fist to chin. He spun to watch a gunship leaving the helipad slung out above his office. Its elliptical outer edge curved massively away, the chunky sci-fi girders supporting it home to numerous roosting starlings whose droppings formed a thick white incrustation. Ever fastidious about cleanliness he decided the shit should be power-washed off. As the gunship swooped to a dot it

149

made no sound because the office was cut off acoustically from the outside world.

Having had time to think through why Hunter sneaked into the alley Driscoll swung back in his chair. Maybe he'd overreacted because his dislike of the bastard meant he'd let him get under his skin. Instead of taking him out now it would be better to see what he did next. But it was probably too late to stop the beating and part of him couldn't give much of a sadistic shit if it was. His logical brain took over nevertheless when he nudged back his cuff to check the time then hit auto-dial at his console and waited while it did its thing.

Hunter had switched on the TV and was standing at the bathroom door, cleaning his teeth.

On TV a narrator was saying, 'Some communities hire private security firms to patrol their streets at night. But some authorities are thinking of making it compulsory for all new residential housing developments to be built with perimeter defence walls.'

The camera panned across such a wall as the narrator prattled on about aesthetics. Everything jumped close to show how coloured brick sets, normally used for paving, had been worked into charming vertical patterns. The guy opined about the prestigious design award the defence scheme had won. He hoped that some English Heritage of the future might acknowledge this splendid example of respectable middle-class citizens protecting themselves from low-life bonebags.

When he'd cleaned his teeth Hunter put on a primrose-yellow leather shirt but left it hanging trendily out of his trousers. As he studded up he was just wondering where

Vanessa had got to when she knocked. Crossing to let her in he wasn't sure if it sounded like her and hoped it wasn't UPS boy coming back for another fucking gander. He knew it wasn't Vanessa when he heard a second, more urgent knock as he got to the door and opened it.

What happened next hit him like an express train. On top of how light-headed he felt from the whiskey on an empty stomach it was like his senses left him for the nanosecond it took everything to sink in. It reminded him of charging excitedly downstairs when he was a kid, to let in some of his mates. He'd hit the steps way too fast, tripped, and taken a serious tumble, nearly going headfirst through the glass front door at the bottom. It was a similar feeling now when the sledgehammer moment got to work and he saw that it wasn't Vanessa who was standing outside his room but another stunningly beautiful woman who'd just come into his life.

Abigail.

He had to look twice.

As the moment stretched, it was her eyes that got to him again. Luminous, enchanting, irresistibly penetrating, gunning for him blatantly now. Her sandy-edged pupils were dilated and he knew the hell why. She watched him intently from the corridor. An old Pet Shop Boys ballad, *Nervously*, was finishing on the overhead speakers. 'I wasn't supposed to come till tomorrow morning,' she said huskily, 'but I couldn't wait.'

She was obviously turned on, which flattered and aroused him too. He realised he hadn't asked her in and quickly moved aside, resting with his back against the door after he'd shut it. He had the feeling that his fly was undone, or that maybe he'd put on odd socks.

151

As she passed him he nosed her scent. It was like Vanessa's fresh soapy smell but laced with clean hair. She was wearing a batwing olive-green leather trenchcoat and held a small purse. Round her neck hung a string of handmade silk beads, similar to the coat in colour but streaked with a wavy pattern. She went to stand in the middle of the room and turned to look at him coyly. Her long hair flowed lustrously under the overhead lights as she sent it back from her shoulder with a sexy head-flick.

'How did you find my room?'

'I asked downstairs,' she said.

'They shouldn't have told you.' He moved away from the door, feeling obliged to switch off the TV. Intimacy crashed in with the silence.

'I told them I was your girlfriend,' she added.

'That was optimistic, wasn't it?'

'Would you like me to leave?'

'No I wouldn't,' he said, amused by the inevitability of what was happening but also curiously moved by it. 'You know I wouldn't.' Then he remembered Vanessa. 'Shit,' he said, crashing back down.

Fuck, he thought, panic cranking.

'What?' she asked, wondering.

He dived across the room and snatched the phone from the bedside cabinet.

Vanessa entered a lift on the twenty-sixth floor. She heard a room phone trill further along the corridor, before the doors pinged shut, but couldn't decide if it was hers.

'Going down,' the sexy lift lady said.

A Pet Shop Boys album track was playing and instantly got Vanessa going. *This must be the place I waited years to*

152

leave, it was called. Symphonic, booming, it worked with the sexy atmosphere of the moment and seemed prescient because she sensed that tonight was going to be special. Neil Tennant sang about having Sunblest in the mornings, making her smile as she flicked her hair from her shoulders and started to descend.

She saw herself in the mirrors and felt unashamedly like the proverbial one million bucks. The powder-blue leather suit worked perfectly with her long platinum hair. The jacket was cut in a mandarin style with small square glass buttons. It was thigh-length but hung lower than the daringly short mini skirt underneath so that when fastened, as it was now, she looked like she wasn't wearing a skirt at all. Her legs were encased in five denier nylon that was so sheer it was impossible to tell it was there, because of the nude tone.

She was late going down because Max had phoned her again. After they'd spoken at lunchtime she thought he'd back off for a few days. What spooked him was her saying that she and Hunter were thinking of moving north to set up shop. It made sense because so much of their work took them there. They were also post-producing more in Manchester because it was cheaper than Soho. Even with hotels and other costs it was more profitable in the long run. For a tiny independent outfit like theirs the savings made by the relative inconvenience of living away soon mounted up over several commissions. But it was the wrong time to have said anything to Max. He was a successful London-based PR consultant and unhappy about her moving, despite him spending much of his time in New York, which was just as accessible from Manchester Airport as it was from Heathrow.

Her mobile went off when she'd dropped a few floors. She got bad vibes when she saw Hunter's face.

17, 16, 15 went the lift's digi panel.

'Can we give it a miss?'

She was KO'd, creaking with new leather. 'I knew something was bothering you,' she said, hearing the words escape before she'd finished thinking them.

'It's because of something that happened last night. I'm sorry for pissing you about.'

'Don't worry.' She knew he was hurting because of what he was doing to her. He was acting way out of character too. 'Are you sure you're OK?' she asked, sensing it must be serious.

9, 8, 7 raced the panel.

'I'll explain in the morning.'

'OK,' she said.

'See you,' he said.

'See you,' she managed back.

But he'd already cut her off, the evening knocked on the head. Just like that.

She looked at his photo. She'd taken it in September, when they'd been to the Lake District on a recce, the day finished off with a candlelit meal at an Indian restaurant in Penrith. That was when she'd first sensed something and knew he'd felt it too. Intimacy had caught them on the hop after a wonderful day together.

5, 4, 3 went the panel.

Then it stopped.

'Third floor,' said the lift lady. His floor.

The doors pinged open.

Still the music came, Neil Tennant singing about the terrible confusion of falling in love.

Now she felt embarrassed by her reflection. The slightest movement made the leather creak. It seemed to mock her. She could see along the corridor leading to Hunter's room and was tempted to go and check if he was OK but thought she'd better not.

A young bald guy in a grey leather trenchcoat walked away from her, obviously lost. He looked as if he had an artificial right hand and turned round when he sensed the open lift behind him. The doors met before he had time to clock her because she'd smacked the button.

'Going up,' said the lift lady over Mr Tennant.

Up she went, eyeing a point in space and mentally kicking herself for being so fucking pitifully silly. The lift felt huge, or she felt tiny, she wasn't sure which and frankly didn't care. Either way, 7, 8, 9 mocked the panel. 10, 11, 12 it went, going pneumatic-ballistic to the sexy music.

Naylor thought he was at Hunter's door but jumped when it opened and a big blonde transvestite muscled out in a black leather mini dress, nearly bowling him over. With brilliant timing she shut the door, gave him the once over, and said in cutting Lily Savage Scouse, 'My God look what the fucking cat's brought in.' She pranced away riding strappy sandals but couldn't resist turning for a second hit. She stopped, eyeballed Naylor up and down, but this time nodded at his bald head. 'I've got a big cock too sonny but it's between my legs.' She stuck a finger down her throat at him then flicked her hair and hit the walk with her butt wagging behind her.

Red rag to a fucking bull time.

Out came Naylor's Sheuze, on went the laser. He began REMing like crazy as he held out the chrome piece and

155

hotspotted the deep split in the tranny's peach. She didn't so much as grace him with a backward glance before she took a corner and disappeared.

Naylor was going doolally at being dissed but then his phone took the piss as it went off inside his coat. He stuck the Sheuze away, nearly dropping the mace clumsily on his foot. His ringtone was a Dalek sampled from *Dr Who*. As he fumbled near his tit the harsh voice shouted mechanically, 'Exterminate! Exterminate!' until he'd killed it and got Addison to his ear.

'Have you done it?'

'No,' he said.

'Back to the car now.'

'But I'm there, for fuck's sake!'

'Just fucking do it!'

Being stopped from dishing shit was like breaking off a bunny hop before you'd splashed. Swearing at the gay boy music being piped over the fucking speakers, he stomped back to the lifts but decided to take the stairs and smashed open the door with his steel fist, debossing a row of holes in the uPVC.

Then he hightailed it down. Uh-oh, or rather whoops, as he missed his clumsy footing. What Addison called the dog shit thing happened, causing Naylor to blow a serious fucking gasket when his ass rode steps.

TWENTY-FOUR

'Shit. That hurt,' Hunter said, grateful for the relief but thrown by what he'd felt after what he'd done to Vanessa. Puffing his cheeks he crossed to the window and drew the curtains. Outside a gunship moved above the rooftops, descending on CPHQ. Further away sirens screamed remotely from across the city.

'Why?' she asked.

'Lying to her.'

'Are you lovers?'

'No,' he snorted dismissively.

'It was the natural thing to assume.'

'She's ten years older than me.'

'Age doesn't matter.'

He shook his head and switched off the overhead spots. Only the bedside lamps lit the room. 'She's my business partner,' he said. 'Conventional wisdom warns you not to sleep with your business partner. Besides which she's been with a guy for years. We're just good friends. Sex never comes into it.' He wasn't convinced of this but felt like he might get away with half believing it now that Abigail was here and he knew what was coming.

157

'You spend a lot of time with her, don't you?'

'She's my best friend.'

'Guys often say that about their wives.'

'I went through a divorce and lost my kids but she was there for me every step of the way. I don't know how I'd have got through it without her.'

He went up to her and eased her coat off from behind. Now he saw what was underneath. A rust-coloured, wool-silk dress that was so short it made the bit of black leather Sarah wore seem like a nun's cassock.

'She knows about you,' he added, letting the coat fall. Still standing behind her, he caressed her shoulders and gently kissed the soft nape of her neck. Kissing a woman's neck had the same effect as stroking a cat at the base of its tail. It was the place where you could kiss a woman, other than the obvious bit, that got her going. 'I told her about you after I saw you on the plane last night,' he said, nuzzling her, turning her, but feeling awkward because they were discussing Vanessa. 'She'd be happy for me if she knew you were here.'

So why didn't you fucking well tell her just now his daemon demanded.

Abigail put her arms round him and kicked off her strappy sandals. The things he'd said confirmed what she'd deduced, leaving her conscience clear about wanting him for herself. As she kissed him back she resigned herself to the wave of sexual excitement that was arresting her body. His dark eyes shone against his beautiful soapy-smelling face. He was one of those guys who smelt squeakily, femininely clean. She'd no time for sweaty hunks or animated hearth-rugs.

'And like I said,' he said, lifting her dress, 'I work with her. We've a joint bank account. She knows stuff about me that my mum and dad don't. And anyway, how come you know I spend so much time with her?'

'I know quite a bit about you.'

'How come when we've only talked briefly, twice, and both times you told me to get stuffed?'

'I didn't tell you to get stuffed.'

'It felt like you did.'

The gunship had got nearer. Any louder and it would be a distraction. Snow flurried at the window.

'You're very honest,' she said, feeling him against her. She reached down and put her hand on it, watching him shudder and close his eyes.

'I usually tell it how it is,' he managed. His breath was fresh from a recent teeth clean.

'Guys don't easily show how they feel to women.'

'I don't assume they're mine to be had.'

'You understand women, don't you?'

'Do I?'

'It's what makes you so attractive.'

His smile became a cryptic grin. 'Are you saying I'm ugly?' he asked, gyrating shamelessly against her before a surge of emotion drove them into a passionate, crushing embrace. Yet still they staved off the inevitable, savouring the build up. He sent his fingers through her hair. Took off her beads and lifted her dress up over her head, making it crackle with static. They were greedy for each other. The room was loaded with their heavy breathing. It went on for a little while longer, till he asked her, 'You haven't answered my question.'

'Which one?'

159

'About how you know so much about me.'

'Are you very patient?' she asked, watching him, seeing lamplight caught in his eyes inches from hers as she undid his trousers.

'I can be,' he said, wincing with pleasure.

'Then maybe I'll answer your questions in the morning.'

That was the starting gun.

Unable to contain himself he swept her up and carried her across to the bed.

The gunship disappeared and for a few moments after they'd got under the quilt the room felt oppressively quiet. The hotel seemed to press down, heavy with its nocturnal embrace, groaning beneath its massive weight and heat. He knew that some relationships began like this but there was almost a weird formality to theirs. They'd exchanged only a few dozen words in all the times they'd spoken to each other yet were going straight into raw animal mating. It was as if they'd needed to break the tension and get the sex out of the way first, before they could get to know each other properly and discuss what had led them to the news conference.

She was impatient and pulled him straight into her. He withdrew to slow her down. He was good in bed but even though it was a while since he'd done it he was none the worse. If anything he was better and felt like a greedy sex machine as he threw back the quilt to kneel over her, his face soon wet with her juices. His priority always was to give himself totally to a woman in bed. His pleasure came by thinking of hers. His HR counsellor had once asked him when he was happiest. You were supposed to say the first thing that came into your head. He answered without hesitation: when his face was between a woman's legs. He'd admitted it when he was still married. Being with his kids would pip the observation now if he were asked the same question because they were the most important thing in his life.

His tongue worked and she contorted with pleasure, clutching him by his hair. He let her come first. She rolled onto him and shagged him greedily, her dark hair and big tits dangling. As she knelt over him, her amazing eyes burned like a frightened cat. Then he felt the stickiness at the base of her spine and she stiffened, swearing so loudly it spooked him when he thought of adjoining rooms. It was as if she were drowning from pleasure. She collapsed onto him, exhausted, but he rolled her over and went straight down again. As he buried some fingers up to the hilt he realised what had been happening this past year and what was behind all the sex stuff with Vanessa. He'd been punishing himself. Deep down, he blamed himself for the failure of his marriage. It was crazy. Vicky had been the adulterous half but he was angry for not spotting her weaknesses before they'd hit the altar. That was what really fucking bugged him. He was smart and on the button in most things but his marriage represented a catastrophic failure of judgment, like being fleeced by a conman. Because of it he blamed himself for what Hayley and Jenny were going through. Their pain was the crisis at the root of his rage. Did it mean he wished he hadn't fathered them? That he could never accept. He loved his kids with a passion that scared him. His failed marriage was a price worth paying to give Hayley and Jenny a life. If it meant he was a selfish bastard like everybody else he didn't give a toss. He accepted the human condition.

When finally he stiffened and swore and kissed her and kissed her and kissed her, he felt liberated with each thrust of his cock, grateful for what Nature had given him as he watched Abigail shut her eyes. When the secondary orgasm happened he consciously pumped every last drop of himself into her. It was a necessary purging.

'That was incredible,' she said, when they laid together in that wonderful drowsy period after love. She gave a little shudder of contentment and he caught the look in her eye. Like him, she knew this relationship would work. It was why it had kicked off on full power.

He'd fucked an amazingly beautiful woman and finally got rid of the guilt hanging over him from his divorce. But what about Vanessa? In the heat of the moment he'd callously dumped her so that he could get laid. Being with Hayley and Jenny might be what made him happiest. But Vanessa was right up there with his girls, because of the value he placed on her friendship, love, and trust. Now, inexplicably, as soon as his old guilt ended an even bigger one began.

TUESDAY

TWENtY-FiVE

Vanessa emerged from her bathroom, wearing baggy silk pyjamas, and ruffled her hair.

Yawning, she opened the door to the corridor and picked up the newspapers that had been left outside. The *Mail* demanded zero-tolerant action from the Government after some more race riots had flared up across the country as surely as if they'd been ignited by fresh petrol running along the motorways.

She stuck the DO NOT DISTURB notice on the outside handle, locked the door and found her glasses, then got back into bed. *The Times* had a more sedate headline referring to a looming Anglo-Asiatic trade row. No sooner had she got down to reading than her mobile rang from the bedside cupboard. She'd been expecting it after last night's balls-up about dinner but her spirits were instantly on a downer when she saw Max's face.

He was at his desk early at his office in Covent Garden. He'd never needed more than a few hours' sleep, which was why he'd been so successful at his job and was able to keep several projects going in his head at once. There were some awkward moments when they sensed the fallout from yesterday's talk about moving north. She couldn't decide if she'd been horrified or amused by what he'd suggested but as she got older she found it easier to take the heavy stuff in her stride. He got straight to it and asked if she'd had chance to think it over.

'No I haven't,' she said. When he wondered why not she added tersely, 'Because I had an early night and it's quarter-to-fucking-eight in the morning.'

'I thought you were going out last night?'

'We were.'

'But you didn't?'

'No.'

'How come?'

'Something came up so he called it off.'

'What did you do about eating?'

'I had something sent up to my room.' She could feel his relief when he knew that she'd been left on her own. 'Look Max, we can't discuss something like this on the phone at this time of the day. It's a big decision so it'll have to wait till I get back. Like I said last night we need to hang on and talk it through properly.'

'We've been hanging on for a year,' he insisted. 'You know it makes sense. We're not kids any more but experienced pros in our forties who spend a lot of time away from home. We've been together long enough to be able to discuss stuff like this on the phone. I want us to be settled, and I want you to be happy. But London's where my life is.' She shook her head at his conceit. At the same time a sense of futility crept into the conversation when she realised he was assuming that he'd get his way. 'Anyway,' he added, going back to something he'd said last night, 'you don't need to work.'

'I work because I want to.'

'On my income you could be a lady of leisure.'

'And do what? I'm a director. I need to be focused. It's why I don't lie on beaches but look at places when we go away. I also enjoy the business side of TV, which I didn't think I would. I'd go crazy if I didn't work Max, you know that.' He did know too after five years. It was because he was trying to cramp her style, as she became more successful, that was pushing them apart. Or rather, pushing her away from him.

'So when will you be back?' he demanded.

'I don't know,' she said. The sense of futility cranked so much it became almost physically painful. 'I promised to spend a week with my dad after we've finished shooting. Then we go straight into pre-production on the 02 film.' Thinking of Hunter made her become assertive and businesslike. 'I might stay up here. Now that Dad's on his own in such a big house he needs Jackie and me. It's not fair for us to leave him.'

'I thought Jackie spent time with him?'

'She does. But he hardly sees me.'

'I'll take that as a "No" then,' he said bluntly, pissed off and turning unexpectedly petulant for a smart professional guy pushing 50.

'I need time to get my head round it,' she said, not committing but knowing in her heart when it sank. Confronted with his obstinacy she suddenly felt defiant. 'It hasn't been right for a long time,' she said, letting off the bomb, amazed how easy it was.

'You're telling me,' he agreed, snorting. He talked the talk a little while longer then, out of desperation, pushed her again. When she put her foot down he started losing his rag. 'Come on love, for fuck's sake,' he said, wanting to get his way because it suited him.

It wasn't how he used to be. But then, she'd changed as well, which maybe was at the root of his jealousy. Since hitting 40 she'd felt better than ever and looked better than ever. She was confident in her early twenties, when the world was her oyster. She'd the same youthful earnestness when she began her thirties but what was missing was the wisdom that comes from living a life, and the sheer confidence of being older.

They finished the call amicably but she shut her phone slowly, listening to it jingle-jangle as it parked. She had no regrets about what she'd said, yet felt as if something beyond her was looming and fracturing. She crossed to stand by the window, hugging her shoulders while the sun came up between the skyscrapers. She knew it was a sign of her emotional maturity and resilience as a strong woman that she hadn't descended into self-pity because of her continuing difficulties with Max. But she still felt obliged to do the feminine thing and reached for a tissue, unfurled it and held it, but didn't lift it.

She knew something was happening, twenty-six storeys below, because of last night's cock-up. But patience was another virtue of getting older, when the years start flying past much more quickly. There was also the asking-the-Universe thing, where you put out for what you want and expect to get it.

TWENTY-SIX

Sunshine streamed through the window onto the wreckage of two Continental breakfasts standing on a tray next to the bed. When he'd woken Hunter felt safe and warm. But as Abigail revealed more about who she was and what she was up to a melancholy morning-after feeling invaded the airy confines of the room. 'You sound like an undercover agent,' he said, watching her cross from the bathroom and get back into bed.

'I know it sounds that way but I'm not. We're like private eyes. We're always running around following people or sitting in restaurants. There's an air of anti-climax hanging over everything we do.'

'Who're "we"?'

'I work with a really clever guy. Mark Halliday. He used to be an industrial chemist.'

'Was he the black guy last night?'

'Yes. There are others like us, scattered across the UK. We meet at big stately homes with our aging mentors but "agents" we definitely aren't.'

He'd discovered she was the same age as him and had worked as an HR exec for some of Britain's top industrial companies. She said it was how she came to Sir Ian's attention. It explained her underlying air of studiousness and appealing scholarly demeanour. It didn't overpower her beauty but if it had been a fraction more predominant it would have quarrelled with her femininity. Like him she was divorced, though unlike him she hadn't had kids. But it was when she explained about whom she was working with, and why, that he got an inkling of what he was embroiled in. She was part of a special group that Churchill had put together to nail corrupt high-profile political and public figures. It tied with what Hunter suspected was behind Greenhalgh's murder.

'We know that some of them had links with him,' she said. She named some prominent Tory backbenchers plus an ugly assortment of cabinet ministers, newspaper editors and odious Labour Party boneheads whose pathetic champagne socialism was a national stock joke. 'His killing took us by surprise,' she went on. 'We'd assumed he was a big enough bastard to be one of them. Because of his business links we were convinced of it. Did you know that he knew Driscoll?'

'No. But I'd a feeling his name was going to crop up.' The melancholia intensified. Maybe he was sexually hung over but at the mention of Driscoll it seemed as if the passionate lovemaking late the previous evening had occurred in a different time and place.

'They knew each other well. Driscoll is a non-exec with one of the City institutions that are implicated.'

'But the police aren't allowed. Especially somebody with his profile.'

'That's the theory but you know how bent everything is. Names can be devised and new ID cards generated when you've friends in the right places. Driscoll is one of a new breed of bent police chiefs. His background is in IT. He's a nasty piece of work and one of the youngest CCs ever appointed, despite joining the force quite late in life. Why do you think he's risen so quickly?'

'Is that why you tried to warn me?'

'Yes, and I've been concerned for your safety ever since. Your insinuations were spot on.'

'What do you mean?'

'There's something else going on but we can't work out what the hell it is. It's to do with a construction firm linked to one of Driscoll's City backers. It seems to involve stainless steel. Serious amounts of it.' Hunter looked puzzled but before he could say anything she added, 'I know it sounds crazy but there's a stainless steel fabricators' mixed up with it, and lorry loads of Polish workers who don't officially exist. We think Driscoll and his cronies might be involved in a nice international earner on the side, funded by the taxpayer.'

Hunter remembered Sarah digging something up about Driscoll when they'd last interviewed him. It didn't mean much because he'd hedged round their questions, threatening to walk out when Vanessa pushed him and insisting he vetted the TX before signing the release. 'Greenhalgh owned a road haulage outfit that does regular runs to Eastern Europe.'

'That's right,' she said. 'But as soon as we got close to finding something we suffered our first fatality. It was the call I took on the plane last night. Polish workers being illegally used as cheap labour would fit, only there isn't any need because they're cheap to begin with.'

He puffed his cheeks as he tried to get his head round it all then filled her in about Samrah and the residue from the shop. 'Christ,' she said. 'If you can dig up anything to show Greenhalgh was murdered by his own people . . .' She got out of bed and picked up her purse. 'I'd like you to meet some of our guys at the weekend. They might seem a bit stuffy but their hearts are in the right place.' She found a car's hands-free card and threw it across. 'I've a meeting at ten. Can you fetch my stuff while I have a shower? I'm parked outside the library.'

Obediently, he got out of bed. She told her watch that somebody was coming down to fetch her stuff and not to stun him. Before he could ask what the fuck that was all about his phone pinged with an e-mail from the dressing table. He picked it up and saw:

> Hope you slept well . . .
> See you in the dining room in 20?
>
> V xxx

He wondered why she'd e-mailed instead of phoning. Smiling to himself he sat on the bed and wrote back, adding a frank PS apologizing about last night. He could see that Abigail had wondered what was going on while he'd typed.

'Vanessa wants to meet me for breakfast,' he said, looking forward to seeing her.

'Can you manage another?'

'She'll wonder if I don't,' he offered.

She went into the bathroom and turned on the shower. 'Why didn't you tell her about the residue?'

'I was going to tell her last night.'

'Can you get back to the IFI without her knowing?'

'She's editing this morning.' Wondering if Abigail was fishing he reached for his shirt. 'I bet you know as much about her as you do about me.' Suddenly he wanted to protect Vanessa.

She came to stand naked at the bathroom door. 'She's a loyal friend. I'd count myself lucky at being in business with her. But underneath the ballsy exterior she's quite vulnerable and *very* feminine.'

'You seemed pretty ballsy till you came here last night and you looked pretty damned feminine to me. Besides,' he added, studding buttons, letting his eyes wander down from her face, 'I prefer getting to know people naturally, not via their OPQ reports.'

Realising what he was looking at she crossed over and put her hand on it. Gyrating playfully she put her arms round him. 'Was last night natural enough?' They kissed but she kept her eyes open to watch him. Because his fingers were still on her he couldn't resist making her jump. He was about to drop to his knees in front of her when she realised the shower was still going and drew back. 'Shall I still come tonight?'

'Why not?'

'Won't she wonder, if you miss dinner again?'

'I'll get round it,' he said, not convinced he would.

She'd asked him not to tell Vanessa about her until he'd met Sir Ian. A necessary precaution, she'd said, yet he felt like they'd hatched a plot to deceive Vanessa and it was beginning to piss him off. Reacting to it he pulled Abigail back and kissed her again deeply, squeezing her so hard against himself by her bum that she moaned and stretched up on her toes when she felt him swelling. Her studious good looks emphasized her elegant sophistication. Stuff about her clicked into place, such as the stylish cut of her hair and clothes. He wanted her again, but the sense of betrayal he still felt from dumping Vanessa last night soured the moment.

She reached down and caught her breath.

'Forget my clothes,' she said greedily. Her eyes burned with anticipation as she unfastened his shirt. 'You'll not have time for a shower when you get back.'

'I had a shower while you were asleep.'

'I know you did.'

Smiling at him seductively she slipped off his shirt and led him naked across to the bathroom, shutting the door after them as they went in.

TWENtY-SEVEN

He never got to fetch her stuff. It was another forty minutes before he'd kissed her goodbye and made it down to the dining room. Although he was late he'd expected Vanessa still to be there but she wasn't.

Wondering, he walked into the noisy clattery conservatory overlooking the atrium but she wasn't through there either. A waiter recognised him and said she'd been in on her own and left fifteen minutes ago. Shit, he thought. It was knocking on twenty-four hours since he'd got the residue but he *still* hadn't told her. Instead of trailing up to her room he went through to Reception and got out his phone, fighting through coach loads of foreign tourists straggling from the desk.

Her phone ran to voicemail. Shit, he thought again, feeling hemmed-in yet increasingly exposed. He found a quiet place near the lifts and called Sarah. 'It's me,' he said. 'Is she with you?'

'Sure.'

Thank fuck, he thought. 'Put her on.'

He could hear their boots working as they went up steps to a street. Cars swished to and fro. An emergency siren split his eardrum close to the phone.

'Good morning,' she shouted over the din.

'Your phone's off.'

'What?'

The *weeooo weeooo weeooo* receded.

'Your phone isn't switched on.'

'We've just come up from the car park.' She meant her signal had been cut off underground across from Sumners.

'You left early.'

'You must have got there late.'

'I needed to see you.'

'I wanted to see you.'

'We both screwed up.'

'You screwed up.'

'I screwed up.'

God how he loved this woman, batting words with him like a game of ping-pong but always staying in the ascendancy. 'Heidi phoned when I was eating,' she said. 'She asked me to go in early. Our Avid packed in last night and there isn't another suite free till Thursday.'

Heidi was their film editor. Vanessa had been due to go in at 11.00 to assemble yesterday's rushes. He was due at the IFI for the same time and intended to join her later.

'Are you coming over?' she asked.

'I've got to go somewhere first.'

There was a terse silence. On the rare occasion he came up against it he felt like a naughty schoolboy who'd upset Miss and been dragged to the front of the class.

'What the fuck's going on, love?'

He shot out his arm to pull back his cuff. His watch was big and chunky. An expensive Rhino made from copper and stainless steel. He needed to move it if he was to make the IFI on time. He was about to tell her everything when cold fear lanced him. Something Abigail said before she'd left. *Your phones might be tapped. E-mail. Room phones. Everything. Surely not*, he'd countered, lulled by sex into a false sense of security after yesterday's emotional rollercoaster ride. *You'd better believe it*, she'd said. *Assume they're listening. Don't say, write, or transmit anything electronically about the samples or what Samrah said.* Meaning they might be listening now. The fear feeling to the gut intensified. Vanessa knew nothing and she'd be safer if it stayed that way. If the bastards were snooping, and it seemed as though she wasn't privy to what was going on, they'd be more likely to leave her alone. Plus, it would throw them off the trail about what had happened at Samrah's, or where he was going that morning.

He came up with a convincing story about meeting a woman he knew from uni when he was in town yesterday. Vanessa wasn't surprised but said she'd sensed sex was in the air when he rang her last night. This was good because it made what he said sound plausible. He apologized for letting her down and promised to make it up over dinner. *Shit*, he thought when he'd said it. *Abigail's coming tonight.* He told her he'd see her later and got to the end of the call. Puffing his cheeks he looked round nervously and shut his phone, feeling more exposed than ever. He tried to reassure himself by watching the busy traffic stacking in the sunny outside and stretching apart when the lights let it go. He needed to get going too. Steve had said the profiles would be ready by eleven.

Like yesterday he drove all over the place to get to the IFI constantly checking his rearview. There wasn't another car behind him within a mile of the institute. The tension eased when he stuck on his shades. He hadn't shaved for a few days and looked lantern-jaw-rugged. Vanessa preferred him like this on camera, saying it made him look sexy and *CSI* cool. He checked his mirror again while he reversed into a space. Still nothing. Just leaves blowing across the deserted avenue loaded with parked cars, and drives winding between rhododendrons with big houses dumped at the top.

Maybe the world was safe after all.

Maybe Abigail was wrong.

TWENTY-EIGHT

Steve was waiting in Reception. He strode over, white-smocked, and held out a large hairy hand. As the automatic door shut out the blustery morning behind him Hunter wondered if the receptionist had caught his eye but passed it off as imaginary.

'Thanks for turning it round so quickly,' he said, as they headed through. They stopped at a vending machine outside the lab. He told Steve what he wanted and watched hot water gush into the plastic cups.

'When do you go back down south?'

'A couple of weeks.'

'Rather you than me.' As he lifted the flap his wedding ring zinged sunlight when he brought up a full cup. 'I enjoyed uni but the thought of staying down there fills me with a sense of dread. London's like a Third World country now. There's still space to move up here. The scenery's better and the women are less priggish. I'm probably too sensitive for my own good.'

Hunter wondered if Steve realised what he was saying as he barged backwards through the rubber doors into the lab, squinting over his big glasses. He seemed not to have

178

changed since they'd filmed with him ten years ago. He was still as lanky as ever. Tan Chelsea boots were still his sartorial trademark. His chestnut-coloured hair was still messy and long. The face it framed still had an expression of youthful scepticism except, now it was older, its square-ness made it look as if it was carved from wood, roughly finished off with sandpaper.

They sat on tall, wheeled stools.

Steve closed the blinds and fired up the kit.

'Have you found anything?' Hunter asked, lubricating his dry mouth with the tasteless muck in the cup.

'Um, sort of,' he said vaguely, 'courtesy of the new fully automatic scanner.'

They were sitting in front of a big touch-sensitive wide-screen monitor fleximounted to chunky steel conduit slung from the ceiling. Blue light from it played with everything in the room. Steve prodded it then kicked himself across to a starship console and got to it. He popped in a DVD, took off his specs, and stuck his eyes to an inverted periscope. 'You got this stuff from a sweet shop, didn't you?' he ask-ed, twiddling something.

'How can you tell?'

'There are loads of sugar fragments.'

He slid back to the screen. Digi chatter kicked in as the chips got to work then a box of stats piled and an image helixed. It was blurred at first but its shape was unmista-keable before it had rendered. It was the last thing Hunter expected. At another time he might have cracked a joke, or bellyached about Sod's idiot fucking Law. But not today. Not when he saw—stating it dumbly, puffing his cheeks in anxious despair—'A mouse . . .'

179

'The *mus musculus*,' Steve said, amused. His eyes were big again now that his face wasn't deprived of his glasses. 'The common house mouse. The computer can generate a full body matrix, right down to the relative elasticity of the rodent's anus.' He didn't provide this but swapped DVDs and repeated the procedure.

Nothing to be amused about this time. OK it was human but he was black, or rather half-caste, with large, not in the least light-coloured, eyes.

'An Anglo-West Indian boy aged nine years,' Steve said, typing something before kicking himself back across to the screen. The kid's body filled in rapidly while the matrix stacked. 'Height, weight, blood type, teeth disorders, vitamin deficiency, shoe size, you name it. And it's all come from a tiny skin flake.' He apologized for the brilliant resolution. 'Of course, these are early days,' he said. 'The technology's bound to get better.' He proudly knuckle-rapped the screen. 'This is the best bit, though. It's what you're really paying for.'

He meant the photofit mug.

The screen blanked and timecodes went crazy along the bottom as fine lines sprang up, leant back, raced away. They strobed while the mouse helix-thing happened again but this time twisted into the shape of a human head. A bump swelled up to make a nose. Depressions sunk for the eyes. Blood vessels raced out across the surface of the head like cracks across concrete. More lines covered it, blocking it in till the divergence reached the seemingly infinitesimal. Inside, something that looked like a gob of snot assumed the shape of a human brain and dropped the medulla oblongata to hang underneath then bent it up to meet the cerebellum, like the stem that supports a bunch of broccoli florets. All the time the outer head was busy with lines as the brain wrapped itself in a multiplicity of different coloured organs. The eyes popped up, two hideous, staring spheres. The skull built in sections, banging into position a phrenologist's panel at a time, faster than Hunter could think. Facial muscles enclosed the eyes. The staring rounds became mild ovals as the head jerked in profile one way, lunged out like a motion-control movie FX shot while it thought for a moment in front of some imaginary camera, then jerked back the other way. A face appeared, the jawbone and teeth exposed at first as a hideous Mr Sardonicus grin. Lips felt their way across it and Mr Sardonicus disappeared. Ears grew from bright-pink ducts strobing, vortexlike, into the centre of the head.

The assembly rendered quickly, leaving a realistic CG human head slowly revolving.

Now for the clever bit.

Steve poked the screen again and the face appeared between them as a life-sized hologram. Hunter paddled with his feet round it on his stool to check it out. Although the colours were a touch loud the staring face would be recognisable to anybody who knew him. His heart sank. It was obviously the kid who'd had the mask. Dope feely time again. As the DVD writer got going he could sense Steve was trying to weigh things up. 'The best way to show how it works is to use blood from the person who's having the profiling done. It's an expensive way to make a point, but I guarantee that you'd recognise yourself and would be able to judge how good the resolution really is.'

'Is he all you got?'

'No,' he said. 'I'm starting with the poorest and working my way up.' He met a laser-print but left it alone when he saw his client wasn't interested. He slid back to the console. 'Subject number two,' he added drily, slotting in another DVD and starting again.

The tension cranked.

Talk about fucking gut rot Hunter thought. These were some of the most stressful minutes of his life.

'Are you gonna tell me what it's about?'

'It's for the film,' he said, avoiding Steve's eye.

'Is that why you told Francine you didn't want it invoicing to your production company?'

Hunter played schtum.

The same sequence as before happened except that it by-passed stage one and went straight to the 3D matrix of the head. When Hunter realised he'd have to watch it render he wondered if Steve was stringing it out to take the piss. Finally, the holographic mug popped up between them. Hunter's heart sank again when he saw dark eyes and skin filling in again.

'A West Indian male,' Steve said. 'His body pretty much destroyed by crack-cocaine.'

Hunter sensed things slipping away. No matter how smart the technology the kid was of the right ethnic origin to have been one of the gang. The DNA couldn't provide the benefit of the fucking doubt. In a way he was relieved. Now that Abigail had come into his life he intended to stop trying to put a corrupt world to rights and take it easy especially with Christmas only a few weeks away. At least he'd done his bit following Samrah's tip-off, for the sake of David's memory.

Then everything sparked again.

'This is interesting,' Steve said. 'You'd have noticed if I'd shown you the full body matrix first.'

'Say again?'

'He's a left-leg amputee.'

Hunter almost cried out with relief. *He couldn't have run very far then, could he?* Suddenly he was back in the frame, his heart going in his chest. 'Is this everything?' Despite the coffee he was sipping, his mouth felt like it had been stuffed full of sand that had absorbed the saliva.

'One more. Of course, if you'd asked when we came in, I'd have told you that we've come up with a mouse, two black kids, and a single male Caucasian. But you didn't. You've just sat there as miserable as sin and been totally bloody impossible to talk to.'

'I was up late last night,' he said feebly. Then came the needle stab to the belly when he digested the words *single male Caucasian*.

He saw Steve poke the screen and heard beeps, beeps, and more fucking beeps as everything hotted up again. 'Most of the stuff from the white guy was made of dried saliva, layered like on the inside of a helmet.' The lines began to party. 'You don't get much from spit because it deteriorates.' He grinned, anticipating the showstopper. 'But there was a single grey hair bulb.' He didn't bother with the screen but wheeled across with folded arms and let it hologram instead.

Hunter knew who it was before the flesh finished forming. As it advanced he was surprised at the accuracy. The computer began with a bald head but defaulted to a crewcut because it couldn't know the length of a profile's hair. If the matrix were being used for police ID work the operator could dip into a photofit library and try out different styles. At first he couldn't believe it. Up came the eyes and the Mr Sardonicus grin. The head danced the motion-control jig as it built itself and swung this way, that way, then another fucking way. Muscles grew and thick rolls of flesh embellished the neck. Still no hair on the domed head, like the computer needed to think a mo, as if it thought maybe the guy was bald. Then it added close-cropped thick grey hair, rubbed it out, tried again, this time with a narrower forehead.

Up the ugly squared-faced bastard came. Hunter swallowed the end of the coffee and metaphorically speaking shat himself. In truth he wanted to run for the hills but it was too late. He'd meddled and the UXB had gone off big time, in front of him. The face pulsed when it had finished rendering and the computer *pinged* to tell them the analysis was done. As the nasty face stared back it seemed to accuse him of finding it. *I will kill you*, it said. *I will blow your fucking head off, like I blew the chauffeur's fucking head off. So say I.* DS Stoneham, Special Branch thug from New Scotland fucking Yard.

'Male Caucasian,' Steve said from somewhere. 'Age 38.' He poked the screen and the face revolved. 'Everything's there including bone fractures, of which this guy has quite a few. Judging by some of his enzymes and some titanium the scanner's picked up I'd guess that one of his limbs is held together with metal pins. In fact, he has quite a few defects.'

Hunter wasn't listening and didn't hear what he said by way of his take at a reply. Instead he sucked his cup again, even though it was empty.

'Well,' Steve said back, 'his left arm's been broken in a few places, and by broken I mean smashed. There's a gunshot scar in his right femur and some other minor fractures and abrasions. He could be a criminal, a mercenary, or a stuntman. It's impossible to tell.' He peered over his glasses. 'Do you want me to go on?'

'No. Just print everybody off. A full matrix on DVD and half-a-dozen prints of each head would be good.'

He tried to stay cool but the groovy sci-fi lab seemed like a big space where he was trapped. He needed to cover his tracks and knew that Steve mustn't suss anything was wrong. When the printer got going again Hunter praised the kit and livened up his conversation. As he did so, the words coming out of his mouth seemed to form independently of the thoughts in his head.

TWENTY-NINE

Emerging from the institute his priority was to speak to Abigail. But he'd left his phone switched off in the Mini's glove compartment, in case the CP could somehow trace it. He couldn't have used it anyway because as soon as it went back on they'd nail him.

As he walked away from the barrier the bitter air stung his face. Since he'd arrived clouds had crossed the sky and scrubbed out the sun. Like yesterday he'd parked a mile away, in case anybody had tailed him. The distance seemed immense. As he lifted his collar and took off along the desolate leaf-encrusted avenue the feeling that he was being watched was stronger than ever.

He thought about Stoneham. Even if he couldn't prove the incriminating residue came from the kidnap scene it *had* come from inside the shop. In conjunction with Samrah's evidence and a statement from the kid who'd found the mask, the laser-prints and DVD meant he'd enough to blow the incident wide open.

As he turned these thoughts over the wind picked up and he noticed that he couldn't see the surface of the pavement he was walking on. All he could see was the concrete kerb, working at masses of dead leaves that were drained of colour because of the lack of sun. They rushed towards him and spooked him, blanking his hearing, making him feel exposed. They settled, changed direction, chased him across the road, sweeping under parked cars. Suddenly the air was alive with golden fragments driven by a roaring gust that whipped them up and slapped them in his face. He checked nervously behind him when he hit the opposite pavement then nipped into an old cobbled footpath that skirted a public Park.

When he turned onto the avenue where he'd parked he brushed the wall and felt something sandwich against his leg in his coat pocket. He stopped and stuck his hand in. It was the cuddly toy from yesterday. He'd forgotten about it after he shoved it away when he met Samrah in the alley. He pulled at it before he'd finished wondering what it was. As it popped out it flew from his freezing hand and rolled under a parked Merc 4x4. Shit, he thought. What now? The Mini faced him from about twenty cars away. Because of its squat shape, its yellow offside front wheel arch nosed the kerb where he'd parked badly. He stooped to try and see under the Merc, knowing he couldn't walk away and leave the cuddly toy. Hayley and Jenny would be mortified. Shaking his head he thanked God for inventing kids. Servicing their precious needs kept silly, sex-crazed, money-obsessed adults on the straight and fucking narrow.

He knelt down but the toy had gone right under, so he'd to sprawl full length to get it. The Merc was stacked on its tyres, making for an easy reach. As he slid back out he was just wondering if he should catch a bus back to town when he saw a pair of big Niked feet crossing the road from his ground-level POV. Maybe it was the tension and the air of wintry desolation hanging over the silent avenue but there was something suspect about how these flippers moved. Breath puffing-panting in a thick mist, Hunter made it to his hands and knees and snuck the toy back in his pocket. Leaves ran away in the gutter, doing perspective with the street, stinking earthy frosty cold. Now the wind had another go at them. The rustling covered him as he crawled across into the gateway of a big Victorian house before the owner of the Nikes got between the cars and hit the pavement up ahead. Inching up the gatepost Hunter peeped round and saw a hoodied kid walking quickly away. Unaware that he was being watched he hugged the cars, thumbing door studs as he passed them.

The next moment he was waving something at the Mini, making a red diode *pip*. Hunter knew it was for disabling the alarm. It also read the onboard computer and overrode the engine immobilizer. There was a *ping* from the Mini as its indicators pulsed. The kid stood back, crunching leaves. He might have knocked out the alarm but he still had to get in to blag it. He pulled out what looked like an animal bolt-gun welded to a pistol grip. Did the tough-guy tosser pose, face set hard, and blasted off the lock then yanked

187

open the door and got in. Hunter was about to set off running to tangle with him but stopped. The car was hired. Why get into a fight when it wasn't his? He could have snapped the kid over his knee like a fucking twig, because he was scrawny, but he was obviously a professional car thief and probably armed.

Before he could put the full stop behind the thought as it finished in his head a young bald guy in a grey leather trenchcoat started tonning it towards him in the middle of the road. Waving a Sheuze he bobbed above the parked cars, shouting and swearing for the kid to get out of the fucking car. Baffled, Hunter crouched back as he sensed the kid hotwire the ignition. The bald guy seemed to trip and fall. At the instant Hunter clocked this and the Mini's ignition squealed—as its onboard computer went live—his senses were smacked between the eyes.

There was a terrific blinding flash. Everything camerashook and a shockwave smashed into him like the splitting-the-atom thing where time mega trips. His eyes jumped ed in their sockets. His fillings jerked in his teeth. His brain seemed to jolt in his skull. The sound effect wasn't up to much, though. No stylized OTT movie *booooom*, more an uninspiring, short, very loud *bang*. The Mini's roof peeled back. Its windows shattered as it went up nose first, tongue-wagging fire, losing doors, wheels, its boot, the bonnet, human limbs, anything that was hinged. Millions of leaves went up too. Thousands anyway, in a riot of autumn colour like tiny birds frenzying at a waterhole. The driver's door smashed through the adjacent wall, followed by a spray of human guts. Partying with the explosion and everything Hunter could see was the sound of metal ripping like paper.

Dozens of car alarms screamed to life and glass crashed and tinkled from surrounding houses, kicking off yet more alarms. Smoke mushroomed up as the Mini subwoof *wunched* down and something boomeranged away that looked like the arm of a hoodie jacket containing the limb it was made to fit. Trailing fresh meat it disappeared through the smoke that was rolling through the trees. The last thing Hunter saw, before he reflex-hit the ground and the nano big bang ended, was the bonnet of the car parked behind his snap up and fly across the road, like a piece of spent cardboard.

THiRtY

Debris was raining everywhere.

Through leaves raging from the blast, what was left of his car blazed furiously. It had morphed into burning yellow scrap with its roof bent up like a Jack-in-the-Box lid. Other bits pointed away. The wheels had gone. One still flew through the air, finding its apogee across the street. As it came down it ploughed through branches and wanged into a greenhouse, popping glass. Hunter saw a shape in the car with bits missing but still recognizably human. Brighter fire enclosed it. It was slumped across the wheel with its jaw hanging off, burning at the heart of the inferno.

Through the billowing smoke he saw the bald guy staggering in the road. Then a red X6 screeched up through the pother and slowed without stopping. A door slid open and hands grabbed the bald guy, yanking him in. When Hunter saw the grey-haired lummox sitting at the wheel he realised he'd seen the X6 and the Yul Brynner clone before. Yesterday when he was walking to the IFI he saw the same two mean-looking bastards gooning at him like sunglassed fuckwits as they tootled past. He got the feeling they'd clocked him by chance and did a runner when they realised he'd eyed them back.

Low-profile tyres smoked and the X6 did the 0-to-60-in-no-seconds pose, dragging leaves. But what gave the game away was a fucking police APC, hovering at the end of the avenue like it was giving the X6 time to haul before it skidded round the corner on its fat Gripper tyres. Its spots tripped out of sync and its blue-flash lightbar partied mute at its roof. As it raced along the street towards Hunter in a blur of blue-and-yellow Battenburg warpaint its siren erupted, throwing up the long piercing drawl before driving out the hideous frenetic scream. He was already crashing through bushes, falling headfirst over a garden wall into the footpath he came out of before he'd dropped the cuddly toy. His ears buzzed from the bang like tinnitus. He'd never been so shit scared in his life. Behind him the world was going fucking spare. Dogs barked. Women screamed. Alarms babble-tangoed. Then a secondary explosion hit. No, the car in front of his fuel-tanked. As he checked the DNA stuff was still in his pocket, and picked himself up ready to hightail it, he glanced back and saw a red Scirocco going up arse first, wrapped in a neat CG fireball that blew it apart, almost in slow-mo. The ground shook as it *wunch-*

ed level, pranging metal. Everywhere fire raged. Bits of car *pinged* and *peeowed*. Heavier stuff *thunked* and v*erdunked*. Transfixed by the mayhem, Hunter backed away watching leaves scribble like a fucking ticker-tape parade. There was no question now that he was a dead man. His hunch that he was being watched was bang on. More sirens wailed in suspiciously fast, fighting with the panicking alarms. The bastards had nearly got him. If the cops sent in the gunships with their infrared heat-seeking paraphernalia and gatling guns he'd fucking had it.

As another fireball erupted he set off, tonning it along the footpath towards what he knew from checking Google Earth before he drove to the IFI yesterday was an abandoned railway. He ran faster than he thought was possible, like the kid at the start of *Trainspotting*, legs going, feet powering, running for all he was worth.

Running for his fucking life.

Driscoll knew they'd blown it straight away. He was descending from his rooftop eyrie when Addison's call came through. Phone at ear he surveyed his kingdom. The girders dividing the hamster tube flicked at him as he went down the outside of the building.

33, 32, 31 went the digi panel.

On the phone everybody was swearing and panicking as the X6 took off. It was depressing to hear yet also rather funny. Even the dark side of British constitutional goings-on had its innate class structure. The relentlessly swearing dumb fucks at the bottom were like labourers and sweaty navvies. Thick as the proverbial two short bits of wood, OK for the heavy stuff, but waving guns instead of picks and shovels.

Far from being angry at it all going tits up he saw it as a minor setback. It was a last minute decision to take Hunter out so spectacularly anyway. The guys had been watching him from way off down the street. First he was there, then he wasn't and a kid was blagging the Mini. They hadn't been able to pull enough people in at such short notice but it wasn't Driscoll who'd ordered the hit, so not his problem. This filled him with a malicious *I told you so* satisfaction. The belief that politicians were arse fucking stupid was fact. Especially if they tried to control stuff from Westminster and knee-jerked boneheaded decisions via subordinate wankers in the same way they banana-skinned into unnecessary fucking wars.

Hunter was on the run but he was super smart. Driscoll knew he wouldn't dare communicate with anybody electronically, or would at least bide his time. As a precaution every phone and e-mail address into every newsroom in the country had been put under surveillance before he'd reached the IFI. Central Matrix made it easy. Within minutes of the hit going wrong every airport and transport interchange would be scanning for Hunter's ID card. Since yesterday afternoon they'd been tapping the phones and e-mail of Vanessa and the film crew. When you'd friends in the right places you could do anything. You could control anything. You could even, Driscoll thought with a wry smile, control democracy, which passed for Western freedom.

Before the semtex was stuck under the Mini its VIC number had been altered by VOSA and its history changed so that it couldn't be traced to Hunter. Even before he got away they'd fabricated a story about his disappearance. It would be released when Forensic had finished at the crime scene. Meddling journalists were always being threatened by some idiot fucking terrorist faction or other. Blowing the bastard to bits was a necessary precaution to ensure that no physical evidence remained to contradict the manufactured story. When you generated the forensic info you could also fix it. Vanessa was next, although they intended to let her live for a few hours, to see if Hunter tried to get to her.

24, 23, 22 went the panel.

As soon as Addison killed the call Driscoll's phone went off again. It was Collins, the Scot from Communications, telling him that Vanessa had just e-mailed Hunter. 'It's her third time today, sir. She's obviously worried about him but I don't think she knows where he went. Surely she'd call Steve Hamer if she did.'

'I find it hard to believe that Hunter wouldn't tell her he was going to the IFI.'

'He didn't tell her when he phoned her before he left the hotel, sir. It was like he didn't want her to know.'

'Hmm,' Driscoll murmured, wondering why. 'And she's had no incoming calls?'

'None.'

'It doesn't surprise me,' he replied, watching the panel flick away the floors. 'The first thing he'll have wanted to do after he'd fled the scene is phone her. But he'll not risk it. He might be less sure about her e-mail, so continue to intercept it and monitor the phones and e-mail of the film crew. We should also watch his ex-wife and especially his children.'

'I sorted it before he got to the IFI, sir.'

'Excellent.'

10, 9, 8 went the panel now.

The lift was nearly there. It was difficult to tell if it was moving, never mind when it started or stopped. 'Did you notify the CP about his AWV?'

'Yes sir. Straight away. Priority red.'

'Let me know if you hear anything.'

They were referring to the sound of Hunter's voice. Central Matrix held a voiceprint of every British citizen as well as their finger and eyeprints that matched their ID cards. The police could liaise with the phone people via the CP and scan the network. Within seconds of a phone call kicking off the CP could trace the author of a voiceprint. Even if Hunter dared to use that nearly defunct species known as the public phone box, and tried to disguise his voice, he couldn't disguise his unique audio waveform. Meaning his exact position would show up instantly, no matter where he was.

3, 2, 1 went the panel.

The lift pinged and the doors split as Driscoll's Jag slid up to meet him. Dr Steven Hamer next, he decided nastily, picking up his case. His driver got out to open the door for him. Technology, he thought smugly. Today's technology made it easy.

THiRtY-ONE

The Avid Symphony had crashed. While Heidi rebooted it and Sarah phoned the kitchen to order three green teas, Vanessa called Hunter again.

The phone carried a severe weather warning of impending heavy snow for northern England. She'd just checked to see if he'd e-mailed her then had e-mailed him again. She swore as the phone call went to voicemail once more. He apologized for being unavailable but asked her to leave a message. The Orange woman said, 'When you've left your message just hang up, or press one for more options at any time.' *Beep.*

'Where are you?' she asked. 'We need your input on the edit. Can you call or e-mail me ASAP?'

She killed the call and looked despondently at the phone in her hand, like it might provide an answer to his whereabouts. Something was wrong. She could sense it. She'd felt it since he phoned her that morning and she'd asked him what the fuck was going on. Some subtle change had affected his voice, as if he'd been about to tell her something mega then decided not to. Most people wouldn't have noticed but she knew him too well. The story about the woman he met yesterday from uni was bullshit. She knew it like a wife knows when her husband's cheating on her. He was always telling her how much better she knew him than Vicky had done because they spent so much time together. And he was right. He'd reminded her of it after they'd sat up talking late the other night and, loosened by wine, he'd stood awkwardly at the door when it was time for him to go.

Something had happened on Sunday evening. Some shift occurred over dinner. It started with how he'd reacted to her when she'd got back from the salad bar, like he'd seen a ghost. He wasn't prone to being broody but it was like he couldn't bring himself to look at her. At first she thought she'd said something to upset him and asked him if he was OK. He said he was fine except that he seemed a hair's breadth from sounding rattled before dragging himself off to fetch more salad. And later, up in her room, he'd been self-conscious, even nervous, which was way out of character, saying how he liked to hear snow romantically touch a window. When he'd talked about the dark-haired woman his eyes gunned for hers the more he'd said about her, leading to the pause at the door. Him hesitating like a clumsy teenager before he finally turned to leave, like he didn't really want to haul, having perhaps caught the look in her eye.

When he came up to her next morning, after she phoned to tell him about David's death, he'd wrapped her in his arms and held her as if the night before hadn't happened. But the shift had taken place, which is why she'd wondered last night if things might have come to a head. Somehow it connected to his cock-and-bull story about meeting some woman from uni.

196

She crossed to the window while the Avid made its fanfare and the green teas arrived with a runner pushing the sweets trolley. She parted the blind. Clouds were massed over the city. The predicted heavy snow had begun and scribbled outside the window, but she sensed something else in the air. The day was fading fast. The clouds looked like they could engulf everything. Weirdly, lightning flashed behind them but she didn't hear any thunder. He'd say it might have been created by Industrial Light and Magic, a cool CGI FX shot just before the aliens landed. Then she heard a distant basso rumble, muted by the double-glazing. It came towards her, an ominous acoustic dragging itself across the land.

The glass responded as the sound rolled overhead. Now she was seriously fucking spooked, on edge, concerned about his absence. In reality she'd been on edge ever since she'd gone to bed on Sunday night.

THiRtY-TWO

Abigail tapped snow from her brown suede ankle boots then eased her legs carefully in and slid shut the door. She pressed the ignition and the Lexus came to life like a jet fighter starting up. Mark always said it was like the Batmobile firing its atomic batteries to power and doing turbines to speed.

While Computer's stack flashed on LEDs chased across the dash, enough to fill the cockpit of a 747. The 4x4 was already warm. Part of its expensive refurb was that it kept itself aired at room temperature while parked in winter. Now it rose on its chassis. Servos (she assumed) whined up, hence the sensation of gearing for a take-off. Its headlights flooded the gardens and caught falling snow. The wiper sensors took their cue and shifted the white piled at the glass. *Schwump* as it fell. All that was missing was the roar of vertical thrust jets.

She did the *clunk-click* thing.

'Good afternoon, Abigail.'

'Good afternoon.'

'And how are you?'

'I feel totally fucking amazing.'

'Totally fucking amazing,' he repeated, wondering but not understanding.

Off he went to think it through.

She caught her face in the mirror. Looked at herself girlishly from under the lids of her dark eyes as she swung the powered wheel coolly with one hand and headed away from the house across the snowy gravel.

Hunter had brought something out in her and had made her feel alive again. She admitted it unashamedly. It didn't matter that she was a highly educated, highly intelligent woman. Love, if it came, would come later. Something else would come first, like the proverbial express train. It had been on her mind all day, filling her with a glorious adolescent excitement that sustained her throughout her long meeting.

I want him to fuck me again.

I want to feel him inside me.

She was wearing a more sedate skirt than last night because she was also wearing stockings. She hadn't worn them much since she was married but Hunter was an animal in bed and seemed to like traditional role-playing between men and women. This excited her. He wasn't the usual fatuous middle-class pillock living in a state of emotional denial with his head stuck up his backside. He knew how to please a woman and she couldn't fail to respond to it. He also had a lovely big cock and she couldn't fail to respond to that. She sensed that stockings would go down a treat, especially the lace-topped kind she was wearing, which subtly enhanced her olive skin and were so sheer that at first glance her legs looked bare.

Mark had left an hour since to go to the Dunford Bridge terminal. His tracks were almost covered by the time she reached the end of the drive. She wasn't too bothered that she hadn't heard from Hunter all day. Before she left him that morning she warned him not to contact her by phone or e-mail, in case the CP was snooping. She'd arranged to meet him at the hotel at seven but needed to drop something off for Sir Ian on the way in and had set off early. But as she turned right at the village church and drove on into the snowy late-afternoon gloom she turned serious, wondering what happened at the IFI or what the samples had revealed.

She couldn't stop thinking about Hunter being inside her and asked Computer to dial his number. It was a risk worth taking because she wanted to tell him what she was going to do to him before they went out to eat. Her SIM was blocked. If goons were tapping Hunter's phone they wouldn't be able to trace her and get a fix on her position. That would really piss them off.

Computer made the call and the first ring happened. 'Is it a private matter, Abigail?'

'Yes it is.'

'Should I go away?'

'Yes,' she said, 'I think you should.'

The second ring.

Computer switched himself off and his vectorscope winked out at the dash.

The third ring.

The wipers worked in front of her and she caught herself in the mirror again. Sly, she thought, clocking the pale-pink lipstick and shaggy scrunch-dried hair via the glow of a passing gritter's partying hazards.

Christ, I want his cock.

The fourth ring.

She was so turned on that butterflies raced in her gut. The effect was amazing. The whole of her lower body was tingling. The soles of her feet. The insides of her legs. Right up her bumhole, which his tongue had shamelessly explored in the shower that morning.

The fifth ring.

Oh God, yes.

Click.

THiRtY-THREE

Hunter lowered himself to a yellow plastic seat in a crappy American fast-food café. He'd needed to eat and it was the best place he'd found. There wasn't enough money in the area for the big franchises to be interested.

16:04 said a clock on the wall.

'Large fries,' said an Uncle Sam shirt behind the counter.

'Large Coke,' said New York City boy.

'*Large fries,*' repeated Uncle Sam, sounding ratty.

16:05 said the clock.

An overweight figure of no obvious sexual denomination shuffled across and stuck a hand through the hole.

Hunter peered out at the snow and at the vacant faces passing through the fluorescent light thrown at the street. He lifted a paper cup of tasteless frothy liquid. Dissolved some sugar to try and give it taste then pondered a slab of stale lemon cake. The seat was too far from the table but when he tried to scrape it forward he found it was bolted down. He looked at the plasma TV padlocked to the wall, nattering with an excruciating late-afternoon soap above the stars-and-stripes no-hopers dishing slop from behind the steel netting.

16:08 said the clock.

16:09 it said, as he lifted the cup again.

A young mother swore at a half-caste toddler as they came in pushing a buggy. The kid's tantrum split everybody's eardrums. The woman might have grown up pretty if God had spun the roulette wheel kindly. Her outburst drew the attention she craved. What did D H Lawrence say about everybody needing to be looked at? A hundred years ago people were the same. Hunter pitied the ugly woman and hated her human nature then thought of his sophisticated women and embraced human nature. He remembered comparing Vanessa to that vile cow Julia Hall yesterday morning. *It's as if they were from two different species.* Sometimes he despised himself for thinking what he thought. Intelligence was a liability. Ignorance really was bliss. But as long as there were beautiful women, and guys who wanted to fuck them, there'd be inequality for the junk food and mass leisure industries to plunder. It was why enlightened souls higher up the pile had time to froth at the mouth about what the hell was wrong. It was the wicked way of a very unpleasant but actually rather wonderful world. Hunter moved in a different world to this one. He didn't belong in it.

16:11 said the clock, time racing, cup going up again, down again, up.

'Large fries,' shouted Uncle Sam.

'Large Pepsi,' said New York City boy.

'Burger.'

'Fries.'

'Vege wrap.'

'Large fries.'

'Fries.'

'Fries.'

And so it fucking went.

History passing.

Robbing time.

16:17 said the clock.

16:18 said the clock.

He kept seeing the kid burning in the Mini. No matter how enlightened you were you couldn't fight a fucking bomb. His first thought after he'd got clear was the overwhelming need to know when it was planted. Did they do it last night at the hotel, waiting to see where he went today before they primed it? Did they bung it under the car while he was at the IFI? The deserted streets would have made it easy. If so, how the hell did they follow him? He'd watched his rearview all the way but saw nothing. Even before Abigail had warned him about the CP he'd avoided contacting Steve by phone or e-mail. Did that mean they'd bugged his car like in the movies? Did somebody at the institute tip them off? Was it the fit receptionist who wasn't there when he took the samples yesterday? She seemed to catch his eye when he arrived that morning but had gone by the time he left.

It didn't matter now but one thing was for sure. If Stoneham was involved, so was Manchester's top fucking cop. At least Steve couldn't identify the DNA profile. Although Central Matrix could instantly match it to Stoneham's biometric data lawyers and the human rights crowd had fixed it so that a reverse-DNA match could only happen if the pathologist went through costly and time-consuming legal bumph first.

16:29 said the clock.

Weary, he puffed his cheeks and got up to leave.

203

'Have a nice day,' Uncle Sam shot across, courtesy of an e-mail directive from LA.

'Yeah,' he said back, waving an arm.

16:30 said the clock.

He'd been travelling for much of the freezing afternoon. From one bus to two, from two buses to three, hands shoved in his coat pockets, half submerged in the smelly seats. At first he was glad to be alive and wanted to get away and not to have to think. Watching the world go about its business and being stuck in a kind of limbo was enough. Then he'd seen himself reflected in a bus window and his survival instinct kicked in. He'd swapped his contact lenses for his glasses, which changed his appearance. Wearing them he felt less exposed. To disguise himself more he got off the bus, went into an RSPCA shop and swapped his beloved trenchcoat for the snorkel-hooded arctic anorak and fleece-lined gloves he was wearing. The only other thing he had on him was the cuddly toy in his pocket. It had become his mascot, his lucky charm, because it had saved his life. If it hadn't made itself known to him when it did the kid wouldn't have blagged his car.

He crossed the road and went into a public Park, which seemed to offer a sanctuary of sorts. He checked over his shoulder for the first few hundred yards, to make sure nobody was following. Ran through a cloud of his breath up some treacherous steps to a big war memorial decked out in graffiti, standing sentinel over a sombre deserted promenade. The Park was immense and undulating, broken by oases of rhododendron and silver birch. He made his way through the still desolation from one side to the other, wondering what the fuck to do. He saw nobody but kept

204

turning to check because of his footprints in the snow. He passed the fortified Park café, defaced by a fury of graffiti, shut down for winter. Further on was a preserved Edwardian tramway used for pleasure trips in the summer, the shed garaging the cars barricaded with steel plate. Further still into the municipal wilderness he came across a frozen lake, peppered with Canada geese roosting forlornly out on the ice, heads tucked under folded wings.

The snow liberated what it touched, bringing a child's-eye view to a dangerous place where everything was on the verge of being blown up or splattered with the guts of dead men. He took off his glasses and stood with his arms held out in a crucifix pose, like the guy on the *Pure* CD cover. Looking up he shut his eyes then opened them and saw millions of snowflakes coming from the white-orange sky. His world had been smashed but how he wished to God he was with his children. He hated Vicky because of what she'd done to him but he loved her for dropping two such wonderful kids. As the day had taken its toll, and it sank in that he'd nearly been blown to bits, he'd started yearning for the security of his life before he became a marked man. Craziest of all, he'd reflected on his marriage with a queasy nostalgia.

Feeling it now he leant against the railing and buried his face in his hands. It wasn't like this in the movies. In the real world the tough guy was fallible, had emotions. His bones broke when he punched somebody's face to the silly sound effect. He knew he was cracking but told himself he wasn't and rubbed his eyes, stuck his glasses back on, and turned to look at the vast white Park. He couldn't communicate with anybody by phone or e-mail and he was cut off from his women. Bent cops had tried to kill him. But for the sake of Hayley and Jenny and screaming kids in shitty cafés, and poor bastards trapped behind steel security netting everywhere, he had to get through this fucking nightmare and expose the bad men behind it.

Suddenly he knew where he needed to go and what he had to do. He left the railing and carried purposefully on, and on and on and on, his legs working under him, his feet crunching snow.

THiRtY-FOUR

When the Jag pulled up at the security barrier Driscoll saw the IFI spotlit through the falling snow. Being made from mirror-finished copper plate it looked incongruous surrounded by detached Victorian houses and tall trees. Framing the entrance were two fat chrome columns. They went up the front, bent backwards, did something on the roof, then ran down each wall and joined the chunky steel uplighters that were buried in the foundations. The building was like a massive architectural parcel tied up with metal ribbon, holding itself against the ground in case the blizzard blew it away.

The driver sent down his window. 'Police,' he said.

A fat guy with an angry red face frowned from his plastic booth. 'You took your time,' he snapped back. 'I should have gone home an hour since.'

'This is the Chief Commissioner's car.'

'I don't care if it's the Queen of bloody Sheba's chariot. He's got legs. You could have parked out on the street and walked a few sodding yards.' Pissed off, he poked a button and the barrier rose.

The driver eased the Jag through like a growling beast. Driscoll assumed the staff still on the premises knew the security code if they needed to get out after five, which was when the guard should have fucked off home.

The driver swung round to park in front of the building and shut his window. 'There's an obnoxious little shit, if you don't mind me saying, sir.'

'I don't mind at all,' Driscoll said from the back. His phone made a tune as they pulled up behind a couple of squad cars. Their lightbars scudded the front of the building, strobing at the windows and making the snowflakes pulse blue. 'Yes?' he asked the phone.

It was Collins. 'She's just rung him again, sir, and left another message.'

'Are you sure it's not Vanessa?'

'Definitely not, sir. Different AWV, and it's scrambled.'

'What did she say this time?' Collins told him, amusing him. 'Bully for him,' Driscoll said, fascinated that a woman could get off doing that to a guy. 'She hasn't by any chance got a husky voice, has she?'

'Actually, yes sir. Very Pussy Galore.'

The penny dropped. 'I think I know who she is. Which suggests they've got friendly since their little confrontation in the car park yesterday.'

'I'm sorry, sir?'

'It doesn't matter. Is there a history of her calls to him and a fix on her position?'

'It's only the second time she's ever called him, sir. And it's still a negative from the CP.'

'Meaning?'

'Her SIM's blocked.'

'Really? Modifying a SIM to block a satellite fix takes specialist knowledge, doesn't it?'

'Yes sir. Practically under lab conditions.'

Driscoll's enthusiasm cranked as everything fell into place. He told Collins to keep him informed then wondered aloud at the thickening plot. Before he got out to join two officers waiting at the top of the snowy steps he hit a number at his phone.

'Addison,' said Addison.

'The good-looking bitch from the news conference went into Hunter's hotel last night, didn't she?'

'That's right.'

'What time did she leave?'

'She didn't.'

'Meaning?'

'The Lexus was still there this morning.'

'Contact the hotel and find out why she went.'

'They'll spin the shit about DP laws.'

'Threaten them with a fucking subpoena if you need to then call me when you know.' The driver had got out to open his door for him. 'But I'll lay bets that two Continental breakfasts were charged to Hunter's room this morning.'

When Driscoll walked into the lab Steve Hamer was sitting on a tall, wheeled stool, looking po-faced with folded arms, devoid of his trendy white smock and frowning at his watch.

The big screen was ready. A screensaver, looking like it was made from gobs of mercury, bounced sluggishly from corner to corner and every so often exploded into numerous small blobs. The IFI website logo was cleverly embedded in each, no doubt animated by some Flash headbanger upstairs.

Hamer had two lawyers with him. Driscoll knew they'd no links professionally but were independent witnesses to each other. The older one was a stocky, white-haired guy stuffed into a crumpled shale-grey suit, sitting on another tall stool, squinting at his phone. The other was a petite young black bitch with short straight hair who looked like she took shit from nobody. When she saw Driscoll and the officers come in she knocked her cuffs back to the elbows and marched up to meet them. Her thigh-length mandarin jacket also went back revealing a short skirt cut from the same steel-coloured fabric. The shiny bare legs and shiny red boots hitting the shiny red plastic floor worked with the shiny red lipstick and the don't-fuck-with-me jackhammer attitude. 'This is not acceptable,' she said. 'Keeping my client waiting is one thing but keeping him waiting for nearly five hours is another.'

Driscoll didn't apologize but set down his laptop and clicked it open. It was an effort to look at her. The two uniforms stood at ease, their podgy male chauvinist mugs a hair's breadth from smirking at the feisty little black bird. The older guy's expression said it.

I wouldn't mind having a bit of black.

'The warrant came through an hour since,' Driscoll said. 'It took us forever to get here.' The laptop lit up and played a tune. 'And don't pretend to be pissed off young lady. At two-hundred-and-seventy-five an hour you've milked

209

another fourteen hundred from the public purse this afternoon for sitting on your arse.'

Hamer stood up bullishly at this, towering over everybody. Like anybody who inhabited a white smock during the day, now that he'd taken it off he looked withdrawn, almost naked. 'This is confidential client information,' he said, angry at what was going to happen. 'There's no point having a tough Data Protection law if the police can walk all over it when it suits them.'

Driscoll didn't rise to the bait. Instead he raised an eyebrow at the view through the window. 'As you'll see, Dr Hamer, the weather isn't good. The sooner we get it over with the sooner we can go home.'

'I'd like to know what's so important to bring you here on a night like this, instead of some subordinate.'

'It's a police matter. Warrants as serious as this can only be authorized by me.'

Disbelieving, Hamer shook his head and gazed down at the tiny woman. His body was so massive next to hers that if they tried to make love they wouldn't be able to kiss and screw at the same time. Nothing would line up.

Driscoll printed off two copies of the warrant, signed them, and handed them to both lawyers. Originals were being sent overnight to their offices. PDFs had been e-mailed. He handed a third piece of paper to the woman. She glanced at it and passed it to Hamer, nodding. He scribbled on it and gave it back. It was a declaration confirming that he'd made no illicit copies of the media stored on the computer.

'I think we're ready,' Driscoll said, dropping the document Hamer signed in his case. He'd no idea what Hamer was going to spill. What Hunter had been up to was also still a mystery. They knew he'd been to the IFI but as yet hadn't found out why. Following the exposure of corruption in forensic science, Data Protection laws had been introduced that carried tough penalties for anybody who broke them. In today's high-tech world you could control anything, fix anything. Provided the info was in the cyber system, or you knew who or what you were looking for, or you could get to somebody first and blow them to bits or blow their fucking brains out. But if the info you were after was stuck in an obstinate scientist's head, and colleagues who were playing it by the book surrounded him at a top forensic science lab, not even the fucking police could corrupt that.

As soon as Hunter left the IFI at lunchtime they'd gone in and quarantined Hamer under armed guard. He was stopped from using phones or e-mail, in case he tried to give Vanessa the heads-up. Some guys at the IFI heard the bomb go off. The officers waited a while then told them it was a gangland hit. The law said that Hamer had to stay at his place of work till the warrant was issued but he could have lawyers present. As usual the public would pick up the bill. But it had taken another four hours to get a special Home Office clearance to force him to reveal why Hunter had been to the IFI. Even in a controlled democracy things took time. Procedures had to look like they were being followed.

Everybody gathered round. Driscoll stood resolute, with folded arms while Hamer fired up the kit. The screen jumped to attention then he brought up a mouse and the first of three human profiles. He went through them quickly and didn't bother with the holograms. Driscoll quizzed him about what Hunter had said the profiling was for but

211

he thought Hamer was saying the minimum he could get away with because he kept insisting that Hunter had been cagey. The woman acted like an interpreter, OK-ing each answer first. The white-haired guy left her to it but kept sniffing catarrh, frowning at the winter wonderland building outside.

When Hamer told them that Hunter got the stuff from a sweet shop Driscoll sussed what must have happened in the alley yesterday. Since the kidnap he'd been concerned about somebody having seen Stoneham's eyes. Because of an allergy he couldn't wear brown contact lenses like the other guys did. Unlikely it would be noticed, flapped the Ministers at the debriefing, like a gaggle of naïve pillocks. But the chances of somebody getting hold of a single hair bulb and having it DNA profiled must have been billions to one against. He couldn't remember if their forensic guy had been into Samrah's shop before or after Hunter but it didn't matter. Hunter had got hold of some shit-hot incriminating evidence.

When he saw Stoneham's face the seriousness of the situation sank in. It was unlikely that Hamer or the lawyers would recognise the Special Branch DS. If he barged into the lab they might. But something about the image was stylized, like a CG face rendered in an old OpenGL computer game. Real without being too real. You had to know who you were looking for to put two-and-two together. But if you did know who you were looking for it would hit you. Like a bullet in the fucking brain.

When they'd finished Driscoll took possession of the original samples and a copy of the profiles on DVD. By law the police were entitled to take them away and have them analyzed by a third party. Driscoll's signature on the bit of paper meant he couldn't destroy them. Not that he'd take any fucking notice. The info archived on the LAN-Share system was a different matter. Every workstation at the IFI could access it.

'Delete the media,' he told Hamer.

'No way,' he scoffed, looking at the woman. They were amazed that he'd been asked.

'You know the rules, Chief Commissioner. You can take a copy but you can't destroy the master.'

Third party digi material was protected under a convoluted law similar to the Distance Selling Regulations that applied to the Internet. Fucking lawyers, Driscoll thought. 20,000 of them in 1979. 250,000 of them calling the shots today but no contribution to GDP.

He nodded at the uniforms. They muscled in at either side while he stood at the console, grabbed the mouse, left-clicked, fast-tapped keys. Up came:

Driscoll left-clicked again. Bang. It was gone forever, kaput in a handful of mega-quick seconds. They'd assumed he was another stupid overpaid cop but had no idea that, with an accomplished background in IT, he knew more about fucking computer kit than everybody in the building put together.

The woman balked from shock then swore. 'Jesus. Did you see that?'

'I saw it,' the older guy said, galvanized.

'Steve?'

'This *must* be fucking serious.'

'Two witnessing lawyers, Chief Commissioner. That's the point of this procedure. We'll throw the book at you.' Her sleeves had been returning from her elbows but now she sent them right back up.

'I do apologize,' he said sarcastically. 'That was an unfortunate slip of the wrist.' He turned to one of his goons. 'What happened just now, officer?'

'I believe they showed you something on the computer, sir. Not being familiar with that particular advanced CAD package you accidentally hit the wrong button and deleted the media.'

Driscoll turned to the other guy as two more fat cops came through from Reception, smirking, chewing gum, stinking of nicotine, sniffing snot. 'I believe you smacked the wrong button, sir,' the other guy said. He overdid a sarky tut-tut and gave a slow shake of his heavy head. His chins joined in. 'I saw it with my own eyes.'

The eyes were closely spaced and particularly nasty and piggy, belonging to what these law-abiding cretins would dismiss as the archetypal bent copper. Or a thug in a uniform. Either way, in a centrally controlled, increasingly bent police state they pretty much meant the same thing. Again the piggy eyes gazed down lecherously at the fuming woman.

I wouldn't mind having a bit of black.

The other guys verified what had happened. Driscoll couldn't resist smirking with them while he shut his case. 'We have procedures too,' he said. 'It's your word against ours.' He shut his laptop and picked up the samples and DVD. Now that he'd got what he wanted, farting around signing bits of paper seemed quaint and absurd. 'Meanwhile, I'm placing you all under house arrest. You'll have no access to phones or e-mail until further notice.'

Everybody's jaws dropped.

'You can't fucking do that!' the woman said.

'Just you fucking watch me!' he said back, looking down his nose at her, inches from her pretty face.

He pulled some prepped legal stuff from his case and threw it on the console. He'd told the Home Office to rubber-stamp the matter as being a serious threat to National Security, which wasn't far from the truth.

Meaning he could nail them.

To the fucking wall.

'Don't bother reading them their rights,' he said casually to the guys while he strolled out.

Shouting erupted behind him when he pushed open the rubber doors and headed through to Reception. He'd told everybody to expect a fuss when he arrived.

THiRtY-FiVE

Addison called him back as he ducked into the Jag. 'She said she was his girlfriend and wanted to surprise him. The manager wasn't on duty but the young guy who was says she was *very* persuasive.'

'At getting Hunter's room number?'

'Yeah.'

'What was he called?'

'Pierre.'

'I'm sure he was,' he said, amused. 'And we talk about how the French bareback the fucking EU.'

Addison didn't clock the joke.

A familiar *squeak* metronomed at the phone.

'What if he's fucked off back to London?'

'I don't think so,' Driscoll said. The vanity light died and the Jag started. 'He hasn't bought an inter-city ticket today and hasn't used his return to Heathrow. He hasn't hired a car since yesterday, either.'

'He could have gotten somebody to hire one for him, or hitched a lift.'

The Jag swept out onto the snowy street, past the obnoxious shit's shuttered booth, the barrier defiantly up.

Squeak.

'He could have,' he said, 'but we're assuming his priority is to get to London. If his priority is to stay alive, he might fuck off on the back roads instead.' He was referring to a new pilot scheme in London where drivers' ID cards were auto-scanned like they were for congestion charges inside the M25. If they didn't carry their ID, overhead gantries clocked the car's position via the barcode in the tax disk and flagged it up to Central Matrix. He added sardonically, repudiating the over-technologisized nature of the age for its inherent failing, 'Which shows how easy it still is to fucking disappear.'

Squeak.

Hunter came out onto another broad avenue running along the edge of the Park. Big Victorian houses stood back against snow-heavy trees. A few cars crept past flicking up

216

slush. At the Park entrance an information sign with pictures said that trams used to run there. Swollen with snow the road looked so much like those he ran through after his car blew up that he wondered if he was back where he'd started.

Parked across from him in a turning circle was an empty pink-and-yellow bus. Idling noisily next to a trashed metal shelter it was like a glorified Transit van with windows. Its big wipers juddered lazily on intermittent. Its digi destination board was restless. Bound for New Central Square, it said. Up came the arm with the watch. Sniff went his cold runny nose. Back went the grey puffa cuff. 18:13 said the Rhino, snow crunching as he headed over.

Because Abigail was due at seven he knew what he was going to do. Yesterday he'd noticed where some streetlights had failed in front of the library cloisters across from the hotel. While he was walking through the Park he'd decided to go there and wait for her, to try and intercept her when she parked in the square. It was risky but he felt sufficiently desperate and disguised enough to try. They'd never expect him to head back to the hotel. They wouldn't know she was coming. Why hadn't he thought of it hours ago, instead of now?

He reached the bus.

The doors were shut.

The driver was ensconced in his cage, getting off on a lad's mag spread at his wheel. Big tits. Lace-top stockings. Pouting lips in hot lesbian love tangles for adolescent tossers. Yawning, he seemed oblivious to impending custom, or else he'd decided to have a bit of laddish fun and ignore it. Sarah said that British bus drivers got nasty at the same time they stopped wearing uniforms.

Hunter knocked at the glass. No reaction. A joker. No, a wanker because he'd have seen him cross the road. Another knock at the glass. Without gracing his only passenger with a turn of his head the driver stuck out a fat hand at the end of a Popeye forearm, blue with tattoos, and poked a button. No, not Popeye Hunter thought angrily. Bluto in a baseball cap. The doors hissed and did the concertina thing. A gust of hot air hit him, like when his car blew up. *I nearly died you bastard.*

He banged snow from his boots and felt for some coins as he went up the steps. 'How long does it take to get to the city centre?'

'In shit weather like this, bud?'

'How long?'

'Twenty-five minutes.' To try and act the tough guy he drew snot up his nose. Before it descended to the stomach dumped at the wheel he said, 'Except I drive like a fucking idiot.' Down went the snot. Now the baseball cap was adjusted and the ugly face turned to regard him, as if he was a pillock. 'Which might cost you extra.'

'A fucking idiot,' Hunter said, parrot fashion. The pear-shaped face turned serious, weighing him up, looking for a fight. It was a nasty, self-absorbed world where everybody was on the verge of looking for a fucking fight. Bus driver rage, Hunter thought, amused by the idea. Twenty-five minutes, meaning he should get there before her. Just. Unless he'd upset the fucking idiot.

He offered the coins.

'This is all the change I've got.'

Until that afternoon it was maybe ten years since he'd used a bus. He'd no comprehension of how much a journey into town should cost. Buses ran in a different world to his, even in London, where the middle classes weren't embarrassed to use them.

'No change,' said the driver, when he'd told him the fare.

'What?'

'I don't give change, bud.'

'Why?'

'What do you mean fucking "why"? Because some fucking idiot would fucking kill me, that's why. What the fuck do you think this is for?' The Bluto hand shook the cage and nodded at the armour-plated thing where the money went.

It wasn't the cost that bugged him. He'd a couple of ten-pound coins in his pocket and some loose change, but it would have to last. How long he didn't know. To get cash from a bank or a cashpoint he'd need to use his ID card, which he couldn't because they'd nail him. Meaning every pound mattered in a way it never had.

Unless he could get to Abigail.

He stuck a ten-pound coin in the slot and heard it drop. He'd just lost a fiver. Five quid had never meant so much. He went to a seat at the back and sat on urine-smelling moquette loaded with dud gaffer tape repairs. On the seat in front was a styrofoam tray half full of cold chips smothered in a curry sauce. The gunk looked more appetizing than what he'd eaten in the stars-and-stripes café.

Now the driver yacked via a convex mirror that let him keep an eye on his cargo. 'What you should have done,' he said sarkily, 'is ask *moi* for a Return. It would have cost you less than a tenner and been OK for a week.'

Hunter saw the guy's self-satisfied reflection grinning at him as he closed the tits and black stockings, slammed the

219

bus into gear, and tried to scare his passenger by pulling out too quickly. The back of the bus slithered into the road. Some amusement to start his evening. Fat bastard, Hunter thought churlishly and sank down with his knees propped up against the seat in front.

THiRtY-siX

Vanessa was alone, wearing her anorak and carrying her case, when she walked into the empty lift on the top floor of Sumners and smacked the button.

Sarah had gone home early because of the snow. Home for Vanessa was a few minutes across town. Sumners ran 24-7. They'd not have charged her for a full day's booked hire if she'd finished early but she'd carried on regardless. If snow blocked the roads she could always walk back to the hotel. She was tempted to walk back anyway because she didn't fancy braving the underground car park down the street.

The lift stopped at the floor below and a tough-looking but smartly dressed woman of about her own age entered. Vanessa knew something wasn't right straight away. The woman had long dark hair and big breasts, stunk of nicotine, and wore a retro clear-plastic mack over a two-piece navy suit. The short skirt would have worked if she'd had legs to speak of but she had fat muscular calves that made her look like a guy in drag. She seemed to be a bonafide female but it was the look Vanessa caught in the bitch's eye that spooked her. She didn't risk checking but sensed she was being ogled. The woman fancied her.

After the doors met and the lift dropped the atmosphere was loaded. An interminable two floors later they stopped and the woman slipped out into the loo across the corridor, her stilettos Foley clacking on the tiles when she went in. A plump young woman from the Sky Newsroom entered the lift, pulling a face and waving a hand over her nose because of the nicotine stink.

Vanessa knew her and said, 'Hi,' as the doors met and the lift went down. 'Who was that?' she wondered.

'Dunno. Never seen her before.'

'Neither have I. It was odd.'

'What, the size of her boobs or the stink?'

'Both. She gave me the creeps.'

'Me too.'

'Was she wearing a security pass?'

'I didn't notice.'

When Vanessa hit the basement she got out her phone to check for messages while she shouldered through the outer door into the cold night and glanced up. Approaching snowflakes were eerily silhouetted in the light being thrown from office windows. 'You have no new messages,' the Orange voice said. Puffing despondently she called Hunter. As the call connected she crouched to open her case with her free hand and got out her vanity umbrella. She'd reached his voicemail.

'Obviously I'm tied up,' he said, as he'd said umpteen times that day. 'Please leave a message and I'll get back to you ASAP.'

221

She shut her case and stood up while the Orange woman said her bit and the beep sounded. 'Where are you?' she asked. 'I wondered what you wanted to do about eating.' She was worried, especially after last night. She'd expected him to join her in the edit suite hours ago. But like many people do if a loved one goes missing she'd kept telling herself that his absence was nothing to get hung up about. But she'd also remembered the dark-haired woman. Maybe he'd bumped into her. The thought was unsettling. Thinking back to late Sunday night she didn't want to admit how else it made her feel because she'd assumed she was above such stuff.

Abigail drove round New Central Square but couldn't see a space. More cars were parked than usual. Their drivers had probably taken the tram home.

She made another circuit with her wipers working at the snow. In the past hour the weather had seriously deteriorated but the blizzard made her feel agreeably sentimental. She slowed as she passed an area of darkness outside the library. Parking spaces ran diagonally in front of the cloisters but the streetlights had failed all the way along, meaning it was difficult to see despite the brightness from the snow. It didn't matter because somebody else was checking via infrared.

'Scanning,' he said.

A CG sim of the parking spaces flashed onto his screen and changed shape while they crept past, like an airport runway meeting a plane coming in to land. She couldn't see any empty bays but the idea was for her to watch the road and let him look instead. It was their second negative pass.

'Still nothing, Abigail. If you'd like to go round again I'll carry out another scan but the cars are so badly parked I can't judge the gaps. Regrettably our generous dimensions leave us at a disadvantage. We must conclude there aren't any spaces.'

'It's because of the weather,' she said. She'd nearly stopped and thought she saw Hunter under the cloisters but decided she was imagining it. 'Where's the nearest secure car park?' Before Computer replied headlights flared behind them, dazzling in her rearview like heat-seeking missiles homing in for the kill. A van driving way too close. It had come from nowhere, almost hitting her. As it flashed her angrily its cross little engine revved.

Computer flew into action. 'Shall I adopt defence mode, Abigail?' Meaning should he blast the wanker with halogen. Mark said she needed machineguns in her back bumper, not shiny fucking lights.

She told Computer not to bother. Checking her mirrors she saw that it wasn't a van but a small pink-and-yellow bus. More like a glorified Transit van with windows, plastered with vinyl ads for sexy babe hotlines and seemingly empty. She could see an ugly fat face frowning from under a baseball cap, mouthing abuse and waving two fingers as the bus pulled over. Computer ran a Web check and said the exhibition centre car park behind the hotel had sixty-three spaces. She wondered why the hell she hadn't gone there first.

The driver carried on swearing after he'd stopped the bus. 'Fucking kerb crawler,' he shouted. Hunter saw tails fade through the snow up ahead but couldn't see what the idiot had been swearing at. 'Off you get, bud.'

223

He got up and walked to the front. Lost in thought he'd ignored the guy's latest outburst because he'd sworn at traffic and pedestrians all the way to the city. Nobody else had got on. As the doors hissed open and snow blew in Hunter wondered about the economics of running an empty bus over such a distance, arctic weather or not. There was no point asking the dickhead driving it.

When he hit the pavement he zipped up his snorkel hood to hide his face and slid back the puffa cuff. 18:39. At least the dickhead had done what he'd said he would and got there on time. As the bus skidded away a light-headedness hit Hunter. Maybe the heat aboard the bus had induced it as he met the cold. He'd struggled to stay awake all the way into Manchester. Every so often he'd nodded off, his head bumping the glass, his eyes on the tray of cold chips reflected in the window.

He set off towards the cloisters but the snow felt heavy underfoot and he stopped and stood out of sight while he tried to get it together. He kept seeing the burning figure that should have been him, its spray of entrails hitting the ground like buckshot. The tangle of bloody sausages was his small intestine, spat out when the lower abdomen blew open. The polythene bag thing dumped on the pavement, looking like a pile of pink-red shit, would have been his stomach. His bollocks would have been blown apart when the bomb went off up his arse. He felt faint, knowing that he was undergoing the after-effects of extreme shock and emotional trauma. All afternoon he'd felt like he was descending into a nightmare. He was confident, educated, middle class, knew what planet he was standing on, and how bent everything was. But he'd never truly tasted fear. He'd nearly been blown to bits and it was his wake-up call. Nobody could go through what he'd been through without suffering a paradigm shift. The ground started coming closer, going further away. He thought about Vanessa. Superimposed was her bubbling flesh, pouring from her face like molten wax. This was what soldiers meant by post-traumatic fucking stress. He was losing it and as soon as he set off he fell between some cars. He'd been set on reaching Abigail but it was Vanessa who was invading his mind. He was sure he'd woken up recently moaning her name. He struggled to his feet and gazed across the snowy square but everything had blurred. He couldn't risk calling Vanessa from a pay phone, much as he was tempted to try. They'd be monitoring her phones and e-mail. Plus, the CP would be scanning for his audioprint and ID card across the phone and cyber networks.

With some effort he set off, the snow missing his face because of the deep hood. Then he remembered needing real money to survive when he'd paid his bus fare and something hit him with a smack. There was cash in his briefcase up in his room. Regardless of the fad for security it often struck him as being piss easy to get into a hotel via a service entrance, or to walk in off the street. In his haste to get away that morning he didn't hand in his keycard. Banknotes were traceable but he could swap them for coins at a post office *without* using his ID card. If the idea of coming back to New Central Square had been irrational, the idea of trying to get up to his room was downright dangerous. But trying to intercept Abigail in the open seemed monumentally difficult. He couldn't even see across the square because of the swirling blizzard. If he was at one end, and she parked at the other, he'd never see her. But upstairs, inside, that would be different.

Feeling confident in his disguise, even affecting a difference in his walk, he made quickly for the street running at the side of the hotel. Round the back was the service entrance he'd used yesterday, where the laundry bins were kept. The last place the bastards would expect him to go would be up to his fucking room.

THiRtY-SEVEN

Abigail refreshed her lipstick in the Ladies then made her way across Reception to the lifts, with her overnight bag slung at her shoulder. Smacking the button she sent back her hair with a kick of her head. As she watched the digi panel eat floors she realised a small, frog-like creature was standing next to her. Looking down she recognised a pair of bulbous eyes gawping up from six inches below hers. It was the young French concierge who'd succumbed to her charms the previous evening.

'Excuse me, madam,' he said, grovellingly, 'but the manager would like a word.'

The lift had arrived. The doors pinged open and a leggy blonde transvestite wearing a short black leather dress hit the walk. She moaned something suggestively under her breath as she clacked past but Abigail didn't clock what. She was busy getting bad vibes as she followed the little Frenchman across to the desk.

The manager hadn't been on duty last night. When she arrived he showed her a dazzling crescent of neat teeth that worked with the whiteness of his shirt to emphasize his starched subservience.

'Sorry to trouble you, madam, but I gather you're not staying at the hotel?'

'No I'm not.'

'Might I ask why you're here?'

'To see a friend.' She felt aloof looking down at such an obnoxious creep. Like many guys she encountered in his position he wasn't being deferential because it was expected of him. It was because his masculinity felt undermined when confronted by a beautiful assertive woman.

'Would it be the same friend you visited last evening?'

'Yes.'

'Might I ask his name?'

'Hunter. Room one-three-two.'

Something was up. If he'd sussed she was visiting the same guest surely he'd know whom. His eyes ogled a pink Applemac dumped on the clear plastic counter. 'Ah yes, of course,' he said. 'The TV filmmaker.'

'Is anything wrong?'

'Your ID card please.' He snapped some fingers impatiently at her. She took it from her bag and put it down. He slotted it into the Mac but as he scrolled through the info she searched his smug expression, wondering what his game really was. A fluorescent blue glow entertained itself with the white teeth and shirt. He broadened his smile as he removed the card and handed it back. 'I'm so sorry to have inconvenienced you. We've had some unauthorized entries recently. The concierge saw you and reminded me that you're not a paying guest.'

227

'Of course,' she said, glancing at the Frenchman. She relaxed, sensing it was nothing more innocuous than him wanting to even a score. 'Have you seen Mr Hunter?' she asked, studying the eyes of both guys closely.

'No I haven't,' he said. 'Would you like me to call his room to check if he's in?'

'No,' she said, widening her eyes suggestively, 'I'll surprise him like I did last night . . .'

'Certainly, madam.' He acknowledged her sly expression in spite of himself and dragged a finger round the inside of his shirt collar, discreetly projecting his Punch-like chin while he tried to get some air to his hot neck. 'Have a good evening.'

She knew his eyes were on her legs as soon as she turned away. When she was in the lift and looked back across she saw him reach for a phone. His face dropped just before the doors met.

Vanessa had reached the security lodge. She snapped open her umbrella. Martin, the studio gateman, was standing in his brightly-lit booth with his glasses perched on the end of his nose and a tabloid spread in front of him. 'How's it going then, love?' he asked, peering at her over his Buddy Holly's as her umbrella inflated and snow swirled.

'Not bad, Martin.'

'Looks like it's gonna be a bad ' un,' he added, nodding up at the loaded sky.

'They've said so.'

'Up here for long?'

'Till Christmas.'

'On your own?'

'Both of us.'

'Very good.' He immersed himself in the sports pages as she clicked through the turnstile out onto the street.

'You haven't seen him have you?' she called back.

'No love.'

'Goodnight then.'

'Goodnight love.'

As she set off she suddenly thought of something. She stopped and got out her phone again, then went back to shelter under the turnstile, shut her umbrella, and scrolled quickly through her address book.

When Abigail knocked at Hunter's door the phone started to ring in the room.

It kept ringing, or rather trilling, but he didn't answer it. She glanced back along the corridor. Near to the lifts a big yellow laundry bin was parked against the wall, with its lid up. Room linen overflowed from it messily, as if somebody had given it the once over. Usually they were in hotel corridors in the mornings, not the evenings. When she'd passed it she noticed fresh mud on a towel, as if whoever had been through the stuff inside used it to clean the crap off their mucky shoes. Yet there weren't any muddy footmarks on the carpet.

Still the phone rang. Eight, nine, maybe ten times. Then it stopped. Wondering, she knocked again. He could be in the shower. She stuck her ear to the door but the room felt dead. No sound from the bathroom, which was on the left when you went in.

'It's me,' she said, drumming her nails tentatively at the pale-green uPVC. After the drive in she was pent up. The disappointment of finding he wasn't there made her feel foolish for being so randy.

It was nearly ten past seven. He said he'd be back for seven but wasn't. She decided to go down to the lounge to wait but as soon as she turned something weird happened. His door opened making a *clunk* as the deadlock shot back. Wondering, she turned. The door opened some more as she got nearer, then some more when she arrived. She saw darkness through the gap. Maybe he'd ignored the phone because he knew she was outside although he didn't strike her as being the type to bother with silly pranks.

She knew he was behind the door. The self-close hinges were sprung. It couldn't stay open on its own unless it had broken since last night. Meaning he must be holding it, ideally in his birthday suit. Relishing the idea she pushed against the door, feeling him resist. 'Let me in,' she whispered. 'I want to make love.'

Through the gap she saw the bathroom light was on and was relieved. Going with the silly game she reached round playfully to feel for him. Suddenly he grabbed her wrist. Everything fast-vision wiped as he yanked her inside and slammed her back hard against the wall. No way was he into a bit of rough stuff. As the door banged shut a stink of nicotine and shit-bad breath hit her. Strong hands held her, a dark shape crushed her, wider than her guy but not as tall. She coughed when she realised the room was thick with cigarette smoke. Then panic kicked in as a lamp came on and she was gobsmacked to see DS Stoneham pinning her to the wall. She'd walked into a trap, meaning something was mega fucking wrong.

Driscoll came out of the bathroom wearing a trendy civilian suit that shimmered mauve in the lamplight. Before he could open his mouth a big grey-haired bastard said to him, 'She's left the studio. It was her that just rang.'

'Kill her,' Driscoll said.

'Did you get that?' the GHB said. Whoever was on the phone obviously did.

'Abigail,' Driscoll said, mocking her. 'How good of you to join us.' She knew from the greedy look on his face that he approved of her long sheer legs.

THiRtY-EiGHt

Hunter turned into a narrow alley behind the hotel. He felt cobbles under the snow. Slipped and nearly fell.

Panting, he legged it into cold darkness, pulling down his hood because he couldn't run and see properly with it up. He was sure they were behind him but had to stop because he was gasping hard and his chest was burning. The snow came straight down, crusting his hair. He was halfway along the alley but heard something and ducked out of sight in a recessed doorway that stunk of shit and piss. Air conditioning units were bolted to the opposite wall, encased in steel mesh. Too high to reach to warm his freezing hands.

He took off his glasses to rub his eyes then put them back and looked up at the snowflakes, millions coming as they had in the Park. He imagined how tonight should have been. Dinner at a cosy Italian overlooking the square. Back to his room with her. The fusing of two naked bodies.

Waking up next to her. Waking up next to a woman, and holding her, was still the most wonderful thing. He'd forgotten how wonderful till he woke that morning. He was an old romantic. Not one of the intended dead men. Not the guy with a price on his fucking stupid meddling head. Two gruff voices broke it. He froze. Not difficult because his body temperature gave him a flying start.

'Somebody went in here,' a Scouser said, waving his torch.

'No they fucking didn't,' said a deep Lancastrian.

'They fucking did.'

Cops' voices. Space age PC Plods with a twenty-first century edge velcroed into *Robocop* body armour. Footsteps, or rather pseudo-Goth, platform-booted size-twelves, crunched snow along the alley towards him. The torch did the searchlight thing and lit everywhere up, sending him back. Radio static cracked and fizzed from shoulderplates. Hunter clocked his own footprints when the beam found them. The cops were bound to see them too. He braced himself. They'd probably do the *Inglourious Basterds* baseball bat thing to his head with their pneumatic truncheons. He was scared shitless when he saw the torch beam getting hotter.

'Driscoll reckons he'll have fucked off out of the area. He'd not risk coming back to the hotel.' This was the other, more sceptical cop shouting from the end of the alley, his voice thud-echoing along it. When Hunter heard what the guy said, it said it all.

When he'd got off the bus he'd half expected to see cop marksmen stationed on the rooftops, like in the movies. But there wasn't anybody. He'd been so knackered that it didn't occur to him how brave he'd been coming back to the hotel, until he'd sussed they weren't waiting for him. *Driscoll reckons I'll have fucked off out of the area.* He couldn't believe how much it lifted his spirits to know the bastards were thinking it.

'I'm telling you I saw somebody,' the Scouser said, getting closer.

'No you fucking didn't.'

'We should fucking check, Pete.'

Trying to do his job so give the guy some credit.

Hunter sensed a snowball being wanged then something hit the back of the cop in the alley, followed by an eruption of swearing and a scrabble of feet. The torch flicked off as another snowball whizzed past. *Fwump* as it bonged something hollow further in the alley. He poked out his head and saw two disappearing figures encased in fluorescent-green body kit, throwing snowballs at each other, laughing and swearing like silly big kids. The relief was overwhelming when their voices faded. He buried his face in his hands and thanked God.

He'd bottled out of trying to get up to his room. It had seemed like a good idea but there were too many people about and he looked too much like something that had been dragged up. A delivery lorry had been parked by the service entrance when he'd got there. Guys were carrying exhibition stuff into the hotel for tomorrow's Women in Business bash. A Jag was parked nearby, the driver obviously waiting for somebody important. A couple of cops had stood about smoking. Hunter thought they'd seen him which spooked him. He'd slipped as he set off and they'd hotfooted after him.

Deep down he wanted to cry, or at least felt obliged to want to cry. But he hadn't wept for years. He no longer felt such emotion. Hadn't done even when he lost Hayley and Jenny. Instead he'd sworn angrily and wanted to kill the fucking judge. Vanessa had cried for him. It was the only time he'd seen her weep.

Always it came back to Vanessa, this incredible woman in his life. He saw it now and knew why, when he looked out at the deep snow. As these terrible events drove him to the limits of his endurance they eclipsed everything. Punishing himself for Hayley and Jenny's suffering was one thing but he knew what else had been happening. OK he'd lost his kids. But the thought of losing the one other person that meant most to him was unbearable. She was his business partner but it was her friendship he valued. What was it he'd told Abigail? *Conventional wisdom warns you not to sleep with your business partner.* But something else warned him too. He took notice because two loving parents had brought him up properly, meaning he wasn't a selfish shit. Max.

He left the doorway, reckoning he must have missed Abigail. She might have parked in an NCP and already be waiting in the hotel while he froze like a noodle outside. Or maybe the snow had been so bad where she was staying that she hadn't risked the journey. He favoured this excuse. He hadn't seen the Lexus when he'd made his way across the square. The snow was piled on the cars so thickly it wasn't easy to tell what most of them were. He guessed she hadn't come.

He made it to the end of the alley. Everybody seemed to have gone home. A muffled quality had descended giving the city a remote feel, as if the blanket of snow oppressed it, absorbing the sound. A tram came at him with its headlights flaring. He ducked out of sight, slid back the sodden cuff. 19:23 said the big watch. He'd one last hope. Try and get to the basement car park under the hotel, to intercept Vanessa when she got back from Sumners.

Vanessa checked the time on her phone.

19:24.

It played its jingle as its screensaver sucked itself back into park mode and she stuck it away. She stepped out from under the turnstile, sent up her umbrella and headed away from the studio gate, crunching snow.

She'd gone back to stand under the turnstile to call the hotel, to see if Hunter was in his room. It was a long shot but worth a try. His phone rang out just before ten past seven. She'd got the guy at the desk to check with all the bars and restaurants and waited for ages. Then a producer friend had rung her. Because she wasn't a member of staff at Sumners she'd had to use a new underground car park that was being built further down the street. Meaning her phone would have got cut off, rooting her overground at the turnstile for another ten minutes. As the call had stretched her thoughts had wandered. She was cool, rational, exceptionally intelligent. But she was human and didn't need a shrink to tell her what the hell was happening. The thought that she might have lost Hunter to another woman, when he might have been ready to come to her, had bugged her all day. She needed to know where she stood, so she could put her feelings to bed.

Fifty yards from the studio she paused to cross the road and saw Martin watching her from his booth. The blizzard worked its magic, scrubbing him out. Before she crossed she waited for a black BMW to pass, which Martin had let out. As it crept past she saw the woman from the lift stuck behind the wheel, peering at her cursorily with a strange masculine intensity, like she'd slowed to eyeball-freak her. Her greedy expression said it. *I want to fuck you, you gorgeous blonde bitch.*

The car made the end of the street and slithered onto the main road, BMs not being good in icy weather due to the rear-wheel drive. Its indicators pulsed at brick and concrete rising sheer against the night. Its tyres had cut the virgin snow. Because Vanessa was a strong, traditionally feminine woman she attracted a certain type of predatory feminine lesbian.

Puffing in despair at this she waited for the BM's tails to fade through the blizzard then hurried across into the dark sidestreet that led to the car park.

Naylor zoomed in to Vanessa through his binocs when she crossed the road towards him.

He was spying on her from the upstairs of a derelict pub opposite the car park. Skulking in the shadows, he'd bent the steel plate out that covered the front window, to poke his binocs through the gap. Loose wallpaper flapped behind him in the wind. Snow blew in through a roof looted of slates. Through the binocs' sight-masking concentric squares did the cool *Star Wars* visor thing from the Death Star trench scene and locked onto their target. Bang. Up the bitch whizzed in 235:1, a tinted red image as bright as day. Her trendy specs kicked back white-hot, like Scotchlite cats' eyes, because of the digi scanner. She had her umbrella tilted back. Even under her thick puffa coat her juicy big knockers jelly-wobbled.

'Look at those fucking tits,' he said, zooming in. He rattled out, 'Cor,' like the nerd in the *Carry On* films, cranking it on purpose to wind everybody up. They took the piss when they heard him over their Bluetooths. The vibe was they could do whatever they wanted with Vanessa as long as they put her six foot under. They'd agreed that Sandra would screw her first because she was the boss. Being the new punk on the block it would be his turn at the end of the night. Anticipating it he howled like a wolf. Not loud enough for Vanessa to hear but loud enough for the guys, including Sandra.

'She's mine, you young nob-headed bastard,' she said at his ear, with a smoker's hoarse drag queen drawl. She was driving round the block, skidding, swearing about BMs not holding the bastard road.

Naylor watched Vanessa swing down her umbrella as she hit the top of the car park steps. Looking forward to tailpiping her he pulled up her fantastic, no doubt virgin-tight ass. When he told the guys she was nearly there they said they were ready, Wakern coming in last with his girly fat-man voice. He was lurking down in the car park, wait-ing to pounce on Vanessa when she came in.

Vanessa shook her umbrella free of snow. The building work meant the top of the steps was an obstacle course of frozen puddles and piles of unlaid brick sets. A temporary security light had been put up. She anticipated its click as infrared sniped her but her heart skipped a beat when the light didn't come on.

She hurried down the dark snowy steps, yanked open the steel door at the bottom, heard it clang shut behind her when she was in. As she passed under the low vaulted ceiling her heels made a curious ricocheting echo. The car park was being built under a massive old Victorian railway warehouse. Sprawling brick catacombs surrounded her, each holding half-a-dozen cars. Rails were buried in the cobbles. As she hurried on she kept hearing eerie rumbling noises, like those before a tube train arrives on the London Underground.

Something wasn't right, making her wonder if she was being watched. Her clumping platform boots were her only companion besides her shadow, which stretched and changed shape with the temp string lighting slung from the walls. It seemed like a lifetime ago since she'd arrived with Sarah in crisp sunshine.

At last she found the Volvo. She was coiled like a spring when she killed the alarm, slid open the back door, threw her case and umbrella on the seat. Then she saw something and froze. The shadow of a fat guy, looming across the barrel wall as he came at her. Instantly she lashed out with her foot and smashed him in the ribs. The bulky figure spluttered as the wind got blasted from him. He was already falling when, snarling, she kicked the bastard between the legs, an incredible direct hit for women who were attacked by pervs in dark places everywhere. As he stumbled back she lashed out again, her hair flying, this time with a Purdey dropkick that hit him in the guts. Her reflexes and amazing physical fitness were a legacy from her ballet training as a teenager and her workouts most weeks at the gym. She could look after herself. Woe betide any dumb fuck who messed with her. But even as her foot sank into his belly and his hands shot up in defence she knew what else was driving her rage. It had eaten away at her all day. Going to bed on Sunday night, thinking how it might have been but waking up alone. *She wanted him, for Christ's sake.*

It was only when her eyes adjusted to the dark that, to her horror, she saw *Hunter* curled in a foetal position on the floor, clutching his groin. She hadn't recognised him. All she could see were glasses, plastered wet hair, heavy stubble, a grimy face. He wasn't wearing his *Matrix* coat either but a Michelin Man anorak that pumped up his size. He looked like a drowned rat. 'Oh my God!' she said, realising what she'd done, her echo thudding back.

'Be quiet,' he croaked.

Instantly she was on her knees, holding him. 'What the fuck are you playing at?'

'You got me.'

He was badly winded, to put it mildly.

'You scared the shit out of me,' she said.

She guessed something was seriously wrong but now that he was with her everything overwhelmed him. Involuntarily he grabbed her and went into a delayed reaction to shock, like a nervous system shutdown caused by prolonged adrenal burnout. The shakes. Violent trembling. Muscular spasms. Nausea. Similar to an epileptic fit. Wondering what the fuck had happened, but sussing what was happening, she managed to get him onto the back seat of the car. It was difficult because he refused to let go of her. His mouth was so numb with cold he couldn't speak properly but instead sort of hummed out the words.

'They tried to fucking kill me,' he moaned. 'I thought I was gonna die.' She pulled him upright, knocking off his glasses, and knelt astride him, stooping under the ceiling. His hands were like ice, the nails blue. She couldn't believe anybody could be so cold and wet and still be conscious. 'It was a kid who tried to blag my car, but it should have been me . . . *They blew him to fucking bits . . .*'

He was hyperventilating. Recognising the symptoms of parasympathetic shock she held him for all she was worth. Something terrible must have happened, which explained his daylong silence. Shivering against her he raged at what was attacking his body, saying he couldn't fucking stop it, his words muffled in her coat, his head buried between her breasts.

'It's OK darling,' she said, rocking him, her eyes filling up. She hugged him tight, watching nervously through the steaming windows. 'I'm with you, love,' she kept saying. 'I'm here . . . I'm here . . .'

She'd heard all about PSS, a delayed physical reaction to extreme emotional trauma that knocked seven bells of shit out of the toughest of guys in war. Clinginess and begging her not to leave him were symptoms. Coldness at the extremities was another, not helped by the sub-zero weather. Driven by severe tiredness, combined with cold and dehydration, it could be dangerous.

Even fatal.

THiRtY-NiNE

But Vanessa knew he was tough, not to mention obstinate, indefatigable. A couple of years ago he'd worked so hard to hit a transmission that he suffered from nervous exhaustion. His doctor said most people would have sat in a corner and indulged in a breakdown. But Hunter was so resilient, had so much stamina, that it never occurred to his subconscious mind to pack in. Instead he drove himself till he literally jammed up mentally. Something similar must have short-circuited his brain just now.

After a few minutes she knew he'd peaked. The car was freezing. Her instinct was to start it to get the heater blowing but he said no. She found a bottle of water and got it to his mouth and wiped his runny nose. He recovered quickly and filled her in on what had happened. After two cops chased him into an alley behind the hotel he'd seen an approaching tram. He'd intended to wait for her in the hotel car park but when the tram stopped in front of him he'd sussed it would go near Sumners. He'd decided to try and find her there because the cops were hanging round and getting past them would be risky. The tram ride had taken less than three minutes.

When he said he'd spent the night with Abigail, Vanessa knew she'd lost him, if she'd ever been going to have him. After the hell he'd been through her needs seemed unimportant. She hoped he fell head over heels in love with Abigail because he deserved it after the strain of the past year. Plus, they were the same age. This made her wonder if her feelings for him had been a kind of crazy toy boy fascination as her life with Max fizzled out. Secondary gain as the psychologists would say. Nine years wasn't much of an age gap but it meant that when Hunter was 60 she'd be pushing 70. At least she knew where she stood now and felt clearheaded. It was the not knowing that usually got you down.

'Are you sure about Stoneham?' she asked, getting back to matters at hand.

'It's him. He must have been one of the gang. They must have been blacked up for God's sake.'

He pulled out a sodden envelope and showed her some laser-prints in the half-light. There was something Spike Milliganishly funny about Stoneham being blacked up. As if on cue they heard somebody approaching and ducked when torchlight filled the car. Hunter grabbed her protectively while a figure spitting two-way radio clumped past. False alarm. It was a car park attendant, kitted out in fluorescent-green, beginning his rounds. They could just see him through the steamy windows.

As the bootsteps faded she climbed off him. 'We've got to go some place to think this through,' she said, slumping back to stretch her legs.

'If we book into another hotel they'll trace us. If they're watching upstairs they'll nail us when we drive out.'

Something was in her mind. Knowing speed was of the essence she checked her watch and opened the door. 'Genny stays in town with Emma during the week. She won't have gone yet. I'll go back up and see if I can borrow her car and the keys to her flat.'

'You can't go back upstairs.'

'I've got to, love.'

'What will you tell her?'

'I'll come up with some story about the shoot.'

'She lives further north.'

'We'll just have to try to and get there. If we get stuck we can always book into an old-fashioned B&B up on the moors as Mr and Mrs Smith.' She managed a smile. Because of their predicament the idea appealed. She turned to slide open the door but he felt for her. 'What?' she said, turning back.

'If they're watching, they'll recognise you when you get back up to the street.'

With a brisk efficiency she got out and set about changing her appearance. She started by turning her anorak inside out then took off her boots and trousers. Underneath she was wearing sheer bronze-coloured tights, a habit of hers to keep warm in winter. By fastening the coat, which hung above her knees, and tying the belt, she looked to be wearing a skirt. Now she went to the back of the car and rooted for her moonboots, which she sometimes wore if they shot outside in icy weather. She put them on then got back in the car to fish in the glove compartment for Sarah's bobble hat. She tucked her hair up inside it and pulled it over her ears.

Finally she swapped her work glasses for her Gucci designer specs, wrapped a thick white scarf round her neck, and drew on matching mittens.

'They shouldn't recognise me now,' she said, crouching by the door to look at him and holding his hands between both of hers. She managed another smile but the atmosphere was thick enough to cut. The danger they were in was immense yet there was the sense of a big gap closing. If they escaped they'd spend the night together. She knew it daunted him as much as her. 'I'll not come back down,' she said. 'Hang on five minutes then go up to wait for me by the Euro car park.' She gave him the Volvo's keycard so he could lock up and described Genny's Smart Car. 'Watch for a nasty-looking cow in a black BMW.'

'What for?'

'Just a hunch. And bring my case.'

He slid across to sit at the open door. 'Go out the front way,' he said. 'And walk differently.' He seemed aware of impending danger and suddenly reached for her, hugging her. 'Shit,' he said to her. 'If this goes tits up, I might never see you again.'

She'd filled up.

'I'm coming back to get you.'

Their faces were inches apart. He held hers between his hands, the most intimate thing he'd ever done. She wondered if he might kiss her. He didn't but something in his eyes fired her determination to live when she slid shut the door and headed off into the unknown.

Naylor was getting impatient and panned quickly up and down the snowy street.

The corner of the car park had been hacked away and a sort of giant steel helter-skelter was driven in the ground. The top was level with the street like a chute, open to the elements. This was where the cars came out. By now the snow covering it was deep and unbroken. Vanessa hadn't driven out. No fucker had driven out. Naylor took in some fresh air via the window to clear his head. Some wino had taken a dump on the rubble behind him. The stink was so bad he could fucking taste it. If he blew this job it wouldn't be the only shit he'd stink tonight.

A snowplough roared past beneath him, flinging light from its strobing hazards. When it had gone he punched out the steel plate that covered his corner of the window and hung through the gap. The juice had nearly gone from his phone so when Vanessa went in he'd cut everybody off. Now it hit him that the guys' phones hadn't been cut off earlier, even though they were underground. The quiet had gone on long enough. Fifteen minutes since Vanessa disappeared.

He patched through to Sandra. 'What gives?' he asked anxiously.

'Where the fuck have you been?' It was Wakern butting in, sounding like a nagging old woman. 'She hasn't come in, that's what fucking gives.'

'Yes she fucking has.'

'No she fucking hasn't.' Pissed off, he was puffing from recent physical exertion.

'Where the hell are you?' Naylor asked, recognoticing that Wakern had a signal.

'On the top floor.'

'What do you mean on the top fucking floor?'

'We're up on the tenth fucking floor. I've been up and down like a bloody yo-yo and I'm telling you she's not in here. There's one pedestrian entrance to this stinking shit-hole of a car park and she never came through it.'

'The car park's underground!'

'No it fucking isn't.'

'Yes it fucking is!'

'It fucking isn't!'

'Which car park are you in?'

'The NCP.'

'Where?'

'On Princess Street.'

Naylor smacked the wall. 'I said Prince's Street, not fucking Princess Street!'

'Jesus fucking Christ, Naylor!'

Everybody started laughing, except Sandra. There was no difference when Naylor yacked each place name, not helped by his nasally Liverpudlian timbre. He was already charging down the rubble-strewn stairs and doing the dog shit thing before he'd got halfway, treading on his fucking leather coat and taking an ass dive. Wakern launched into a fit of swearing at his ear, slagging him off because of his stupid lousy idiot shitty toss-arsed Scouse accent and saying he was gonna fucking kill him.

FORtY

Abigail couldn't breathe because of the cigarette smoke filling Hunter's room. Her throat was dry because of it. She could smell it on her hair, face, and clothes. To her, one of life's great mysteries was why people smoked. It ranked with eating shit.

She knew something must have happened to Hunter. The bastards hadn't said what but she guessed the samples had thrown up something deadly serious when he'd got to the IFI. Meanwhile, Driscoll had subjected her to the classic prisoner interrogation. Plonk her on a chair. Ask questions. Don't believe the answers. Ask the same questions again.

'Where is he?'

'I don't know.'

'Yes you do.'

'I don't.'

'Did you know he went to the IFI?'

'No.'

'You do.'

246

'I don't.'

'How much do you know?'

'About what?'

'How well do you know him?'

'I don't.'

'You've shagged him.'

'I slept with him once.'

'When?'

'Last night.'

'Here?'

'Yes.'

'In this bed?'

'Yes.'

'Fuck you hard, did he?'

Resentment in his voice when he glowered at her. His eyes kept going to her legs, which she held defensively together at the knees.

The brawny grey-haired guy, wearing cordless headphones and smoking like a chimney, was standing in front of the chest-of-drawers gawping at a laptop. Abigail could see it was linked to three hidden CCTV cameras. The first showed a shot of the snowy pavement in front of the hotel. Headlights and a tram streaked through a top frame corner. The second looked across the Reception hall. The third was fish-eye, the tiny camera stuck to the ceiling outside the room, aimed back at the lifts and the laundry bin. That was how they'd timed the game with the door. Driscoll said they'd watched her from the moment she entered the building. They hadn't seriously expected Hunter to come back to his room. The surveillance kit was for her. The CP had picked up her call to him and they'd put two-and-two together. She kicked herself for being careless.

Stoneham was the nastiest looking but the least intimidating of the bunch. He had a kind of compassion on his face when he looked at her. She got the feeling he was a hired hand. The smoke surrounding his head went up to a spot sunk in the ceiling. He looked to be smouldering, as if he might spontaneously combust.

Driscoll emptied her overnight bag out on the bed and found her ID card then slotted it into another laptop and scrolled through the info. When he got to the bogus History and Politics stuff, masquerading as her dud literary front, her heart was in her mouth. Frowning, he got out his phone and asked somebody to check if her ID and who she worked for were legit. When it was confirmed they were she breathed easy. Kareem's skills had paid off the first time they'd truly been needed.

The grey haired bastard with the CCTV laptop didn't buy it. He'd called himself Addison when he'd taken a phone call. The contents of Hunter's case were spread at his big feet, the photos of two sweet little girls on top. The dark one looked like Hunter, the blonde one like the photo of his ex-wife, whom Abigail had seen in his divorce file. 'She's bullshitting,' Addison said, stubbing his latest cigarette. 'I've come across her type before. She's tough as old boots. We should fucking thump it out of her.'

'Violence is your answer to everything, isn't it?' Driscoll said disapprovingly. 'But there's no need yet. You heard what she said outside the door. She thought he'd be here.' He was halfway through making a circuit round her but suddenly swung her chair and lunged to say in her face, through foul breath, 'What if I told you Hunter was dead?' Assuming it was a shock tactic she didn't shoot anything back. 'You don't believe me, do you?'

'No I don't,' she said. 'You've spent twenty minutes asking me to tell you where he is.'

'Very good,' he said, fastidiously returning the chair to its correct position. 'Excellent, in fact. But let me show you something.' He switched on the TV with the remote, found *Channel 4 News*. 'Let me suggest that you haven't heard from him today. You've not been too concerned but surprised nevertheless. Am I correct?' The bastard had hit the nail on the head. He nudged at his cuff to check the time. On the TV a young black guy fronted a report about the trade row that was brewing with the Economic Alliance of Asiatic Nations (EAAN). Two had announced they were going to manufacture high-tech products they'd agreed to buy exclusively from Britain, after it had shut down most of its manufacturing industry and depended on EAAN for its low-tech stuff.

The report ended and the presenter said they were going back to the Manchester car bomb story from the start of the programme. While they'd been on air the police had released the name of the victim. Although the body had to be formally identified they believed it was a former current affairs journalist who'd been shooting a documentary for the BBC. Hunter was named and his mug shot flashed up as an overview of his career began. Abigail was knocked for six. Driscoll turned to check how the story was affecting her but her training and resilience meant that cold logic auto-kicked in. Why grill her if they knew Hunter was dead? She began to wonder nevertheless. Because of her daylong meeting she hadn't seen the news. Kareem wouldn't have made the connection with the bomb, anyway, and the cops had obviously kept the location strictly *sub rosa* till now.

249

She saw a telephoto shot of a smoking lump of metal. It was the remains of a yellow Mini filmed earlier in the day, before the snow came. The shot zoomed in to some guys in white suits, kneeling on a leafy avenue. A clip from *Crime in Britain* superseded it. When Hunter spoke, amazingly clear in HD, she started to feel something as the story sank in. Looking younger, thinner, he was intercut with archive footage of the previous PM-but-one arriving at Number 10 and being bombarded by photoflashes. The VO said the Tories' historic landslide General Election victory was the first story Hunter covered as a fledgling provincial journalist. The report ended and Driscoll killed the TV. Abigail didn't know what to think. Maybe he was dead, or maybe not. Something didn't stack up.

Driscoll stood gloating over her, the light plying his ugly mug. There was no expression on it, and no emotion in his voice, when he said, 'Your reaction looks authentic to me. So you'll be pleased to hear that I believe you when you say you don't know where he is, seeing as all that's left of him are a few burnt scraps of meat on a slab at the police mortuary.' Still he eyed her as he said to Addison, 'Do you see how violence isn't necessary? You have to appeal to a woman's instincts.'

Stoneham stayed serious, asking, 'What the fuck are we gonna do with her?'

'What I said we'd do when she came upstairs.'

Addison scoffed. 'But that involves violence,' he said, amused.

'Then I refute my earlier observation. If you recall, I said that violence wasn't necessary *yet*.' He was impressed by his irony. 'Fetch the laundry bin then let's kill her and get the fuck out of here.'

Abigail's heart kicked off and blood started pounding in her ears. Your life was supposed to flash in front of you but hers didn't. It was seeing her private feminine things strewn on the bed that threw into perspective what would happen. New M&S underwear. Two unopened pairs of PP Ultimate 5 Naturals. Bausch & Lomb lens fluid. Bathroom bag and make-up pouch. Forzieri tissues. Loeffler Randall strappy sandals. Pink polka-dot socks and a pair of Nikes in case she'd got stranded in the snow. Her work clothes, some Wranglers, and a sweatshirt were in a suit carrier in the Lexus never to be worn again. Her NLP training meant she could cope with stuff like this but in the closing moments of her life she was resigned to a sick desolation. All she could think about was how they'd do it and the amount of physical pain. She looked at Addison's laptop and saw the laundry bin at the end of the corridor. Now she remembered what she'd thought when she arrived. *They were usually in hotel corridors in the mornings.* A throwaway observation portending her murder.

'Yes,' Driscoll said knowingly. 'I had it brought up just for you. I'm sorry it's not more dignified but as you'll be dead it won't matter.'

Stoneham got out a Sheuze and smacked in a cartridge. He seemed put out when Driscoll snapped his fingers impatiently to make him give up the gun and told her to get up. Addison smoked a fresh cigarette sombrely and yawned. Obviously another routine murder to him. She hadn't really thought they might kill her when they sat her down. Gang rape had been her big concern.

Stoneham dragged the chair away from behind her, so that she could fall, then leant against the wall with folded arms. The colour seemed to be leaving his face.

251

Driscoll flicked on the laser and aimed the red spot. Tying everything up, he observed, 'You were going to fall in love with Hunter, weren't you? In which case, you should know something.' He eyed her smarmily along the laser. It sent a thin red shaft through the cigarette smoke, joining to her forehead. 'If it's any consolation,' he went on, 'he *isn't* dead. I needed to know if you were telling the truth. The news report is false. The TV people don't know because they're reporting what we've told them we believe are the facts.'

Before she could get her head round this he primed the gun and held it out at arm's length in both hands, standing like a wanker posing in a cop show, to see if she'd break. She knew that her stoicism impressed him. No, seriously fucking annoyed him.

Then he swung the gun down and she heard it go off. Thought he'd shot her between the legs but felt her belly tear apart. The pain seemed to rip through her and out the other side. Instantly her legs went from under her and the floor came up fast, slamming into the back of her head, making her hair fly. Shocked at the callous cold-bloodedness of her murder she tried to get up but her strength had gone. She crashed down, lay still. Stoneham towered massively away. Patterns from the billboard across the square winked at the ceiling. Everything swirled. She couldn't get up but there came a feeling of relief as pain expanded in her chest and held her down. She knew she was dying yet there was an amazing sense of calm. Something ran from her nose round to her neck then left for the carpet. Sound faded as a deepening calm avalanched in. She sensed her heartbeat slowing when the pain became an all-consuming numbness.

Finally, a tidal wave of panic hit her with the terrifying moment when her life really did flash before her. An accumulation of key scenes. The fast-action edit job, topped off with a desperate need to stay awake and be with her mum and dad. But she couldn't stay awake because her life was nearly over. It echoed away from her slowly but quickly, did her life.

She knew she was dying.

She knew she was . . . dying.

She knew she . . . was . . . dying.

She knew . . . she . . . was . . .

Dead.

PARt TWO

FORtY-ONE

Vanessa kept a low profile as she pulled up at the studio gate. Her hair was still stuffed under her bobble hat and the windows had steamed up. Every second counted and she didn't want Martin quizzing her about how she'd got back into the building and why the hell she was driving out in Genny's car. While she waited for the gate to slide away she switched off the wipers and let snow cover the glass.

She'd made it back to Sumners' without a hiccup. After leaving Hunter she'd come out of the car park by the main Pay Station onto Oxford Road. When she arrived a bendy bus was pulling up in front of the door, blocking it from the black BM, which was parked in a sidestreet opposite. All she had to do when the bus set off was step outside, mingle with the disgorged passengers, and walk through the blizzard to Sumners' front door on the next street corner. The fact that she'd got there safely, got the stuff from Genny, and was driving back out in one piece, proved that her plan, her disguise, and the diffusing effect of the snow was working.

She nudged the wipers back on as soon as she set off so that if Martin glanced across he couldn't get a proper look. None the wiser he waved her through and got back to his paper before the back wheels of the tiny Smart Car had hit the threshold.

She was buzzing. She was in a terrible hole with Hunter. She was on a mission to save their lives but in a crazy way was enjoying it because of the potential pay-off. The door was open but she sensed it was up to her to go through it. Maybe that was why he hadn't kissed her in the car park. They had a special understanding. Not many guys could handle her because she always wanted to be in control and usually dominated conversations. This sometimes pissed off other strong women she encountered and some public school dodos in the politically charged world of TV. Hunter was a control freak but took her at face value. In a way he treated her like another guy, which made him easy to be with. It was at the root of her problems with Max, who no longer liked giving her the space she needed to be the kind of woman she was.

She drove the opposite way to when she'd walked to the car park earlier. When she got to the end of the street the lights hit red. She needed to turn right onto Oxford Road, past the front of the car park, to drive round the block to pick up Hunter. While she waited, she saw a young bald guy in a grey leather trenchcoat charge out of the same door she'd used when she hid behind the bus. It looked like the bloke with the artificial hand she'd seen from the lift in the hotel last night. He scuttled across the road like a startled rabbit and disappeared into the street where the BMW was parked.

Wondering, Vanessa set off. When she passed the street the guy ran into she saw him talking to the dyke from the lift, next to the BM. Seeing the bitch confirmed that something fishy was going on. The dyke looked angry with the bald guy and threw a punch at him but he jumped out of the way and she fell flat on her face in the snow. It was like the weight of her immense boobs had pulled her over, so hard that Vanessa felt her hit the deck and winced. It was a surrealistic moment but as she stuck her foot down she felt a grim satisfaction.

Less than a minute later she picked Hunter up safely at the rendezvous place and they hightailed it away from the city. Genny had got them two cans of coffee, a couple of bottles of water, some fresh fruit, and some biscuits from Sumners' kitchen. Vanessa knew that Hunter had recovered because his sense of humour started working overtime. As he dived into the bag and she told him what she'd just seen he guessed the bald guy was the fuckwit he saw running in the road after the Mini blew up. He suggested that if they'd had the new Sheuze hand-held rocket launcher with them, which they'd made a film about in July, they

259

could have driven back round and blown the BMW, the bald tosser, and the strap-on addict off the fucking face of the earth.

FORtY-TWO

In the exhibition centre car park a young black attendant was midway through his evening walkabout. He was kitted out in yellow safety togs striped with Scotchlite. Two-way radio static spat from his shoulder as he yawned and passed the silver Lexus that had parked earlier.

Massive, dwarfing the other cars, most of the snow piled on it had melted over the past hour forming pools around it. He was impressed by such a cool machine and decided to take a gander. Nice wheels, he thought, squeezing between it and the next car on the driver's side. Doing his job you did a ton of window-shopping for pricy motors you could never fucking have. All he could see in this one were a copy of *Woman and Home* and a box of Forzieri hankies. Must be a slick chick owner. Probably sexy and *very* classy. He felt a certain longing as he was reminded of his place in the scheme of things. But he wasn't bitter, just an ordinary guy getting on with life, the conformist kind that extremist nutters hated. He'd just become a proud young dad. Lennox they'd called him, only a week old. Dad was permanently on top of the world.

The Lexus winked its red alarm diode at him as he came out from the gap and, blowing into his cold hands, got on with his rounds.

Computer came to life as soon as the attendant's bootsteps faded. Digi chatter kicked in, his 747 displays got to work, his vectorscope winked on at the dash. Kareem was activating him by remote but Computer wasn't taking chances and kept his audio low. He didn't engage in witty chat but got straight to the requested dialogue.

'Computer?'

'Yes Kareem?'

'Situation please.'

'Abigail parked me fifty eight minutes ago in the exhibition centre car park.'

'Overnight?'

'Yes Kareem.'

'It *must* be the hotel where she went.' This wasn't Kareem but Mark, patched from the XJS via a three-way split. 'Did she say where she was going?'

'She confirmed that she was liaising with an unnamed gentleman.'

'Fuck it,' Mark said knowingly. 'I knew it.'

Kareem again: 'Can you get a fix?'

'Scanning.'

On his screen a CG image of the Lexus and the nearby streets and buildings twisted round in 3D. The guys could see it back at base. Two spots of light flashed red almost on top of each other, in a building less than a block away. Its interior floors throbbed and lunged in as he got a fix. He beeped when the spots of light joined to the Lexus and everything zinged green.

261

'Affirmative,' he said. 'Fix confirmed.'

'Approximate distance?'

'Two thousand metres.'

He'd picked up two signals, one from Abigail's phone, the other from her watch, each independent of the other in case they ever parted company.

Kareem typed at his end. 'The grid reference is the hotel. Room one-three-two.'

'It'll be Hunter's room,' Mark said, 'I can fucking guarantee it.' He was seriously pissed off.

Kareem again: 'I'm on the hotel computers and can confirm it's Hunter's room.'

'Shit,' Mark said. 'I knew she was shagging him.'

'If it was announced on TV that he was killed at lunchtime, why's she in his room eight hours later?'

Computer had scanned the mainframe back at base and uploaded recent updates, so that he knew the score. 'That pre-supposes Hunter is dead,' he noted. 'Until sufficient forensic evidence is provided to the contrary, the identity of the bomb victim remains open to speculation.' Kareem started to say something but Computer cut in. 'Forgive me but Abigail is on the move.'

Mark thanked God. 'She's probably on her way back to you, man.'

'Pardon me, Mark, but her phone and watch signals are one-point-six metres apart. The phone is stationary but her watch is moving independently. Distance increasing. Two metres. Three. I would speculate that her phone is still in Hunter's room but she is walking away.' On his screen the two red spots were parting.

Kareem, cranking the pace: 'Maybe she's going down to fetch something.'

Computer: 'Correction. Her phone is following. I would speculate that somebody has picked up the phone and is trailing her.' On screen the second red spot was tailing the first, each pulsing-pinging as it went.

Mark: 'If Hunter *is* dead it must be somebody else who's in his room.'

Kareem: 'Computer? I've patched you into the hotel server.' Because he could compute faster than human fingers could hit keys. 'Where's she headed?'

'Scanning.' He'd instantly hacked into the hotel computers. 'She's entered the service lift on the third floor.'

Mark, amazed: 'Why the fucking service lift?'

Computer: 'Now she's descending. Her likely destination is the hotel service entrance.' On screen the CG image shifted round as the first red spot dropped between the 3D floors, highlighted in a lift shaft and pulsing-pinging as it went. As the guys watched at their end Mark thought of something.

'Hey, what about the hotel CCTVs?'

'Good idea,' Kareem said. 'Computer?'

'Patching in camera seven.'

Another beep. On his screen a high, wide-angle POV of the service entrance at the back of the hotel replaced the CG image. Now that he controlled the camera he zoomed out further. Fat snowflakes dithered close to the lens. The camera was bolted way up on the outside wall and aimed down at the steps and snowy pavement, exaggerating the perspective. Several uniformed cops stood about smoking. Everybody was oblivious to the CCTV creeping round on its bracket to spy on them.

A police APC was parked. The service entrance doors were open, flooding light. Computer jumped to another

CCTV inside the doorway as some lift doors parted and a big grey-haired guy wheeled out a yellow laundry bin. He nodded at two cops outside just as Computer flicked back to the exterior POV. The cops went up the steps, lifted the bin lid, and reached in. Now Driscoll appeared, followed by Stoneham carrying Abigail's overnight bag. They turned as somebody came up behind them. Mark swore when he saw the creepy hotel manager squeeze past Driscoll and Stoneham to stand in the doorway, unzipping his teeth. The grey-haired guy stuffed a wad of cash in the creep's hand then told him to fuck off over the audio. Driscoll tailed the cops when they came outside with a bodybag slung between them and carried it down the steps to load it in the back of the APC.

'Jesus fucking Christ,' Mark said, reading the situation. 'It's got to be her.' Panic loaded his voice but Computer was already scanning.

'I regret to confirm,' he said, 'that the grid reference and the position of the tracer suggest the contents of the body-bag are Abigail.'

Mark swore again, feeling it now. 'It's because she was shadowing Driscoll, I know it. But why the hell were they in Hunter's fucking room?'

Kareem stayed cool. 'Computer? This is turning serious. I'm authorizing you to drive up to the street. As long as Abigail's tracer is transmitting you can track and pursue. Stay out of visual range and relay back to base. Wherever they take her I want you to follow. How are you for fuel?'

'Nearly full, Kareem.'

'Remember you're in a manned car park. You'll need to exercise protocol when you leave.'

'Yes Kareem.'

'Fast as you can.'

He got to it and brought the Lexus to life, doing what Abigail called the aircraft take-off build-up thing. He eased out of the parking space, turning the steering wheel by invisible hands, and crept along Sub-Level 1 with his four-litre engine growling. Exercising caution in case of pedestrians he reached the exit ramp leading up to the ground floor and turned. His tyres squeaked at the shiny grey-painted concrete floor as he drove the Lexus with a strange controlled precision, like he was running it on a laser rail. Which in a way he was, seeing as a glorified satnav was driving.

Young Dad heard approaching wheels and turned to see the Lexus bumping up the ramp behind him. Still in good spirits he thought hey, a chance to eyeball the nice lady. Squeaking rubber the big machine hit level and turned towards him, like an X-bomber gunning for take-off, with its headlights dropping back to dip and its engine throbbing super-cool.

But Young Dad sussed something wasn't fucking right straight away. Squinting he pulled a face, thinking surely not man. Concluding Jesus H Christ he grabbed his shoulder radio and hit open frequency.

'Hey you guys?'

The Lexus passed him slowly. He gazed inside, spooked by what he saw. *Nobody was driving.* Or else the nice lady was the Invisible fucking Woman.

It had to go round the outside edge of the floor to get to the barriers so Young Dad took off, short-cutting between cars, arriving just as the Lexus got within ten yards of the exit and stopped. Two day-glow-clad Euro Joes arrived, their reflectors hotting as the Lexus headlit everybody and gave it some seriously mean rev.

Mexican moment time.

Young Dad edged forward saying, 'I'm telling you guys! It's driving its fucking self!'

'No way,' said Euro Joe # 1. He'd stooped uncertainly, trying to see in the Lexus without going closer.

A black guy Joe shouted in amazement from the booth. 'It's fucking paid, man!'

'What?'

'It's just paid! By Swiss CC!'

'How?'

'It's overridden the fucking PC that's how! It's paid us fifty quid, tipping us a fucking tenner each! It's the same registration ID!'

'Jesus!'

'Don't let it through!'

The Lexus revved again.

Young Dad heard booth guy going apeshit as he whacked dead PC keys. 'Shit, man!' The barrier folded away. 'What the fuck?'

'Don't let it out!' This was Euro Joe # 2. A short-arse.

'It's letting its fucking self out!' said booth guy, coming out with open mouth and upturned pink palms.

They rallied by the barrier to form a human wall. Young Dad got out his phone and started to video the Lexus, but it revved again, pissed off now. The phone fried and puffed smoke in Young Dad's hand. He swore, *yeeowwed*, and dropped it. The Lexus revved ominously and reversed. Its headlights flicked on halogen hot, making everybody fling hands up to eyes and swear as their reflectors did their thing. Now a genteel English voice boomed from speakers buried in the 4x4's mean-looking brushed-steel radiator. 'Please stand aside, gentlemen. I've paid and tipped you generously. I'm leaving the car park.'

The Lexus burnt rubber and set off at a serious fucking speed. Everybody dived aside as it swept past and up the ramp so fast it took off from the top, spraying snow when it landed with a protracted *wunch*, and was away.

The guys rolled about, panting. Young Dad saw his frazzled, smoking phone and heard short-arse swear in Polish. Snow swirled beyond the barriers, diffusing the city lights as the sound of the Lexus faded.

'Way to fucking rock, man!' booth guy said, cackling as he got up, clacking some fingers. At the top of the ramp an old hanging metal NCP sign swayed and creaked from when the Lexus had caught it.

FORtY-THREE

They reached Genny's flat at ten. The snow had stopped and the vast white panorama made the night bright. When they got out of the car Hunter saw numerous lit windows scattered romantically across a glacial hillside. A muffled quietness held it, making him think of the magic of winter during childhood. It wasn't like the unpredictable quietness of the city because tingeing it was the wild presence of the moors.

They crunched across to the door and stood under the portico spots while Vanessa got out the swipecard. The apartment was in a large converted woollen mill opposite a preserved steam railway. The only evidence of this was a snow-covered semaphore signal at the top of an embankment overlooking the car park. As she waved the card the red panel went green, locks *fdunked,* and the door popped open. When they went inside Hunter couldn't help thinking their old life was ending.

During the drive there she'd told him everything about Max. It was as good as over and had been for much of the past year. There'd been no animosity, she said, just a slow drifting apart. As Max got older and more successful he'd changed. She'd didn't know if it was a mid-life crisis thing, as he shot towards 50, or power and money going to his head. But the less time he spent with her the more possessive he'd become. Yesterday he'd asked her to marry him, to save the relationship, but that wasn't her idea of a reason to take the plunge. What pissed her off was his attitude, suggesting it like a business proposal on the phone. Things had come to a head when he'd phoned her again that morning, to see if she'd made up her mind. When she said she hadn't he'd pushed her and she'd told him it was finished. Hunter had caught the look in her eye and asked her why she'd never said anything to him. Because he'd enough extra-marital problems of his own, she said, without taking hers on board too.

While they waited for a lift, and the panel counted the floors from four down to three to two, he wondered if he'd ever noticed a lack of affection between her and Max. If he wasn't in New York, Max did seem to have mastered the art of putting a distance between himself and any visitors.

He'd move about the kitchen rattling crockery, or go up to his office to use the phone. But such oblique behaviour suited his restless personality.

As they entered the lift she said, 'Weather permitting I think we should leave first thing in the morning and head north. They'll expect us to head south.'

'Where shall we go?'

'Wherever it takes us. It's easier to disappear these days than most people think.'

He couldn't deny that being on the run with her in the snow was taking on a special kind of excitement. Or maybe it was the prospect of finally shagging her that had turned him on as their arctic odyssey progressed. But Max still held him back. Not like before. But, after what she'd told him, Hunter couldn't escape the uneasy feeling that if he made the first move he'd be taking advantage. Absurdly, he'd his dignity to think of. She'd say it was his fucking obstinacy.

The apartment was on the sixth floor. When they reached it they were a little breathless. She slotted in the card with difficulty because her hand seemed to be shaking. As they went in, and the door slid shut, all he could hear was the creak of central heating. They crossed to the open-plan lounge and dumped their stuff. With its blend of Moonbase Alpha set design, transparent furniture, and primary colours, the apartment was pure Modernist Revival. Small and neat enough, but trying to give an air of convenience to hide how it had been snapped together like Lego on a tight budget in a tight space.

A glass coffee table stood on a deep white sheepskin rug in front of an inflatable clear plastic sofa. Hunter threw off his coat and started going on about Scandinavian acrylic flat-pack houses but wondered two things simultaneously. The first was if Vanessa looked seriously hassled like she'd suddenly got the world pressing down on her shoulders. The second was why the hell was she dragging the table off the rug? Then he knew the fuck why because she grabbed him and went for him, big time.

She kissed him greedily, moaning as her suppressed desire exploded. He joined in but was so knackered his legs started to go from under him. Because of her workouts at the gym she easily held him up. His hard-on erupted between them. She pressed her hand against it and said huskily, 'I want that inside me. Now,' then pushed him down onto his back on the rug. It was symbolic because he'd be on his back for much of the night. She knelt over him and yanked her clothes off untidily over her head. Her glasses got lost in the tangle. She kicked off her boots, leaving only her pants, bra, and tights to come off. There was wildness in her eyes as she yanked off his boots and socks and tore at his trousers. It was like she was raping him but it was a mega crazy turn-on. Seemed like the right outcome to the past few years, never mind the past few hours.

His main concern was BO. Because of the running he'd done that day he was convinced he stunk but all he could smell was his deodorant as his clothes came off. Meaning it was doing what it said on the tin. He hadn't wanted it to be like this but had hoped to have a shower and take his time. He knew he was in love with her but it was the same as what happened with Abigail. Intelligent guys needed to go straight into hard sex and release the horny animal tension. Their lives being in danger didn't help rational behaviour. The tender lovemaking and intellectual chat would come later.

She pulled off his shirt, snapped loose her bra, ripped off her pants and tights. They were nude. She knelt over him on all fours, blocking out the overhead ceiling spots, everything dangling, like an animal ready to devour its prey. Then she took aim and fed him into her as she came down. They cried out at the moment of penetration. She locked onto him and rode him with a frantic desperation, gulping and swearing as he fucked her. Or rather, as she fucked him, spreading his arms in a crucifix pose, rearing up on her elbows and grinding his arse into the rug. He'd never seen such unadulterated greed on a woman's face as when she slid off and went down to him.

They went wild with desire. It was as if they were suffocating on each other. The accrued emotion of all the years they'd known each other assaulted them with its cumulative wisdom and blew their feelings apart. He was usually good at delaying his orgasm but tonight he started coming almost immediately. Realising this she climbed off him to take a breather. They were panting, balanced on the edge of the moment. 'Your heart's beating like mad,' he said to her, looking up at her. He flattened his hand between her breasts and saw an expression of it's-now-or-never resolve in her beautiful sparkling eyes.

'I'm scared of losing you as a friend,' she said, reciprocating his thoughts. It was the only intellectual exchange of their lovemaking that night but it facilitated the multiple detonations of physical pleasure that followed. He rolled her over and gave it everything he'd got.

FORtY-FOUR

Mark lifted his binocs when he heard the rig coming but decided to wait till it had passed through the village before he took off.

Christmas tree lights shone in the XJS's windscreen from across the quaint cobbled square. One of Gary Numan's coolest B sides, *Shame*, was going at the CD, not too loud in case it woke the village, which was dead at that hour with few windows lit. To try and stop worrying about Abigail Mark goosebumped to the music and sang with the backing girls when they hit the abandon me bit. His lit cigarette bobbed at his mouth as he nudged Numan back and said to Kareem, 'It's just gone through but that was a fucking hairy chance I took back there.'

The rig hadn't shown at Dunford Bridge terminal. He'd waited till half-fucking-ten in the blizzard then followed it across Thurlstone Moor and down the Stocksbridge link towards the M1. But it came off at the first exit and stopped at an all-night transport caf. When it got going again it avoided the main road but slewed across the Strines, of all fucking places, and made a beeline for Ladybower at the northern edge of the Peak District. Suggesting that rig # 3 was cutting across country instead. Because of its size and the deep snow it had stuck to the wider roads so Mark had looped round and kept going to the next village, hoping it would take the same route.

He fired up the XJS and took off, saying to Kareem, 'It's come ten miles from the terminal. I don't know anything about this area but I'm sure there used to be an old army camp somewhere. Lancasters flew here during the war because the hilliness suited target practice for the Dambuster raids over the Ruhr. They reckon one crashed and is lost out on the moors.'

Shame finished as he skidded out of the village square and took the unlit road to the south. The snow had finally stopped and the night was clear. Up ahead white hills outlined the horizon. Reservoirs glinted like silver bars beneath the moonlight where they trailed off through a long valley. Now Mark's favourite Numan single kicked in, a hi-octane ball of energy called *I Can't Stop*. In a just world it would have made number one instead of only number twenty-fucking-seven. Abigail had heard him playing the 10" Club Mix so often she loved it too. Thinking about this upset him. As he took the snow-drifted lane way too fast, back came the big volume, especially for Abby, when Tessa Niles let rip.

An hour later, Mark was standing at the edge of a deep snowy field scanning the arctic landscape through his binocs. The night was starlit and bitterly cold. A wind blew from the moors as awesomely as a sound effect in an old Hammer horror movie. It dusted snow from the drystone walls and sent it scurrying in eddies across the fields. He'd just heard the rig horning in the distance like a ship lost in fog. Steadying himself against a metal gate he hit cinema-scope scan. Up came an infrared 235:1. HD image, so clear in might have been a hundred feet away. The rig reached a narrow unadopted road and negotiated the turn with difficulty, its headlights flaring. Red marker bulbs outlined its trailer and cab as it crept between the pines, clanking and crunching ice, till it crested a hill then disappeared into a fir plantation over the other side.

Mark said to Kareem, 'Back at the café I saw guys in the trailer, like yesterday. I'm going in on foot. I'll stop transmitting in case they're scanning the area.' Before cutting off he asked if there was any news.

Kareem told him that when Abigail's tracer had got to CPHQ it stopped moving. The APC carrying her body left an hour later but with no signal to follow Computer lost it. They'd hacked into the main road CCTVs, to try and work out where the APC had gone. But the logical conclusion was to assume they'd disposed of her body and that she'd gone forever.

As the icy wind pushed at his face, Mark gazed off abstractedly and tried to come to terms with not seeing Abigail again. Behind their chiding and his constant worrying about her safety they were close. The prospect of the long night ahead, stuck in the middle of nowhere in the freezing fucking cold, was bad enough. But the thought of his wedding next summer without her was infinitely worse. He said he'd see the guys later and killed the call.

Blowing into his gloved hands he trudged back through the snow to where the XJS was hidden in some trees. He needed to focus on the job at hand and see it to the bitter end, for Abigail as much as anybody. Getting killed was a risk they ran. Sir Ian paid them accordingly and they all agreed it beat working for a living. The shit Driscoll was up to meant they could hardly go to the cops and demand a fucking explanation.

Before setting off on foot he checked he'd got everything in his rucksack and hitched it on, then locked up and kicked snow to hide the XJS's chunky tyre tracks where they'd swung off the road. It was nearly midnight. He lit another cigarette and walked into the darkness, still trying to get to grips with what had happened to Abby. Everywhere was bright from the snow, making it easy to see. A myriad of stars sparkled above him against the clear night.

WEDNESDAY

FORtY-FiVE

Forty minutes later Mark was lying on his belly in Alpine-deep snow at the edge of an industrial stockyard, scanning the red-tinted view through his binocs.

The blue-and-yellow rig, kicking chrome in the night spots and as big as the monsters that carried SHADO mobiles, had reversed up to an old warehouse clad in ribbed asbestos sheeting. Piles of junk and a knackered caravan made shapes from the snowy shadows.

Figures materialized from the gloom, shaft-waving torches, clouding breath. They opened the back doors of the rig and a fork-lift started zipping about, loading up orange plastic shipping crates. About a dozen guys helped, most smoking. Their cigarettes burnt at the darkness, their puffs of backlit breath hung in the lit doorway. As the forklift came up with a new load two of the guys jumped on, larking about. Somebody in charge swore at them and they fell into line. Their subservience gave the game away, but even from where he was crouched Mark knew the accents were Polish.

When they'd loaded all the crates the Poles disappeared into the building. Through his binocs Mark checked a digi map reference and realised this wasn't the old army camp. According to Google he should be in the middle of a reservoir. The place didn't exist even though the decrepit buildings looked as if they'd been up since the war. Still wondering, he heard noises coming from round the other side of the site. He made his way cautiously along the perimeter fence, trying not to crunch snow, till more spots came into view, as hot as floods blasting a soccer pitch. Feeling exposed he dropped to walk on his elbows and knees, like an escaping POW. Lattice shadows from the fence stretched towards him across the snow, the diamonds getting bigger and more blurred the nearer they came.

He stopped and zoomed in through his binocs when he saw two guys talking at the edge of a large spot-lit hole in the ground. Through an open loading door behind them something big, made from stainless steel, caught light in the shadows. Some portacabins stood in the yard, probably makeshift dormitories for the Poles. Trying to weigh it up Mark lit a cigarette and hit Record for a while till about two-dozen Poles trudged outside. As they pushed through a yellow PVC strip curtain some more stainless-steel stuff showed behind them before a rollershutter started clattering down. Kareem's guys would take apart the HD footage and analyse it properly.

The men carried shovels and were driven towards the hole by an English-speaking chargehand, who ducked under the descending shutter. It looked like they were going to fill in the hole. Mark set his binocs to audio-record and was tuning his earpiece when he heard approaching vehicles and saw headlights flaring as a short wheelbase box lorry appeared, and a slick 4x4 Jag. The Jag stopped while the lorry moved nearer to the hole. The Poles were lined up in front of it, leaning docilely on their shovels, their lit cigarettes waving under a big smoke-breath cloud. Mark was spooked when he saw who got out of the fucking Jag. Driscoll, not in uniform but wearing the shiny civvies he'd worn when they'd watched him on the CCTVs outside the hotel. He'd a phone stuck at his ear.

Mark heard him say, 'Right, that's it. Is everything good at your end?'

A voice must have A-OK'd.

'Tell him I accept his apologies.' He laughed then told the chargehand: 'The new one isn't needed till next summer. Tell them their work is done.'

The chargehand spoke to the men in Polish then Driscoll nodded at the lorry. Immediately the men became agitated and Mark clocked the fuck why. The back of the lorry shot up with a rollermetal clatter. A helmeted guy in padded X-Men leathers and chunky Goth boots swung a double-barrelled machinegun from a pneumatic steadiharness.

Its red laser swept the snow.

281

Down came the guy's digi night visor.

Into the back of the gun went his hand.

Then he let fucking fast-action rip, mowing down the Poles in cold blood.

Muzzle-flash strobed but the gun made hardly a noise, only a relentless basso-silencered thudding. It emphasized the sickening *thwipp* and *phut* of the bodies being blown to bits and the men's screams as they were blasted back into the hole. Snow flew up among a spray of guts. Some of the men tried to run away but were instantly shot to pieces. It was like a scene updated from the Holocaust, or some appalling Nazi slaughter in a snowy forest.

When it was over, Mark saw intestinal steam rise in the shafts of blue-white light hitting the hole. Blood soaked the snow around it. Unaffected by what he'd seen Driscoll held up his phone and casually took some photos. The flash flashed then a Bobcat digger rumbled into view and fussed about, its hazards partying as it cleared up the corpses that hadn't fallen in the hole. It scraped at them as if they were garbage, making elbows and knees buckle obscenely as it drove at the pile. Some other guys used snow shovels to clear the red snow. When they'd finished the chargehand dragged out a hosepipe and swilled away the gory residuum. Finally, the Bobcat ate at the pyramid of soil and started filling in the hole.

Mark had stuck his lit cigarette in the snow while he'd videoed the massacre. When he lowered the binocs he realised his hands were shaking. Something mega fucking serious was happening. Whatever Abigail had suspected about Driscoll's dodgy business dealings must be bang on. He knew for certain now that she was dead. It induced a sudden panic. He wanted to get back to the car and get the fuck outta there. It was only as he reached for his cigarette that he saw a second hotspot of light pricking the snow in front of it. He turned and saw a figure standing silhouetted in the moonlight, laser-sight at eye. Mark was dazzled by the red hotspot but sensed it shift up from the snow to settle on his forehead.

The figure aimed right between his eyes as a gruff voice said, 'Say prayers, black boy.'

In the split second before the bullet split open his skull Mark wondered if he'd heard its echo chase harshly across the snowy valley, like an audio missile splitting the white night.

FORtY-siX

It was the early hours before Hunter and Vanessa had finished. She fell asleep quickly but he lay awake for ages, exhausted and aching, staring at the bright red numbers of the bedside clock.

He hugged her from behind, curling with her under the quilt in a natural foetal embrace. Only the hum of the central heating, left on low to dry his clothes, disturbed the peace of the room. Then, as her sleep deepened, her stentorian breathing and occasional snoring worked at the hermetic silence of a strange ebony limbo where he was somehow stranded with his thoughts.

The clock threw the time at the opposite wall, the numbers distorted due to the angle. 01:49 when he next looked. The colon flashed away the minutes quickly. He felt agitated, oppressed, emotionally shellshocked but couldn't put his finger on the hell why. He'd enough excuses but there was something else besides the bomb and the kid being blown to bits and him fretting over Abigail's whereabouts and finally making love with Vanessa. Maybe the bottle of Terra Vecchio they'd drunk had hyped him. After they'd orgasmed in the sheepskin they'd showered and eaten two Quorn shepherd's pies she found in the freezer. She stuck his clothes in the wash then they'd sat talking on the see-through sofa and popped the wine. She in a too-small pink bathrobe of Genny's that was shorter on her than a mini-skirt, him wrapped in a big white bath towel.

It seemed right for her to have taken the dominant role and seduced him. She was an assertive woman who could run circles round most guys. But when they'd gone to bed she'd shown her true colours and revealed an unexpected feminine submissiveness as they became more intimate. At the same time she participated in lovemaking more than any woman he'd been with. Most would just lie there and let him get on with it, which was OK because their pleasure was his pleasure. But Vanessa was at him all the time and in control during sex. It was like she couldn't stop herself running the show in the same way she called the shots in their business life, or directed a shoot. She was a more complex character than he'd thought.

As though disliking herself for it she'd grown upset for having taken him so roughly on the floor. It should have been a beautiful moment, she'd said. He'd assured her that it was, and meant it. They were pent up and in danger and had needed a quick physical payoff. But still she beat herself up emotionally. When he'd kissed the tears from her eyes, and comforted her, far from feeling that she was ten years older than him he felt ten years older than her. He remembered what Abigail said about her yesterday morning and felt guilty for knowing it. *Underneath the assertive exterior she's quite vulnerable and* very *feminine.*

Eventually, swirling images conquered the ache in his head and carried him away into some semblance of a fitful slumber. He knew this because his mouth tasted of sleep when he felt her shifting his arm and getting out of bed. Something rustled from the darkness then the door opened and closed. Soon, he heard a cistern hiss through the wall. For a few moments he was at peace with himself and unexpectedly happy, until the explosive events of yesterday bulged back. With them came a nagging fear in the pit of his stomach. It collided with a vision of Abigail writhing under him as he emptied himself into her, knowing he'd deliberately abandoned her after shagging the arse off her. Then he heard a blind rattling. After what could have been a minute or an hour came the reassuring sound of water filling a kettle and a teaspoon clattering in a mug. He lifted an arm to his eyes when sunlight flooded in and she stood silhouetted in the doorway.

'We'd better move,' she said.

While doing stuff in the kitchen she'd been compelled to wear, as a sort of mandatory badge of honour, his clean shirt. It was unfastened and crinkle-dry from being hung on a radiator.

Smiling, she padded across to sit on the bed and kissed him, to help bring him round. 'Did you sleep?' she asked, caressing his heavily stubbled face.

'Not really.'

'Neither did I.'

'Yes you did,' he said, scoffing. 'You kept me awake half the night with your bloody snoring.' Puckering her face she poked him affectionately as he eased himself up into a sitting position. 'I guess this has been a shock for both of us,' he noted through a yawn.

'I suppose it has,' she agreed, climbing over to kneel astride him. He'd made love to two different women in as many days, both of them beautiful, one blonde, one brunette, both of them uninhibited in bed, both similar in their sexual needs. But welded to Vanessa he'd attained a level of physical gratification he'd not known. He wanted to explain it logically but couldn't. Nature had the upper hand. 'What?' she asked, prompting him as his silent scrutiny of her continued.

Bewildered, he shook his head. 'What was it somebody once said about eating sawdust all your life thinking it was bread?'

She was touched and looked unusually bashful from under the lids of her pale eyes. 'I suppose it makes a difference because we know each other.'

'I have other women friends who I know like you, but the thought of going to bed with them never enters my head. It doesn't devalue their importance to me as women intellectually.'

'Did you ever wonder about us?' she asked. She started to stroke him gently, as if she were comforting a favourite pet laid between her hands.

'Not really,' he said. 'You weren't available so it was a line I didn't cross.'

'You're very moral, you know.'

286

'So are you. It's because we're so fucking moral that it's taken so damned long for this to happen.' He sighed and caressed her breasts when her stroking took effect. 'Sometimes I fancied you like fuck though.' He was resigned to a sudden desolation as a memory of how he used to see her crashed into more pressing worries.

'A tension's left your face,' she said. 'I don't mean because of yesterday but from as far back as I can remember.' He was gazing off, staring at a hideous daffodil lamp that dominated the bedroom and fought the purple wallpaper printed with Electric Warrior LP covers. 'I'm sorry,' she said realising.

'I wish you were their mother,' he said mulishly.

'No,' she said, shaking her head. 'I love them as much as I love you but something I've always known is that I don't want kids. I'm too selfish.'

'No you're not.'

'Yes I am. My career's too important. It wouldn't be fair to have kids unless I could bring them up.' Always she put the welfare of others before her own, meaning she was the exact opposite of what she'd said. 'This feels right though, doesn't it?' she added. Her eye twinkled impishly at the *double entendre* as he swelled in her hands.

Despite their imminent danger he agreed. 'Now that it's happened I can't get over how right it feels.'

'I wonder why?'

'Because it's not just about sex?'

At that moment it was all about sex. She suddenly reared up, with a familiar wildness in her eyes, and gripped what she'd brought alive. Without letting go, she yanked him round onto his back then knelt astride him and came down swiftly. Her eyes momentarily bulged.

He remembered hearing the kettle boiling and clicking off when it reheated. A short time later, as she stiffened in his arms with an epileptic potency and swore as savagely as him, the microwave beeped, reminding her of the bread she'd been defrosting.

FORtY-SEVEN

Ten minutes later, looking like a cat that had just found the cream (or had been impregnated with it) Vanessa slid off the bed and headed back to the kitchen.

Hunter heard the whistle of a steam train. Feeling as if danger had passed them by, he reached for his specs and hurried through to the sun-drenched lounge. 'This age we live in gets more ridiculous by the day,' he said, pulling on a guy's bathrobe he'd found last night and crossing to the window. Spraying snow, the train blasted out of a tunnel across from the apartment. As the shiny black loco chuffed past, shoving out a massive plume of steam, figures hung from the maroon carriages incongruously wielding cam-corders. 'Did you know it takes three hours to steam an engine?' he threw across.

'No I didn't,' she said, setting a full cafetiere on a tray and busying herself with toast. She set a jug of milk going in the microwave. 'At least the snow's stopped so the main roads should be clear.'

Hunter saw a photo on the windowsill showing a film crew shooting a scene in a movie. Judging by the period costumes of two boy actors it was set during the 1950s. He realised the photo had been taken on a bridge across from the apartment. In the background was the massive mill he was standing in, presumably when it was still in the business of weaving cloth. He recognised somebody. 'Is this Genny?' he asked, turning.

She looked across and spoke above the *bweee weee weee* of the microwave. 'Yes,' she said. 'It's a low-budget lesbian feature she worked on. She was a clapper-loader then. The boy in the yellow jumper is the director's son.' She named the film. 'There's probably a DVD somewhere.'

She brought some toast across and stood by the window to drink a cappuccino, gazing at the brilliant winter landscape from the top-floor view. Hunter was surprised to see by the cooker clock that it was as late as 10:43am. Before eating any toast he nosied in a cupboard but stopped dead when he saw a portable fucking TV.

'Shit, there's a telly,' he said, pulling stuff off, dragging it out. When they'd arrived they assumed there wasn't a TV because they couldn't see one. Following the demise of analogue, and the short-lived blip of digital, most people had Internet TVs or used their laptops or phones. Vanessa's phone was in her case but even though it received TV signals it was still a mobile. If they switched it on their location would show up if the CP were scanning for her IP address and phone numbers.

He couldn't switch on the TV fast enough. There was no remote. He dumped it on the worktop that split the kitchen from the lounge and swore at it as he manually flipped through channels. Eventually he found *BBC News*. Swore again when, to his amazement, he saw a photo of himself and his blown-up car with BREAKING NEWS wiping the bottom of the screen.

Two Newscasters took turns to explain that mystery surrounded the Manchester car bomb from yesterday afternoon. An anonymous witness had phoned the BBC to say she saw a hoodied kid getting in the car just before it blew up. She saw another guy dive into an X6 straight after the explosion, while a third guy in a long black coat tonned it away down a footpath.

Vanessa was standing next to Hunter, with the mug of coffee between her hands. Initially encouraged he put his arms round her from behind and squeezed her. The Newscasters said that he'd been seen in Lincoln and Norwich. It was weird to hear them discussing him, like they were talking about somebody else. But as he wondered about Driscoll's ulterior motive for making his "death" public, he sensed a force outside himself, which had been manipulating him since the bomb went off, was finally closing in for the kill. He quickly pushed aside any concern for his feelings when something else hit him. The effect of the story on his mum and dad.

As if in response to this they flashed live on screen, standing sombrely at the gates of their Cotswolds farmhouse. Hunter was pole-axed. His mother, from whom he got his looks, had a deeply distressed expression, as if, having just seen a ghost, she'd been told that it might not have been a ghost after all. Hunter's father, a broad soldierly man from whom his son got his height, drew his wife protectively against himself and said solemnly, 'This is a difficult time for us both but we hope and pray this new information is genuine.'

Hunter swore because he couldn't be with them, then a babble of voices bombarded them from off camera before the woman Newscaster came back. 'Mystery also surrounds the disappearance of Mr Hunter's 41 year old business partner, Vanessa Aysgarth. She was last seen leaving a Manchester TV post-production house at about seven-fifteen last evening but failed to return to her hotel.' Up popped her photo followed by Martin the studio gateman, devoid of his specs, insisting he saw her leave and head for the car park further down the street.

Hunter still held her. 'Didn't he see you after you went back inside?'

'No,' she said, shaking her head. 'Nobody did, except for Genny. I went in the front way and made sure Martin didn't see me when I drove back out.'

The report ended and celebrity crap kicked in. Hunter killed the sound, feeling exposed like when he left the IFI. 'Let's hope to God that Genny's kept her nerve,' he said. Puffing his cheeks with a nick-of-time jadedness he crossed to gaze from the window. Last night the snow acted as a leaven to the seriousness of what they were caught up in. Now it seemed like an insurmountable obstacle, jeopardizing their ability to get away.

'Surely we can phone in,' Vanessa said. 'Even if the CP track where we are the cops'll never get here before we've told somebody about what's been going on. And now that it's been made public . . .'

He turned to face her, firmly shaking his head. After the uncertainty of yesterday this morning he felt focused and revitalised. 'Our priority is to stay alive,' he said. 'They could kill us but come up with some fucking cock-and-bull story.'

'Not now they couldn't. There'd be too many questions. We're in the public domain.'

'It doesn't matter. If they find us they could still get rid of us. As far as the public's concerned we've disappeared and we're not known faces. If we knocked on somebody's door, and told them everything, we could still disappear after the cops arrive. You know as well as I do that these things happen, in full view of the media. They don't give a shit but just lie. If we make TV programmes about them they sit in front of the camera and keep fucking lying because it suits them. They're even coached to lie with the right body language.' He mentioned a Government scientist whose suspect death had never been properly explained. 'All that matters is that we stay alive. We've got to get to a live TV studio before they get to us.'

She watched him from a shaft of hot sunshine. Now that the euphoria of their sexual union had passed he could see from the look on her face how their true predicament was sinking in. She put down her coffee and reached for him. He held her and kissed her forehead gently but when he looked into her eyes they were wet. He'd never seen her looking so afraid.

She recovered quickly and said, 'Let's get dressed and drive back into town and walk into ITV and show the bastards.' He agreed and released her. She picked up the tray to take it back to the kitchen, adding, 'You must eat something before we go.'

He said he would and reached for his jeans, which were drying on the radiator under the window. He looked out at a brilliant blue sky above a magnificent steep white hillside. Earlier, Vanessa had opened an air-vent. The sound of playing schoolchildren drifted cheerily in.

Driscoll, he thought. Fuck Driscoll. But Hunter couldn't deny that if Driscoll hadn't tried to kill him he wouldn't have slept with Vanessa. The compensation was bitterly ironical. His spirits went up as his bare foot went down a crinkly-dry trouser leg.

FORty-EiGHt

What happened next was so unexpected it was like when his car blew up. Everything seemed to hang in a state of suspension lasting for a nanosecond, starting with his foot going into his jeans.

Through the window he saw a frustrated geometry of shapeless white rooftops. Terraced houses raked down the hillside opposite, street after street of them, testimony to the mills that once ploughed the landscape with dormitory lives. Being near open country there wasn't the menacing air of the inner cities. The impression was of an enduring English neighbourhood absolved from the celebrity-mad culture and unremitting corruptibility of modern life.

As the nanosecond progressed his eyes went to his foot slotting into the trouser leg. On the windowsill sat a lump of crystal with two thin chrome strips bolted to a face that was machined flat. He decided it was a clock and guessed from the position of the chrome strips that it was eleven-fifteen. Now the big audio dynamite. First, rooks calling

293

funereally, as they had been since dawn, floating like black rags round the mill chimney. Then a mega noise collided with his nanosecond observations torpedoing this pleasant documentary snapshot of a bright snowy northern morning. The apartment's outer door exploded inwards. Somehow Hunter sensed it coming, thinking the fuck *no*. Vanessa heard it too and spun as the door smacked into her, sending her and the tray and its contents flying. She threw out her hands to stop herself, dark liquid from the cafetiere and milk from the jug stretching in a kind of viscous slow-mo as everything headed for the clear sofa. Armed cops filled the apartment before Vanessa or the other stuff landed. As she slammed down, real time seemed to kick back in, speeding up as Driscoll blustered in, in uniform. Stoneham and a bunch of armour-plated cops brought up the rear. Two of them grabbed Vanessa by her arms and threw her onto the sofa. The other cops overdid arrest procedure, hitting Hunter with their lasers as they aimed their machineguns. Before he could react, two of them rushed him and pinioned his arms.

'Surprised you, did we?' Driscoll said, unable to contain his exuberance.

'How the fuck did you find us?' he said incredulously, trying to take everything in. He struggled as his arms were shoved up behind him, hurting his bruised ribs from when Vanessa had booted him in the car park.

'A tenant saw you arrive last night,' Driscoll said. 'He knew that Miss Atlas was away. Somebody he met in the car park when he left this morning said he'd heard adventurous noises coming from this apartment during the early hours.' He frowned at the walls, as though some failure of the builders to provide adequate acoustic impunity had asserted itself. 'You can usually count on sex to trip people up,' he added, tut-tutting theatrically. 'As a precaution the tenant called us.'

Stoneham picked up the laser-prints and passed one to Driscoll who, scrutinizing the mug-shot style image of the DS, went across to Hunter and whacked his head with it dismissively. 'You don't know what the fuck you've stumbled onto do you?'

'I can imagine,' he said, unflinching.

'Oh no you can't. This goes way beyond you unearthing the truth about a couple of recent high-profile deaths. Now things take a nasty turn for the fucking worse.' He scowled at Vanessa, dovetailing his outgoing observation into what crashed in. 'Which reminds me. Abigail came to your hotel room last night, only she bumped into us. She must have thought you'd stood her up. Judging by what went on in here this morning she was probably right.'

To make the point he held up his phone and hit a button. An MP3 of Hunter and Vanessa making love kicked off as she said something private and poignant. The cops sniggered. When Driscoll jumped to the raunchiest bit the cops laughed. Driscoll enjoyed the power kick. Anxious to continue with his narrative, he said, 'We were outside listening till back-up arrived.' He shoved the phone in Hunter's face when Vanessa hit her orgasm, her cries filling the room. Hunter looked at her but she'd covered her eyes. Driscoll noted sarcastically, 'You're thinking what a complete bastard I am, aren't you?'

'You said it, not me,' he replied, fuming. 'Only I'd have made the observation nastier still.'

'I'm sure you would,' he said, killing the MP3. 'I also neglected to mention that we didn't know what to do with

295

your dear, beautiful Abigail.' He paused for effect. 'So we shot her.'

After such amazing sex with Vanessa, Hunter had felt an awkward detachedness from Abigail, because of how he sensed their relationship might have been. It had lurked at the back of his mind since he and Vanessa took off from Manchester. But to know Abigail had been murdered when she went to his room to be with him was another sledgehammer moment. He might as well have stuck a Sheuze to her head and pulled the fucking trigger. He saw Vanessa searching his expression. 'I'm so sorry,' she said, making him feel like an even bigger shit.

Events had suddenly intensified. A sadistic Tarantinoesque side to Driscoll was emerging that Hunter hadn't seen before. It drove home the horror of their predicament and what was no doubt going to happen. He looked at everybody and demanded, 'What now?'

Driscoll was amused but there was a hint of psychotic madness in his dark button eyes. 'You've pissed me off for a long time,' he said. 'As a consequence your story enters a disturbing period of torture and extreme violence, making your demise protracted and painful.'

'I'm delighted that you find me so annoying.'

He thought he saw a smirk tugging at Stoneham's bricklike Jack Kirby face. Distracted by it he failed to anticipate Driscoll's fist as it smashed into his own face, knocking him senseless, knocking off his glasses. It made the cops who were holding him jump. Hunter heard Vanessa gasp. He couldn't remember ever being punched in his life. Not even at school. He really could see stars flashing. The only bird noises were the rooks yattering outside.

'That got you, didn't it?'

'Fuck you!' he said, his senses still reeling.

'Yes, fuck me,' he said with contempt as Hunter pedalled the carpet and the cops struggled to hold him up. Only one foot had made it into his jeans, which flapped off as he kicked. 'Your arrogance typifies the sniggering, anti-authoritarian attitude of our age, driven by a naïve preoccupation with human fucking rights.' Hunter thought Driscoll was going to slap him again but he grabbed his throat instead. 'But let me tell you something Mr smart arse, big TV man. I can fucking swear and I can hit back and your human fucking rights just fucking ended.'

Hunter's nose had burst. 'You'll never get away with it,' he said feebly, spitting blood. His front teeth were going numb and he seemed to be falling backwards but forwards but down.

Driscoll inhaled, more from weary scepticism than from his lungs needing air. 'Why do you assume the law will save you when we are the law? You're an experienced observer. These are desperate times. You found out something you shouldn't so you'll be killed.'

'What about Vanessa?'

'What about her?'

'What will you do with her?'

'We'll kill her as well, although she doesn't piss me off as much as you.'

Hunter couldn't see her expression now that his glasses had gone. It had been the best twelve hours of his life but Abigail's melting face superimposed itself accusingly. *She was somebody's daughter, for Christ's sake.* He shut his eyes, saw the light finally going out in her eyes, imagined the horror of her final moments. Her amazing glowing eyes dead, dead, fucking dead. 'Just tell me one thing,' he managed. He ran his tongue across his front teeth and found they were still there. 'Why was Greenhalgh killed?'

'Things are going on in this country of constitutional significance. We've been straightjacketed for too fucking long. Greenhalgh was involved but his working-class belligerence got the better of him.'

'What do you mean by "constitutional significance"?'

'You'll find out soon enough.' He told the two goons to get him out of there and got out his phone.

A skinny blonde policewoman appeared and hooked a pair of plastic medical slippers onto Hunter's bare feet. As the goons stuck his specs back on his face and frogmarched him out he wondered if the events of the past few days had cruelly led up to this scene in Genny's flat. Realised that his nagging sense of impending danger hadn't been born of the fear of death but of not knowing what the fuck would happen next. Now he knew. He tried to look back at Vanessa as he went through the door but a fat mitt slapped on top of his head and spun it face-forward.

When Hunter had gone, Vanessa found it hard to look at his bloody skidmarks on the yellow carpet but managed to lid her rage. Driscoll said to somebody, 'Go and put on the blue flashing lights. We might as well make it look authentic,' then told Vanessa to get dressed.

'I haven't got any clothes,' she told him back.

She sat huddled on the sofa, trying to cover herself with Hunter's shirt. Last night she left her trousers in the Volvo after she took them off. All she had were her blouse, vest, coat, boots.

'Then wear some of Miss Atlas's clothes,' Driscoll said impetuously, thumbing phone buttons.

'She's six inches shorter than me!'

'Then put *his* fucking clothes on!' he said, sussing that she was wearing his shirt, seeing his jeans on the floor. 'He won't need them where he's going.'

The policewoman picked up the jeans. She saw Vanessa's pants and bra hanging on the radiator, picked them up also, then followed her across to the bedroom.

FORtY-NiNE

Fifteen minutes later Vanessa was sitting in the back of a red X6, reversing out of a space. Her wrists were bound with Duck tape on her knee. Don't waste 'cuffs, somebody had joked.

Two bozos sat in front. Cops wearing plain clothes, she presumed. She recognised the young bald sidekick at the wheel. He'd run out of the car park last night and nearly got popped by the bitch next to the BMW. Naylor, he was called. He'd a black eye. The other guy was big, grey-haired, mean looking, with the iron face of a merciless killer. His seat didn't seem big enough. His wiry hair scraped the ceiling. He called himself Addison when he took a call before they set off while his punk tried to outstare her, chomping gum. They were both smoking like fucking chimneys. The 4x4 stunk of it and of ugly masculinity. These bastards were for real.

As they drove across the car park she steeled herself for the horrors that must lie ahead and glanced up at the huge mill. It had been sandblasted and fitted with plastic windows. Looked as new as it would have done when the Victorians had built it. The winter sun gave it the Cotswolds colour of honey. Blue flashing lights scudded from the remaining APC but she wondered at the zero interest from the tenants about what was happening. Either everybody was at work, or it was another symptom of a world that no longer gave a shit.

They took the main road away from the town. It curved up the hill, leading eventually to the moors. Beneath them the railway snaked through an arctic wilderness of allotments and dilapidated hen runs. Rows of houses flickered past at either side, braced against the incline, the narrow streets thick with snow. Vanessa could see for miles. In the distance a few surviving mill chimneys poked with some high rise at the clear sky.

After five minutes she asked the bastards, 'Where have they taken him?' No response, just the continuous drone of the X6. 'Why won't you tell me?'

'Because you don't want to fucking know,' Addison said ominously, blowing smoke.

'I care about him.'

'I'm sure you did.'

He laughed at his past-tense wisecrack and slapped the punk's arm. Five minutes of this stalemate crap became ten, splashing slush, passing endless urban clutter buried under top-heavy white.

She looked at her subtly varnished almond shaped nails and was aware of her naked body under Hunter's clothes, of the abuse in store for it. The punk turned to stare at her chest when they'd stopped behind a bus that was grinding up the hill. Banged up by support cups her boobs literally burst out of her shirt, nearly as big as watermelons, with a cleavage to die for. The dumb blonde bitch who'd watched her get dressed back at the flat had eyeballed them jealously. Her body armour didn't help but even without it her chest would have been fair game for a spirit level.

As the bus shifted and Naylor trod the pedal she asked, 'Where are you taking me?'

'The inevitable question.' Addison speaking, turning to give her the evil eye. He'd a matchstick stuck between his teeth but something loaded his smug expression. Not sex but the threat of sadistic violence.

'What are you going to do with me?' she insisted, when a new minute went live at the dash clock.

'Not surprisingly it involves sex,' Addison said. 'Most things in life do. Our orders are to kill you, and as far as they're concerned that's what we'll do. But we're going to keep you alive as our bit of stuff on the side. We'll feed you and look after you but we won't hurt you or make you suffer because *we're* nice guys.' He winked at his punk. 'What Sandra will do to you is another matter. Have you ever been laid by a woman?' The answer was an emphatic no, but she didn't say anything. His matchstick stuck out as his head went to profile. 'Most guys get off seeing a pair of birds humping but it's a scary spectacle. I never realised that, if they're both feminine, one of 'em still likes to play the bloke. That's the fucking weird bit. And the girl bird likes to be stuffed by a king-size dick. So why not by the real thing, instead of by a lump of fucking rubber made in China? It still comes back to a guy's codger. What a fucked-up race of depraved creatures we are.' He made a noise

301

through his teeth. 'Whether you're male or female, gay or straight, life boils down to the shagging of a hole.'

As if on cue his phone went off at his tit. He fished in his coat for it. It was a woman giving orders. Vanessa knew who it was straight away. She couldn't tell what the bitch said but heard something about plenty of rope to loosen her up. Rope was cop-speak for Rohypnol. Date rape drug. If they got that into her she'd fucking had it.

The moors got nearer, the snow got thicker, whipped into crazy shapes where it had fought the wind. At a cross-roads up ahead traffic lights changed from green to amber. Naylor eased on the brake as the gap closed, the lights hit red, and everything outside stopped moving. There was so much new snow up there it reflected the sun and lit up the inside of the car, dazzling Vanessa. The bastards stubbed their cigarettes and stuck on shades. Addison reached in his pocket for a woman's wafer-thin gold watch, the expensive kind that clips to her wrist like a bangle. Vanessa saw tiny jewels glinting instead of numbers, on a face not much bigger than her own little fingernail.

'You fucking thief,' Naylor said.

Addison smacked his lips like a bum retard.

'It's to placate the fucking wife,' he said, hula-hooping it round two fat forefingers. 'There's an inscription on the back but it'll buff off.' He squinted at it in his giant hands. 'Christ knows how she saw the fucking time.'

Sunshine flooded into the X6 through its back window. Vanessa sensed it shift as something got nearer. She turn-ed to look. A big silver 4x4 whizzed up close, dwarfing the X6 when it arrived. It was a Lexus, white with salt spray. As it pulled up its four litres growled like a pent-up beast. No, like a Porsche turbo on acid. A pretty young black girl

sat at the wheel. High cheekbones. Great Dusty Spring-
field bob hair. A good-looking young blond hunk filled the
seat next to her. Lantern-jawed. Scarred left cheek. Bunched fists like rocks at folded arms. His perfect suede crewcut made him resemble a life-size Action Man. Both guy
and gal wore white leather snow fatigues and wraparound
mirror shades.

Sensing something was afoot Vanessa checked up front.
The dickheads were oblivious, lighting fresh cigarettes and
talking Sky Sports. Still wondering, she turned back. The
blond hunk pulled on a white baseball cap then took off
his shades, so she could see his intense sea-blue eyes, and
discreetly pointed down. She did as asked, in time to see
the Lexus's number plate do a back flip. Green digi words
scrolled against black:

> **< WE'RE WITH YOU VANESSA! >**
> **< DON'T WORRY IF WE DISAPPEAR >**

As the plate flipped back the guy made sure that Laurel
and Hardy weren't watching then grinned, held up a reassuring thumb, showed teeth as white as the snowy verge,
coolly hooked back his shades. Bang. An adrenalin rush
hit Vanessa. Last night Hunter had said that Abigail drove
a silver Lexus loaded with weapons. This must be it, with
her guys, but how? *How?*

Addison's voice smashed in.

'What the fuck are you doing?'

'Nothing,' she said, turning back quickly.

Naylor was about to jump the lights when they changed. 'At fucking last,' he swore. He stuck his foot down and
screeched round to the right, towards the moors. Vanessa
saw the Lexus going off the other way. So did Addison.

He turned and watched it uncertainly till it disappeared, his eyes blanked by his cool tosser shades.

We're with you Vanessa.

Don't worry if we disappear.

But how the fuck had they followed her?

Hairs pricked at her neck and tears pricked her eyes. As they drove into what seemed like vast white space euphoria swept over her. Revitalized, all she could think about was the moment last night when Hunter had kissed her breasts as contentedly as a baby suckling from its mother. The world knew that guys loved breasts but it wasn't interested in how it felt for women. When a guy kissed and petted a woman's breasts it struck at what it meant to be female. Maybe it went back to the intimate thing male and female shared at the start of life.

She knew they'd come to save her but she was scared of looking back. The snow was getting thicker. The bastards' smoke stunk fucking awful. But now there was hope, for him as well as for her.

FiFtY

Hunter knew where they were taking him as soon as they came off the motorway. They entered a sprawling industrial park north of Manchester where he kept seeing signs for HM Central Prison. He was curiously resigned to his fate but wondered why they were taking him there instead of killing him at Genny's flat.

He knew a bit about it. Had even filmed it, which was when he'd had his first run-in with Driscoll. It was the biggest prison in Europe being built in phases over a five year period. As they headed up the snowy approach road the massive Phase 3 administration block, fat perimeter wall, and yellow trim of the buildings gave it a sci-fi audacity. It looked like a big SFX model covered in flour. Every time he saw it he thought of those chunky concrete buildings in *Thunderbirds* that slid back to reveal supersonic airliners. It had the same retro angles and top-heavy control towers, which were the architectural stamp of the Modernist Revival. Even the air vents, handrails, and other relief details looked like Airfix bits stuck on for effect.

Controversy surrounded the new twenty-storey Phase 3, which was under construction. When the APC stopped at the gates he looked up at the massive scaffolding-loaded tower, looming in the clear sky. It was skinned with ribbed blue plastic laminate that colluded with stainless-steel trim hotspotting for the afternoon sun. Huge chrome letters ran its height, ominously proclaiming:

MATRIX

CM was scheduled to relocate from Glasgow in 2019, meaning the world's most comprehensive DNA database would be on the same site as the world's biggest ultra-modern prison. Rumour had it that a new high-security wing was also being built underground. He hadn't heard if the helipad atop Phase 3 had been commissioned yet but saw a police gunship fly away from it as the APC set off and started hitting bumps.

They arrived at a service bay under the tower where two goons unloaded him and frogmarched him through a building site of bare breezeblock, exposed cables, and fresh plaster. They put him in a lift and took him down to an isolation wing three storeys underground where *Star Trek* sliding doors, worked by keypad codes, zipped open and closed and everything was clinically stark and minimalist in its lack of aesthetic fuss. Grey studded-rubber matting covered the floors, dulling the sound of the goons' snow-booted feet. He got the feeling the place was strictly out-of-bounds, which seemed to confirm the new HS wing rumours. The copious amount of stainless steel made him remember what Abigail had said about Driscoll being linked to a construction firm.

The sci-fi theme continued in the modular futuristic cell they put him in, which was like the autodoc from the remake of *Alien*. A cot jutted from the wall like a grey plastic shelf. Facing it was a small table, which also sprouted from the wall, as did a pair of matching bucket seats at either side. At the other end of the cell a touch-operated WC and a small stainless-steel washbasin were set in blow-mould-ed casings growing from the floor. Everything was fixed down so it couldn't be used to assault the warders or for self-harm by inmates. Two sliding doors squared off, be-sides the one where he'd been brought in. Fingerprint-sen-sitive keypads worked them both.

Driscoll had warned of extreme violence and impending torture. As Hunter tried to get his head round it, and took in his surroundings, it was as if a spark inside was snuffed out. Trying to stay cool he sat on the bed while one of the goons fetched him some water from a cooler set in the wall outside. When he came back, and Hunter had drained the paper cup, his mouth still felt parched. He asked what had happened to Vanessa.

The second guy looked amenable, with less of a nasty glint in his eye than his beefy sidekick, who was a grunt doing a job. 'They're gonna shoot her in the head,' he said, in nasally Scouse. 'At least it'll be quick.' He stabbed some fingers at his own head and popped open his eyes. 'Bang! I'm not taking the piss, mate, but if it's any consolation she won't feel a fucking thing. They're gonna bury her up on the moors. That's all we know.'

They shuffled out and the door slid shut, sealing him in. He felt a spasm of anger then of utter despair as he psych-ed himself. His only companion was a low rumble that he felt through his feet, like the distant engine room of a ship. He sat, elbows to knees, and tried to get to grips with both his women being dead because he'd meddled in stuff he should have fucking well left alone. He was cold, hungry, shit scared, wearing only his glasses, a bathrobe, and some elasticated slippers. He stood up then sat down then stood up. The blow-moulded, battleship grey walls seemed to be closing in. He imagined them splattered with his blood. Regardless of this, and the shit coming his way, the fact that he could rationalize his thoughts made him more determined to fight when—for the first time in his life—he faced a terrifying, stomach-churning reality. Knowing that he'd need to kill, to try and stay alive.

FiFtY-ONE

Naylor turned into an access lane leading down to a gigantic reservoir. Vanessa had seen it glimmering through the pines and sensed it was their destination before they'd left the main road. The concrete retaining wall holding it back swept away at the head of a wooded valley. The moors all around it were thick with snow. They might have been in northern Canada, not at the roof of the world in northern England. The bastards had switched on the radio and were arguing about a pop song. Naylor said he liked it but Addison swore at it and said how much he hated the homogenous pap that passed for modern music. He fished in the glove compartment for a CD, shoved it in the player, and pumped up the volume.

Naylor relented as The Cult's 1985 hit *She Sells Sanctuary* kicked in. It was the 12" Howling Mix, which began with wolves howling. And as the X6 got serious with the drifts and bumped down the hillside towards a parking area in 4x4 snow mode, these idiots howled, like a pair of happy slapping teenage tossers. Naylor chewed his gum stupidly and eyeballed Vanessa's chest in his rearview when music boomed from the Xplōds behind her.

Before Anna stopped, Steve dived out of the Lexus, high-jumped the snowy wall, and tonned it through the pines carrying his machinegun.

He was glad they were onto Vanessa. Three hours ago Abigail's watch had started moving, after being stuck at CPHQ for fourteen hours. Hoping to find her alive they'd tracked it to the edge of the Yorkshire Dales. Reached the mill to find it crawling with cops. Trained their binocs on a top floor window from a snowy backstreet at the other side of the railway. Saw Vanessa. Saw Hunter. Wondered what the fuck was going on. Hunter supposedly blown up. Abigail in his hotel room eight hours later. Driscoll and his goons disposing of her body then abducting Hunter and Vanessa miles from the city. They saw Hunter being loaded into an APC. Fifteen minutes later Vanessa was bundled into the X6. When it set off they pursued, Computer tracking Abigail's watch signal being beamed from the big tosser's pocket. But when they caught up with them at the crossroads, and were about to take out the X6, Sir Ian told them to hang fire, in case the thugs were taking Vanessa to where they might be keeping Abigail and Mark. Less than a minute ago, the X6 had unexpectedly turned off the main road. By the time they'd caught up it was going down the reservoir lane. It was too dangerous to follow, in case the jerk at the wheel saw them and they harmed Vanessa.

Steve made it to the trees overlooking the reservoir. He threw down his machinegun and *fwumped* onto his belly in the snow, just as the X6 arrived at a parking area a hundred metres below. He locked on to it through his binocs as it pulled up, stark and blood red against so much white. Its thudding music died, then its engine. The only sound left was the big roar of water gushing from an overflow at the bottom of the dam wall. The frozen snow was gilded with winter sunshine.

Steve zoomed in as the big guy got out waving a Sheuze then opened the back door and dragged Vanessa out with his free hand. Bang. Up she came in 235:1, her breath puffing backlit for the sun. She flicked her hair from her eyes with a horsy jerk of her head and flared her nostrils at the big guy as he stuck the Sheuze in her gut. Steve reckoned she was old enough to be his mum. Just. It made him want to protect her even more, although she looked well capable of looking after herself. His mother had died when he was a kid, before he really knew her. It had left a big hole in his life.

In the Lexus, Computer was scanning. Anna sipped a can of Nescafé, watching the screen and praying for Vanessa's safety. The POV through Steve's binocs was relayed back. Computer minimized it then brought up Google Earth. An aerial view of the reservoir lunged close, trees blurring as he whizzed in to get a bearing.

'There's a farmhouse in the valley,' he said, 'at the edge of the trees. I'd surmise it is their likely destination.' As he said this, a CG image of the house jumped up then minimized over the Google image. At the end of the dam wall a flight of steep narrow steps led down a sheer cliff. Computer zapped a red line along the wall and down the steps, to the house. 'The lanes leading to it are blocked,' he went on. 'This is probably a back way in on foot, because the trunk route is still open.'

'I see it,' Steve said over the speakers. He was still panting from running. Computer patched through his Google image to Steve so that it minimized in his binocs.

Anna asked Steve, 'Why don't you fire a warning shot? Or let Computer blow up the X6?'

'Too dangerous. They're armed and might throw her over if they know we're here. We'll have to sit tight till the cavalry arrives. If they're taking her down to the house it'll buy us some time.'

Sir Ian had reckoned they needed some heavy support to see Vanessa's rescue through to a successful conclusion out there in Alaska. He'd enlisted the aid of David Kowalski's brother-in-law, one very unbent cop who was an AS in the Air Police and headed up some serious fucking firepower. He was on his way with his guys in a gunship but they were a good ten minutes away because they had to drop some nob off at CPHQ first. Everybody had assumed the X6 was heading for Yorkshire, till it had done a bunk at the border.

Kareem said, 'I'm on Central Matrix. Hmm. The owner of the house is one DS Sandra Blake, ex-PI, age forty-three. I'm pulling up her ID.' Anna heard him type before he bemoaned, 'Shit.'

'What?' everybody asked.

'One Miss Sandra Blake used to be known as Mr Roger fucking Blake.'

Everybody groaned, including Computer, reflecting the straight thinking of the all-action he-guys who'd programmed him. Anna puffed her cheeks at the thought of genital surgery and guys growing estrogen induced boobs as she knocked back her Nescafé.

On Computer's screen Steve panned from the house to the X6 when the driver's door opened.

Vanessa watched Naylor get out of the X6 sucking his butt before he flicked it away. His shiner sung against the snow as he turned to look nervously at a motorway spanning a gulley in the distance. 'This is fucking crazy,' he said, turning back.

'What is?' Addison asked.

'What if somebody sees us from the motorway?'

Addison looked at Vanessa with the despair of Oliver Hardy confiding in the camera, but said to Naylor, 'Can you do something for me?'

'Sure,' he said, like an obedient dog waiting to fetch a stick. Vanessa thought he looked like a nasty piece of work but she also knew that not all his slates were nailed down. Addison obviously enjoyed taking the piss, to give himself some comedy relief.

'Stand over there and look at the motorway.' He winked at Vanessa. Naylor duly went across puffing steam, which pulsed gold for the sun. Addison was lighting a cigarette and asked him through it, making it bob, 'Can you see the drivers in the cars?' Smoke and his breath clouded as he shook the match.

'No I can't,' he said, and shook his head.

'No you can't you stupid fucking bastard. Just like they can't see you.'

312

The cars and lorries were vague dots, moving this way and that in a soundless steady rhythm.

Vanessa realised she was nearly as tall as the guys in her moonboots with their heated three-inch-thick solid rubber soles, powered by batteries that snapped into each heel. What the bastards didn't know was that standing in the boots switched them on, keeping her feet snug and warm. Addison turned her round, dug his gun in her back, and shoved her across the car park towards the vast angled wall. It swept away from them in a wide, curved grey arc for maybe a quarter-of-a-mile.

As they hit the wall crunching snow and the yellow handrail began, Addison said to her, 'I said that we intend to keep you alive as our bit of stuff on the side. This young bastard would like to give you one but I'll boot polish his other eye for him if he tries.' Naylor frowned, obviously unsure of what was being implied. One of his shoes had started squeaking as the foot inside got soggy from a leak. Addison went on, 'But I'm not interested in having sex with you. Believe it or not I've never been unfaithful to my wife. I'm a businessman and you're my latest proposition. Have you noticed how the minority of shit at the top of our society is as corrupt and morally bankrupt as the minority of criminal scum at the bottom? They're incestuous. They do drugs. They don't care who or what they shag. To sustain themselves, both groups exploit the huge body of honest folk in the middle. So I intend to exploit the tossers at the top by catering for their squalid perversions. Guys who'll pay to have a bird as posh as you are high-fliers, into all sorts of crazy fucking things whose wives won't play ball. As for the birds.' He named a prominent Tory MP's wife. 'Her eyes popped out when I e-mailed her your

313

photo. She'll pay well to gobble you for an hour.' He despaired and shook his big head. 'They're all at it, the birds more than the fucking guys. I'm beginning to feel like a closet heterosexual. But it means we can clear five grand a week from you. Are you on the pill?'

She didn't say anything. She was wondering where the Lexus was. It was maybe twenty minutes since she'd seen it but the spinning number plate seemed like a sicker joke than Addison's ranting.

He stopped her and jabbed the Sheuze into her, asking nastily at her ear, 'Are you on the fucking pill?'

'Yes I am,' she said, half wondering if now might be the time to Glasgow Kiss him and tip him over the railing. She thought better of it as the gun dug deeper and he set her going again.

'Good,' he said. 'And that's how we'll keep it. The last thing we need is a fucking sprog buggering up the cash flow.'

FiFtY-TWO

Hunter typed randomly at the keypads but nothing happened. He spat at his hands and tried to force the doors then dropped to his knees to look under the gaps but there weren't any. The doors ran in shallow steel channels lined with airtight rubber seals.

Tanked on adrenalin he got up and rushed about the cell banging the walls, to see if they sounded hollow. Nothing. There was no way out. He half expected Driscoll would be spying and would kick off laughing any second now from a hidden speaker. Then he sensed movement through the door where they brought him in. It hissed open and Driscoll swept in, still in uniform. Two uniformed goons tailed him and took up positions by the door, their squat, square young faces impassive.

'Aren't you impressed?' Driscoll asked, poking the keypad to close the door. As it glided shut he glanced approvingly at the cell like a salesman unveiling a world-beating product. No, like a madman, Hunter thought. 'It would make a great TV film for you, like discovering the existence of UFOs.' Smirking, he paced round Hunter with his hands knitted behind his back.

'Nobody's told me where I am,' he said, turning to keep the bastard in his sights.

'I'm tempted to say you're about to enter your worst nightmare,' he said. 'But surely you've worked it out? You said at the news conference the other day what the Police Federation is lobbying for.'

Jesus Christ, he thought as it hit him. He'd half thought it when they brought him down in the lift but hadn't believed it because his thoughts were all over the place and he assumed the world abided by the old rules. How naïve and ridiculously middle class. He remembered some brilliant song lyrics from his student days. Their searing indictment of the modern world. Of progress being a rapist. Of the world of tomorrow being here to stay.

The old world was dead and had been dying for a long time. Bastards like Driscoll were making the new rules.

What drove it home was something Hunter thought when he came into the cell and realised there was more than one door. He'd seen this before when, as a student, he filmed in the old condemned prisoner's cell at Wandsworth jail, just before Britain's last working gallows was decommissioned. Now his eyes flipped between the other doors and it hit him like a brick in the face. 'Jesus fucking Christ,' he said, feeling a definite chill.

'Yes,' Driscoll said, relishing the moment. 'You're in the condemned prisoner's cell of Britain's first brand-new state-of-the-art execution facility. It's the first of its type and the most advanced in the world. It was planned five years ago and its construction over the past two has been the most closely guarded Official Secret of modern times. It's because of its existence that Ministers will push Greenhalgh's bill through.'

'Let me guess,' he said, discreetly checking the concentration of the goons over Driscoll's shoulder. 'I'm the first condemned prisoner.'

'You're our prototype. We need to test it. Break it in, so to speak. It would be easy to pick up some dope addicts on a Saturday night and do the world a favour. But for something this important I want to christen it with somebody against whom I hold a grievance.' He set off again. 'Note the two other doors. That one'—he waved a hand—'leads to an infirmary kitted out with the latest technology where the inmate is prepared for execution. The door behind you leads to the execution chamber proper. Note also the studded-rubber flooring. It deadens the approach of the secondary warders as they arrive to assist an inmate through to the gallows. In the old days they used coconut matting.' He stopped pacing. 'You see, apart from such practical considerations, and the fact that this place has been built to kill people, the inevitable Human Rights tosh means we're obliged to make sure it doesn't intimidate prisoners while they await disposal. What won't surprise you, as an educated man, is that we nicknamed this cell Room 101 while it was being built.'

Hunter was reeling from hearing such a nonchalant use of the word *disposal*.

Again, Driscoll picked up his expression and ran. 'Yes, I like the term "disposal" myself. It sounds more up-to-date, don't you think? And don't look so put out because things do go on which neither the media nor the public know about. Bastards like you think you control the world nowadays through your fucking sneering and via TV and the fucking press but you know only what you're allowed to know. It was the same when secret underground bunkers were built to protect the Government in case of nuclear war. The construction of this place was no different. And there you were, getting worked up about a worthless dead MP when something far more high concept than a humble fucking murder mystery was unfolding.'

'I'm not one of the sneerers,' Hunter reminded him.

'No you're not. But you keep digging at stuff and beavering away when you'd be better off leaving well alone. There's a natural balance to be maintained if the Western world is to survive. The police see it because we're on the front line. Violent criminals are a disease that should be cut out like a cancer. If a vicious dog attacks or kills somebody it's immediately destroyed. When the same instinct surfaces in human beings we absolve them from any responsibility for their actions. This place is a long overdue reaction against such fucking liberal lunacy.'

317

'It's the matter of "constitutional importance" is it?'

'Correct. My involvement is because I'm a director of the construction outfit that built it. It isn't finished and no date has been set for when it'll become operational. In truth, it's been built as part of a feasibility study and may be moth-balled and never commissioned. But who the fuck cares? We've created it and made a fat profit courtesy of the tax-payer. It's a terrifying glimpse of our inevitable future as it becomes ever more criminogenic.' He was obviously enjoying the intellectual exchange. 'You could say it's the trad-itional Victorian gallows brought up to the computer age by a bunch of cyber lunatics.'

'So Abigail was right,' Hunter observed.

'In what way?'

'She'd been watching you for a year. She knew all about your nice little business connections.'

'Did she?' Seeming pissed off he folded his arms, pro-cessing something internally that seemed to be a source of great irritation. He paced this way and that with compres-sed lips and narrowed eyes. 'And she convinced *me* she was a humble fucking writer . . .'

'And Greenhalgh and David Kowalski?'

'Their elimination was an unfortunate precaution to en-sure everything was completed on schedule and in total secrecy. Greenhalgh got greedy and Kowalski might have sussed the kidnappers weren't what they'd seemed. So, strictly speaking, a little PR assistance was necessary.' He seemed to become aware of time slipping by and flicked back his cuff to eye his watch. Crossed to the keypad on the wall by the main door and jabbed a button. 'Tell them to come down will you?'

'They're on their way, sir.'

Hunter's heart started going, now that he realised they were coming to kill him. Through blood pounding in his ears he heard Driscoll say, 'Everybody assumed that if the death penalty were ever reintroduced it would be carried out by lethal injection. Needles seem so much more humane, more in keeping with our high-tech world. The belief is quite misguided because as long ago as 1953 a Royal Commission concluded that hanging was the most reliable and humane method of execution.' He paused for effect. Hunter found the coldly formal history lesson as unnerving as his approaching death. 'Provided that certain precautions are taken, as I'm sure you're aware.' They heard movement outside. Driscoll stood aside, telling his goons, 'Hold him.' They crossed over and grabbed Hunter, wrenching his arms up his back.

Over the past few minutes his determination to survive had taken a reality-check. He was underground in a high-security jail, surrounded by machineguns, guards, electric fences, the works. He could no more hope to escape than he could punch his fist through a sheet of steel or lead next year's first manned flight to Mars. These thoughts ganged up as he decided his time was up when the cell door did the cool *Star Trek* thing and hissed open. But then, totally unexpectedly, it was nanosecond time, somehow in crazy fast-action slow-mo with a few freeze-frames thrown in for effect, like when the door blew off at Genny's flat and tons of observations hit him.

It started with the colour-coded studded-rubber flooring in the corridor. It was light grey but slate grey in a strip a foot wide at the edges. A fat red stripe ran along the walls, at waist height, with a big white letter C spaced at intervals. Makes sense, he thought. Third sub-level, third letter of the alphabet. He was still taking this in when he saw a grey something else. A human leg coming into the cell, encased in a utilitarian boilersuit with an incongruous-looking ankle boot at the end. Now his eyes jibbed up the body when the leg supporting it arrived with the other leg and stopped. This was the fucking weird bit because he sussed he'd been here before and taken the same sledgehammer hit between the eyes, two days ago.

Like last time he tried to take everything in, only to have the living fucking daylights knocked out of his senses. Call it shock, call it pain, even a kind of fright. His eyes made it to a beautiful face, passing a couple of generous bumps on the way. Amazing dark eyes, smudged with mascara from crying, gazed back. As before, they wanted to come to him except this time hurt instead of excitement loaded the eyes in this cell full of nasty, smelly men. *She's alive* he thought, over the moon at whom he saw, yet still disbelieving. But joy became pain became terror because he knew they'd have kept her alive for a nasty fucking reason. What was it the ugly dome-headed bastard in front of him had said in the apartment? *Now things take a nasty turn for the fucking worse.* An old 70s movie title flew back. No, a tatty paperback film tie-in he'd bought at a garage sale when he was a kid. On the cover was a bloody face with its eyes gouged out. The image had haunted him for days, trashing his sleep. He'd not forgotten the author's name. David Case. Published by Pan in 1973.

And Now The Screaming Starts.

Inside, he started screaming when it sank in whom he could see. He knew from her expression that she wanted to scream too. Stoneham was with her, digging a Sheuze in her gut. The evil dome-headed bastard called Driscoll had brilliantly engineered the emotional explosion of the moment and was revelling in it. *Abigail was still alive.* She was so beautiful it hurt. Hunter wanted to go to her but when he tried to move the goons held him. He rewound to getting off the crappy little bus in the blizzard the other night and a feeling of utter futility hit him. He must have missed her after all. If he hadn't, they wouldn't both be trapped with these bastards.

FiFtY-THREE

Abigail didn't suss it was Hunter because she wasn't fully compos mentis. She saw a tall, hairy guy in a bloody bathrobe that was too small. He wore glasses and was heavily stubbled, with a swollen mouth. His nose was caked with dried blood. Then it hit her who it was and she knew what people meant about time standing still.

'Ah yes,' Driscoll said, sensing the effect she was having on the struggling figure, obviously savouring it, 'the proverbial catch in the story.' He taunted Hunter with, 'Did I neglect to mention that when we shot her we used a new tranquillizer?'

'You said you'd killed her!'

'No I didn't. I told you that we'd shot her. I won't deny I said it in such a way to make you jump to the wrong conclusion. But I never said we'd killed her.'

She could feel that her hair was messy. Some was hanging across her face. As Driscoll nudged it back fastidiously she clocked the look in his eye. She'd seen it when he'd interrogated her in Hunter's room last night and kept gawping at her legs. She'd seen it when he'd deliberately made her think they were going to kill her and he'd stood like a tosser with the gun, eyeballing her along the laser to see if she'd break. She knew what was in his mind right now, and what he'd do to her before the day was out. She'd instinctively flinched when he'd touched her and said, 'Keep your filthy hands off me,' as if she'd ticked off a troublesome brat.

She saw him chewing at her insulting tone as he took a half step away. He'd done the same when she'd put him in his place while he'd stood gloating over her first thing that morning, when she woke up. He said calmly, 'I told you not to speak to me like that again,' but before his half step made it to a full step he whipped back and something exploded. It was pain in her bruised belly. She remembered seeing hate in his eyes when he thumped her and saw his fist swing again but her legs gave way before the second hit. Driven down by such a savage blow the floor zoomed up. Embossed grey studs got big. Impact. As the new-rubber smell hit her something crunched. Her nose felt like it had broken and nerves jumped in her front teeth because she'd hit the deck face down.

She heard a shocked Stoneham despair angrily, 'Jesus fucking Christ,' as her tongue went to her teeth, to check they were there.

Knocked for six, she scrabbled about and tried to get up but couldn't. She saw legs and trendy pseudo-Goth booted goon feet then flopped onto her back and saw big guys going away in perspective to the backlit sci-fi panels running across the ceiling. Hunter was struggling, snarling, swearing at what Driscoll had done. For a few moments his feet kicked as they were hoisted off the floor. She saw Driscoll closing. He was going to lace into her. With no expression, with a vicious brute strength that seemed disproportionate to his weedy build, he grabbed her by the scruff of the neck and lifted her. She tried to curl into a ball to defend herself. Fighting with her, losing it when his top blew, he manhandled her across the room and dumped her by the door where she'd come in. When he lifted her again and smacked her hard across the face she realised her nose had burst from the floor collision. Blood splashed the walls and Driscoll's shirt. He drew up his fist ready to go for it then suddenly backed off when Stoneham moved forward like he'd decided enough was fucking enough.

Driscoll threw her down and stood aside, demanding that Stoneham get her out of the fucking room. She coughed hoarsely, her head swimming as Stoneham helped her to her feet, hooking her arm over his shoulder, and reached up to open the door. Driscoll was a maniac. She knew he'd a history of violence against women but something else was happening and she couldn't put her finger on what. She'd got an inkling last night, like some realisation had dawned on him while he'd grilled her about Hunter. She was drowsy from the drug but as she mentally flipped back over his OPQ report it hit her when she remembered what she knew about his fucked-up childhood.

Hunter had felt the assault as much as her and was only grateful that Driscoll hadn't used his feet. It was a pitiful moment when Stoneham opened the main door and helped her out of the cell. When Hunter saw the skidmarks she'd left in her blood, and heard her gulping and retching from the corridor after the door hissed shut, he got a handle on what flipped Bruce Banner enough to turn him into the Hulk.

Driscoll seemed hyped and was shaking with rage as he wiped his bloody hands across his blood-spattered white bent cop's shirt. Hunter could see that Abigail had got to him but he couldn't put his finger on the fuck why. He obviously fancied her but it was like he resented himself for it. Glowering at Hunter he got it together and said, 'You're thinking how you'd like to fucking kill me, aren't you? But do you know why you can't fucking kill me, apart from the fact that I'm about to fucking kill you? Because you'd never sleep decently again. Cardboard heroes can kill as the finale approaches and walk away and feel no remorse. But not real human beings like you. Oh no. This is the real world. The reality of this cell, the reality of the events in which you're embroiled, is the reality of a boot stamping on a human face *forever!*'

He stood back and nodded at the goons. To their credit, Hunter knew they hadn't liked it when they saw Abigail being fragged. No guy in his right mind could bear to see another guy beating up a woman. Sensing it was execution time the smellier, spottier goon tightened the bathrobe-belt but Driscoll intervened. 'No,' he said. 'I think it would be symbolic if we hanged him naked.'

He tore off the bathrobe then knelt and ripped off the medi-slippers. Hunter felt exposed, limp penis and all. The goons held him in their vice-like grip and turned him to face the death chamber. He'd lost his specs in the scuffle when Abigail was beaten. Through the open door he saw a blurred futuristic noose hanging spotlit against darkness, swaying almost imperceptibly above the gallows. Some fancy piece of kit was fitted to the knot but he couldn't tell what it was. Black-and-yellow safety tape marked the centreboards sending a chill down his spine, carrying on the sci-fi theme he'd clocked since coming underground.

Before he'd got to grips with what was going to happen the goons had hoisted him up. Then in true penal tradition they pinioned the prisoner's arms, to stop him struggling, and frogmarched him through.

FiFtY-FOUR

They'd made it to the far side of the reservoir.

Vanessa could see a flight of steep narrow steps leading down to the valley. Hidden in the trees at the bottom was a farmhouse. Under thick snow its stone-slated roof had sagged with age. An abandoned railway ran in the background, its embankment visible as a horizontal white shelf through wintry branches. Water roared hundreds of feet below. She saw it shooting from a short fat pipe, throwing up spray. Before they descended she stopped. The snow was deep on the steps, making them treacherous because they were hidden. Only blurred declivities suggested they were there. She knew she'd slip. 'I'll fall,' she said, holding up her bound hands.

Addison got out a Swiss knife and cut the tape. 'Don't even think about it,' he said, catching the look in her eye and waving his Sheuze. 'You're going down first. I'll kick you over if you so much as fucking flinch.'

On the dangerous side of the steps was a sturdy galvanized-metal banister, running at waist height. No railings under it. Instead posts supported it every few feet. At the other side a steep snowy slope, tufted with heather, fell to another cliff.

They went down sideways in convoy. She led the way, gripping the banister firmly to support herself, her hair dangling. The dickheads slotted their feet in the holes she left in the snow, which gave her a satisfying feeling of control. The sound of rushing water steadily grew. Because of it Addison raised his voice to ask her, 'You're not scared of heights are you?'

'No,' she said, concentrating on her hands. As she looked up through her shaggy hair she wondered if she should have lied. The sun blazed overhead, dazzling low from a clear sky. As she squinted up at it she saw the black-eye-kid behind her and sussed he was doing some nervy REM thing. Bingo, she thought, clocking his acrophobic mug. *He was shit scared of heights.* His latest cigarette smoked at his goofy gob. He wouldn't want bastard features to know. As she turned back to the banister she glanced across the valley but saw only the red blob of the parked X6. Maybe the guys in the Lexus were waiting down at the house. Hoping so she crunched snow slowly, trying to find the next step, and the next.

Steve zoomed in through his binocs from the pines above the car park and scanned the three figures puffing steam.

Vanessa kept flicking back her hair with kicks of her head so she could check where she was going. She gripped the banister confidently, holding it like dirt-bike handlebars. Tension was cranking and Steve was getting cold lying in the snow. The backlit trees behind him spoked shadows out before him. He hit scan and filled the sight-masking with the bald kid's pale HD face. He looked like he was scared of heights and was about to indulge in a technicolor yawn. The approaching chopper thudded in the distance. They'd decided to sit tight till Vanessa and the guys hit the bottom of the steps. Spooking them halfway was asking for trouble. They'd probably shoot her, or throw her over. Computer had scanned the reservoir and calculated that the noise of the water at the bottom of the steps would cancel the sound of the approaching gunship. Giving them a tactical advantage.

When they were maybe a quarter of the way down Vanessa heard Addison's phone ring.

Dismayed at the timing he fished for it and snapped it open saying, 'For fuck's sake,' then told her to stop as he stuck it at his ear. Because of the overflow din he'd difficulty hearing and had to jam some fingers in his other ear. He leant awkwardly against the banister shouting, 'What? Pardon? I can't fucking hear you.'

Vanessa's mind raced. She saw the immense concave wall bending away from the cliff, giving the Hoover Dam a run for its money. If looking at it made her feel giddy it would be squeezing shit out of the gun-poking punk behind her. Despite the Lexus being around, she felt totally alone and sensed that time was running out. When she'd trained as a ballerina in her teens she used to show off to the boys in the village by kicking up her long legs. Joanna Lumley once played a cult 70s TV character, who'd also trained as a ballerina but adapted it like kung-fu. Vanessa clung to the memory as she came to terms with her life or death ordeal. Her weekly gym sessions meant she was still super-fit. Unknown to these boneheads it was her trump card, as her gorgeous guy found out the hard way last night in the car park.

Naylor's smoking cigarette smarted his eyes. It had been marooned at his gob since it went in. He tried to aim his piece at her while he supported himself against the banister and the REM thing cranked.

Vanessa heard Addison yack to his phone that Hunter had been taken to Central fucking Prison and that somebody else should go there. When he'd finished he stuck his phone away and told her to keep going. She was mightily relieved to think Hunter must still be alive and shouted up, 'Why's he been taken there?'

'Just keep fucking going,' he shouted back.

She did but Naylor didn't.

'Fucking come on,' Addison said impatiently.

The punk didn't move.

Addison shouted, 'Stop,' to her.

She stopped, looking up at two pointing Sheuzes. Naylor was rooted to the spot, his face losing colour, his eyes doing the big squeeze. He looked puke sick.

'Move it!' Addison shouted, losing it, snorting steam like a restless bull.

Naylor shook his head. Said through his bobbing cigarette, 'I fucking can't.'

'What do you mean you fucking can't?'

'I can't fucking move!'

Addison booted him straight up the arse. Naylor cried out as his legs went from under him and he struggled to keep his footing in the snow. Kick number two made him let go of the banister. In the split second it took him to grab it again his Sheuze had flown away from his hand towards Vanessa, six or eight steps down. She saw it spinning, a chrome bit kicking sun. Addison saw what was happening straight away as her survival instinct kicked in. It was one of those crazy slow-mo CGI moments. Addison posing to aim his Sheuze at her. Naylor's Sheuze reaching its apogee. When it started falling, her hand flew out to grab it. Addison had instinctively let go of the banister to aim his piece with both hands, like some movie poser fart-face on two fat sticks. Big mistake. His clodhoppers went from under him in the slippery snow and his vast body tipped forward, making for the horizontal.

At the same time, Vanessa thought she heard a missile whiz in across the valley followed by an immense fucking *bang* from the car park. She saw the X6 lifting, partying with fire. Snow blew out from it in a centrifugal circle like the ring-of-Saturn thing at the start of Hiroshima. Up the red mess went, arse-first, as it came apart. A second explosion expelled wheels, the bonnet, a tangle of torn red metal. The doors ripped off bullet-fast through spreading flames. The lump of burning scrap cartwheeled through the air with a fantastic agility for something so big, like a toy thrown by a giant's angry kid.

Vanessa snatched the Sheuze as it arrived, knowing that her life depended on it. Out of the corner of her eye, the X6 nosedived down the opposite cliff, dragging fire and the railings from the car park. Her right forefinger slotted into the Sheuze's trigger guard. Her palm received the sweaty, still-warm grip. *Somebody's looking after me.* Inexplicably, she thought of David Kowalski but something else drove her. *I have a life to live with the guy I love and I'm gonna fucking live it.* She half saw the X6 fireballing through snowy trees, the fencing clattering behind it like metal drainpipes, doing dumbbell acoustics.

Knowing she'd no time to flick on the gun's laser all she could do was crouch and aim. Addison was still falling towards her. Naylor still scrabbled between them, scratching grubby digits at the sky as he also fell. A few seconds had passed since the gun left his hand. Addison fired his piece from mid-fall, the slug leaving as Naylor found his footing and shot upright in front of Vanessa. Uh-oh, she thought. Mr and Mrs Naylor's piss-ugly brat just pulled the short fucking straw.

The poor bastard never knew what hit him as the nasty dumdum slug blew away his left shoulder in a spray of gore, demolishing his humerus and scapula, meaning his arm no longer joined. He looked lost as he went headfirst under the banister, devoid of the arm, kicking snow. Instead of shouting he sort of barked as his cigarette flew from his mouth. His severed limb got left behind. It still held the banister by its badly nail-bitten fingers when the rest of him had gone. Then some stray fabric that must still have been joined from his coat tugged at the sleeve still wrapping the dismembered arm and took it with it. Vanessa sensed rather than heard him as he started bouncing, screaming hysterically, down the cliff. His arm did some gymnastics as it boomeranged away to open space, trailing raw meat.

She'd shot at Addison but narrowly missed. By now he'd hit steps and was falling messily towards her, filling the space left by Naylor. He lost his Sheuze as he tried to steady himself and came at her so fast he might have been sledging down the slope. Snarling he changed his fall to a dive and collided with her before she knew what hit her. Unable to stop him she pulled his big weight on top of her and fell backwards, her Sheuze flying. As they went tumbling down the steps, grappling violently, he tried to grab her throat and knocked off her glasses. Somehow she was able to take advantage of the momentum and use her legs like a pole-vaulter's stick. She levered him up in the air so that he rose vertically right over her, through a hundred-and-eighty, and slammed onto his back behind her. But the force of lifting him on a steep slope took her with him. Panicking, she somersaulted backwards and also did a hundred-and-eighty. Felt a terrific pain crack her right ankle as she came face-down, hard on the steps.

Addison slid away feet-first, ploughing snow, *veering under the banister*. Panic flashed at his face when he realised he was joining his punk. Vanessa was still sliding down the steps and flipped onto her back to steady herself. But as Addison shot away from her *he grabbed one of her feet, taking her with him*. Realising, she cried out. They were sliding to their deaths, bobsleigh crazying down the hillside. Addison reached the grassy tufty bit at the cliff edge and kept going. White spray fizzed up, hitting her face. She saw a flash of blue sky and grey dam wall. *They were going over*. Then, as she went between two fence support posts on her back something else flashed above her. A silver bar, slicing across blue. She shot up her hands and grabbed it, bringing them to a sudden stop.

Her legs felt like they were ripping from her pelvis and her shoulders like they were wrenching from their sockets.

331

She was holding onto the banister and Addison was holding onto her legs. Maybe fifteen stone of him, flailing and snarling, hanging on for his life. They were dangling over open space but she rested partly on the cliff edge, *taking their combined weight*. She pictured the weights she shoved up and down at the gym and screamed not from pain but from the will to live. *Then from pain*. Searing pain from the ankle that took the hit as Addison thrashed on the end of her. She looked down her chest and saw the bastard looking up at her, wild-eyed. Snow fell away as they struggled. Because her glasses had gone everything further than ten or twelve feet away was blurry. She couldn't kick him free because he was clinging to her legs.

She looked up at the steel bar. Her knuckles were white. Bones and veins bulged. Her arm muscles felt to be tearing loose and she was slipping. Addison got spooked when he sensed it, sliding right out to open space as they crept ever nearer the precipice. She felt herself going but managed to grab the left post with her left hand as it fell. For a few moments, crying from pain, she held their combined weight on one hand till she'd locked her elbow round the post. Mega pain kicked in when her bicep tendon hit raw metal. She swung her other arm across to the support post on her right and did the same with her right elbow, thanking God for her puffa coat. She managed to slap her hands round the posts at each side and held on. Her elbows locked her in position, in the gap between two ice-cold posts. She felt like she could hang on for England, if her hands didn't freeze from holding bare sub-zero fucking metal first. The snowy sloping cliff supported her bum and back but Addison dangled right out. She felt him struggling and swinging and kicking at midair.

Then something smashed into her belly. He'd lunged up to grab her belt, locking his hand round it to support himself. His heavy weight pulling dug it into her hourglass bit. Ankle pain ripped through her while he made triumphant ugly noises and started *climbing up her*. He swung again with his free hand, whacking it into her chest, grabbing the shirt under her breasts. But the studs popped loose due to his weight and he slumped back, clinging to the belt, leaving the shirt ripped open and her breasts exposed in their big white support bra.

For the first time in her life her chest was a hindrance due to its size. She couldn't see Addison properly because her boobs were in the fucking way.

FiFtY-FiVE

Steve was on his way, powering along the dam wall. He'd dived down the snowy slope from the trees as soon as the kid fell. Told Computer to go for the big guy's feet, to ensure he didn't hit Vanessa. He carried his machinegun. His binocs were velcroed to his tunic to stop them flapping up into his face. As he ran he looked across the reservoir and saw the gunship zooming in low above the water, driving a concussion wave before it. He had to fucking save her. She was his responsibility. They'd let her down, big time. They'd cockily told her not to worry via the clever number

333

plate trick and she'd nearly died. As he ran for all he was worth he shouted to his Bluetooth, 'We've fucked this one up, guys!'

'Pardon me Steve,' Computer noted, as he skidded the Lexus round to the top of the access lane, 'but Sir Ian instructed us not to attack. We couldn't anticipate that the X6 would turn off the main road. Nor could we speculate that the young man would accidentally end up being shot and fall to his death. Events unfolded arbitrarily.'

Steve heard Kareem saying, 'Computer, you're bullshitting when you should be saving Vanessa!'

'Pardon me Kareem,' he replied, 'I'm driving as fast as I can towards the access road leading to the reservoir. I was able to fire missiles without being in visual range, because they were heat seeking. To act on the present instruction I need to see the target. I haven't increased the odds against Vanessa surviving by even part of one second by pointing out the inconsistencies of Steve's analysis.'

In the Lexus Anna sat with folded arms and let Computer drive. She heard Kareem and a panting Steve swearing at him as he justified what he'd done and his 'scope spirographed at the dash. He was running the show, setting off as soon as the big guy took a dive.

They'd stayed out of sight behind the trees in case they were visible from across the valley. Computer blew up the X6 the moment the kid took the first hit up the ass, to distract the big guy and give the Sheuze time to reach Vanessa's hand. Only a super-computer could have scanned the situation, plotted the gun's trajectory, and reacted before the nanosecond knew it existed. He'd thrown her a lifeline but now things were going seriously fucking wrong.

As the Lexus bulldozed snow and hit the access lane the cliff steps came into view. The big guy zoomed in on Computer's screen when he took aim. Bang. Up came the kicking, booted feet, real tight in crystal-clear HD.

Anna knew her combat gear and recognised the black and dark-grey whoppers with trendy multi-grip soles as being like a cross between a Nike and a Helka GTX. Everything zinged portentously red. Goodbye feet, she thought. She watched them, anticipating, snarling, 'Die, you ugly bastard,' but feeling no remorse. This dodo was mean. She enjoyed doing the Robert Shaw *Jaws* thing with the empty Nescafé can in her hand, her red nail-varnish stark against so much sexy white leather. As she finished crushing the can Computer got to work. She heard him fire the gatling gun that was embedded in the Lexus's front bumper. Then a foot on the screen blew off the big guy's leg in a sickening bloody detonation.

Vanessa felt Addison jerk, heard him scream in agony. She saw a blurred silver blob across the valley, at the top of the lane. Realised it was the Lexus and thanked God.

She looked down and saw a booted foot boomeranging away in a splash of red, then sensed another impact. The same thing happened except this time the boot contained the lower half of a shattered leg bone flapping soggy, hairy flesh. Jesus Christ. They were shooting his fucking legs off like when the guy got shot to bits in *Robocop*.

Addison screamed and juddered again as bits of bone and meat flew up. The roar of the water killed the noise of the gunfire. Still he held onto her belt but now his other hand flailed helplessly. At last her good leg was free. She looked down and started booting him in the chest. Hated herself for wanting to kill him but knew she'd no choice because he'd kill her. She stuck the boot in again and again but the big bastard would not fucking drop. It hurt her other ankle each time she kicked. Then something spooky happened. She felt herself slipping but everything froze as time seemed to suspend itself. Sound faded to be replaced by her intense mental focus.

I have a life to live with the guy I love.

And I'm gonna fucking live it.

She looked down between her breasts at Addison's pleading face as his legs disintegrated under him. His nicotine-stained teeth split each time he cried, yet she pitied him with his hard pockmarked face and his short, thick grey hair. He was a nasty bastard but he was still somebody's kid. A mother had suckled him, feeling that unique feminine bond with her baby even though it grew into this fucking evil monster.

Then as their eyes met David Kowalski was in her mind again. *Kick his face. Hit his head. He blew mine off.* A shiver went down her spine. The pain in her right ankle was excruciating and her numb hands were so frozen they were turning blue at the posts. She knew she'd fall any second and stopped kicking. Instead she raised her foot. Suddenly she knew this lummox had killed David. She didn't know how she knew but she did. It was him she'd heard on the phone over David's intercom the other night. She drove her heel into his face and felt something crack but kept on kicking. Felt his front teeth cave in. Heard him spluttering and gurgling till something else gave way with her final, almighty downward kick and at last he let go. The relief when his weight ended was awesome.

He shrieked as he fell.

'Elaine!'

It sent another chill down Vanessa's spine, then a spasm of guilt. *I've killed a woman's husband. But he'd have killed you*, the voice said. *He's a merciless killing machine who'd have sold you for perverted sex.*

There was a moment when all she heard was the huge gushing of water from the pipe. She thought she heard another big rushing noise coming from the dam and was relieved to see the blond hunk from the Lexus coming down the steps. Before she turned back she saw something glint in the snow but couldn't tell what it was. Then, as happened to the punk, she sensed rather than heard Addison's impact hundreds of feet below. What she saw clearly, as she gazed down, was the effect of his body hitting concrete and exploding outwards in a visceral spray, somewhere at the bottom of the huge retaining wall.

FiFtY-siX

Minutes later the gunship flew away from the steps with Vanessa dangling from a cable in a harness. Her ankle was killing. An air cop shouted down from the open fuselage door that they'd got medical stuff aboard but she guessed rather than heard what he'd said because of the din. She'd to claw her hair from her face because of the downdraught from the chopper blades.

The lovely young blond guy, Steve, looked at her from the hillside and made a thumbs-up sign as she swung to open space and the valley opened out massively beneath her. He headed back to the top surrounded by snow flung up by the gunship. It had swooped from above the dam when she'd heard the big noise as Steve arrived. Even before he'd pulled her back up to safety she'd shouted frantically over the din about Hunter and Central Prison. Steve relayed the info to his guys, when he'd fetched her glasses, and assured her the cavalry was going in while he'd clipped her into the harness.

What she'd seen shining in the snow was the watch that Addison had looked at when they drove up. It must have fallen from his pocket while they fought. Steve said it was Abigail's and because of it they'd been able to track the X6. He was devastated when she confirmed that Driscoll had killed Abigail. He told her she could keep the watch as a lucky charm and that maybe Abigail had been watching over her. As she hung suspended across the dam wall she remembered Addison saying something about an engraving on the back of the watch. The bastard callously said he'd buff it off before he gave it to his wife. She turned it over and, squinting, saw:

To our wonderful daughter Abigail
Love always
Mum and Dad

Emotion crashed in. Vanessa had lived because Abigail had died and these loving parents no longer had their precious daughter. It was too much to bear. Through her tears she saw the vast dam lake, shimmering from the whipping blades where it swept back from the walkway. Sheer dirty concrete stretched beneath her, vertigo inducing because of its immense scale. Rusty yellow girders sprouted from a pump station at the bottom, where the water shot from its fat pipe in a long white column.

Then she saw Addison's Rorschach splurge, staining the concrete where the water hadn't washed it off. She could see another twisted bloody heap that was the smashed remains of the punk, surrounded by frenzied feeding birds. The X6 burned at the foot of the opposite cliff. She shut her eyes to try and get it together then realised her nose was bleeding. She stuck Abigail's watch away and waved up at the cop, putting some effort into it when she held her nose to stem the flow of blood. He did an OK sign with a thumb and forefinger and spoke to his mouthpiece. Another helmeted face appeared next to him and the cable began to rise quickly.

She felt nauseous, dizzy. Maybe it was the pain in her foot combined with the after-effects of shock as everything that had happened sank in. The pounding blades created a thunderous echo across the face of the reservoir. She looked up at the flashing hazards, which began to have a weird hypnotic effect. She tried to cancel the din by sticking her hands over her ears but when she let go of her nose blood poured from it. Everything was fading. She didn't want to resist because it seemed to be taking her closer to her loved ones. She started to cry as memories of last night at the apartment flashed before her, then frame grabs of her dad weeping at her mum's grave. She wanted desperately to be with Hunter, to get away from this nightmare, to spend Christmas with him at her dad's big old house, to live this wonderful thing called life.

Her life had been saved but even though Steve had assured her the good guys were on their way in, she'd a premonition they'd be too late. After coming so close, the prospect of life without Hunter was too much. Blood sprayed centrifugally from her nose in the downdraught and her hair swirled about her face. Panic hit her when key events from her life started playing in fast-action slow-mo and a numb blackness engulfed her. She felt her head flop forward and passed out.

FiFtY-seVeN

Hunter prayed that he didn't pass out while Driscoll tortured him like a cat toying with a wounded mouse. A motor hidden in the ceiling worked the noose. For the umpteenth time it had hoisted him to the point just before he'd swing off the floor, leaving him tiptoeing to stop himself pirouetting. He snorted and gasped as the weight of his body pulling at his head slowly strangled him. Not enough to KO him but enough to traumatize the thyroids and major blood vessels of his neck.

He knew about the effects of hanging on a human body. Although capital punishment for murder ended in 1965 it stayed on the statute till 1998 for acts of treason and mutiny in the armed forces. That's why he'd filmed in Wandsworth Prison. He knew from his research that not much pressure to the carotid arteries could induce unconscious-ness, even death. Driscoll knew it too. He was standing a few feet away at the executioner's control podium, which dominated the gallows like a bizarre futuristic pulpit. With his bloody shirtsleeves shoved back he poked a touch-sensitive plasma screen fleximounted to the console, looking as though he should be in the Transporter Room aboard the fucking Enterprise.

Hunter guessed Driscoll was taking him to the limits of physical endurance to monitor the results. His throat was rupturing. Some kind of hernia pain was being resurrected from his constant straining. As he crept higher his airwaves jammed up. He found it tough to believe that nutcases who were into autoerotic asphyxiation deliberately induced what he was going through to heighten sexual stimulation. He was being throttled but the last thing he could imagine was getting off on it. It made him realise what a fucking insane world he lived in, for how much longer he didn't know.

His toes only just touched the centreboards, which were slippery because they were covered in blood running from his nose. It had started bleeding again from the relentless aggro. As he was slowly strung up yet again he focused on Hayley and Jenny's happy young faces. Visualizing them gave him the will to live, fuelling his determination to see them grow up. Whenever he went back to his old home to collect them for the weekend he felt like a fucking pariah invading the picture postcard cottage that *he'd* bought. But the pain of losing them always eased as soon as they ran out to meet him and were in his arms. Nothing on God's earth beat the magic of receiving love and affection from your own kids.

341

But another reality crashed back in now because they always wanted to know where Aunty Vanessa was. *Vanessa is dead.* Rage made his eyes fill up as his feet went *en pointe,* cramping his calf muscles. Except this time he didn't stop going up. He tried to gulp air but couldn't.

As he swung away completely his weight was immense, hanging from his head. He sensed himself going an inch off the floor, two inches, five, ten. Panic kicked in with the onset of a red blackness. His eyes felt like they'd pop. He knew all about petechia, how strain from severe pressure could burst blood capillaries in the retinas. Earlier Driscoll had blabbed about the differing effects of death by short or long drop hanging. He'd got scientific and yacked about cerebral ischemia, carotid reflex, cerebral hypoxia, while he'd fingered his fucking fancy screen. The bastard had even lectured him on the super-sophisticated noose. It was basically an advanced kermantle rope similar to those first used in parachutes during the war. A bright-orange sheath encased numerous fine nylon threads. The properties of each stayed constant because they were made from plastic. Meaning the length of rope needed to snap a neck cleanly could be computed unerringly in relation to bodyweight. Such precision was unknown during the primitive days of horsehair rope hangings, when a bag of sand was dropped first to stretch it. If you didn't work out the correct length things could get messy.

Decorpitatingly so.

Still Hunter went up, choking. Now his spine was going and excruciating pain hit him. Something happened up his arse and even to the nerves in his teeth. Only the spotlight above the gallows lit the death chamber, dazzling him as he gasped and spun on the end of the rope like a spider dangling on a web. Out of the corner of his eye he saw Driscoll calmly knock back a bottle of water. The bastard watched him along it as he tipped it. Even took the time to smack back the nozzle and wipe his mouth before jabbing the screen when the computer beeped a warning. Then the rope dropped and there came a whole wonderful second of weightlessness as the centreboards shot up from eight or ten feet away.

Hunter couldn't have slammed into them faster if he'd been stuck to a rubber band that had stretched and snapped in a Road Runner cartoon.

FiFtY-EiGHt

When Stoneham ushered Abigail into the lift and took her back down to watch Hunter die she sussed what Driscoll's frenzied attack had been about.

Because she'd shadowed him for a year she knew more about him than he knew about himself. For starters, she knew from his psychometric profile that he equated violence with sexual satisfaction. As usual with the screwball elements of Britain's depraved ruling elite, it went back to his public school, where a teacher who later committed suicide had sexually abused him. As far as she knew Driscoll wasn't gay but he'd been deeply traumatized by what happened to him during his formative years. His suppressed anger had manifested itself by incorporating extreme violence into his sexual psychology. Beating a woman to make her submit, as he'd beaten her earlier—as he'd been beaten while he was raped—turned him on. It was the sick emotional template he'd absorbed. Fighting it seemed to have driven him, in some cockeyed way, to his top job. She even sympathized because like any sane person she hated cruelty to kids and thought convicted paedophiles should be put against a wall and shot.

But as the lift door hissed aside and they stepped across to the death chamber she realised something else was going on. Computer had dug it up after Kareem got hold of Driscoll's illustrated back story. *His mother was very beautiful, Abigail. She bore a startling resemblance to you when she was younger.*

It meant nothing till her subsequent digging led her to suspect that behind Driscoll's sexual anxiety was a mother complex. He'd grown to hate his mother but Abigail didn't know why. It went deeper than a bright kid being shunted off to boarding school and getting buggered by a monster who eventually did the world a favour. Something else had scarred him mentally, dooming him to a life of resentment and unhappiness. It had turned him into a vicious killer and a despiser of beautiful brunettes. Violence was his aphrodisiac.

As Stoneham typed at the panel she braced herself and focused on remaining calm, collected, super-cool. But the scene that met her when the door slid away was straight out of a Hobbesian fucking nightmare. It took her a few moments to absorb it while her eyes adjusted to the darkness and Stoneham ushered her across. Upstairs in her cell she'd done a deep breathing exercise to slow her heartbeat and induce a kind of controlled self-hypnosis. She did the same thing in Hunter's hotel room last night. It didn't prevent the shock of the denouement but got her to it with some semblance of womanly dignity.

The surroundings were simple, stark, more so than the rest of the facility. Embossed steel treadplate shone from the shadows. Industrial hazard tape zigzagged across the floor. Blue Expamet steps disappeared down behind yellow safety handrails at the back. She knew they led to the secondary chamber underneath. After a judicial hanging the body was left suspended for an hour till muscular contractions had stopped.

A clammy smell of new rubber hit her at the gallows. So did the stink of human suffering and the coppery stench of fresh blood. She didn't know where to look when she saw Hunter standing naked on the centreboards with a hi-tech noose round his neck and his hands tied behind him with a velcro strap. He tried to meet her eye but couldn't due to the angle of his head. He was suffering terribly. Veins embossed his forehead. His limp cock swung. He was covered in so much blood from his burst nose that it gave shock meaning to the term *blood bath*. It was matted on his hairy chest and skidmarked where it had dripped.

Stoneham went to a rack on the wall and unhooked two velcro straps then came back to bind her ankles and wrists. He went out via the condemned cell, but turned in the open doorway, where Hunter's bathrobe was in a heap, to finger the panel. Driscoll told him not to let anybody come down till it was finished. Stoneham nodded before slapping the keypad. Abigail noticed how he avoided her eye but as the door was about to cut him off he looked straight at her. His expression the same as when he'd gazed down at her on the cot when he'd taken her back up to her cell, after Driscoll beat her, and the same as when Driscoll was about to shoot her last night.

When the doors met the only sound was Hunter struggling on the end of the rope. Driscoll also avoided her eye, even seemed self-conscious as he poked the screen. It told her a lot. She sensed that he knew she was watching him, which told her even more.

Stoneham was alone when he came out of the lift. He switched off his phone, so it couldn't make noise, and took off along the empty corridor.

He'd made his decision after Driscoll had beaten her up. Violence was sometimes the only answer to difficult problems in a cruel world. Britain's whacko governing classes were no longer motivated to lead by setting a good example and could only hang onto power through being bent. Why? Because the moral strength needed for a society to behave itself and halt the slow decent into barbarism was in freefall as the West's rulers became ever more decadent and let their civilisation go the way of the Roman Empire. It meant that guys like Stoneham had got roped in to do some dirty work. But violence for kicks was unacceptable. He wondered if he'd try to stop it if Driscoll only intended to kill Hunter. Maybe. Hunter was a swell guy. He knew who'd shot at Greenhalgh's car but Driscoll had wiped the media at the IFI and had the lasers and the DVD. What impressed Stoneham about Abigail was that she hadn't asked him to stop what Driscoll was doing, probably because she thought it would be a waste of time. Regardless of the shit that was in store for her she seemed to know more about the true meaning of courage than most guys.

He got to where he was going. Set back in an alcove was the door to the Computer Room and UPS area. He typed at the keypad. Thought he heard a dull thud upstairs and a faint vibration in the suspended ceiling. As the steel door slid away he wondered if he sensed another thud but decided it was the builders jackhammering.

A slick pneumatic hiss sucked the door shut. The room hummed with live kit. Driscoll's droning voice and Hunter's choking down in the death chamber came up through a small hole in the floor. Everything was switched on because Ministers were flying up from London to check out the facility. Banks of computer cabinets went back in rows. At the end was the sheave mechanism controlling the rope leading to the gallows. It looked like a miniature lift pulley system with anything metallic still shiny-new. The titanium spindle slowly turned as it lifted the orange nylon rope with Hunter snuffling on the end.

Stoneham wasn't taking chances and pulled on a pair of surgeon's gloves. Took out a Bosch powered screwdriver and knelt to the sheave to flick back the housing. Through the hole he saw Driscoll standing at the podium, his bony face catching light from the spot like a death's head mask. Hunter dangled spotlit directly beneath. Abigail stood at the end of the centreboards, looking like she was in some kind of trance. Still the spindle turned. There was nothing Stoneham could do but wait till it stopped.

FiFtY-NiNE

Driscoll knew why he found her alluring.

She'd the same intense dark eyes and long dark hair, the same immaculate figure and amazing long legs. Her husky voice had the same educated confidence, giving her a commanding presence. Any discomfort he'd felt because of the physical resemblance had gone.

He'd popped a couple of pills before Stoneham brought her down. His body tingled with anticipation, as it used to when he walked down the long back garden to the summerhouse. Standing at the gallows he saw himself and his memories like an external observer, looking back at that long hot summer of 1976. It was always the same when he got ready to have a woman and strangle the life out of her while he did it. But as the drugs raced through his blood and kicked the neurocentres of his brain his past became less painful. He wasn't ashamed at being defiled by a dead pervert after forty years. It had scarred him but he accepted it and channelled it, building an accomplished career round it. Creating this magnificent execution facility was part of his healing process, eliminating vile diseased scum four decades on.

Abigail's lover, who'd given it to her with the lump of meat flapping as he strained on the end of the rope, was also due for elimination. Set into the podium console was a computer keypad but Driscoll preferred the touch-sensitive screen. He ran his finger up a CG diagram of the gallows and the naked figure lifted, spitting blood as it snorted in the light shafting down at the centreboards. When he'd gone high enough Driscoll poked the diagram to immobilize him then looked at Abigail. Her eyes were on his when they arrived. She obviously knew his vendetta was against her, not Hunter. Round one to the beautiful bitch, he decided, as the drugs hit and he saw her sitting on his bed on the rare occasion she noticed her son. He was the first to look away from her strange glowing eyes during that fateful summer.

Will you paint with me, Mother?

No, I'm reading my book.

For a few weeks a year he shared a house with a strange man and woman who were so cold emotionally they were incapable of knowing any intimacy with their offspring, treating him like an adolescent fucking lodger. The drugs helped blur the pain of this and their smarmy toffee-nosed voices echoing dismissively across the decades, while he floated across his father's hot study to Hunter carrying a roll of Duck-tape.

Will you play with me, Dad?

No, I'm busy. Go and play with yourself.

So he did, in the summerhouse usually. Sometimes he did it into articles of his mother's silk underwear, which he stole from her dressing-table drawer. It compensated for what happened in the musty attic during term time, when he was forced to be girly.

He stood behind Hunter, calmly raised a foot to shove the body, then stepped out of the way as it tried to swing back like a pendulum. Hunter managed to keep his toes touching the floor and steadied himself, twisting painfully from the effort. 'The only reason you can do this,' he snarled, watching Driscoll down his nose, 'is because you've strung me up. If I wasn't, I'd fucking kill you. And I would have,' he added, trying to swallow, coughing blood, 'no fucking qualms.'

'I'm sure you wouldn't,' Driscoll replied, tearing off a strip of tape and binding Hunter's mouth, garrotte-style, from behind. The naked figure panicked, as though it were drowning, skidding in its blood. 'Most of us are capable of killing if we're driven into a nasty enough corner.' He casually unwound more tape, wrapping it round the bloody face. 'It's the dilemma at the root of our so-called civilized society. It's to do with adrenalin. Perhaps this will galvanize yours.' When he'd gagged him he threw away the tape. Came round to face him and dropkicked him in the belly. Hard. 'Or this?' He lashed out harder when he saw his father load his golf clubs into the boot of the car while the gardener sucked his tatty roll-up slyly from across the vast parched lawn. Hunter snarled from behind the tape but he couldn't get away. His cock flew up with each kick as Driscoll's mother watched his father head off down the drive from her bedroom window. 'Or this?' He took a run at it this time and kicked Hunter savagely in the balls, angry when he saw the gardener throw down his spade and pull off his sweaty vest.

His mother had gone from the upstairs window with its 1930s lead patterning, the sky hazy blue above green Cumberland slate. He wandered down the sultry back garden across the gallows towards her an hour after his father had pissed off, wondering where she'd gone.

Where are you, Mother? Creeping up to the summerhouse window when he heard moaning cumming from inside. He arrived in front of her at the gallows. Saw her eyes drill into his from across the centreboards, as he grabbed her chin, in time to see the gardener kneeling behind her in the *bad position*. That's not how men and women are supposed to do it, he'd thought, recoiling from the dusty old window, his innocence abused, his sleep that night trashed by his mother taking it in the nasty place too. But going back to watch despite himself, jealously fascinated as he gazed into her eyes and confronted his shagging daemon forever knelt up behind him. *She won't love me but she'll let an ugly working-class shit do* that *to her?*

He took out the Sheuze that was stuffed down his belt. Snapped off the safety of his steel-and-chrome cock. Made it do digi chatter. Really fucking buzzing now, wading through the cum that splashed his life like snot saying, 'Does my behaviour repulse you? Surely not because I'm an intelligent man. I'm an *educated* man.' Circling her, stalking her, cranking to insane evangelical when he saw her kneeling on all fours in the summerhouse with her big tits and long hair dangling. 'But I'm also living proof of something more sinister. What did Yeats say?' Back in front of her, grabbing her chin again, contorting her mouth, hating her rhythmic gasping noises while the beetroot-faced gardener gunned her thighs and fucked the arse off her class with contempt. '*The ceremony of innocence is drowned,*' he quoted. '*The best lack all conviction while the worst Are full of passionate intensity*. Are you impressed that I can analyze my motives?'

It was what he saw when the gardener withdrew that sent him away crying. The image had haunted his life. He squeezed her mouth hatefully. Made her snuffle and snort through her nose. 'Does it, bitch?' he demanded, watching her at arm's length, running full pelt across the lawn, into the kitchen, up the oak-grained staircase, diving into her dressing-table drawer then straight onto the bed in his nice cool room to give it some wrist.

Abigail knew that he was aroused and wondered if he was hashed on spunk. He seemed hyped and out of breath, like he'd been running. As he let go of her chin his greedy expression said it. *I'm going to fuck you and then I'm going to kill you.*

Once, driving over the Yorkshire moors at night, she'd hit black ice and skidded off the road. Crashed sixty foot down an embankment. Rolled over and over and finally stopped when her trusty BMW 318i, her friend for 200,000 miles, fatally wrapped itself round a tree. Yet she'd walked away unscathed, convinced that her car had tried to save her by how it landed. What had happened was that her subconscious survival-driver kicked in. She'd never forgotten how she felt after that near-death experience. Triumphant. Pissed off only by the heather muddying her legs as she'd trudged back up the freezing hillside in her high heels. Two drivers who'd stopped were amazed at her calmness. The recovery guys said the shock would hit later but it never did and she knew it never would. She wasn't engrossed in herself enough to let it. She remembered heading into the black unknown, after she'd left the road, but saw herself walking away unharmed even while her car did the big flip.

She felt the same determination now, staring into the eyes of her killer. She drew on the NLP creative visualization techniques used by top sportsmen and the motivational coaches she'd trained with in the States. Basketball players who imagined throwing the ball into the net before they played consistently scored better when they did it for real. As though antagonized by her resolve Driscoll waved his gun, to warn her against making an unexpected move, then ripped the strap from her ankles and drove her across to the podium with the Sheuze dug in her belly.

'I'd like to show you something,' he said. Her heels banged treadplate. Blue light from the screen hit their faces when they arrived. He kept the Sheuze in her gut and typed, saying spitefully at her ear, 'Do you know what'll happen if we don't compute a length of rope that's proportionate to Hunter's weight?' She knew but didn't answer. 'Well, let me tell you. Either it'll be too short, meaning he'll dangle on the end of it and die of asphyxiation because his body won't jerk at his head violently enough to snap his neck. Or, if I feed too much rope from the ceiling'—he typed, whacked Enter—'*this* will happen.'

Words flashed at them:

He mocked her. 'What does it say, Abigail?' The stink of his shit-bad breath was so strong she could almost taste it. 'Let's hear it.' Still behind her he stuck the gun against her head and shouted, *'What does it fucking well say?'*

'It says he'll be decapitated,' she said coolly, seeing herself being free, feeling Hunter deep inside her.

'What was that?'

'His head will come off.'

'I'm sorry Abigail but I can't hear you. I don't think your lover can hear you either.' He jabbed her with the gun and groped her breasts, snarling through gritted teeth, *'What does it say you fucking lousy bitch!'*

She yelled, *'It says, "Subject decapitation imminent! Compute correct fucking rope length"!'* Hunter was paralyzed on the end of it. Spooked by her shouting his eyes popped open above the tape covering the bottom of his face when he'd digested what she said.

Driscoll knew she was cracking and dragged her back over to the summerhouse window, really crunked now, getting higher as the hot summer faded. 'You brute,' his mother said to the gardener through Hunter's contorting bloody mouth. 'You vulgar working-class brute.'

He pointed the Sheuze at Hunter at arm's length, fired off six or eight rounds, but deliberately missed him. Something pinged around the summerhouse after each *phut*. He grabbed Abigail's chin again, deforming her face when the last ping ricocheted from treadplate. He jammed the gun to her forehead, ripped open her boilersuit with his free hand, exposed her tits as he emptied himself into her silk knickers on his bed. *I wanted to love you, Mother,* he told her accusingly as he lay back, watching flies move at the green mottled-glass shade hanging on its old twin-flex fucking wire. *For you not to send me away again.* What was it a fucked-up Norman Bates had once said, in scratchy black-and-white?

A boy's best friend is his mother.
In the normal world is.
See you at Christmas, darling.

Bang went the black car doors at the scrag-end of the chrome bumpered era. *I don't want to go back, Dad*, as they went down the drive, the car stinking of his father's cigar smoke, his *Daily* fucking *Telegraph* folded neatly on the back fucking seat.

You're not being bullied are you? No answer as the Rover turned left at the gates. He looked back, in time to see the gardener throw down his spade and rip open his shirt. *Hit the buggers back if you are*, said the ex-military man next to him, doing his smug ho-ho fucking laugh.

Driscoll slid the gun barrel down and forced open Abigail's mouth with it, now that she was kneeling in front of the gardener and the summer was rewinding to its final painful blow. *No Mother*, he pleaded as she opened her mouth and the Sheuze went in, depraving herself. *Please Mummy*. He shook his head, revolted yet fascinated, unable to stop watching. It spat in her face before he could pull the trigger. The fucking repulsive thing that raped his life from behind, through never-ending cum tears dripping from the end of his mother's nose. He ripped the boilersuit off her shoulders but couldn't get it down because of her tied hands. He quickly went behind her to pop the waist studs holding the boilersuit top to the bottom. Then he peeled down her pants ready to force her into position. Hunter snarled and thrashed on the rope when he clocked what was happening.

'Kneel down,' Driscoll said hoarsely, his voice loaded with anticipation while scenes from his past gang raped him. 'If you don't, I'll blow your fucking head off.'

He stuck the gun to her neck and made to push her to the floor but something was seriously fucking wrong. The gun in his hand had changed. His mother wasn't in front of him. He saw a plastic case with its lid up. Inside were several small bottles and a hypodermic gun set in contour sponge foam. He lifted an ampoule, drew clear liquid into a vessel that formed the barrel of the gun then took it out and assembled it. Felt for his jugular, stuck the gun at his neck, and fired. But it just fucking *clicked*.

Baffled, he aimed at Hunter and kept firing but the bastard just mocked him with a giant swaying cock that fisted then CGI'd across and punched Driscoll in the face. Hunter laughed at him but suddenly fell as the rope holding him snapped. He slammed onto the rubber matting, nonplussed as he unexpectedly did a George Bush and landed flat on his back. After he'd hit the deck the end of the rope fell limply towards him, like a great big Indian trick gone wrong.

siXtY

When Abigail saw the rope break she knew it distracted Driscoll and grabbed her chance. She turned to check over her shoulder then kicked out with her left foot as hard as she could behind her and hit him with the back of her heel on the shin. So hard she thought the bone cracked. Taking a hit on the shin was incredibly painful, and didn't he know it. He'd obviously OD'd on spunk but still cried out, his face whipping down as he auto-keeled and the breath got blasted out of him.

She spun and stepped back. Her hands were tied behind her but she steadied herself and got ready to take a drop-kick that would win Hunter and her the game of life. Driscoll's head was the football, heading straight towards her. She needed to kick it the length of the pitch first time. No, right out of the fucking stadium. Still the ugly puss came down as nanotime stretched and she aimed her foot, kicking harder than she thought was possible. She cried out triumphantly with the impact, her hair flying. The relief of hitting the bullseye was awesome. She was sure his front teeth had caved in because something spattered the floor. Barking as his head snapped up, he spat snot and staggered backwards through the shaft of light.

Hunter was on his feet, wondering what the fuck had happened. When the rope broke it threw back his head. He couldn't see clearly without his specs but thought he saw somebody move through the hole in the ceiling.

He ran across to Abigail and they stood back-to-back to untie their wrist straps. When his hands were free he unhooked the noose from his raw neck and ripped the Duck-tape from his mouth, grateful to breathe through it again. She drew the boilersuit back onto her shoulders and threw her arms round him. Driscoll thrashed about on the floor next to the podium. Hunter knew he was out of his head on spunk, going further under the more turned on by Abigail he'd become. The final pill had topped him. Now he squealed and started throwing up.

'He's OD'd,' Abigail said, studding her boilersuit back together but staying near Hunter.

'Why did he get tanked?'

'He must have been reliving something pretty horrific,' she said. 'He kept mumbling to me as if he thought I was his mother.'

Spunk was a Japanese sex stimulant known as the rich man's Coke-Viagra. The addict could relive memories like they were for real and get hit by multiple anal-genital orgasms. The pills were five hundred a pop, favoured by rich socialites and assorted tossers in the entertainment industries, compensating for the pointless vacuum of their self-indulgent lives.

Driscoll struggled to his feet but angrily tied the cut end of the noose round the fleximount bracket bolted to the podium. Then, still holding the Sheuze, he smashed his fist into the keypad. The centreboards split open, sending up a volcano blast of light from the chamber below. He blinked confusedly, like he thought Hunter might have been hanged. Then he saw him and aimed the Sheuze, swearing deliriously when the trigger multi clicked. Hunter knew the gun was empty. When the bastard chucked his spaz earlier and shot wide of the centreboards he'd fired off all eight rounds without realising.

They were distracted by movement from the corridor. With almost comical late timing the door zipped open and half-a-dozen blue-helmeted air cops rushed in. *Robocop*'d in scuffed Kevlar, waving machineguns, still panting from running, they hit strike positions and scored red laser hits straight at Driscoll.

Sensing the good guys had arrived Hunter felt immense relief but noted sardonically, 'You timed that pretty badly guys.' Turning to Abigail, he wondered why they were there. 'Stoneham?'

'Maybe,' she said, gratefully linking his arm.

The big burly Scouser in charge ignored Hunter but told Driscoll to freeze. 'Put down the gun, Chief Commissioner,' he said, creeping closer.

Driscoll ignored the order. 'I'm your commanding fucking officer,' he snarled, exposing his wrecked, toothless maw. His words were slurred, his strength fading quickly. The words had lisped because of his missing front teeth. With the posey chrome gun in his hand and his white shirt such a soaking cherry-red, puke-splattered mess he looked like a meathead who'd walked out of *Reservoir Dogs*. Still stunned from being kicked in the face, he blinked hard as he tried to brandish his piece.

'Put down the gun,' the cop said again.

'It's empty,' Hunter told him.

'What?'

'He zeroed it earlier.'

Furious, Driscoll kept pulling the trigger, swearing with each *click*. Despite the knife-edged tension it was a sign of the cops' training that they didn't flinch when they heard the empty chamber doing its thing.

Driscoll fell to his knees and knocked the Sheuze away from himself as he crouched on all fours, moaning. There was a welcome lull filled with heavy breathing as the guys did a Jack Bauer with their weapons. Suddenly there was fresh movement from the podium. It was Driscoll, snarling with renewed energy. The all fours thing had been a trick. Snatching up the noose from the floor he hooked it over his head then scrambled across and took a dive feet-first towards the open centreboards.

Everybody jumped but Hunter was in pole position. With amazing speed he leapt at Driscoll as he started to go through the hole. Being a filmmaker he saw what happened like a fast-action-cut in an old *CSI* cop show. Saw himself move lightning fast to a funky *whooshing* sound when he reached out and up whipped Driscoll's wrist, super close, to a stylized *wunch* and a pop of white light. Grabbing the hairy forearm with both hands he braced his bare feet against the long edges of the hole while the flailing figure swung under him.

The cops froze.

All eyes were on the naked Hunter but nobody was going to laser him after what he'd been through. Or maybe, he wondered, favouring the possibility, they were willing him to drop him.

In a crazy twist of fate Driscoll's life was now literally in Hunter's hands. The other end of the rope was tied to the podium. The noose was round his neck. If Hunter let the bastard go his head would probably get torn off, as Driscoll would have done to him if he hadn't OD'd. Where the strength to hold him was coming from he didn't know, especially with the increasing pain in his spine. But in that moment of triumph Driscoll felt as puny as a puffed-up young street tosser.

Hunter knew it was his call. Weighing it up he looked at everybody till something hit him like a bomb going off, the sense of loss blinding him with rage. Spending last night with the most wonderful woman he'd known. The private stuff they'd shared over the years, growing together and falling slowly, inevitably in love. The life they might have had. His eyes filled up as he looked down at the bastard who'd killed her. The physical pain racking his body after being strung up was nothing compared to the emotional agony and sleepless nights that lay ahead. But there was other stuff to consider. What dangled under him wasn't human in the normal sense. It had tried to kill him, twice. There was also the depraved act it would have committed against Abigail, not forgetting the week's roll call of murder and mayhem it had greenlit. And yet crazily, because of it, Hunter knew he'd grown. He'd been on an amazing emotional journey. It could be argued that Driscoll had thrown him the fucking map.

The bloody face grimaced with the noose still round its neck, still tanked, lacking the strength to struggle. He just hung there, defeated and pathetic, expecting, waiting to die. Hunter looked at the cops but they gazed at him, entranced. Through his tears he looked at Abigail, who looked at him knowingly, slowly shaking her heard. His sense of power over the life of this fucked-up uniformed animal was electrifying but he didn't like it. It wasn't in his nature to exploit the suffering of others, even when they deserved it. The floor of the secondary chamber was a good ten or fifteen foot away. The least he could do was unhook the noose and drop him, hoping he'd break his useless fucking legs. But he couldn't lower himself to the level of a brute. Nor could Abigail. Which is why she stepped up to him and gently squeezed his shoulder, when she sussed what was in his mind. Five minutes ago, yes, when it was a fight to the death. But killing him now would be cruel. Hunter looked down and said reluctantly, 'You were right, you bastard. I'd never sleep decently again.'

It was a signal to the cops. One of them untied the rope from the podium as Hunter hoisted Driscoll up and threw him on the floor next to the hole. The moaning, grovelling

361

mess tried to crawl back to the gallows before several cops engulfed him. Bits of his teeth showed in the bloody puke where he'd sprawled. He deliriously insisted he was their commanding fucking officer and waved at Abigail when a couple of the cops pulled him to his feet and frogmarched him out, treading bloody bootprints.

SiXtY-ONE

Hunter was lying on his back in the infirmary next door to the condemned cell. It was clinically white, packed with futuristic hardware and other sci-fi looking stuff. He wondered if the dead PC screens fleximounted to the consoles would ever be switched on.

The cops had left him alone with Abigail, who was standing over him, cleaning him up. She'd filled a melamine bowl with hot water and was washing off the caked blood from his face and chest with antiseptic wipes. They hadn't said much. He was thankful they were still alive and content to watch her wonderful glowing eyes search his while she fussed over him. When she got to his mouth he winced and asked if he looked a mess. She shook her head. 'The swelling's going down,' she said.

At another time they might have cracked a joke. Instead she gently wiped under his nose then dunked the cloth in the red water and wrung it out.

He was glad they were together but he knew she was trying to weigh everything up. After their ordeal it seemed crazy to think it but he wasn't sure how he felt about her now. He could see how she felt about him because it was in her eyes. A few days ago he'd been besotted with her. She was one of the most beautiful women he'd ever met, with an intense, even formidable presence that drew him like a magnet. One minute she'd unexpectedly come to his hotel room and spent the night with him. The next minute he thought she was dead after he was thrust into the same situation with Vanessa. Then he discovered that Vanessa was dead, only to find out that Abigail was still alive. Fly-in-a-bottle time emotionally. But the thought of scurrying back to Abigail when they were both vulnerable would be disrespectful to the memory of Vanessa. He suspected that he'd end up in a committed relationship with Abigail but would need time to shoehorn himself into it. He couldn't go through what he did with Vanessa in bed last night and switch his feelings back to another woman as if nothing had happened.

Earlier he'd told her what they'd done to Vanessa and wondered if it was why she'd gone quiet. Her tears had stoked it up for him and he'd felt himself going when it all started to hit home. Now that he was entering the fallout period he knew he'd have to come to terms with the biggest loss of his life, worse even than losing his kids because at least they were still alive. As emotion welled he decided that losing Vanessa might eventually destroy him. He sought solace knowing the real grief would come later, when he was alone.

Then he wasn't so sure. A young black air cop appeared at the cell door, minus his helmet, knocking back coffee.

363

He'd a shiny shaved head and a stand-up comic's cocky, squashed-up mug. He blurted in nasally Scouse, 'Vanessa wants you guys to know she's safe.'

A bomb detonated in Hunter's head. With a vehemence that had no effect on the cop he fired back, 'This had better not be a fucking wind-up!'

The guy grinned and strode across, making his boots clump rubber studs. 'She said you'd swear and accuse me of taking the piss. She's on her way down with a fractured ankle. Apparently two bozos got demmied. It was in self-defence because they were gonna snuff her. Our guys saw it from the air. So did the young guy who pulled her back up from the cliff.' He slurped coffee and swallowed a burp but couldn't resist winking.

The next few minutes unravelled through a daze. Hunter wasn't religious. The world was much too nasty a place for him to believe his God could be so irresponsible as to let his wonderful creation slowly fuck itself, without intervening and kicking some serious ass. But when he thanked God this time he knew he meant it, the closest he'd come to believing the words. No sooner had he thought it than the other door slid open and Vanessa hobbled in, wincing with pain but still bossing the two young cops who supported her. Hunter struggled to hold everything back. She was wearing his clothes but they were soaked in so much blood that Abigail gasped. It looked worse than it was. He found out later it was because of her nosebleed, suspended under the gunship in its downdraught. He didn't know this then. Instead, it tormented him to think what they'd done to make such a mess of her.

He'd been on an emotional rollercoaster ride but had repeatedly careered off the rails. First Abigail was dead then she was alive. Then Vanessa was dead, now she was alive. Everything stockcar raced in his brain. No, absolute fucking euphoria hit him, thrown into the bloody omnium-gatherum of seeing a kid getting blown to bits and his own life nearly going kaput.

Now, after he'd nearly been slaughtered with Abigail in a subterranean hellhole, events felt to be reaching a satisfying close because both his women were still alive. Nothing else mattered. Realising it whacked him so hard it seemed to blank itself before it began. He knew Vanessa was overjoyed to find Abigail was still alive. But he knew she was also being sensitive to a potentially awkward situation and was careful not to give anything away about what happened at Genny's flat. As they all three consoled each other, jubilant that their tribulations were over, Hunter sensed an impending emotional abyss. Half-an-hour ago he was on the verge of being murdered. Such a short time later a new plight loomed. In its own bizarre way it was as terrible to confront as death.

He drew both his women against himself and wondered what the fuck he was gonna do.

siX MONTHS
LATER

siXtY-TWO

The hot sun blazed from high in the sky.

Songbirds were calling.

Fields stretched away from Hunter, smothered with buttercups. The trees and grass were a rich lime colour. For the first time in months his spirits were up. This was his favourite time of year. In the valley below he could see the mill where he'd stayed that snowy night with Vanessa. A steam train chuffed past it, whistling distantly.

369

The cottage stood on raised ground, its roof disproportionately large in relation to the height of its ancient stone walls. It was neat rather than charming. To anybody with an ounce of aesthetic awareness the small plastic windows seemed incongruous and ugly. At least the landlord had gone for oak-effect, instead of the garish white that blighted the other houses scattered about. Such things used to piss Hunter off. But the older he got, and the more important his kids were to his life, the less such petty environmental shit mattered. Or maybe a shift took place if you'd flirted with death. You stopped bellyaching but accepted stuff for what it was because you knew that life itself was the most precious thing of all.

There'd been little mention in the media of what happened to him before Christmas. At first this had angered him but then he'd resigned himself to a familiar cynicism. TV cameras, photographers, and reporters had been prevented from seeing the execution facility. The prison was effectively quarantined, suggesting powerful forces were still at work. No denial of the gallows had been made but neither had its existence been confirmed. He'd uncovered a matter of constitutional importance but the predictable whitewash accompanying the scandal known as Driscoll soon pushed it out of the news. This had worked to Hunter's advantage. In a televisual age written words had become the best way of conveying what he'd seen, massively increasing their value. Within days of his ordeal a bunch of literary agents had started falling over themselves, wanting him as a client. By the end of the week he'd signed a lucrative publishing deal, meaning that for the first time in his life money wasn't an issue. Nowadays the media was straightjacketed but books seemed exempt, suggesting that those drafting legislation assumed the public was too stup-id to read. Or, as seemed more likely, wasn't literate in big enough numbers to threaten their accountability.

Since early spring he'd been writing his book, living it up in some style in a rented cottage at the edge of the Yor-kshire moors. Each morning he opened the blinds and saw the mill in the valley. He saw it now, as he sipped a bottle of Perrier. The car park was as empty as it had been when the goons marched him out to the APC back in December. It was hard to believe what happened with Vanessa under the stone-slated roof. Even harder to imagine them arriv-ing in thick snow when everything now baked under the glorious June heat. In its own crazy way thinking back to being on the run with her held a weird nostalgic appeal. It had intensified the more into his writing he'd got. It was like recalling a wonderful dream, no doubt helped by the sense of adventure that heavy snow brings.

With the weather being so good he'd been sitting on the terrace working all morning. When his visitors unexpect-edly showed up half-an-hour ago he was writing about the drive to the apartment with Vanessa. His laptop was open on the ornate cast-iron table in front of him.

He turned it and read:

> As we neared Genny's apartment the landscape got hilly and the motorway went down to a single lane. We pulled off at the next junction and entered an old industrial district comprised mainly of mill-terraced houses and steep backstreets.
>
> So many phone boxes had been decommissioned since the mobile revolution they were few and far between. As we passed one, near a railway viaduct, I was tempted to ask Vanessa to pull over so that I could call Abigail. But if she'd called me today Dris-coll would have got a return trace and they'd be

monitoring her number. Incoming calls would be
picked up, including those from phone boxes,
giving away our location.

It was OK as a first draft but it wasn't how it happened.
Something was missing. He'd been through an astonishing
sequence of events and survived but there was no proof
because of reporting restrictions. The effect of this embar-
go was that, for the first few weeks, it left him feeling as if
he'd been recovering from a bereavement. The sobriety of
his life had fractured and in the process something of importance slipped away as deeper disillusionment hit him.
Until he got this into his story he wouldn't be telling the
truth. But something else was missing, which was at the
root of his problem, which he couldn't face in print. It was
as if a canyon yawned under him with a safe destination at
each side. He was stuck on a flimsy bridge in the middle,
knew he could go either way, but couldn't decide. Which-
ever way he turned he'd be consumed with immense fucking guilt.

He shut the laptop when he heard her emerge from the
house. Showing his manners he stood up as she crossed
the lawn towards him, smiling with her long hair flowing.
She was wearing a lightweight silk summer dress. The sun
caught it from behind, sending it translucent. When the
breeze rippled it he saw her hourglass bit. He'd had the
pleasure of exploring every inch of that wonderful body,
understanding himself better. As he held her, and gently
kissed her forehead, he felt privileged to have known her.
They were silent for several long moments. A final, quiet
contemplation was all that mattered. They'd said what
needed to be said the last time they'd met. He'd tried fucking hard but had pretty much ended it. Months ago he felt

as if his life were fizzling out. It happened to their relation-ship instead. He loved her, of that there was no question, but it was a different type of love to true love. He couldn't fail to love the woman who'd saved his life and he knew that she'd be a part of his life for the rest of his life. Every time he was with her, he felt an enormous debt although she was usually quick to point out who had really saved them both.

She'd known the break was coming.

They'd had some wonderful times together, especially an idyllic week spent walking in the Dales at the start of spring. But she knew that his heart was elsewhere. In her own heart she'd known this ever since he answered Van-essa's e-mail that first morning in his hotel room. The way he'd wanted to go walking so recently through the Wharf-edale landscape that bore her was one thing. But renting a cottage overlooking the mill where he'd stayed with her said it all. It was as if, by trying to escape from whatever troubled him, he'd inveigled himself with this cottage in readiness for whom he really wanted to be with. Now it was inevitable. Six weeks ago Vanessa had split from Max. They'd been living apart since the end of March, Vanessa with her dad near Harrogate. This was what had done it for Abigail. The sale of Vanessa's house in Hampstead and her decision to move back north permanently had forma-lized everything. She knew it was only a matter of time be-fore she lost Hunter.

She was smaller than him today because she was wear-ing flat-heeled strappy sandals. 'Thanks for coming,' he said again. 'It's been great to see you.' The only thing they hadn't discussed was his TV work.

'How long will you stay up here?' She knew. What she really meant was how long he'd stay, now that he was going to be with Vanessa.

'For a while,' he said. 'There's more opportunity than what there used to be. And with Internet TV killing the old broadcasting monopoly, everything's changing.'

They heard somebody blowing their nose and Mark appeared, stuffing a handkerchief in his trouser pocket. He'd used the cloakroom toilet while Abigail used the bathroom upstairs, before they set off on the long drive back south. He came across in a bright orange t-shirt, beige chinos, and brand-new Space Nikes.

'Cheers again Mark,' Hunter said, holding out his hand. 'All the best for the wedding.'

'Cheers,' he said, taking the proffered hand warmly.

Hunter had said that Mark's story should be a subplot in his book. When the laser hotspot had hit his forehead he hadn't been shot but was taken prisoner. He thought he'd heard the slug echo round the valley just before it split his skull because he had. The goon aimed above Marks's head to alert the other guys. From what Vanessa had since told them, they'd worked out that the phone call Addison took on the dam steps before he died was about what should be done with Mark. Hunter had constantly spoken of his indebtedness to his women. But for six months Mark had wondered if he believed in miracles. And to his surprise, more than anybody else's, he'd stopped smoking.

When Hunter heard the Volvo arriving with the crew he gave Abigail another hug, reminding her they should see each other soon. He let her go and watched her have a few words with Vanessa at the wooden gate. They hugged and kissed and said some private things they didn't want anybody to hear. Their affection for each other was plain to see. Part of Hunter's healing process was that he felt like he'd been blessed with them both.

Vanessa came across to him smiling. She was wearing a loose cream cotton voile blouse, a short brown suede skirt, and flat-heeled peep-toe shoes. She wasn't wearing high heels yet because she still had a vague limp. The doctors had said it would disappear.

Harry followed with Gordon, their hamster-faced cameraman of long standing, and Sarah. In the background the XJS reversed off the gravel with Abigail and Mark waving through the open windows. They disappeared with some beeps of the horn. A few moments later Hunter saw the silver car kicking sun through the trees as it raced away down the hill. Mark might have knocked smoking on the head but he still drove like a fucking lunatic.

There was a welcome lull, broken by the skylarks from way on high. Hunter felt as if a line had been drawn. The crew sensed he needed to be alone with Vanessa and lingered self-consciously on the lawn at the side of the house. It overlooked a scattering of quaint stone weavers' cottages. Most were three storey, less imposing than his seventeenth century merchant's house. They trailed, arbitrarily it seemed, down the cobbled lane.

Vanessa took the bottle of Perrier, when he held it out, and sat with him on the arbour bench seat. Her hair was shorter and he wondered if he could see some new lines in her face. She'd started wearing skirts a lot more. Today's rode nicely above the knee, not quite a mini because she wasn't a forty-something tart, but it showed off her perfect bare tanned legs, which shone for the sun.

'What are you gawping at?' she asked, grinning as she passed back the Perrier.

'What the hell do you think,' he said, smirking, deliberately looking at her legs. He puffed his cheeks before knocking back water then waved a hand, as if he'd overheated. His flirtatiousness was the starting gun. Her eyes twinkled as she shuffled closer and tickled him, making him spurt water when he laughed. He felt so fucking happy as he took her hand, feeling her shudder with anticipation when their fingers interlocked.

Turning serious, he gazed off and shook his head. Bees buzzed lazily about them while he measured a pause, saying, 'It seems so bloody long ago.'

'I know,' she said.

'But I don't regret what we did.'

They discussed their new film. They'd had a coup. Not long after they'd set up Real Life Pictures they'd approached Buckingham Palace about making a film following the Queen on the new Amtrak Royal Train. The Royals had vetted them for three years but finally consented in the spring. The resultant commission was greenlit on the basis of an excited one-word e-mail to their wimpish young exec at the BBC saying: BINGO!

It was fifty years that summer since the steam railway down below reopened nearly a decade after Beeching axed it. The Queen was coming in two weeks on the Royal Train to unveil a plaque for the anniversary, before crossing the Pennines by rail to open the new Olympic Stadium. It was a change from their investigative work but they'd decided it was necessary. Being allowed to travel with the Queen had renewed Hunter's faith in things and eased his scepticism after the whitewash of last winter. Shooting an intro that afternoon at the plaque site would be his first time on camera for six months.

When the crew had got in the car Hunter put on the house alarm and locked the front door but couldn't contain himself any longer. He embraced Vanessa on the flags and kissed her, taking her by surprise. As the kiss continued she let her bag slowly fall, moaning as she went heavy in his arms. He paused and saw the sun catching her beautiful sparkling eyes, inches from his. Searching yet submissive they aroused his natural protective masculine instincts, making him realise what a truly wonderful thing sexual love between men and women was.

'This is the moment,' he said, 'when you should say, "Where've you been?"' Realising he'd dropped a bollock by opening his stupid fucking mouth he added, 'Shit. That was incredibly selfish.' He shut his eyes tight and, deprecating himself more, spat out, 'Fuck!'

Laughing, prodding him because of his swearing, she tightened her grip and said, 'Yes, and I should say, "You took your bloody time didn't you?"' And yet it was a sign of her emotional maturity and her uncomplicated goodness as a human being that she'd given him his space. She hadn't hankered once, so conscious was she of the importance of their friendship.

'Did you always know?' he asked.

'Always.'

'No doubts?'

'None.'

'You're amazing.'

'No,' she said, giving no offence, 'a little older than you and maybe a touch wiser.'

He kissed her again then lowered his hands to her bum and pulled her by it against himself suggestively as he felt himself swelling.

'Will you stay with me tonight?'

'Of course I will,' she said. 'You know I will.'

And in that moment he knew he'd be with her for the rest of his life. The doubts, the insecurities, the emptiness, all disappeared in the blink of an eye.

He realised what was missing from his book. He'd deliberately kept his personal voyage of discovery out of it because it hadn't been resolved till now. He knew that he must go back and revise. Theirs had been a tale of action and adventure, of that there was no doubt. But by building everything around the framework of his love story, as the terrible events unfolded that led to the death chamber horror, he'd engage his readers emotionally.

There was an agreeable stillness. Perhaps he'd engineered it. 'I love you,' he told her, at last, finally at peace. Unable to contain herself she reciprocated before smothering his face with kisses. He'd never seen her looking so happy. Then everything hit her and for a few moments she lost it and became small, vulnerable, exquisitely feminine. He kissed the tears from her eyes and kissed her again deeply on the mouth, lifting her up off the stone flags. He wanted to devour her on the spot and wondered, stupidly, if they might come up with some excuse to the crew and unlock the house and go back in.

When they got to the car a short debate kicked off about who should drive. On the advice of her doctors Vanessa had been easing back into it, to strengthen her ankle.

'I don't mind,' she said.

'Neither do I,' he said.

Harry said, from the back seat, 'Why don't you toss a coin?'

'Good idea, Harry,' Hunter said.

He fished in his pocket for a coin and threw it up. They both stood back to watch it land. Typically, it rolled under the car. Everybody laughed.

'I'll drive,' Hunter said to Vanessa. 'I want to drive,' he told her.

When they were driving away down the hill *It's My Life*, by Talk Talk, started playing on the radio.

Coming next

To Kill the Queen

Turn the page for a sneak peek . . .

Picks up where the book you've just read leaves off. The Queen is heading north on the new Royal Train to open Manchester's Olympic Stadium. Hunter and Vanessa have been granted special permission to travel with Her Majesty to shoot a TV doc.

But before they can board the train it does the Bermuda Triangle thing and disappears. Dark anti-Royalist forces are at work. There are terrorists, big guns, ex-Soviet missile launchers, shamelessly bent politicians - and one helluva tough US mercenary who's built like a brick s***house!

It's Rambo meets the Great Train Robbery. They don't come much bigger, more explosive, more daring than this!

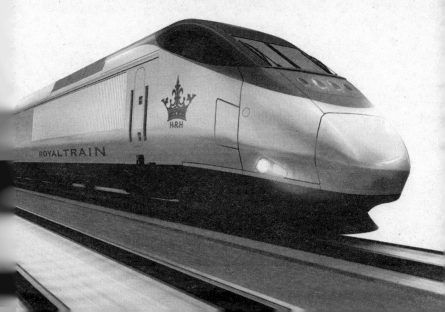

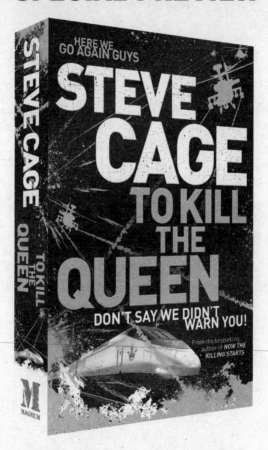

1

Craig Connors stuck his foot on the brake but it was too late. As he shot out of the mountain tunnel the road suddenly went AWOL off to his left while he carried straight on. To counter it he threw back the wheel, hard, but hit a serious fucking skid, heard rubber burn, saw double yellows snake crazying under him. Still the car refused to tango and slewed across the hairpin screeching blue smoke, towards the cliff.

1

He knew that to correct a tailspin you swung the wheel the other way but before he'd finished doing it he crashed through the guardrail out to where birds flew, seeing bits of shit crack his windshield. As a mile-deep canyon yawned he clocked the fierce revving of the car's turbo, now that it had no blacktop to chew. Saw the Alpine road he'd left getting tiny in his rearview and got ready to smash to smithereens. Before he'd set off Hartman had mentioned a stock shot in those 60s Brit TV cop shows where a white Mark 2 Jag crashed off a cliff. Connors was doing the same move more fast-and-up-to-date-furious, more Hollywood OT fucking T. Plus, he was going into it with attitude at a 120mph high in some sunny Grossglockner pass, not some crappy low-budget quarry in Hartman's dismal English Home fucking Counties.

The car nosedived then Connors saw pines coming from nowhere. He ripped through them vortex-fast and slammed into solid rock. Felt his legs trash as the car crumpled big time and slid down ass first, breaking up. He saw the engine pop from under the flapping hood and begin partying before glass shattered round him and fire rolled in. He was being totalled. Stunk himself doing the sizzly bacon thing in his fat as the fireball ploughed through branches taking half the fucking Austrian cliff with it. The last thing he saw before he died was a king-size boulder, meteorite-spinning at him CG fast. Then it was over and he got crunked by the big rock before a nanopause sparked the mega whiteout that topped him.

Or should have topped him, he thought smugly, or at least KO'd him. That was a neat trick with the surprise cliff the computer had rendered nanoquick. But even while he was being splattered he clocked the digi panel at the dash, coolly noting his pulse still rocking-and-rolling at a steady seventy-eight—the same as when he climbed into the simulator. That would piss the doc off. Chan, the sweet Thai pixie assistant, would be mightily impressed, as she had been by his six-pack when she'd exfoliated his chest with the abrasive pad before she stuck the electrodes to it that measured his HB.

The lights came on and the sim's gears whined slickly as it repositioned itself ready for the next punishment sucker. Thousands of tiny air jets and skin surface stimulators that had made it feel as if everything had hit him and fire had fried him shut down. As fans sucked away the toxin-free smoke clogging the cabin Connors snapped loose his harness and slid open the door. Not only had he pushed himself to the fucking edge he'd taken off from it. 'Seventy-eight,' he shouted across, grinning and making a fist at the guys, 'on the fucking button.'

'Impossible,' Doc Hartman's tinny voice said from the speakers. 'Not with settings so critical.'

'Nothing's impossible for the US of A's finest,' he threw back. As he stood up from the sim he karate-chop saluted the bony Brit face gooning at him through the sloping tinted glass but kept his grin going and held up a straight middle finger.

The control booth door slid open and the yellow-smocked Hartman emerged, still shaking his head in disbelief. Freeman was in tow, steel browed, steel faced, shiny fucking steel-suited, always looking like he needed to be some place else. Chan tagged on with that expectant *fuck me* look daubed across her pretty oriental face and seemingly half the height of Freeman, who ducked under the jamb as the doc yacked his stuff.

3

'The conscious mind knows it's not real but the subconscious doesn't. It's the same principle as an optical illusion. No matter how strong-willed we think we are, our senses cannot shut off completely from external stimuli. And with virtual reality sims being this sophisticated nowadays any normal person should black out with settings so dangerous. For it not to touch his pulse indicates an iron will. I'd say he's your man, even if he's otherwise another jumped up, sweaty beefy yank.'

'Tell me it didn't go one note over, you slimy over-educated pompous English shit,' Connors joked, overhearing Hartman's quip while he clumped down the blue Expamet steps.

'That's the upshot,' Hartman confessed. 'And physical stresses don't come much tougher. Oh yes, and I went to a mixed comprehensive, you big Arizona tosser,' he added, eye-winking as he punch-lined a wisecrack he'd left dangling earlier.

Connors got the joke and showed his teeth while he pulled off his t-shirt and let Chan unpluck the electrodes. Doc Hartman had a sense of humour. Ice-cold Freeman didn't. 'You're not even perspiring, Mr Connors,' Chan said, looking up at him with her narrow, silver-shadowed eyes. Her long fingers took their time at his bronze chest, tugging at the clear-rubber suckers.

'OK you've made your point, Craig,' Freeman butted in, clearly tiring of the macho tough-speak. He popped a plastic cup from the wall dispenser and stuck it in the cooler to make the sensor boogie and gush water. To Connors, well spoken but humourless English toffs like Freeman always seemed spooked by the grunt stuff. This particular streak of gnat's piss used to aid a very bent PM before opting for a life in the British SS. Now he picked up the full cup and, conscious of Hartman and the petite broad, handed it to the American brick shit-house who matched his height but was twice his width and three times his weight, then filled cup number two saying, 'Let's talk, shall we?'

They headed out onto a rooftop garden that baked in the midday sun. Vapour trails raking the blue sky pointed accusingly at Heathrow. After air-con, the greenhouse heat of the hottest British summer since '76 made Freeman puff his cheeks. Connors knew heat and strode through it to the balcony sticking on wraparound mirror shades and knocking back his ice water. Freeman hooked on retro Raybans like the specs Oscar Goldman wore when he briefed Steve Austin back in the 70s. He set his laptop on the concrete ledge. The grass framing the gov.uk complex had morphed to straw. Toy cars parked way over by the admin block simmered through a haze.

'You were determined to get the job, weren't you?' Freeman told him, firing the kit, loosening his necktie.

'I wanted to prove why I'm your guy,' he said. 'Under the circumstances you don't have a choice. I mean to make the hit, not to hire me for two million bucks.'

'I think we can take it as read that you're our man. Delegating an assignment that strikes at the heart of the British constitution to a kick-ass foreigner with, uh-hum, biceps excites the powers-that-be. But they still feel dirty because of the daringness of the plan.'

'Glad to know they got feelings,' he said, sipping water. 'I feel like an A lister who's been brought in to give US box office to one of your subsidized little social issue movies about which nobody gives a shit.' Definitely no sense of humour he decided, as Freeman gazed off, his eyes blanked by his shades while he tugged an earlobe, an oddball habit of his when he mulled.

'The dangers of this mission are—how would you put it?—"awesome",' he said, failing to match the observation with enough voice cool. 'They don't come much more high concept either because there hasn't been a serious plot to take out a reigning British Monarch since the days of Francis Walsingham in 1586. It'll bring the country to its knees and plunge us into a crisis of the first order, which is of course what we want.'

Connors was amused. Over the past ten years governments had hired him to do their dirty work, ostensibly for political gain but really to stockpile their financial booty. Nothing wrong with that. Western politics was now a kind of upmarket crime, but at least guys like Freeman stuck within the parameters set by 'democracy'. The alternative was to abide by the laws of the jungle, which nobody wanted. Connors decided when he was still a marine, and sussed how the West really worked, that its two political systems were opposing forms of corruption. All that mattered was which one best gave ordinary folks decent freedoms and living standards. Guys like him exploited financially the swift boaters at the top who, come election times, vied to dupe the unsuspecting masses with either bent system. He suggested this to Freeman while they watched a Virgin helijet drop towards Heathrow, hotspotting sun. 'Besides,' he said, turning serious, 'you thought you'd scored in the Fall but you sure as hell hadn't.' He meant the shit hitting the fan after the Michael Greenhalgh hoo-ha and the pro-hanging stuff going tits up.

'It's because of that little episode that we've upped the ante and that you and I are talking. Speaking of which, or

6

rather whom,' he said, poking the laptop screen and turning it so Connors could eye it in the dazzling sun. Up popped a grab of a good-looking dark-haired guy with longish hair. Next came an older, sexy silver-blonde broad with a ton of chest. 'Don't let their looks fool you. You'll need to give them a wide berth.'

'Hey, Hunter. Isn't he Mr Bolloxbag?'

'Yes he is, and he's been writing a book about it since March. As far as we're concerned it won't make publication but that's a bridge we'll cross when we get to it.' He fingered keys and made Central Matrix pile stuff about the broad down her side of the screen. 'He's breaking off to shoot a TV doc with her, not knowing that, uh-hum—how would you put it?—"big time shit" is headed his way yet again. She's his business partner but he's now her toyboy in the other sense because he's split from the sexy brunette who gave Driscoll his dentures. As award-winning filmmakers they've been granted special access to travel with Her Majesty aboard the Royal Train but had to wait three years for the privilege because the Royals do their homework and like to know who the fuck they let breathe their air. As a matter of fact,' he said, wrecking his neat silk cuff to eye his Rolex, 'they'll have just finished shooting the Yorkshire plaque Her Majesty thinks she's going to unveil later this week.'

'How come they're dangerous, if they're TV guys?'

'It's not so much them being dangerous as you needing to ensure the hijack happens before they get to Her Majesty. They're not due aboard the Royal Train till it leaves Manchester but are filming some trackside flypast stuff to the south of the city first. They're using two film crews because they'll only get one shot. Meaning we have a narrow window to make the Bermuda Triangle thing happen, on the main line north of Crewe.'

'So I got the job?'

'My dear chap,' he said, slipping back to Brit toff speak, 'there was never any doubt you'd be our man in the field. Meanwhile you've something else to contend with.' Two good-looking young Asian guys popped onto the screen. 'Others who are plotting to make life difficult for Her illustrious Majesty when she takes the train.'

'Reece told me about this. Shades of 9-11, huh?'

'Something like that,' he said, still fastidiously smoothing his cuff. 'It would be easy if they were the usual brainwashed simpletons holed up in some impoverished northern backstreet. But they're not. They're clever, well-bred types festering within.'

'Go figure,' Connors said, meaning it.

'Yes, 'Freeman agreed, this time with enough voice cool when he slipped into US lingo. 'Go fucking figure.'

2

Randeep pulled over to wait when he saw Nahid scrim up through the heather at the side of the road. With it being midnight in high summer, some daylight still played with the horizon where the South Yorkshire moors rolled up like tundra to kiss it.

The verge fell steeply to the Dunford Bridge Freightliner Terminal, blazing at the darkness in the valley bottom and as out-of-place in such a barren spot as a McDonald's on the moon. It was a bleak outpost, built in the middle of nowhere because of the cheap land. Chunky sci-fi container cranes straddled a mess of floodlit railway sidings outside the three-mile Woodhead Tunnel on the reopened Manchester-Sheffield railway. Randeep knew the line had closed controversially in 1981. Eurorail rebuilt it in 2014—this time under attack from environmental nuts instead of rail activists—to ease congestion on the Trans-Pennine motorways. The concrete-lined tunnel was the only one in the UK built to Continental standards. Tax breaks urged road hauliers to piggyback their rigs through it by train to avoid the Draconian road tolls.

Nahid was puffing when he got in the Range Rover. 'It's arrived,' he said. 'Take the old farm track. He's knocked out the infrared sensors along the fence.'

As Randeep set off it struck him that, since Oxford ten years ago, thanks to his smart, rich, third generation dad, he seemed to have been picking Nahid up late at night in flashy 4x4s.

When he hit the track he kept company with the terminal's twin electric security fence, bumping ruts till they made Gate 5, where they got out and crunched limestone gravel. The triple pointed aluminium palisade they arrived at meant business. Five-metres high, sizzling with 240,000 volts of lethal live juice, according to the pictures of a guy getting fried. Half-a-mile away a train was being loaded at the terminal hub, meaning it was a good time to sneak into the compound. Heavy switchgear oscillated across the hot muggy night as rigs were shoved about like toys with the air of a robo-production line at a fáctory. Partying hazards bounced off every shiny surface.

They clocked an approaching stocky figure, farting un-selfconsciously as it waddled between trashed ship containers stacked five and six high. Torchlight flared in their faces when the guy's feet stopped making noise. A gruff Middle Eastern voice struggled with a few words of English. 'You got here, huh?'

'What would you do if we said we hadn't fucking got here?' Randeep hit back, raising a manicured hand at the glare. Bearing in mind why they were there it was right for him to have put the fuckwit in his place using the Queen's Very Best. As the torch died he clocked the lecherous look in the dark piggy eyes.

'Not just a pretty boy but a fucking comedian too, huh?' the fuckwit insisted in better, nastier English. He typed at a panel in the gate-frame and made it *fdunk* open then ushered them across to a reefer-trailered rig with its twin vari axles slung off the ground. Fancy vinyl self-stick and loud candy stripes cramming the trailer sides hid the rig's black market long-task. A fat middle-aged Arab paced tarmac in front of it, his cigarette-glow waving, his bloated gut wobbling. He seemed more amenable, nodding uncertainly before he shot bolts at the trailer's side door and pulled out some Expamet steps. Randeep followed him up them with Nahid and the fuckwit tagging.

Inside the trailer they were hit by the acrid stink of piss cut by the faecal reek of filthy humanity. Up front, walkthrough clear vinyl door strips split the main storage area from the bulkhead refrigerator. They squeezed down the side of it into a compartment where everything had been stripped out to make a secret bunny hole. The air was as humid as in a hothouse, the stink so godawful ammonia-bad Randeep could taste it. It was like landing in a pigsty. A dozen exhausted, unshaven young Asian guys slobbed up against the bulkhead. The fuckwit swore at them and stuck the boot in. 'Stand up all of you bastards,' he snarled. 'Come on! Fucking get up!'

As they shuffled to their feet the fuckwit dragged them roughly into line so they could do the police ID thing. Randeep paced in front of them slowly. He might be related to the poor bastards back down his bloodline but he felt no affinity with the sweaty submissive faces. They were little more than slaves. Or lambs to the bloodiest slaughter. 'I'll take him, him, and him,' he said, then turned.

'You mean you'll take them or you'll *have* them?' the fuckwit asked seedily, through shit-stink breath. Randeep didn't take the bait but went back through to the main part of the trailer, this time clocking shitty handprints smearing the walls. 'I see you go for good-looking guys with beards, huh?' the fuckwit said. He came up behind Randeep and smacked him up the arse, squeezing it suggestively. 'I bet you like them nice and hairy too, huh?' he added, showing titanium buck teeth to try and goad his handsome young Pakistani guest.

When they were back on terra firma Randeep pulled a fat envelope from the breast pocket of his tracker vest and threw it at the fuckwit. 'Three thousand sterling.' He was sticking to the deal because he couldn't be arsed getting excited on such a hot night by whipping out his Sheuze to blow the ugly bastard away.

Nahid ushered the three bought guys through the gate. The loitering fat Arab struggled up into the rig's cab, revved it, and stuck it in gear.

'I thought we said four thousand,' the fuckwit shouted, taking the piss as the rig hauled pronto. Still Randeep stayed cool. If you were educated and English you didn't get wound up when shit dissed you. He tailed Nahid through the gate across to the RR. The fuckwit threw the envelope into a new open-top Warrior then tough-guyed over to lock up. 'Hey,' he said, whacking across a galvanized bolt, 'what you gonna do with those bastards, huh? Train them to kill the Queen of England?'

It was like a bomb had gone off. Randeep heard his own feet crunch gravel while he digested what the fuckwit had said. In the background another train had arrived at the terminal. As the waiting rigs entered the holding area they were shunted sideways onto flatbed loaders. At the same time safety clamps sprang up behind the wheels and locked. Randeep heard them *fdunk*, falling dominoes fashion, along the length of the train. It was impressive stuff, backed up by some serious kit, gracefully big yet energetically clunky, like movie CG work happening for real.

He reached the RR, opened the driver's door, but shut it. The three guys dived in the back and ransacked the fridge, popping Red Bulls.

'Kill him,' Randeep told Nahid icily.

'He was only joking, for God's sake.' An unlit cigarette bobbed at his mouth.

'It doesn't matter. The thought's in his head. Kill him.' Saying no more he got in the RR and sent down the windows because of the stink. He watched Nahid walk gravel back to the gate, calling to the fuckwit for a light. The loco gave a throaty roar from the terminal and shot fumes like a whale spurting through its blowhole as it got ready to leave. From that distance its growling engine and the con-

12

stant moaning and squeaking of gears from the overhead cranes sounded like a building site. The noise covered the *phut* of the Sheuze when it fired but stood no chance at hiding the sound of a dumdum bullet when it made the fat bastard's head go pop.

3

It was 2.03am when Bill Martin eased the brand-new Class 68 loco across the maze of points into Wolverton MPD. He took her past the Royal Train prep sheds into a siding and brought her nearly up to the buffers then shut her down and reached for his snapbag.

Unlike the old Class 66, the Class 68 was a joy to drive. Air-conditioned, a practical console layout, with a computer that did what the tin said. Bill had been driving for thirty-five years, switching latterly to freight because the pay was better and the HSE Gestapo less of a bind. During his time he'd seen the kit go from clockwork to microchip but he'd also seen Britain's railways go from the wreckage Beeching left to a few mainline routes. Too many crooks on both sides of the Commons had vested interests in the road industries, as they had since the days of black-and-white telly when an allegedly Conservative Government installed a rail-hating Minister of Transport who happened to own a motorway building company.

Bill's dad had been a driver during steam's heyday. Till Beeching he'd voted Tory but never forgave them for what they did to the railways after 1963. Shaking his head at this Bill stuck his backside through the cab door and climbed down backwards with his bag slung at his shoulder, thanking God that he was close to retirement and would be out of it soon. He puffed his cheeks at the humid night as he hit the ground and crossed oily tracks. The MPD was still a hive of activity at such a godforsaken hour because trains needed maintaining 24-7. Southern England was lucky. It had kept some semblance of a railway because of its white-collar voting power.

When he reached the Timekeeping Office, Pete Robbins was there with his teenage son, who was researching some project for sixth form. Self-consciousness worked at his spotty face because of the fluorescent-green togs he'd been given to wear on site. He was a good kid, computer savvy, headed for a life in IT, but brought up the traditional English way in a neat suburban semi with Hornby trains in the loft and an awareness of Britain's industrial past. His step dad was rotund from spending too many nights propping up the bar of Wolverton Railwaymen's Sports and Social Club. He puffed at the stifling heat and wiped sweat from his beetroot-red face with his cuff, nodding for Bill to stick his ID card in the Payclock.

'I hear it's your big day on Thursday, Bill.'

'It is,' he said, waiting for Central Matrix to ping his eye-print green and confirm his Euro citizenship.

'ID confirmed,' said the sexy husky lady.

'It's my last time, though,' Bill said, taking his card. 'I'm out of it in September.'

'Retiring somewhere good?'

'Tuscany. Pauline's over there now with the brother-in-law and his wife. I should be with them but I couldn't let the old girl down, not with it being my last call. They only told me on Friday morning. An hour away from us getting a cab to the station.'

Pete laughed at the mention of the *old girl* and told his son, 'Bill's one of a select few who're allowed to drive the Royal Train for the Queen.'

'Somebody has to do it,' Bill said, turning to the door as a loco rumbled past outside, its wheels hissing-binding. 'Only trouble is they don't let you know till a few days before. Security I guess.'

'How cool is that?' the lad said, taking a step back in his dayglow waistcoat.

'Tell him about the six-inch thing,' Pete said, sticking in his ID card, making the Payclock do digi chatter.

'To become her driver you've to be able to stop within six inches of a mark,' Bill told the lad, 'so that Her Majesty ends up smack bang in front of the waiting nobs lined up on the station platform.' He winked his near eye. 'Except she knows I can make it closer to an inch.'

To be continued

MAGNUM

Books crying out for you to read.

Taking the British crime adventure thriller to new turbo-charged cinematic heights.

Entertaining you. Saving lives - with your help.

£1 from <u>EVERY</u> copy of this book that's sold helps in the fight against male cancer.

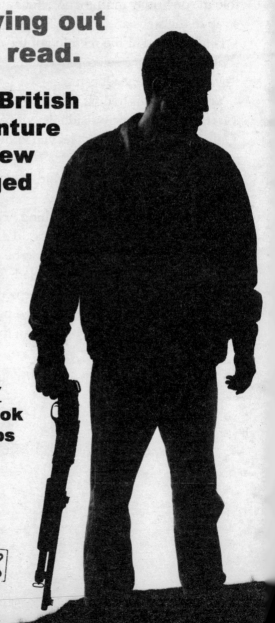